PRAISE FOR **ALL TRUE NOT A LIE IN IT**

Longlisted for the Scotiabank Giller Prize
Winner of the Amazon.ca First Novel Award

"Hawley's skills are impressive indeed. In her hands, Boone comes to life in a way that even longtime aficionados will find surprising and affecting. . . . *All True Not a Lie in It* is a powerful reminder of the fact behind the legend, of how fiction can arrive at fundamental, troubling human truths. The manner in which the book ends . . . leaves one almost breathless for the sequel, which Hawley is apparently [illegible] can't come soon enough." [illegible] *ald*

"Hawley masterfully creates [illegible] a fearful fantasy. We get to know [illegible] intimately. . . . The book's magic, however, is in Hawley's treatment of Boone's inner life. *All True Not a Lie In It* . . . may come closer to disclosing the 'real' Daniel Boone than those who originally manufactured and perpetuated his myth."

Quill & Quire (starred review)

"I fell in love with Alix Hawley's Daniel Boone, a man drawn to the beating heart of the wild landscape that stretches beyond his known world, and who risks recklessly to preserve his freedom." Frances Greenslade, author of *Shelter*

"A book of great sympathy and sadness. Hawley's intimate version of Daniel Boone is a wonderful character, intelligent and self-aware, even if he can't stop himself from being himself."

Nick Mount, *The Walrus*
(Amazon.ca First Novel Award citation)

"An extraordinary feat of backwoods ventriloquism, carried off with great flair and conviction, across the boundaries of custom, time and gender. Alix Hawley invests afresh in the voice of Daniel Boone and his tough familiars, bringing shock and sensuality, but also surprising tenderness, to the famously rugged frontier myth."

Richard Holmes, author of *The Age of Wonder*

"Hawley balances a poetic appreciation of her characters, the weather, the landscape, and her storytelling imperative. . . . Hawley's prose underlines the hallucinogenic sensation of Boone in the wilderness—her words and her sentences jar each other with their abrasive imagery. . . . Hawley's ability to convey the menace of paradise is overwhelming, as well as her ability to make the reader share in the sorrows of her hero."

National Post

"A brilliant conjuring of Daniel's Boone's life. . . . An exceptional example of the historical novel. Exquisitely written, with a wonderful sense of place and dialogue. . . . More fascinating is the portrayal of Boone's inner spiritual life, his evolving self-awareness that had him, for a while, understanding himself and his place in the world as an Indian. Let us hope this is the first of many fine novels from Hawley."

The Record (Waterloo)

"Alix Hawley's debut novel is audacious and bold, like an early Ondaatje, with writing that is luscious, lyrical, and bloodthirsty. Like Hawley's narrator, Daniel Boone, *All True Not a Lie In It* constantly seeks out new ground, wrapping the reader in a landscape of language and dream."

Alexi Zentner, author of *The Lobster Kings* and *Touch*

ALL TRUE NOT A LIE IN IT

ALIX HAWLEY

Vintage Canada

VINTAGE CANADA EDITION, 2015

Published in Canada by Vintage Canada, a division of Penguin Random House Canada Limited, Toronto, in 2015. Originally published in hardcover in Canada by Knopf Canada, a division of Penguin Random House Canada Limited, in 2014. Distributed in Canada by Penguin Random House Canada Limited.

Vintage Canada with colophon is a registered trademark.

www.penguinrandomhouse.ca

Library and Archives Canada Cataloguing in Publication

Hawley, Alix, 1975–, author
All true not a lie in it / Alix Hawley.

ISBN 978-0-345-80856-1

1. Boone, Daniel, 1734–1820—Fiction. I. Title.

PS8615.A821A64 2016 C813'.54 C2014-902491-6

Book design by Five Seventeen

Cover images: (buffalo sign) © Tom Marks / Corbis; (holes) vesna cvorovic / Shutterstock.com; (sky) © lostandtaken.com; (flaps) texturelib.com
Interior images: (map) courtesy of the David Rumsey Map Collection, www.davidrumsey.com; (dirt texture) © texturelib.com

Printed and bound in the United States of America

2 4 6 8 9 7 5 3 1

For Mike, Theo, and Kate,
and for Jocelyn and Peter

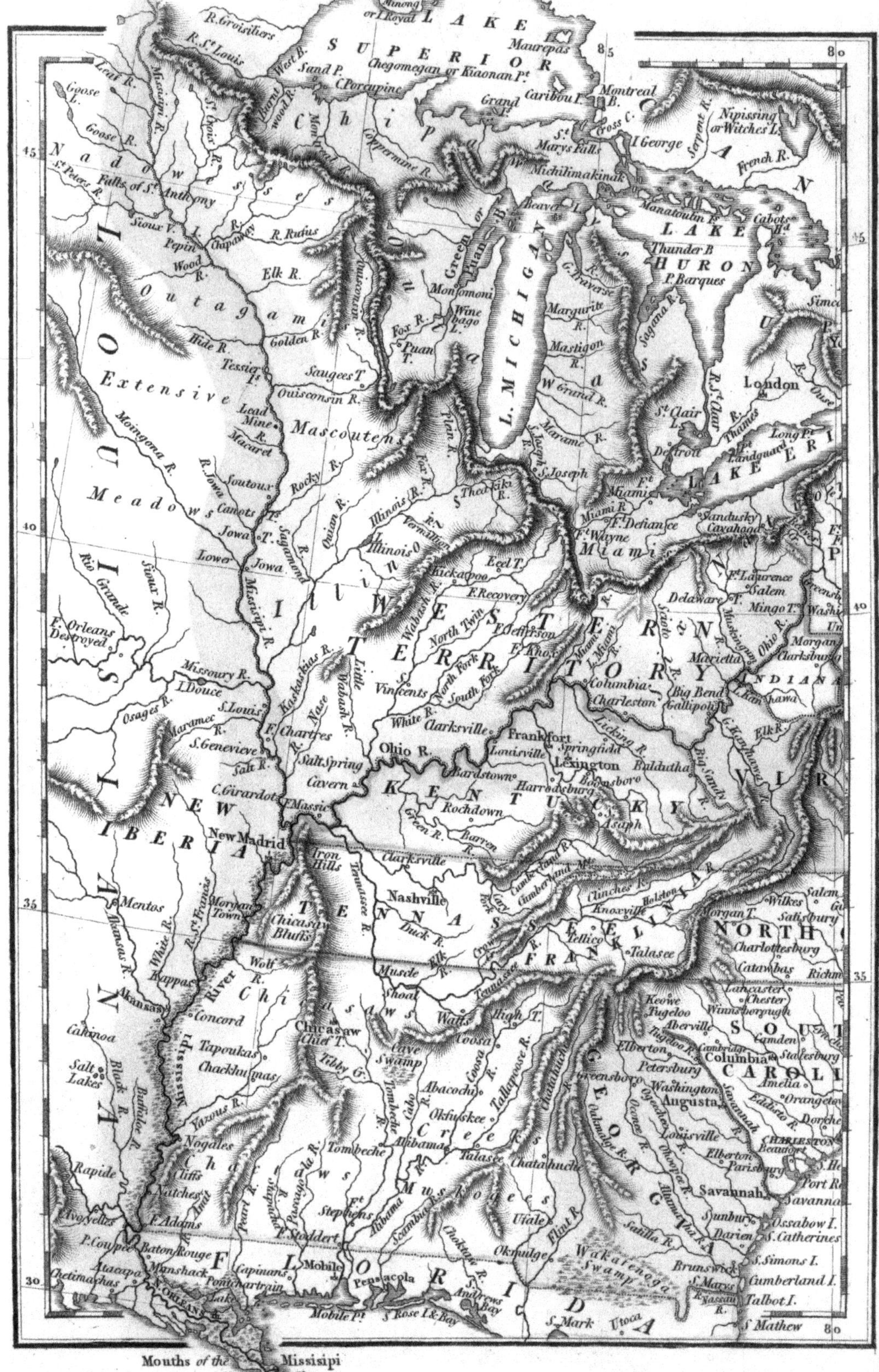

LAKE SUPERIOR
Long Lakes
Philipeau I.
Minong or I. Royal
Maurepas
R. Groisiliers
R. St. Louis
West B.
Sand P.
C. Porcupine
Chegomegan or Kiaonan Pt.
Grand I.
Caribou I.
Montreal B.
Gross C.
St. Marys Falls
I George
Nipissing or Witches L.
Serpent R.
French R.
Leaf R.
Goose L.
Goose R.
Misisipi R.
St. Croix R.
Burntwood R.
Montreal R.
Copermine R.
Chippawa
Nadowesses
St. Peters R.
Falls of St. Anthony
Sioux V.
Pepin L.
Chapaway R.
R. Rufus
Wood R.
Elk R.
Ouisconsin R.
Green or Puan B.
Michilimakinak
Beaver I.
Monomoni
Wine bago L.
Fox R.
Puan T.
L. MICHIGAN
G. Traverse
Marguritte R.
Mastigon R.
W. Grand R.
Marame R.
St. Josephs
S. Joseph
Manatoulin I.
Cabots Hd.
LAKE HURON
Thunder B.
P. Barques
Sagana R.
R. St. Clair
St. Clair L.
Detroit
London
Thames R.
Ouse R.
Long Pt.
Landguard Pt.
LAKE ERIE
Outagamies
Louisiana
Hide R.
Golden R.
Tessiq R.
Saugees T.
Ouisconsin R.
Extensive Meadows
Lead Mine
Macaret R.
Moingona R.
Mascoutens
Plein R.
Fox R.
R. Jowa
Soutoux
Rocky R.
Canots
Jowa T.
Lower Jowa
Sagamond R.
Quiaz R.
Illinois R.
Vermillion R.
Illinois O.
S. Theakiki R.
Ft. Miami
Miami R.
Ft. Defiance
Ft. Wayne
Miamis
Sandusky
Cayahoga
Kickapoo
Egel T.
F. Recovery
Ft. Laurence
Salem
Delaware
Mingo T.
Sioux R.
Rio Grande
F. Orleans Destroyed
Misisipi R.
Illinois
WESTERN TERRITORY
Wabash R.
North Twin
Ft. Jefferson
Ft. Knox
Miami R.
L. Miami
Sioto R.
Muskingum R.
Ohio R.
Morgan
Clarksburg
Marietta
INDIANA
Missoury R.
I. Douce
S. Louis
Osages R.
Kaskaskias R.
Little Wabash R.
Vincents
North Fork
South Fork
Columbia
Charleston
Big Bend
Gallipoli
Kanhawa
Maramec R.
S. Genevieve
F. Chartres
Nase R.
White R.
Clarksville
Frankfort
Springfield
Lexington
Licking R.
Balduthan
Big Sandy R.
G. Kanhawa R.
Elk R.
Salt R.
Salt Spring
Ohio R.
Louisville
Bardstown
Harrodsburg
Boonsboro
Cavern
C. Girardot
F. Massic
KENTUCKY
Rochdown
Green R.
Barren R.
Asaph
VIRGINIA
NEW IBERIA
New Madrid
Iron Hills
Tenassee R.
Clarksville
Cumberland R.
Cumberland Mts.
Clinches R.
Holston
Nashville
Knoxville
Mentos
White R.
R. St. Francis
Morgan Town
Chicasaw Bluffs
TENNASSEE
Duck R.
Tellico
Talasee
FRANKLIN
Wilkes
Salisbury
Morgan T.
NORTH
Charlottesburg
Catawbas
Akansas R.
Kappas
Wolf R.
River
Muscle Shoal
Elk R.
Tenassee R.
Akansas
Chicasaws
Concord
Walls
High T.
Keowe
Tugeloo
Lancaster
Chester
Winnsborough
Aberville
Camden
Cahinoa
Tapoukas
Chicasaw Chief T.
Cave Swamp
Coosa
Coosa R.
Tallapoose R.
Chatahuchi R.
Elberton
Tugeloo R.
Cambridge
Columbia
Statesburg
SOUTH CAROLINA
Salt Lakes
Mississipi
Chacklumnas
Tibby G.
Tombeche R.
Cabo R.
Abacochi
Greensboro
Petersburg
Washington
Augusta
Savannah R.
Edisto R.
Amelia
Orangeburg
Black R.
Buffaloe R.
Yazous R.
Okfuskee
Creeks
Oconee R.
Ogechee R.
Oakmulge R.
Louisville
GEORGIA
Nogales
Chactaws
Tombeche
Allibama
Talasee
Chatahuchi
Elberton
Parisburg
Beaufort
CHARLESTON
Rapide
Cliffs
Natches
Amit R.
Pearl R.
Pascagoula R.
Stephens
Alabama R.
Muskogees
Escambia R.
Ufale
Savannah
Port Royal
Avoyelles
F. Adams
P. Coupee
Baton Rouge
F. Stoddert
Choktau R.
Flint R.
Okmulge
Wakatenoga Swamp
Satilla R.
Sunbury
Darien
Ossabow I.
S. Catherines
Atacapa
Chetimachas
Manshack
Ponchartrain Lake
N. Orleans
FLORIDA
Capinans
Mobile
Pensacola
S. Andrews Bay
Brunswick
S. Marys
Nassau R.
S. Simons I.
Cumberland I.
Talbot I.
Mobile Pt.
S. Rose I. & Bay
S. Mark
Utoca
S. Mathew
Mouths of the Missisipi
Balise
C. Lodo
45
40
35
30
85
80

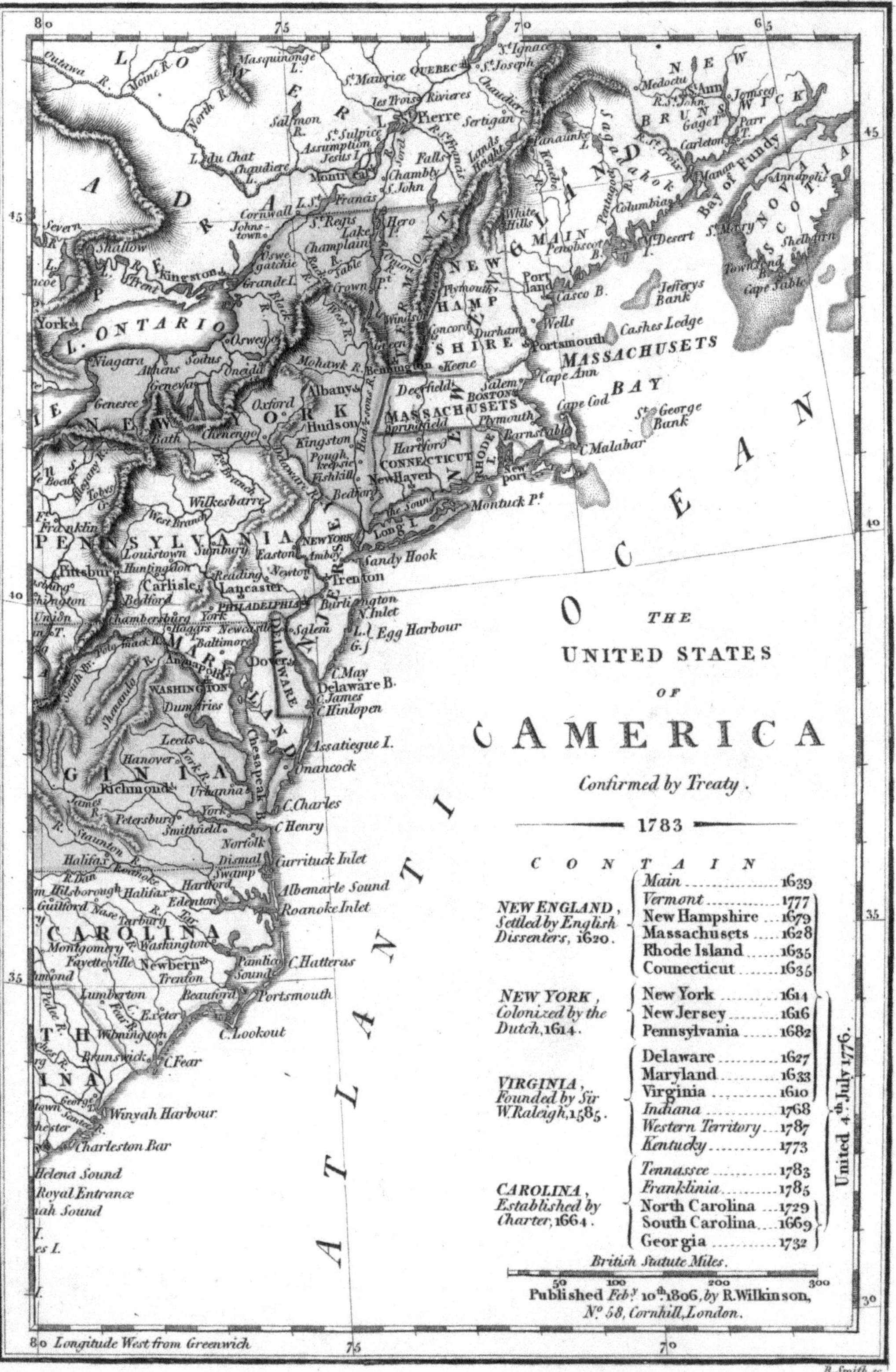
THE
UNITED STATES
OF
AMERICA
Confirmed by Treaty.
1783
CONTAIN
NEW ENGLAND, Settled by English Dissenters, 1620.
Main 1639
Vermont 1777
New Hampshire ... 1679
Massachusets 1628
Rhode Island 1635
Counecticut 1635
NEW YORK, Colonized by the Dutch, 1614.
New York 1614
New Jersey 1616
Pennsylvania 1682
VIRGINIA, Founded by Sir W. Raleigh, 1585.
Delaware 1627
Maryland 1633
Virginia 1610
Indiana 1768
Western Territory .. 1787
Kentucky 1773
CAROLINA, Established by Charter, 1664.
Tennassee 1783
Franklinia 1785
North Carolina 1729
South Carolina 1669
Georgia 1732
United 4th July 1776.
British Statute Miles.
50 100 200 300
Published Feby 10th 1806, by R. Wilkinson, No 58, Cornhill, London.
80 Longitude West from Greenwich
75
70
B. Smith sc.
ATLANTIC OCEAN
MASSACHUSETS BAY
L. ONTARIO
NEW YORK
PENNSYLVANIA
NEW HAMPSHIRE
NEW ENGLAND
MASSACHUSETS
CONNECTICUT
RHODE I.
NEW JERSEY
DELAWARE
MARYLAND
CAROLINA
NEW BRUNSWICK
NOVA SCOTIA
Bay of Fundy
QUEBEC
Albany
Hudson
Boston
New Haven
Philadelphia
Baltimore
Washington
Richmond
Norfolk
Trenton
Sandy Hook
Long I.
Montuck Pt
Cape Cod
Cape Ann
C. Malabar
St George Bank
Jefferys Bank
Cashes Ledge
Portsmouth
Casco B.
Cape Sable
Chesapeak B.
C. Charles
C. Henry
C. May
C. Hinlopen
Delaware B.
Egg Harbour
Assatiegue I.
Onancock
Currituck Inlet
Albemarle Sound
Roanoke Inlet
Pamlico Sound
C. Hatteras
Portsmouth
C. Lookout
C. Fear
Winyah Harbour
Charleston Bar
Helena Sound
Royal Entrance

AUTHOR'S NOTE

I didn't know much about Daniel Boone when I started writing this book. An image of him burst across my brain: an illustration from a *National Geographic* article, which I hadn't seen since I was nine. I don't think I'd thought of him since. But once I saw that painting of him again, I couldn't stop.

American schoolchildren might learn his name in history lessons, but ask most people what he actually did, and you aren't likely to get much of an answer. He is a slippery character, a peculiar mix of famous and forgotten. The known facts of his life are gripping enough, but he became a myth even during his own time, when wild stories about him spread around the world. Even Lord Byron included him in a poem. My novel continues this myth-making tradition, moving some of the dates of Boone's chronology, making guesses. So who was he? He left almost no writing. Some say the body dug up and reburied under a monument in Kentucky years after his death isn't his.

Certain people have a charisma that imprints itself on time. They don't disappear. Perhaps they don't want to. His voice has haunted me for the last few years. My story is about trying to find him. His story is about trying to find paradise, and about what happened when he brought about its ruin.

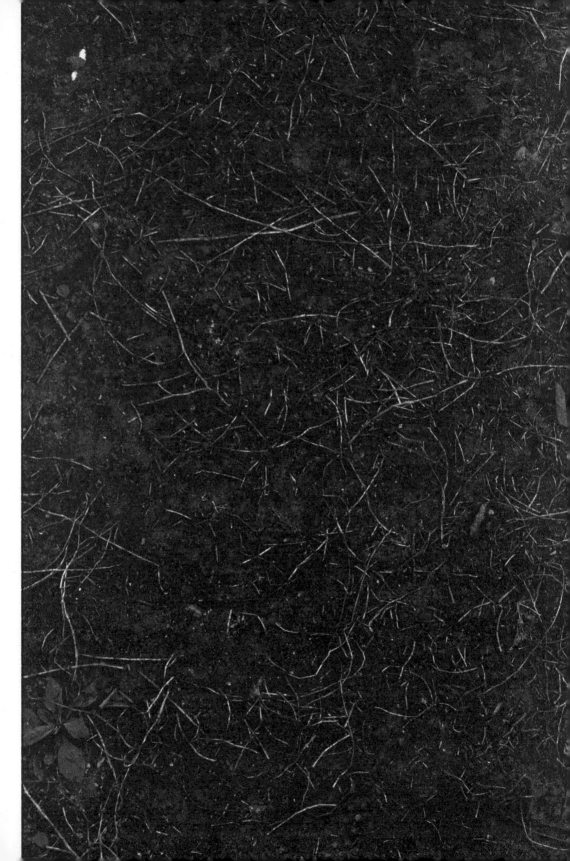

PART ONE

WHEN I AM GOOD

—YOUR SISTER is a whore.

—Your sister is a whore.

—Your sister is a whore.

This they bawl beneath the creek bridge like hogs all stuck. I hear it often enough when I am seven years of age. I sing back down:

—Which makes me a whoresbrother.

An eye shines up through a crack in the boards, a rock comes for my head and I duck it, but one of the boys sees fit to add low as a judge:

—His granddaddy had a famous whore.

—Which makes me a famous—

Then we fight. I kick one boy's shins and give the chin of another a crack with my elbow. A hard fist strikes my cheek and I hit out again unseeing with my little bird club. William Hill, who stands to one side watching and grinning, is fetched a bloody nose with the knob of it. Ha. He steps back covering his face and I run shouting insults of my own devising: *dungflower* is one. I win the fights generally. And what famous thing does that make me? Well.

But Hill pounds along behind me calling: Dan, Dan. I turn and shout:

—You know nothing! The King of the Delawares stopped at my granddaddy's house when I was two! For a cake! King Sassanoon! He had wives enough! And could have killed you all! I was there, I was two years old!

Hill stops on the path and bellows, all joy:

—You will be famous, Dan! I will make a book of you!

I know he is grinning through the blood on his face and his hair like dry straw in his eyes. I know he will not catch me. And I know he has told the other boys what his father told him, what is in the Exeter Meeting records, that whoring is in our blood. *Your granddaddy had whores in England.* The low voice beneath the bridge was his, it is just the same as his father's when he leads Meeting. Hill will make up any tale, but this tale is true.

—Dan, I see you! I will catch you up!

I go faster. I feel his eyes on my back, the curious unclouded grey eyes of Hill. I have known him all my life. It is too long. When I see him I feel tied to him and to this place with a rope. My Fate has tied me and made a pair of Hill and me, like dumb white oxen bent to the plough. We are built the same way, not tall but strong. We are both clever enough but he is clever in my Uncle James's school, and I have had enough of school. Our fathers are both in the weaving trade, but his father began in England as a rich woollen merchant, my Daddy has a few looms in the barn here and a little forge that does no good. Sometimes Hill and I are friends, most times we are not, so far as I am concerned. But he watches what I am doing, trying to do just the same if I am throwing my club or pretending to shoot, as though he has no interest in his own life and only wishes to catch mine like a fish. He will never leave me alone.

I run. At this time it seems to me that I can outrun my Fate.

—Your sister is a whore! And your daddy's sister is a whore!

I am far from the Owatin bridge to town where I left them, the path is narrowing. A branch catches my ear. Two of the boys are running a way behind now, I hear their yelling, but I am faster than anyone. My elbow aches, my feet burn, I hate my shoes. Hill is calling still: Dan, Dan. He thinks I am going up the hills to the pastures but he does not know, he knows nothing.

When I see the lane beyond the holly bushes I dodge down it and run hard all the way up to Granddaddy's square stone house, where I never go. No one goes here. The boys will not see me, I am too quick. The house is built of the same brown stones as Meeting House in the township, though it has the look of a sick cousin. Granddaddy's hounds bark and tug on their chains outside the old cabin he never knocked down. My heart thumps. I suck in the kitchen-garden smell of onions and graves.

Once inside the big house I bang the door and I stamp my feet on the flagstones. I have never been here without Ma or Daddy. I hear my heart in my ears. The indoor air is quiet and queer and has a mossy smell. I say:

—Hello.

No one answers. Aunt Sarah, that is to say one of the whores, must be in back of the house spreading out the washing. She goes nowhere else, she is cast out of Meeting and the Friends only suffer her to live with Granddaddy because he needs looking after. Perhaps she is sat down in the grass sniffing up the grave smell of the garden and sniffling over her husband the outsider. He left her and took up with another woman, but then came back when he got sick. This husband is now dead, and sad at being stuck in the earth alone, as I imagine. Daddy could not allow an outsider into the Friends' burying ground. The Meeting leaders have put him in charge of it, which is a satisfaction to him. He is not satisfied with much else. He makes sure the ground is flat after buryings. He walks about on it with his bandy legs.

I go along the hall singing "I Care for Nobody," my oldest brother Israel's favourite song. I toss my club as he does, and I think of the Delaware king walking on this floor with all his wives. I was here then and I did see, though all I recall is a red blanket on someone and a lot of moccasins. I am struck by a wish for moccasins. I go quietly as an Indian now over the floor. No sound in the house. Perhaps Granddaddy has died.

I stop in the doorway to the right. The room beyond is dim and stinking with the curtains drawn. They have put Granddaddy's bed there. He is in it, twisted and bony. I look hard. He is breathing. When again I say hello, he starts and tugs up his face, as though I might be a Meeting leader, or perhaps the spirit of King Sassanoon popped out of the wall with a scarlet blanket on and feathers in my hair.

Do you see me, Granddaddy? I do wonder. He squints under his brows, snarled and white as roots. His wet mouth hangs low on the left side. I keep where I am. Up and down goes his chest. Daddy told me all proud that Granddaddy was born in 1666 when the city of London burned down, and now he is so old, and still breathing. Think of him whoring and all unclean before he came on a ship here to Pennsylvania and had to tell Meeting everything he had done before they would allow him in. He had the new Meeting House built as penance, straight at the centre of the township, with all the roads running off from it. And he named the town Exeter after his old home in England. But perhaps this was wrong, it was there he did his whoring. It is not a lucky town, I think.

People smile when Granddaddy is mentioned, and they nod kindly as they do about wise old men, but it is false. He was all right until Aunt Sarah married out and people began to talk of our bad blood. His crooked old right thumb slips about upon his quilt as if he is running the weaving shuttle back and forth, as if he still keeps up his old trade, as if he were still quite a young man inside. As if he still had all his money and had not spent it on the whores of his youth and on this new place, as if he could fornicate any time he chose. As if he were in paradise. He dreamed of it when he turned up in this new world. This gives a queer feeling in my guts and so I call goodbye, but Granddaddy coughs and waves his arm towards the pot beside the bed.

—Fetchit.

I fetch it from under the great carved black cabinet. I am glad the pot is clean. While he sits up and scrabbles at his nightshirt I say quiet:

—You had a whore.

—Eh?

He has a baby smell, milk and piss, but more sour. His arm trembles. I breathe in and I say:

—But—you had fights. You saved two Indian girls when a gang stole them.

My Daddy has told us this story, it was before the new Meeting House was built, and the Delawares and Catawbas came along their old trail and stopped all the time to trade here. Some bad white men snatched the girls, but Granddaddy spoke hard to the men and gave some money and got them back. I think of a young Granddaddy winning all the fights. I say:

—I fought a gang. I did it just now. Look.

I hold up my bloodied elbow. Granddaddy is filling the pot loudly. His face is half dead and he stares at me as if I am full of lies. I steal a glance at his parts, they have a sad lifeless look. Piss drips from him onto the sheet. He holds out the pot with his shaking arm. It will tip, it will all tip out. He says in a rough voice:

—What do you want here? Eh? Who are you?

My stomach leaps into my throat and I near shout: I will not be old, I will not be like you. I will win all the fights, I will never tell my secrets. I will not go rotten like you in this place. I will find a real paradise. You never did.

Aunt Sarah is clicking along the passage on her wooden heels. Granddaddy rocks his head in the direction of her noise and frowns.

He had to beg forgiveness in Meeting for her marriage to the outsider. I think of that man buried in some unfriendly ground, all bones now. Again I say goodbye. And now I run out the back door of the house and over the grass and the sheets going white in the sun.

I run up into the hills and into the woods. With my club I get a squirrel down from a secret elm I know. The squirrel is a red one with a fair-sized tail. I sit in the tree for some time in hope of getting a wild pig for my Ma, but I have never got one yet, and there is nothing more about worth having. I want to go farther but the night is coming now. I wait until the shadows are stretched, and I make my way down the side of the valley and back along the creek bottom, through my two uncles' farms and across to the back of ours. My body is all aches and scuffs and bruises from fighting and hunting.

As I come round to the front of the house, Ma steps out holding up the lantern, which makes her look ghastly. She touches my sore cheek but she does not ask what has happened. I show her the squirrel tail and she smiles as she turns her face to the dark. As I put the tail down the front of my breeches I think again of Granddaddy and his parts, and of how his life has gone, and how my Daddy's has gone too, slowly rotten all through like an old egg.

Oh Ma and you others all gone now, all of my dead, you know that I begin well.

I

The Whores of Pennsylvania

My sister the whore is shown before all the Friends at Exeter Meeting like a grub spaded up. She stands at the centre of the room, and we all sit up on the benches round her to see. Sallie has got her confession prepared. She holds the paper before her face and talks as if she has got a mouthful of chewed potato. Unusual for her to talk so flat, she could run a blab-school if she liked. Heels-up Sallie, the boys say. Give her a tap and over she goes. Always the last to leave a bonfire or someone's new barn in the dark.

I watch her tip back and forth on her famous heels. Her cap is slipping to one side, she tugs a curl out over her ear and lifts her eyes to see who is watching. Her fellow stands a few feet away looking out the window. I listen for words of interest but the only ones I catch are *I was too conversant* and *fornication*. She admits to all of it though it is evident enough to anyone who takes one look at her belly from the side. And everyone does look.

This is not usual Meeting. The air has a stunned feel as if a shot has just gone through it. The leaders have summoned all of the Friends. The benches are full. Even the Friends from the country farms have driven to town for it.

Daddy bursts into sad perspiring, his smell rises up like bread. He is set to get up and walk off. But Ma's fingers tap upon little

Neddy's head, and so Daddy sets his jaw and keeps himself on the bench beside her. I slide my feet in circles. I want to laugh. My sister Bets creases her nose like a fox, and my oldest brother Israel does laugh under his breath.

—This is my confession.

So Sal finishes, but one of the widows near the door begins to swat her haunch and complain of ill winds. Bets chokes a giggle and whispers in Ma's voice:

—Do you suffer from wind, my dear Danny?

I give her a poke. Hill's father carries on with Sallie and her fellow:

—In truth you were too conversant with one another before this day.

His voice is a wealthy man's voice, every word rings like a coin falling. His face has its usual rosy look, but it becomes imaginative for a spell. I become imaginative also. I have not at this time witnessed any conversant doings at our house beyond those of the cows and bull, which are not entirely interesting, being so brief. At this time I am an innocent boy, but I am interested in many things in my mind.

Hill's father asks Sallie will she now be married before all these Friends.

She says she will. Her fellow takes a sip of air through his teeth and says he will take her to wife.

Well it is done. Easy. Sal sneaks a look at us, she is thinking, That is that. Her eyes are bright. I hear her give her finger joint a pop, as is her way. Not a whore any longer. A wife. Safe, like magic. Well. God is not immune to performing tricks, perhaps He pops his finger joints also.

—And your confession? Plenty of time.

Hill's father has turned to the fellow, his voice is kindly enough in asking. In his mind, we might sit here all day, but Sallie's new husband says a brisk no thank you! He is not a Friend, he is an outsider.

Perhaps he is not so certain he wishes to be inside the Boone family after all. But too late. He twists his feeble beard like a wick and squints, though I know he is not squint-eyed. He is keeping his eyes from his new wife's lower half. Everyone else is still looking.

Hill's father walks a few paces across the centre of the room and then turns in quick hope to Daddy:

—The truth is all that we seek in this life. Confession makes us new. You will confess now, Friend Boone?

Daddy rises, just as Granddaddy had to when his own daughter did the same:

—My daughter was too conversant. This is true, yes. I am very sorry for allowing it.

For a moment Daddy stretches his neck like one prepared to say more. He looks at Hill's father's legs. His fingers twitch as if they might test the weight of that good heavy cloth suit. Daddy is a poor enough weaver himself, though he cannot understand why. He can see this cloth is good. He would like it not to be. The leader's life has gone right, his suit says so. The deep grey of it defeats Daddy and he says:

—In the future we will be more c-careful.

His stammer noses out of its dark rabbit-hutch as it does at such times. His face goes hard, he touches the top of his head where his hair is gone. He has a love of escape and a love of being angry. See the ship thundering off from the grey English shore, young Daddy's chin thrust over the bowsprit, away from other people and their ideas and money and churches to find a home for Granddaddy and himself and his brothers and sisters. It was meant to be better here.

Israel snorts. But Ma's eyes are like glass, all breakable. She squeezes young Squire, who frowns, and Daddy thumps down onto the bench again and breathes against his fist. Ma is a true lover of God. She turns back to Sallie, who is trying to keep up her meek countenance as though she has been brained like a cow by Him.

Bets laughs into the crook of her arm and makes out as though it is coughing, but I know.

I squint like the new husband, I turn my face upward to make everyone vanish. I have no liking for Meeting, the people in rows, the gap at the centre where Sallie and her fellow stand to be gawped at, and the long spells of quiet when everyone contemplates each other's sniffling. Bets is singing under her breath: Wind in my bow-ow-owels. She pokes me again but I pay her no heed. I am the first to see it. A bird at the highest window, a martin with a dark head and body. It flies straight in and sits for a moment on the sill until it flaps up to the rafters. I see every turn it makes, every shift of its wings. I see every feather of its body, and I see its small black eye.

A few hands rise and point. The martin rushes and flutters in the silence. It beats like a heart against the ceiling. Israel says:

—It will shit on Sal.

I believe Israel, I always do. He is sixteen years of age and has whiskery cheeks. I cannot help a look at them. I suppose I will have whiskers at some time. He crosses his arms and raises an eyebrow and gives a smirk. It is the first interest he has shown today. I look up with my mouth shut. Bets laughs loud this time:

—It will! Or piddle.

Daddy casts her a look from his loose eye and so she saws her cap strings back and forth between her teeth. I keep my eye on the bird. I feel Israel's idle interest, he is following it too, he could have it down before it twitched.

The martin crosses the rafters back and forth, as if it is stitching them up with a thread. It lands on a window ledge and pants, it opens its beak but it says nothing. I know I could get that bird if I had my club. Or an arrow. Or a stick. I could make a path straight to its head from where I sit. Israel would see me do it.

At a cough from below, the martin dives straight down as if it has fallen but now swings up again to the ceiling. Its head and breast strike the roof again and again, all dull thuds. I want it to look at me. I am sorry for it. If Daddy would let me have a proper gun, I would shoot a little hole through the martin's head and its suffering would be ended. I have clubbed plenty of birds dead. I know already that their eyes stay open but lose their wet shine, though their feathers do not for some time. I have held them until their bodies go all cold. It takes longer than you might imagine.

The martin bangs on. Hill's father knows he has no grip on anyone's brains now, and so he folds his hands and says Meeting is at an end for this day. Plenty of talk and hand-shaking as the rest make their way out, all looking quite relieved and able to be kindly again now that the marrying is done. I feel my Ma's relief and Daddy's grimness as the Friends nod to them. I am thinking to take this opportunity to ask Daddy about that gun when a finger arrives in my ear.

I stretch my foot backward to crunch William Hill's toe. He pulls his finger out but not before he says with great cheer:

—A baby is going to come out of your sister. Out her stomach.

—Out her big arse, Hill. Like a chicken. I know you love to look at chicken's arses.

I see Hill grin wide but I walk on with Bets behind our brothers. Once out the door, Israel turns and says loud:

—How can you stand and watch her go? And never speak to her again. Nothing about this wedding is right. It is nothing! None of these people can say we are wrong—

Ma hushes Israel as though he were young Squire. Daddy shakes his head but keeps quiet. Israel stalks off and my legs burn to follow. I know he will be going to fetch his gun, he will go up to the hills away from all of this, perhaps he will not come back until morning.

I am about to set off after him when Ma grips me and says:

—Hold little Neddy now. Stop him going into the road.

And my young brother smiles, he is always smiling. Sweet Neddy. I lift him. He has a high smell like Granddaddy. I say:

—Now look.

I hold him up so he might see Sallie's arse as it retreats to the cart in which it will travel to a new house to lay an infant. Cast out, married to her squinting outsider husband. Neddy calls:

—Gone. Gone.

—Yes.

I set him down, his face is perplexed but he does not cry. Ma and Daddy stand still looking after Sallie as though they do not know what to do with themselves now, but they go on looking as though some answer will appear. I turn as the bird flies out the open door of Meeting House, it leaves a pile of purple droppings on the threshold. The only answer we get.

—Bets. Bets.

The night of the wedding I do not sleep, though the house is silent. Ma and Daddy are quiet in the loft upstairs. I think to get Bets out of the bed next to mine and Neddy's, but she is heavy in her sleep and only rolls flat onto her back when I whisper. And I recall she threw shad guts over me the last time we went night fishing. So I tug the sheet over her face and leave her like a corpse.

I crawl past Sal's empty bed. I know it is empty for ever and this gives me an odd prickling about my heart. I feel my way along the floor and I find Israel's bed empty also, which is a disappointment to me. He has not come back. But perhaps I will find him.

Once I am free of the house I go over the kitchen-garden fence with a pail, thinking to get worms. The moon and a few stars are showing themselves. I trot over the Owatin Creek bridge and down towards the river, I can hear its quiet rush. For a moment I am quite happy.

A thick rustling comes out of the night before I get to the water. I say:

—Israel?

A shadow crashes from the birches and snatches my arm. My happiness peels away from me.

—Are you fishing, Dan? I thought you might come out. I will go with you.

It is not Israel, it is William Hill. His mouth smells of iron, I know he is smiling in the dark, as if he has eaten my happiness. He is only one year older than I am. He sits before me in my Uncle James's school and turns about to breathe on me with this breath. Sometimes he whispers answers at me if he thinks I do not know them. I do not listen, I would rather sit blindfolded on the one-legged stool in the corner than listen to him. Uncle James is always sorry for punishing me and gives me sweets at home later.

But Hill has money, it tumbles from his pockets, he is careless with it. Sometimes he gives me some of his money for a dead squirrel or a walk with me up the creek to a fishing place. His pleased face over the fence or around the edge of the door.

I say:

—You do not know where I am going.

—To your granddaddy's? I do not mind. I would like a look inside his house. Does he keep whores in all the rooms?

And again I run, again he follows me. He thinks he knows where I will go but he does not. I take a long winding way over the fields. I will not go to Granddaddy's, though I cannot think of anywhere else in particular. I only want to run Hill until he is too tired to go on. I race through dark pasture and corn and flax until the moon ducks in back of the clouds and I can only make my way by knowing the fields in my mind, not by seeing them.

I run in grass up to my knees for some time. Soon enough the back of my hand catches a farm fence, all rough split rails. I know it is the Blacks' fence and I know they all have the summer fever. It has given Ma something safe to talk about with the other women. Well, I have no care for sickness. I am sick worse of William Hill.

I follow along the fence towards the yard. A horse has got out of the stable and is standing by the front step. I put my hand over its soft nostrils as I pass, it puffs in my palm. I will find the root cellar and hide there with the turnips until Hill goes. But I hear him lumping along into the yard and so I go up the front step of the house. I find the door, the sick-rope is knotted on the latch, but I hear Hill talking to the horse as if to me: Where are you? And so I go in.

In the thicker dark of the room I stand, keeping myself still. I am not afraid, I am afraid of nothing. I hold my breath in. A curious noise comes from across the floor, a rattle.

I pick my way over the floor to the far wall, but soon enough Hill's breath is on the back of my head and I stop. He says:

—Go on.

—Do you want to catch it?

—Do you?

The Blacks have only daughters. One of the youngest lies beneath the open window hot as a pie, her teeth clacking and her eyes bound up with a white cloth to save them from the fever. I lean closer to see. Hill shoulders me down beside her and takes up a lock of her hair, then presses the end of it into my ear. In his father's low kindly Meeting tones again, he whispers that Molly Black and I are now married till death do us part.

—Kiss her. Hug her.

My brother Israel told me at one time that sick hair will lay bad eggs in your ears. I do not know if this is true but the hair pricks me horribly. I make my shoulders stiff. I do not wish to wake the sick girl. Though I will not have Hill think me a coward.

I bend and put my lips to Molly's burning cheek. Her teeth rattle on. I laugh and roll away but Hill says then reasonably:

—Or breed her. I will watch.

—No.

—Go on, Dan. I am trying to help you. I will save you from whoring, you will need a wife.

—No.

—Dan.

I jab him and again I say:

—No.

He sighs up another lungful of helpfulness. Molly's teeth give a great rattle and I reach out to cover her mouth. Hill bends with his face big and close:

—I want to see what you will do now.

I break free of his iron breath, I fly out the door and this time he cannot keep up. I run as the stars watch blinking. This time I will run for ever.

My chest burns but I pound on and do not stop. The moon is up now, and I run back to the river by another way, past some cabins of a few of the praying Indians who come to Meeting. I see the dull white of two of their ponies in a grassy patch, I smell the smoke of their fires. A door opens, but I keep on. I skirt round a field. I will run up the river, farther than I have ever gone, perhaps farther than anyone has gone.

I hear the river at last. As I am crouched on the bank to catch my breath, a short low call comes. It is not a bird, I know.

I crawl along a way until I hear a small splashing. Someone is just upstream, stepping into the water. I see how tall he is. His dark hair hides against the sky and trees, but his pale legs show. He has no breeches on and his shirt is loose and open. He takes up a thin stick and snaps its end. He turns his face.

Israel. He has seen me already, I know, but now he is looking up the bank behind him, where the sound of light steps moves away into the woods. I say low:

—Is that a deer? Will you get it?

I know he could get it easy if he wished to. I have followed him plenty of times in the early morning, I have seen the way his eye roams in a dark, lazy fashion over the dawn sky until at once it goes still and he shoots. He can get jays and crows, and sometimes deer. He does not know all the times I follow him. But sometimes he catches me out and shows me the way to look for the marks of deer hooves on grass, or for their droppings, or their hair snagged on branches. When he is home in the evening, he often lets me measure out his powder. Four times he has let me scrape his deer hides. Twice he has let me shoot squirrels with his gun. He gave me an old broken barrel without a stock, I have it beneath the pallet of my bed. I dream of it, though it is unsatisfactory dreaming. I would like to be as good a shot as Israel. He is Daddy's favourite, and Daddy has set him free to hunt. He will not mind the bellows in the forge or work the looms at any rate, he goes where he pleases and has no care for what anybody says. He cares only for hunting and getting away from the town. He has shown me how to hide my steps and keep my weight even on my feet and go silent. I know the deer traces no one else but Israel has seen, and some he has not seen. But I do not know what he does at night.

With the water rushing round his legs he looks at me. He says very quiet:

—No deer here. What are you doing about tonight, Danny?

I do not wish to tell him about Hill and little sick Molly Black. I say:

—Hunting. What is it then, that noise?

He raises his head. He spikes a fish with his stick, its body gives a brief shine in the moonlight as he turns it in the air. In his calm fashion he says:

—Hunting, are you? With what? Only fish here. And you.

A ball rises into my throat. He knows about every animal and where it goes and how to find it. Everything is easy for him. I say:

—Where have you been? You have not been here long, you only have one fish. Did you hunt already? What did you get?

He turns and his face goes silvery where the moon catches it. I say:

—Why are you out again? You are always leaving your bed. Come on, we can get a deer. I will help.

But he says nothing. He pulls the shad off his stick and goes on fishing as if I am not here.

—Israel!

—Go home now, Dan.

He is walking up the river against the current, lifting his bare feet. I shout:

—I hate this place! I hate Exeter. I will get something without you.

He says nothing, he only looks up briefly, and I run on. I think of running again, but it is darker now, and alone I have no hope of any deer or any escape. I go home and thump dirty into bed beside little Neddy, who sleeps as hard as Bets does. Anger thumps in my blood, anger that Israel is so free and I am so pinned and so young. I am angry too at Hill for following me and wanting to see what I will do now. I see his big face. William Hill, trotting about in my mind as if it is his own field. Dunghole. I am ready to shoot anything. But as yet I have no gun.

Israel steals in sometime before dawn. I hear him settle into his bed and breathe slow. I will find out where he goes. I will follow him. I turn over and put my hands over my eyes, and I am struck by a thought of the blindfolded girl with her skin on fire and the prickle of her hair like hay.

I wonder whether I crept into her sick dreams, a little husband. Molly, I did catch your slow fever when I kissed you, though not badly. I am alive yet. But you know this. You dead know about me and what I have done.

2

Gone

EVERY NIGHT I want to follow my brother Israel, but the boys who follow me are out at night also. On and on they go in soft voices outside our window: You whoresbrother, you ape, you arse, you toadstool, you stew-brains, you shit-stew, you fathead, you wart, you cuckoo, you maggoty bastard son of a whore.

One night I throw a pot out at them. My teeth ache with hating, but we continue on in Exeter for five years after my sister Sallie leaves it with her fellow. At Meeting, the looks the Friends give are pitying. We might smother in pity and kindness. Daddy and Ma keep themselves sweet there. Daddy stalks about the burying ground, flattening the earth and making sure the grass grows over the newer graves so everyone is hidden for good. He says:

—We were here first.

He means the burying ground and the town. Daddy is never one to give up. He buys five more acres of rough pasturage up in the hills and puts up a sign with our name on it. Some of the boys scratch it out with *WHORES*. I scratch that into *HORSE*. I fight anyone until my ribs hurt and I laugh until it is the only sound in my head.

And now Israel vanishes for days at a time, bringing back meat and skins every so often. He will not say how far he goes or just where. I think of him finding a marvellous place where he is quite alone and where all the birds and deer show themselves and say: *Shoot us, here we are.* In my mind I can quite see this place. Some days I try to track my brother up the hills and deeper into the woods, but I have no success. I will find my own place, I think. As yet I do not give it a name.

I do find new animal traces and very old Indian trails where the trees are blazed with signs. I find a worn-out hunter's lean-to and have a talk with two old Catawba men there who tell me where they have seen beaver on one of the streams. We have a talk together though they do not speak many English words, and they offer me a smoke, but I say no thank you, and I go on. I practise with my club until I can get any bird at the first throw, even pheasants. Once I get a raccoon that is crouching to drink, it falls into the stream dead without having seen me.

I keep myself to myself. I keep right away from my Uncle James's school and his lessons. I avoid the boys and Hill and his kindnesses, unless he has money or tobacco. Until he gets a new-made gun for his fourteenth birthday. It is a good gun, with a scene of lilies carved into its oak stock. He brings it to the house to show me. I say:

—Let me use it and I will let you watch.

With his usual grin he shoves his hair from his eyes and hands it to me. It has a good feel, it shoots straight. I tell him I will oil all the parts for him, but I take it and go to our summer pastures up the valley. I suppose I have stolen it, and I am sorry but not so very sorry. Hill does not come up here, he is keeping on with school to please his father, and his father does not wish him to be near me. I try not to think of Hill, but at times I think of the night he married me to little Molly Black, now dead of the fever. I think of my lip on Molly's cheek. I am sorry she is gone.

With Ma I stay in the scratchy grassland for months while the rest of the family is at home. I look after the cows and take the milk and butter down the hills to the spring cellar at home for her.

I wheedle her to tell me her old Welsh story about wolves stealing into houses in the night and picking up babies in their teeth, then taking them off to their dens to live as wolf children. She does not like this tale, especially up here near the woods, but I do. Sitting at our fire we hear cold howls far away on occasion. Ma always goes into the little cabin then, but I wheel about slowly with Hill's gun, looking into the trees with one eye shut. I would shoot a wolf if I saw one. Israel got one once after it killed a sheep and tore open the chicken house at Uncle James's place. Its eyes were yellow. I did not like to look at it when he dragged it home, though dead wolves are worth quite a lot of money from a magistrate. Granddaddy is a magistrate still, even in his aged condition, but I will not go to his house alone again, even if I get a wolf.

Ma touches my shoulder as I sit beside her. She misses Sallie, her first child, and she thinks of the younger ones at home, Neddy and Squire and little Hannah. So it gives her pleasure to coddle me for a short time. She tells the wolf story and strokes my head and says:

—Such hair. Sweet Neddy got the rest. And now what have I left?

Her hair has thinned, it is full of white threads. I was born with a black thatch, thick as hers once was. Her favourite boy Neddy has the same. He is like me but with a sweeter countenance. The rest are like Daddy, paler and gingery, though Israel's hair is a dark brown with red in it like embers, as I recall. We have not seen him in more than a month.

With my club I fell a red finch and then two more birds on their way to their trees. I pluck and gut them and cook them on a stick for Ma. The birds' legs stand out straight, crisped in the smoke. She says:

—A pity to eat the little singers.

But she does eat them. The evening smells of warm grass and cows' bodies. I can see the horseshoe-shaped valley below, the Schuylkill River at the end and the creeks running along like threads, and the house no more than a stump. I say:

—Ma, where do you think Israel is?

Without answering, she gets up to bring in the herd for evening milking. She calls:

—Ah. Here with you, you Ham.

I have given this name to all the cows. Ma humours me. The bells clank round her, she hums a flat little tune. She is worried about Israel and about what will become of us in Exeter, I know, though she keeps up a calm appearance. The corn and wheat did not come good this year, and Daddy says we must get fresh land for planting. For now I will stay. I will hunt and get her anything she wishes. So I think to myself. I am happy here alone with her in the fields, perhaps it is the happiest time of my life. Perhaps we get happy times to measure our unhappiness against later. Ma, I remember you.

It is September and cooler when a grey shape appears out of the higher hills across the pasturage. The sun is just coming up, Ma is still in the little dairy cabin fetching the pails. I stand up with the gun and aim. A sharp laugh comes:

—Do not shoot me yet. You do not even know who I am.

But I do know. Israel comes with his hands up and then sets his bag outside the cabin door. He grins through his beard and lies down in the grass with his gun beside him. He is wearing a breechcloth and leggings under his hunting shirt, which has tiny bright beads sewn all over it. His hips and thighs show bare. He kicks off his moccasins and a sharp smell comes from his feet. Another smell comes from his skin, a leafy smoky smell, the sort of tobacco the Indians use. Israel closes his eyes and goes limp as the pheasants and pigeons in his bag. I sit watching for quite a long time. When Ma comes out, he yawns in a great breath, as if his life is just starting itself. He sits up and asks what we have for breakfast, his hair rumpled and wild and his whiskers piercing out from his skin. Ma embraces him and says he looks quite a warrior in his outfit. I say:

—Have you got any skins?

—Back in my camp. Traded some with the Delawares.

—For what?

—For the shirt.

He points to the beading on his chest. His mouth is full of the bread Ma gives him. She begins to spoon out some of last night's stew and he eats as if he is starved. I say:

—Where did you find Delawares? I met some Catawbas. Where is your camp?

To Ma he says:

—Who gave you this meat?

He points the spoon at the bowl and Ma says:

—Our Daniel got it.

He looks at me properly. His eyes tighten. I say:

—Is beaver tail too fat for you now?

He begins to smile around the meat. He laughs and says:

—Well, well, the young master got himself a beaver. Got the pelt?

—Yes.

I do not tell him I shot the beaver and made a great hole in the skin. I have no traps as yet. He laughs again and chews off another great bite and takes another look at me. He says:

—You will have to come with me. We will get something else.

He sleeps all day in the grass. I help Ma but my heart is banging all the time. I want to go with him. I club a few squirrels and shine the gun and prepare my powder and shot. When Ma brings the cows in for the night, Israel wakes and stretches in the twilight. The moon is coming up already, a fat moon tonight. A wolf gives a yipping cry far in the woods. Israel finds a pitch-pine branch and makes a torch of it at the campfire. His eyes shine. He says:

—Coming?

He speaks as if he has not been asleep at all and does not much care whether I come along. I say:

—I am ready. Are you?

With our guns we cross the grass and go into the woods. I do not look back at Ma. The fire from the torch flips and shivers in the breeze. I am glad to be with him but I do not wish to show how glad, so I keep silent for some time until I cannot help myself, and I say:

—Are we going to your camp?

He says nothing as we hike up a hill. I say:

—Where is it?

He says:

—Anywhere I like.

He is silent again, I say nothing also.

When we reach a flat place with few trees about, he hands me the torch and walks on. I say:

—Is this it?

He does not answer. He gathers heaps of dried leaves and sticks and piles them as he walks about through the trees. For some time I do not see him, I only hear his light steps far off. I keep to where I am. It is darker when he returns. He takes the torch and says:

—Ever fire-hunted yet?

He touches the flame to the leaves at my feet. Fire runs along the trail he has made, a great circle a quarter-mile wide, snapping and leaping between the trees. We back up outside the round. The smoke is quick and heavy and stinking, my eyes run. He says:

—Now we wait. We might get a wolf or two. That would please Ma.

—Do you eat wolves in your camp? Do you not get anything else? We can have beaver all the time in the pastures, you know. I know where they are.

He is not looking at me. He says:

—Take the first shot. Anything that comes along. The fire will make it easy for you.

—I will take anything better than a wolf.

His teeth show in the blazing light as he grins. My heart bangs harder. I have no wish for a wolf, I do not like wolves. I feel Israel's eyes narrowing at me. I raise my gun and I keep it steady.

A crashing begins, light at first and then furious. Something is running back and forth at the centre of the fire. The smoke is choking, I tighten my eyes to see through it. Israel throws an armload of branches before me, the flame jumps high as my face and I step back from the heat. But Israel is watching still, and so I move forward again with my hands tight on the gun. Now is a terrible sound, a weeping, like the sound of a woman. I look to Israel but he only squints. The weeping and crashing come closer. Perhaps it is a young wolf, perhaps it is trying to howl but can only weep in this unfair fight. I have the gun up but I cannot shoot. The fire gleams off two eyes ducking up and down behind the flames. Something breathes in, a wretched gasp. My finger moves on the trigger. And leaping straight through the fire, straight at us, is a big doe. I see the scorch marks on her pale underbelly and her tail as she leaps, I feel her gasp and I feel Israel's watching. She is running. I turn and I shoot her through the neck and she goes down.

I feel your surprise, Israel. You did not think I could do it. You stand for a moment and you say:

—Easy.

It is too easy, it is a child's game, and I am not a child. It is wrong. I pull myself up and I say:

—Where else have you been? Have you been farther than this?

He laughs and says:

—You want to know everything.

He takes my gun and has a look at it and runs his hand along the stock. I say:

—You can use it if you will show me where you go. You want to get out. You have found better places, I know you have. That is why you never come back here.

—Maybe.

—I can shoot. I could go with you. I want to get out too.

He smiles and says nothing. He only takes up the doe's hind leg and cocks a brow at me. I take the other leg and we drag the animal back to Ma. I know I can do better than this, and better than you, Israel. To myself I say I will never fire-hunt again. I listen half the night for wolves while you sleep. And the next morning you are gone again without me.

I do not see Israel again until one evening late in the month, not long before we take the cows down to the farm again for the autumn. It is a hot thundery evening. Ma sends me home with the milk before the rain. I go down the valley side with the cans on their yoke over my shoulders, across the back of our place and round the side to the spring cellar door.

On the first step of the stairs beneath our house, I stand waiting for my eyes to wake to the dark. The yoke is heavy. The cold of the cellar hits my chest, the smell is slightly sour. Shapes press themselves out of the shadow at last and this is when I see my brother. I truly see him.

He has his gun propped against the wall and his bag set on the floor. A pelt hangs out of it, beaver or otter. His face is hidden from me. I see a hand is spread against the damp wall as if seeking relief there. It is not his hand, it is a girl's, and Israel is bent with his forehead pressed against hers. My first thought is that this girl has an aching head and that Israel is doctoring her. Though I have never known him to show any talent for doctoring.

A whisper slides out from them, a wet hungry sound. The thought strikes me that they are thieving butter and gobbling lumps of it together in a hurry to be gone. Then I hear their catching breath. I see her white cap on the floor with its strings in limp circles. I see her shawl beside it. I see her dark hair down over her shoulders, and I see Israel's bare thighs above his leggings as his shirt shifts upward. Her apron slides down to the flagstones. I do not move an inch. The damp ceiling weeps on my head. The damp floor weeps up through my shoes.

Israel's hand hovers just above her breast. Now his fingers are on her, they move up to her collarbone and back down to her bosom. His mouth is against her cheek as he opens the top of her bodice. He says:

—Does it feel nice? I know it does.

I have never heard Israel speak so soft and so kind. His voice is strange and private, as if he has stolen it. Then he speaks some words I do not know. They are not English, they are Indian words. *Quetit* is one. She says something back in a gentle way. The words near knock me down though I do not know what they are. His hands are all up and down her. I feel myself shut off inside a clanking armour of milk cans. My legs shake. I want this, the touching and the sounds and the privacy. The want rises up high in my throat, I can never tell of it.

The girl gasps as the doe did in the fire. At once I think again of my little wife Molly Black, but she is dead. This girl is living and her arms are round Israel's back. I drop the cans in the doorway, one clangs down the stairs and milk flies everywhere. I do not care. Full of my want, I am running. I want to go where you have been, but the only place I can go is back up to the pastures. The rain has begun but you do not come, Israel. I think of you in the spring cellar, you and the girl. You have everything you want. You have a gun and a free life and now this.

I know what you have been doing all this time. You do not know what I have seen. I have seen your wish for a secret life, your own life. My hope of going with you is finished. And I wish to have your life. I wish and wish for it all night. Israel, I am sorry for it now, perhaps I wished too hard.

The night is cold and wet. When Ma and I wake in the damp morning, Neddy appears at the cabin door. I say:

—Have you seen Israel?

Rubbing his sleepy eyes, he says with his sweet smile:

—No. Daddy says I have to tell you he will be a magistrate now, and Granddaddy is dead.

3

Tied

Granddaddy is put in the Friends' burying ground behind Meeting House and covered over without a marker, like everyone else. Daddy is in charge of the burial. He gives a proper nod to everyone who comes. But he is not made a magistrate yet and Granddaddy has not left him much. All his children want money. He leaves most to Aunt Sarah, who is alone now in the stone house and quite outcast without him. He does leave Daddy his carved black cabinet from England, very heavy and very old. When Daddy rumbles home with it in the wagon I say:

—You can keep your night pot in it and think of Granddaddy whenever you need it.

Daddy swats at me. To Ma he says:

—It will come. It will come right.

He is bright enough, striding home from the burying in the autumn sun. Uncle James walks along with him. He is a big man with a bald head and a wide red face and a schoolmasterish voice. With the money he does get, Daddy plans to buy another few acres to the south of our farm from him. All the burying party stops at our house to drink. I duck away from Uncle James but I hear him say to Daddy:

—You are planting yourself deeply here. Our old father would be proud, rest his soul. A good old man. He would be proud indeed.

Daddy sips his ale and says:

—Yes. Yes.

He looks as if he quite believes this, but I know Uncle James's words are only a thing people say when someone has died. Uncle James gets up and looks out the window. He says:

—At times like this I confess to feeling as the people of the city of Troy must have felt in ancient times, waiting for the Greeks to attack and believing they would win.

Daddy laughs:

—Showing your learning again, Master Jimmy. Have the Indians been giving you wind of plans for a secret attack? Or have they joined up with the Greeks now?

Uncle James smiles and shakes his head and says:

—You ought to ensure your Daniel gets to school. He has more learning to do yet. He could do many things.

He wags a big finger in my direction. Turning back to the window he says:

—It is an odd feeling one gets after a burial, a sense of waiting for things to improve, and then to end.

Hill's father comes over with his hand outstretched and takes Daddy's. With his eyes shining, he says in his most earnest manner:

—Friend Boone, we know this world will end someday. We can only hope to improve ourselves while we are in it.

Daddy roars out a laugh now. He says:

—I will improve my children's lot. They will all have part of the land my father and I settled. My Dan here will be a lawyer, I can see it in his hand.

Daddy sometimes lines us up and peers at our hands with his good eye, hoping to catch at a sign there. He takes my hand now, his breath damp in my palm. I snatch it away. William Hill, arriving beside his father, laughs and slaps my shoulder and looks me full in the face with his curious grey eyes as if he can read my life there also. My heart falls down. He is going to ask for his gun back.

—Hello.

I turn, and it is Israel coming through the back door with the sun behind him. He has been gone again since I saw him breathing in the cellar. He missed the burial. His hunting outfit is a shock against all the grey coats and frocks. The beads on his shirt gleam when the light touches them. The cloth is streaked with dried animal blood. He has a rough beard, his hair is plaited up and greased and his moccasins are dirty. The talk in the room stops. He wipes his mouth and extends his hand to Hill's father. He says:

—Well. Who is dead, aside from the deer I left in the yard?

Daddy hands him a drink and he raises his mug and says:

—I am alive. Are you?

Daddy nods, puffing himself up. Well we are all right. Until the next whore, who is worse, being a whore and Indian.

Winter comes, and it is not long before everyone knows of her. And how can I help staring? I am not the only one. The girl's neck is thin and pretty below her cap. My body and legs ache when I see it. Standing at the centre of Meeting she looks at the door as though to say: *Deliver me from these apes.* She does not look at me.

It is cold. The snow comes down outside the window. Beside me Ma is fretful, this wedding is her doing, a real marriage in our own Meeting for the sake of the child, as she said. She wraps her shawl tight about her shoulders. We are a bad lot. Bad blood. Very bad now. The women Friends sneak looks at us, Ma keeps up her small smile that says: *We are harmless, we mean no harm.*

I see the girl's knot of coppery hair and her warm brown skin. I know these parts, and more of her, from the cellar. I know Israel has been with her there more than once, and elsewhere in the woods. I have seen him cross the river, stopping to spear some fish to take to her in the Delaware cabins. He has been giving her skins and pelts she can trade for money. She is part Delaware, maybe half, maybe more. I know her soft voice though she has said nothing here yet. Friend Jones on the bench behind me says low:

—A half-breed will produce what? Quarter-breeds?

This is meant to sound kind, it has a slow drip like jelly. But Jones is picturing the mixing of blood. And of other parts. This I know because I am picturing it also. I have many such thoughts now.

A heavy countrywoman says deafly to her husband:

—Blood will out.

This may mean the Indian blood, or ours. She is old, her old face says she knows all about Granddaddy. One of the boys who is not far from where I sit sings soft, but not so soft that I cannot hear it: Blood will out out out, blood will out out out. Hill turns and smiles at me with what he believes is a sympathetic face, though he looks as though he has a needle between his teeth. He mimes holding a gun up to his shoulder, he tugs his arm back and mouths *bang bang*. I see his breath puff out in clouds. I suppose he wishes to go shooting with me, I am miserable thinking about it. His gun has only tied me tighter to him.

Israel looks set to kill anything that comes near. His eyes snap. He is in usual clothing, not his hunting outfit, but he stands with his feet apart and easy, as if he were in his leggings and moccasins, as if he were quite at home. His fingers curl at his belt and then retreat. I wish I had my little knife or my bird club. I would need no gun to deal with anyone here.

My boots bite into my heels as I rock my feet back, the bad blood outs and wets my stockings. I am not fond of boots and I feel myself trapped inside a giant one, all stinking and chafing. Even Bets keeps silent but she has her eye on a bony fellow across the room. I give Bets an elbow to the ribs but she is too flabby in spirit to jump. She sits thinking that nobody, bony or not, will marry her now, sprung as she has from this Boone family flower bed.

William Hill's father calls for Daddy to come forward. His voice is like a bell ringing the same ring all the time, it makes the back teeth ache.

Daddy stands but moves no farther. His mouth is calm but I can smell his black humour. Hill's father speaks:

—Friend Boone, you know a father's duty. Correct your son and make your confession before the Friends gathered here.

The leader holds out his white hand. It puts me in mind of a drowned thing dredged up with its legs all splayed and limp. Who would take such a thing? Daddy stares with his brows locked until his bad eye slopes off to a corner. He breathes in as if to speak and then coughs too loud and spends a time seeking a handkerchief to drag across his mouth. Israel is not a good son, he does not listen, he does only as he pleases. But Daddy loves him, he is helpless with it, Israel is his favourite, his first boy. Looking upon him, Daddy sets his arms about his stomach as though he is the one with child.

Everyone is picturing fornication. I see all the pictures rolling and turning in all the heads. The silence grows fat. The snow keeps falling. Ma's lips are tight, she is squeezing young Hannah who is fortunately not given to shouting. Neddy is slipping his hand into her pocket in search of sweets. Daddy's front hair grows damp, but even his wandering left eye does not deign to wander in the direction of the boy singing about our blood. Do not give in legs or eye: so I think. And Hill's father goes on smiling towards Daddy with his drowned hand out. The kindness that cannot be ignored.

Women begin to fan their faces faintly with their hands to show they are aware of the sweaty smell and that it does not come from them. Ma is nailing Israel in place with her smile, though he throws back his head. Hill's father keeps his hand out and speaks as if he knows everything and owns everything:

—Come. Can you not beg forgiveness, as your own father did, for allowing your child's fornication to occur?

Looking again at the hand, Daddy appears to conclude something, for his nostrils gape:

—P-nah. I do not choose to do so. Not t-today.

In spite of the stammering, he speaks like a man who can do whatever he likes on any day, like a man who has every choice in the world. I know he is thinking of Granddaddy standing here in the Meeting House he built, saying sorry for everything in his life. I know he is thinking that he will not go to his grave having done the same. Daddy, when I first see a buffalo bluffing a charge, spinning and snorting itself mad, I will think at once of you.

Israel is grinning now. He whistles a few notes: *I care for nobody, no not I.* Daddy's legs creak as he stiffens them. Bets has taken her miserable eye from the object of her affections and shoots me a look that says: *See Daddy's bandy legs.*

Daddy does not take the hand. He whistles lightly between his teeth also, I hear it. Israel barks out, Ha!

What else can one say at such a time, I suppose. He turns and everyone sets to bustling on the benches. I see Daddy's rough angry eye looking for a landing place, I see Ma's pale smile. Again it is done. The bride and bridegroom stalk out into the snow together. No congratulating this time. Although there is again a baby, five months later.

Daddy keeps up his defiance of Meeting though he insists we all continue to attend. He is letting his anger puff up like a toad. He will not condemn his son, he will not beg forgiveness, he will not beg for anything. He is waiting. Like the people in the city of Troy, as Uncle James said. *Go on and attack us.*

From round the door at the forge, I see Daddy's arm banging at something small. A cowbell. He often makes little things, not very useful things. He is not much of a blacksmith. He is worse since Israel's marriage. His trade has declined. Some Delawares from the little settlements and some travelling Catawbas come for horseshoes, but no Friends come. The crops are worse, the earth is being used up. Daddy is no magistrate. And he has near given up weaving, as if the good suits of Hill and his father haunt the looms and mock him. He looks up and catches me.

—What do you want? Come in here.

This seems an opportunity. And so I do go in, though I never like the smell of hot weeping from the metal and I have no wish to run the bellows. He once beat my backside with a stick when I refused to help here, I ran off singing to the woods with my breeches still down, and looked back once to see him all angry and helpless. He has had to take an apprentice, none of his sons is any good for this work. But he is happy having someone tied to him, who will take his orders. The skinny apprentice, Miller, scowls at me from where he is pumping away with his long arms. He is one of the boys who shouts after me sometimes still: *Whores*. I have fought him before and he is no fighter.

To Daddy I say:

—Well, I want a new ramrod. Can I have one?

He puts down his hammer. I feel myself surveyed like a field. He is set to lecture me, I know, and so improve his temper. He comes round the table to take me by the arm. He says:

—You come along, Dan. Miller, keep it hot.

I do not ask him where we are going when he takes off his apron and gets his hat. We walk quietly down the lanes. The leaves overhead are like dark stars against the sky.

Though it is forbidden, it turns out we are going to see Israel's baby. He is a big baby and appears to fancy brawling, which seems to me a good quality in Exeter. He waves his red fists at me and, not knowing what else to say, I say:

—How do.

Israel's new house is full of the sharp smell of new wood. Daddy sits down with a thump at the table, he bumps it and jigs his joints about like an old man, darting his eyes in all directions. Jig jig jig goes his foot on the knee of his opposite leg. He makes an irritated remark:

—This time of year is fickle. The air is not what it might be. That is what disappoints, that it is not what it might be. N-nah-no. Like all of this place.

He laughs without mirth and goes on jigging. Israel stares at him as though he is too tired even to move his eyes elsewhere. I want to ask him what is wrong but I do not.

Israel's wife is calm by contrast and offers us tea and flatbread and jam. The jam is very good and I say so. She smiles at me. She is thin as a stick now though her bosom is round. Her eyes are circled by purple shadows, but the eyes themselves are very bright. She piles more jam on my bread, as women do when you praise their cooking, until the baby sets up howling. Israel does not move. Though I am still hungry, I get up to rock the cradle but I knock the table worse than Daddy did, and I spill some tea. The baby howls all the more for my efforts, and so his mother is forced to take him up the stairs to tend to him. I hear her voice, it is husky and pleasant. She has him at her bosom, I know. She says Goodboy, Goodboy. I am uncertain of the ways of Indians in naming children and so I ask Israel:

—Is Goodboy the boy's name?

—No. It is Jesse.

Israel adds that the child is indeed a good boy, however. A very good boy. It might as well be his name! He says so boomingly as if I might not believe him. The baby bawls on upstairs.

I look around. There is a cut of new sacking stiff across the entry in place of a door. Daddy keeps up the jigging of his foot until he takes himself off to the privy.

I look at the jam pot and have to stop myself from taking more when there is so little here. I hear Israel's wife coughing above. I think further about her bosom. She is lovely, she gave me plenty of jam. I say to Israel:

—You off hunting again soon?

He rubs at his chin and laughs, all helpless. A poor pile of deerskins is lumped beneath the table. He has got no furs worth having this year. He says:

—My luck is going.

I say:

—Maybe you need to go farther south. Or west. You could settle anywhere you like.

He looks hard at me. His cheeks are thin, his bones show. He says:

—Is that so?

His voice is hard also. I shift about in the chair and I say:

—Well. I would like to have a wife and a house like yours.

He picks up a gun barrel he has been making a new stock for, then he throws out his hands and drops it. His wife coughs harder upstairs, the baby lets out a bawl. He laughs again and says:

—Do as you like, Dan. That is all I can tell you.

Daddy and I continue to visit, let Meeting say what it might, and I go on my own also. I hold baby Jesse, and soon I am helping him stand and walk and run about after a leather ball I make. Then there is another boy, and a little girl quick enough. Their mother is tired always, but at her table she teaches me some proper spelling and ciphering and some of the Delaware language, which has a musical sound. She used to have a little dame-school for the Indian children in a little settlement somewhere outside town. She tells me some Delaware stories about odd creatures and reads to me from *Gulliver's Travels*, which has plenty of odd creatures also. When

I am better at reading, I read it to her. Yahoos and Lilliputians. The half-circles under her eyes grow darker and her body grows thinner. She coughs and sometimes she cannot stop the coughing. Israel goes on hunts but never comes back with much. I take the little family a deer joint or some bear meat when I get any. I am fifteen years of age, I feel life springing and surging all through me and I see her smile to look at me.

But she is sick. After the last child, she lives for a time, thin as a whip and big-eyed in bed, but then she is dead. Daddy thinks to try to bury her in the Friends' ground but he will not go quite so far, and we put her in a grave at the edge of our place. Israel brings the children to live with us at Ma and Daddy's house. The poor little girl's breathing is troubled like their mother's. Israel is thin too and he is weak. He tries to help Daddy at one of the looms in the barn but his heart has flown out of him and his hands are not quick. Everything is always coming undone, he says, and he laughs and coughs as the loom beam thumps down on his fingers.

I hunt to feed everyone at home. I have no trouble getting deer or anything else.

Some of the women Friends come to Ma. They say the children must attend Meeting for their own sake, if Daddy and Israel will only confess and beg forgiveness as they have been asked again and again. They say it reasonably and then they say it with damp eyes. Ma drops her head and reaches for Israel's little daughter. Daddy hears and says:

—Get off my land, you pack of crows and buzzards. Off!

In my mind I still see Israel's wife's hand spelling the words on the slate for me to puzzle out, and I hear her soft voice reading to me. I see the dark freckles in a *V* down her neck. I have a liking for freckles still and for the letter *V*, which she showed me how to write with little wings at the top. *V* is for *victory*! I do not forget her laugh when I spelled out *friend* as *f-i-e-n-d*. At that time I was astonished that it is possible to spell out untrue things.

But I know now it is possible to spell out anything you wish. I return from a hunt with a doe and find Daddy standing in the door of the house with Israel behind him. I see William Hill in our yard holding out a notice between his hands. His father is a few paces away looking more scrubbed than ever. He does not hold out his hand to Daddy now. Ma at the window has her own hand to her throat, and her face is dreadful.

Here is Exeter Meeting's last judgement on us: *Against the Order and Discipline of Friends in General. 26 March 1750.* I remember all of this trumpeting across the page in great letters, and I remember laughing as Daddy stood repeating it. Israel coughed and spat a bloody bubble in Hill's direction and Ma tugged him indoors. I hear her soft fretful question: Where? Where? Daddy rips off coat buttons and sends them skittering over the floor, saying there is no answer to such a stupid word, why talk, why not go anywhere other! The buttons bouncing off to all corners and Israel coughing and coughing and falling to his knees sick and laughing.

Outside, Hill shouts:

—Dan, I wanted to tell you first. I will not forget you.

A hot flint seems to be striking against my breastbone, trying to kindle all my bones. Hill, it is true. Hill, I am sorry. What is this but the true desire to murder you, the first time it is sparked in my own body. I shout back through the window:

—Use that paper for your arse.

Hill's father beside him shakes his head and walks on all solemn in his good grey cloth, but Hill turns back to see me. He stops and fumbles in his pocket and sets a little stack of coins down on the ground. He points to them and to me, and he nods. Then he stands staring in dull sorrow at our all being cast out this time. I see what he is thinking: *What will you do now?*

4

Carolina

I KICK THE money into the dirt but I keep Hill's gun. All the long journey away from Exeter I walk with it before the fat flock of wagons. Ma and Daddy and Bets are in them, and Ned and Squire and Hannah, and Israel and his children, and my sister Sallie and her small outcast family. Granddaddy's black cabinet creaks and takes up half the room in the last wagon. I walk the horses across the shallow ford up the Schuylkill as we leave the valley. My young brother Squire and I swim the animals across the broad Susquehanna in Virginia. Though he is not yet nine years of age, he is a good swimmer, pulling the horses into the water one by one and making sure the wagons keep upright. His little dark head bobs in and out of the river, dipping under a wagon and showing up on the other side. I say:

—There you are.

He nods and walks with me as I make our trail until we get to the old Indian road southwest, which is quite a high road now, scattered with travellers. We are not the only ones in search of a better place.

I watch for anything to shoot. Anything. I watch for signs, for tracks, for moving shadows, for twitches in the trees and grass, for William Hill-shaped things, though I am glad enough to think we are going to a new place without Hill and without Friends, with any luck.

I get turkey and deer and my first bull elk. It noses out into the bright Virginia morning and I shoot it clean through the brain.

Squire watches. I give him half the liver and we jerk the meat together. Elk liver is very fine. I could eat fifty. I know I will get more.

At times I am visited by thoughts of Israel's wife in the spring cellar with her bodice open in the dark and the sound of the cold water trickling. She is in the ground now, truly gone. But above this current of thoughts my eyes and ears keep sharp. Out in the air I feel my skin drying and blowing off like a snake's. This is what I have wanted all my life.

At first I imagine that I have my brother Israel's hunting eyes, but soon enough they are my own eyes. Israel is lying in one of the wagons. He coughs roughly into the night, he does not stop. I sit awake at the campfire and listen for his raggedy breath. Ma asks a passing Moravian priest for medicine, for any help, but he has nothing to offer but a spittly prayer in German.

I do not go to look at Israel. He does not come out. I can feel him thinning and vanishing, I can hardly bear to think of it. I hear Ma's weeping and Daddy's silence, it is full of disbelief.

I will get game, I will be a better hunter than Israel is, and he will live to see! So I say to myself. The thought charges through my blood. I cannot sit still. I ask Ma for Israel's hunting shirt with the Indian beads, and I put it on and tie up my hair in a plait like his. His little boys, Jesse and Jonathan, peer at me out of the flap of their wagon. They let it drop when I catch them looking. I go off on a three days' hunt.

I do not forget you, Israel, though when I return you are dead in the wagon, your body gone cold and hard, as I imagine, and your eyes finished, just as the eyes of birds go. I do not go in to see you before Ma wraps you up. Thinking of seeing you this way makes me feel sick. I do not wish to see Death sitting at your shoulder, breathing cold on what is left of you. I do not wish it to get near me. At this time I do not know how close Death can come.

Ma and Daddy remain in the wagon with the body of their firstborn son for some time. When Ma stumbles out at last, a cry rips out of her:

—It came from her, from *her*. It was never in our family. It never was!

Even sweet Ma is marked by Death's cruelty. She means the consumption came from Israel's wife. Ma cannot look at Israel's little girl, who is dark like her mother, and very sick now also. The girl is called Sarah Sallie, after our aunt and our sister. Soon she too is gone.

Again I remember the mother. She was a kinder teacher than most. I am sorry to this day that I cannot recall her right name, though I can picture her hair and other parts of her. Israel called her Little Girl. In the Delaware language he would sometimes say it, *Quetit*. I know it now.

Israel, Ma tells me through her tears that you wished me to have your guns, and your quarter-breed boys to raise once I have my own house. You leave me your life, or perhaps I took it from you in wishing for it.

But for the time I am emptied out without you alive. I hunt in the hills a few days more before we move on. There is nothing to me now but the smell of powder, the loose shake of it in the horn, the dust caught on my fingers when I tip it into the measure and out into the pan. The cool of the lead in my hand and then in the barrel. The hesitation before the catch, the hot spark and crack, the speed of the shot. And the resistance of flesh when the knife goes in and the skin peeling itself back when the cut line is made.

All of it comes from you. In my mind you are a grey shadow always coming across the field with the sun, as you did in the summer pastures. We leave you in a grave near where some Germans have made a little village in Maryland. I put up a marker, which the Friends do not allow, but I have no care for that. It is a poor enough marker, only a plank with your name spelled out on it, but I could find it now if I wished to.

I cannot see you fully but I imagine you telling me there is more to find, and I always wish to follow you, Israel. I do not know at this time that you will follow me always, trying to get your life back.

We carry on, we find places we might settle. But no place is right. Daddy wishes to be farther from everyone, from everything, from all he remembers. I wish to be farther from where Israel died. I walk far ahead of the wagons, I never sleep in them now. We move on again and again, following the Indian road that bows round with the Allegheny Mountains, until we find ourselves in the Yadkin Valley in Carolina. The earth is a deep rusty red here, it clays up my moccasins as I walk. It seems a good place, with meadows and plenty of forest all round.

Daddy spots a thin man dragging a scythe across the flats near the Yadkin River. He pulls up the horses and shouts to stop the rest of us. Climbing down, he stalks after this man and speaks to him for some time. I see the man nodding, I see the sun trying to flash off the spotted scythe blade. When he returns, he says sharp to Ma:

—Three shillings the mile. What do you say, my girl?

Ma says yes, what else can she say? This sort of land would cost a hundred pounds in Exeter. Daddy buys twelve hundred acres. We stop and begin to unload. It is a pretty enough place, a long empty patch near the forking of the river, with the bluish hills rising to the west. And cheap, yes. She tries to keep her face sweet, though I know she is thinking of the lonesomeness of the situation. No friends here. And no Friends.

We stay. As soon as I can, I get out the gun and ready myself to set off exploring. Daddy looks up from where he is splitting shingles for the new house, though there is no house yet. He is set to hurl his axe at me.

—Where do you think you are going?

—Anywhere other.

After I serve him up his own words he sits down heavy upon a stone. The land needs clearing, the logs need building into a cabin. The wagons where Ma and the others and all the children are living need unloading. Granddaddy's cabinet is the one piece Daddy has taken out. It sits crooked and black on the ground. Daddy eyes it, his face hard. He is still full of Israel's death. His hands are set upon his bandy knees.

—Had you not better get to work here?

I think to say: N-nah, not today, his words again. But instead I say:

—I am going on a long-hunt. A month at least.

This is all that I will say now. I keep my countenance pleasant and still, what can one say to it? His face sinks as he watches Lawyer Daniel, the son of his old dreams, drown forever. I am lucky that my hands said nothing of blacksmithing and weaving when he used to try to read them. Daddy often stares at his own hands and says, as if he is arguing with someone: I have no sympathy for the materials, none at all.

Here in the Carolina backcountry, he is casting his loose eye about to establish us and to grow himself again like a cabbage. He does not wish to talk of Israel again. And we do not talk of the past, though Neddy sometimes mentions Pennsylvania and old times with a wistful air. I see him down at the creek now where young Squire is crouching, intent on fishing. Ned is trying to dry his feet, standing on one and swabbing at the other. He was made for happiness. He has always been happy, he has always pleased everyone with his company. This dragging discomfort is not to his taste, but he tosses a careless smile at me when he sees me. He sings in his pure sweet voice, it carries over the twilit flats:

The sun was sunk beneath the hill,

The western clouds were lined with gold.

When Ma touches her eyes and says he sang this for her in the old house in Exeter, Daddy says very loud that it is all sold now, it might as well never have been built, there is no such house! And Ma goes sadder at the thought of her homeless children and goes down to Neddy with a cake, trying to make her darling boy happy again.

Daddy, you never liked to be reminded of old times, as I know. You thought there were always better things coming. But the past keeps sniffing after us here.

Daddy appears fatigued. He blows his nose and peers into his handkerchief in case an answer has emerged there, he looks at his hands again as if they will change. But he has no choice with me, as he can see. He understands me to mean I am good for nothing else. His eyes say, *You in those clothes. You are not my first son. Israel was to be the hunter.* I hear a slight shudder in his breath. He scratches all round his neck and says slowly:

—Do not vanish entirely, Dan.

But I do think of vanishing. Daddy knows it. He sends his blacksmith apprentice Miller along when I go off for my hunt. Miller is eager and glad to be away from Daddy and all the land-clearing and homestead-building, but he is unsure of himself in the backwoods, and his arms are too long for the poor short-rifle he has. So I leave him to keep camp and I go alone through the bright autumn forests, trapping all along the Yadkin and hiking up into the foothills of the Blue Ridge Mountains, where the air is indeed bluer and thinner. In this air I can follow the animals' thoughts and I know which way they will run. I know which way I will find them lying in the trap and which way they will gnaw at their caught legs. They do not think, they do not have the words for thoughts, they are driven about by their blood's whispers. I listen until I can hear the hissing. I remember Israel first showing me how to find their marks on the ground or in the trees. He seems far off now, a memory only. I look at the animals' blood when it goes from wet to thick, I smell it. I keep a tally: thirty deer in a single day. At the camp, Miller keeps firing off the numbers of skins hurriedly under his breath. For some time I am near happy.

Over the next several years, I travel all through the forests whenever the weather is warm, and I hunt through the autumns and winters. I bring the meat to my family, I sell the hides down in Salisbury. Selling the hides takes the shine from it. The traders' fingers are blunt and unseeing. If there were a way, I would slap the skins back on the carcasses and send the creatures off, to have the more to catch again. Selling them does bring me plenty of money, enough to bring home and keep some over. I buy a new gun. I am fond of money. And I wish for more than I have. More of everything.

One night Miller wishes to go to the frolic at old Morgan Bryan's big place upriver. He is curious, as apprentices are not meant to go. And charming Neddy, smiling and smoothing his black hair, with no care for trouble, says:

—Why not?

I will admit I am happy enough to be persuaded. Ned and I steal out of the house as dark falls and get on Daddy's favourite horse, Jezebel, barebacked. She is a good mare, light on her feet in spite of our double weight. Miller follows wary on the pony. All the way Ned sings "Courting" and "Women and Wine" in his sweet clear voice. I laugh and try to sing along but I cannot get into Neddy's key.

Some at Bryan's are taking it in turns to shoot at a straw target. The echo of the shots quivers across the dusk.

—Here at last. The famous marksman. King of the tomahawk.

This from one of the many big well-off Bryan boys, his hair like a banner on fire in the torchlight. He holds up his hands as if in surrender. Miller and Ned laugh and I say:

—Then you have been waiting for us. Your party so bad as that?

Bryan grins and crosses his arms and says:

—Give your tomahawk a twirl. Get it out, give the girls a good look.

One of his brothers says:

—Keep your weapon to yourself in public if you can, Boone, ha!

I say:

—Send me word when you learn how to leave yours alone.

The brother grabs at his parts and thrusts out his hips. Ned laughs again as he dismounts. He turns towards the barn at the side of the big double house, where there is dancing. People in pairs spin past the open doors in the gold torchlight. Miller keeps himself well back, hoping nobody will notice him and tell Daddy later. I get down too and watch. But just to the left of the door my eye catches a face against the wall, turned just slightly, as if it were a painting on the wall, a painting of a face only. Her hair and dress both black and hidden. She is not moving even her toe to the music, not moving at all. She will not look at me, though I continue to look at her.

I raise my rifle at a black movement far across the field, and I shoot it clean. A whoop goes up with the flash of my gun. Another Bryan gives my back a violent slap. The girl does not move.

A young boy runs back with the dead animal limp over his arm, a grey owl. He hoots: Tu whit tu whoo! He spreads the owl's wings wide, clicking the joints, the feathers fanning against one another and the head lolling back. Some of the others hoot back. Ned takes the bird and holds it out to the girl. Wordless, she turns and walks into the warm noisy depth of the barn. Another girl spins out and stops in the loop of light from the door, just before Ned. She looks similar to the other girl, likely a sister. Someone in the barn shouts for Neddy to come in and sing, and he hands the owl to this girl. She is confused, but she takes it and holds it to her breast. I whoop also, I am too happy.

Miller vanishes at some time, I do not know when, and I lose sight of Ned in the dancing. When I find Ned, it is getting on for dawn, and I say:

—We had best get home.

We mount Jezebel and set off. I have the reins. I ought to have seen it, but I am half-dreaming of girls dancing, and one girl standing still. I gallop Jezebel and she keeps her head down against the boughs and twigs across the path. Ned gives a shout and I feel him stab his heels into Jezebel's sides, *jump*, but she is going down already, the ground is flying up to meet us as she falls hard onto her knees and over onto her back. A shape in the path looms up out of the dark.

My heart seems to stop. No sound. Then a wet snap of bone, a rickety crack like a child's leg breaking. I roll clear.

—Ned.

I am against heat and mossy breath. I listen, but there is nothing to hear. My hand scrabbles for anything, my gun or my knife.

—Ned. Neddy.

—What? I am here, I am all right.

Ned is kneeling at the side of the path. It is Jezebel's neck twisted and broken, like a fish leaping back on itself. I find myself standing over her, my arm slashing stupid at the dark. White patches begin to move against the night.

Only when it heaves itself up onto its legs does it make a noise and then I know it is a cow, a living one. It walks off. Who would have guessed that a cow could fell a mare so handily? Without trying. Ned laughs all helpless until he empties his drunken stomach all over the path. I laugh madly too until rain begins to tap at my face. I sit down then against the dead horse feeling sorry.

But Jezebel is not dead, not yet. No. She is breathing, her side moving up and down. I crawl up towards her face and I peer close. The lashes feather my cheek, I see a slight shine as the eye rolls towards me. It disappears behind a slow blink but then comes back. I find her nose, I touch her lips with the flat of my hand and put my ear to them. She does not snap at me, perhaps she could not do so even if she wished to, but she was always a gentle girl. I listen to her gentle breath, my throat clenched. I cannot see enough to load a shot, and at any rate my horn has spilled in the fall. I whisper:

—Ned. Ned. Have you any powder?

But he has none, he dropped his gun somewhere and is dizzy and sick with drink. And so I have to find the centre of Jezebel's throat with my knife. It is not difficult, her throat is bent back. She seems to be offering it up. She is patient. I feel for the place where her neck meets her chest, and I find the notch between. The knife slips in without hitting bone. I hold it there. She shudders twice. I move back to keep her blood from my good shirt, but I bend to keep my ear near her mouth. Jezebel, I hear your last breath.

I thought I heard it. I smelled it, hay-scented. I stand, and out of the night, for a burning instant, I see Israel's face, his sharp smile and eyes, his mouth opening, before all of it is wiped out.

Words seem to hiss in the rain. They hang in the air a moment but are quickly gone. I do not know what the words are. My ears strain for them. The hairs are standing on my neck. Neddy is still crouched, laughing and coughing. He has not seen, I know it without asking him. He has not heard. Part of me wishes to see our dead brother's face again, to ask him what he is telling me, but I am afraid.

—Ned. Come on.

Neddy and I creep home without speaking in the wet dark and crawl back into the house. As I slide into bed, Squire remarks with his usual precision:

—You are damp and you smell of wet horse.

He puts his feet on mine to warm them but they cannot be warmed. I think of the horse and I think of Israel. My face is wet with tears I cannot stop. I turn it from Squire.

In the morning Daddy goes out and finds his best horse missing. He rides the pony out through the woods until he comes upon her body. He comes home asking:

—How did she get out? How did she break her own neck? How—how did she cut her throat?

I say:

—I cannot think how.

I remain calm as Ned is, eating his bread. I lie and I am not struck by lightning. Untruth is no calamity. Keeping quiet is no calamity. As I think at this time.

I go back to the forest to try to see Israel again or hear some echo of what he said. Israel, if I had listened harder, I might have known what was coming. But there is nothing. At this time I do not know how many dead followers I will have.

5

The Whores of Philadelphia

I DO NOT sleep well for weeks after I see Israel's face. It does not come back. I sleep outside the new cabin and stare back at the stars. Israel, I am full of confusion. I am afraid of seeing you, and I am afraid you are gone.

It is Miller's idea to go to Philadelphia. He pleads with me to go along for two nights and not to tell Daddy. Squatting on his heels, he says we can make more money selling a pack of skins here and enjoy ourselves spending some of it. I say:

—All right.

Another city, somewhere Israel never went, seems a reasonable thought.

The tavern's bedsheets are innocent though grimy enough. The first night, we have to share the room with a travelling Frenchman who tells us of a woman he had seen in Paris, kept in a glass box quite nude. He stretches out the word in sleepy tones: newwwd. He is half asleep, his eyes are slits. I ask him to say more, but he looks at Miller with a snaky smile and says:

—Have you not dipped your wick yet, ah, poor young man?

He reaches out to touch Miller, who goes pale and turns his back and leaves for home in the early morning. The Frenchman leaves too and I get the bed to myself, though I do think on the quite nude woman. I picture her gratefully loosed from her glass box into this bed.

In the wet evening, I go north some streets into Hell Town, closer to the river and all its slapping noise. I keep myself to myself but I keep my eyes open also. There is plenty of trade here, plenty of people coming and going in boats and along the alleys. Always the smell of fish and the sad little moons of their old scales all over the walk. My skin pricks up here. I like being in a new city, not knowing what is coming. I like feeling my knife.

I stand looking at the river. I am looking for Israel's face again, in spite of myself. This is what I am doing in Pennsylvania. I look at every face to see if one is his. He is not dead, or not fully dead, I am sure. I am watching the shifting of the water and thinking so when a man runs at me, his arm hanging like a dragging wing, I cannot see his face in the shadows of the buildings. He puffs a rough, unshapen word, it is not *help,* though it is something like it. He stumbles and reaches out as if he would take my arm in trade for his broken one. I step back but he falls and clutches my knees. Now I see his upturned face, his eyes are full of tears, pale blue with starry lashes all round. Not Israel's eyes. The man kneels panting before me. I get out my knife. I see his unshaven throat, the bobbling lump at the front of it, and I am full of quick anger that he is not my brother. I raise the blade. I believe by this time that I could kill someone if I had to. Perhaps I believe I could fight Death itself, now that it has been close to me. Most young men believe so perhaps. I grip the handle and keep the blade above him. I stare into his face, I am ready, but he straggles back up and runs on, no longer looking at me. He is calling for mermaids. Show yourselves: so he cries in the direction of the stale water.

I laugh and quiet my heart and I walk on up a street away from the river. The cobbles have a wet sheen, the air is damp. It is quite dark here but for the lights in some of the windows, and not many people are about. And no ghosts. This is what you are now, Israel, I know. And what do you want of me?

I walk slow. Under the splintery red face on the sign for The Indian Queen tavern, a man pukes neatly and then deposits a backgammon piece in the puddle. A horse nips my hair and its drunken rider brushes my neck with dry fingers. I slide my own finger up my knife again and it seems a lonely flat thing.

I close my eyes to the streets. A sniff of green wood burning, a sniff of pickle, a sniff of deep armpit. I sit inside the doorway of a shut bakery, which has a cindery smell and gives me a sad thought of hunting, my campfire sinking to ash and the owls going about their night business. I pull myself up, I feel the cool of the step under my backside and my feet. I force my eyes open to watch the people come and go. People like this life. People like this city, they live in it all the time. But the bells here have a tired sound.

I begin the walk southward back to my inn. Two lights in another tavern burn upon parts of women as they move past the door, lighting their faces when they pause against the wall. One of the women yawns hugely, showing her wide throat. A pair stands blowing smoke into the air and another drags her gown about. When they look at men their faces turn to wood, with carved wooden smiles. Whores. I think of the story of Gulliver, the best story. Israel's wife did not read all of it aloud, not about the whores, but I read it myself. O Gulliver, you did not know what to do with them either.

—The boy! The boy himself, the very boy!

I catch a lick of his smell on the boarded walk. Smells do not disappear from memory, as I find. His broad face and the slope of his shoulders remain the same. As do his voice and his iron breath.

My thoughts of the past seem to have conjured him out of old darkness. William Hill. Perhaps he is what has been coming for me. Not Israel. I am somewhat relieved, I will admit. And he is very pleased at any rate and clutches at my hand:

—Always a pleasure and a delight to see an old friend, friendship is a gift! How do, Boone?

—I do all right.

Hill hardly hears me, so glad is he to be pumping my hand up and down in muscular fashion and crying:

—What brings you here?

I do not tell him that I am looking for my dead brother. He is still gripping my hand and talking:

—The companion of my youth! Happy days, happy days. Though you seem to be in search of other happiness this evening, ha!

He eyes one of the larger whores up the street, and I think of him in youth cheerfully singing under the bridge with the rest: *Your sister is a whore.* Perhaps it was with hope that he used to say it. He puts his arm about my shoulders and presses me forward. Nodding towards the capacious woman, he says:

—We might go in together, have a share. She has plenty to go around, look! Here, let it be my gift. What else is there to do in this city?

He jangles coins about in his palm. He smiles me up and down with his old pointed curiosity mixed with affection. His eyes are clear, his offer is quite sincere. His belief seems to be that we have always been great friends. He makes no mention of the fact that I stole his gun, or that my family was cast out, and I do not wish to bring it up. I suppose it is better to be friends after all. It is better to forget bad times. Hill seems entirely able to do it. And still he has money, which he is used to having, and it seems better than my own money, which at once seems miserable.

He begins to sing "The Green Fields of Home," opening his arms to the lady and the whole night.

I feel sick as a pig. But interested also. I go with him.

We feel our way up the tilted steps to get to her room. It is at the top of the house, and is dim and smells of cold tallow. She settles herself upon her bed, which creaks as if afraid of what is coming for it. We can hear her hard breathing there, we see her broad outlines. She says that she will save her candle, but Hill cajoles her to light it, saying that he wishes to inspect all of her charms closely, and that he will buy her all the candles she wants. And so she lights it and in the guttering glow I watch her get herself out of her bodice and skirts. She huffs and adjusts her flesh as Hill hums and throws his heavy arm about my shoulder. He tells her we are brothers. I burn with a quick wish to strike him for saying so and I pull back, but the woman says dully:

—Brothers. The singer first? Or keep singing while the other has his go. Pass the time.

The singer first. I watch Hill attach himself to her, singing an old song about jolliness of all sorts. Brothers indeed. Hill is rewriting my life for me. It seems easily done. I watch as Hill carries on, running his fingers up and down and in the woman. He turns to slant a joyful eye at me. What would your father say, Hill? *Confess to your Friends here today.* So I think. And Hill would do so, he would tell anyone anything.

Through the cracked shutter I can see the street, it is still there, it helps me to feel less strange. I look down at the earth until my eye lights on a woman in the shadow of the building. She steps forward as a cart passes, and I see her copper-coloured hair in the light from the tavern below us. Israel's wife, her cap off on the cellar floor. My heart fills. The past is with me here. The cart veers on and when the woman turns back she looks up briefly and her eyes flash.

I begin to think that whores are no bad thing.

I go out while Hill is occupied with his face in the woman's backside, singing on in smothered fashion:

I'll roar and I'll groan,
Till I'm bone of your bone,

And asleep in your bed.

Down in the street I offer my hand to the dark-haired woman and I say:

—How do.

As it turns out, she also has red stockings and the most beautiful dimples in the flesh of her thighs. Still I remember her face in the flicker of her own bad candle, as though she were passing in and out of the shade of a tree on a bright day. I remember her pointed chin and her hair curling before her ears. She tells me that her name is Maria and that she lost her virtue at the top of a volcano in Italy. Then she laughs in snapping fashion. But she is kind in spite of my innocence and my hurry. She makes me forget. Thank you, Maria, if that is your name. Are you still in that city, I wonder, or have you vanished like so many.

When I go out the next afternoon I hope to evade Hill, but I go back to that inn to seek her out. It is too early perhaps, she is not there and so I introduce myself to another lady. She is a very long lady and has no dimples but does smile and I will say no more of my trip to Philadelphia.

When I am back in Carolina, that city becomes a loose dream to me, not a real place. It has eaten my money. Miller has kept his share of our hunting proceeds safe. He looks upon me, his face like soap, all clean and disgusted with my dirt.

I had thought myself lucky. But so did Israel. I do not know what I am to do.

The hunting and trapping are poor as the summer comes, and so I earn my keep driving wagons to market in Salisbury. It is dull enough work. I think only of escape, my brains thump with the thought in the day's heat. All the worse because the Yadkin Valley seemed a good place when we first settled here. But my happiness is gone, and where may I go to now? My legs are heavy as lead. I cannot live this way, rolling about with lead legs in a wagon. A fear creeps along, a fear that I will disappear entire into this life. At times I feel Israel's breath, his laugh, at the back of my neck. But when I turn he is not there. Never.

On my way back from market when the daylight is low, I stop at Lowrance's tavern some miles out of town. After a drink I go outdoors to relieve myself, and round the side of the house I see a bundle of hay set on sticks with a slap of red paint at its centre. It has the look of a square pig without its head. Headless it stares at me.

A sign.

I do not relieve myself. I join the queue before the target though I am fatigued and arse-sore from sitting. The evening is windy. It is only a small shooting contest, hardly a contest at all. But I know that I will win it. The wind nips at my eyes but I know. I get out Hill's old gun and I shoot the dead centre of the red paint, the eye of the straw pig. My prize is a tomahawk prised from the death grip of a fallen Iroquois, as old Lowrance says grandly, which makes a group of Catawba Indians who have stopped to watch hoot with laughter.

—White Indian, ha ha ha ha.

They laugh on into the wind. Their eyes glint. One of them is drunk and laughs so hard he falls sideways to the ground.

For a time I carry the tomahawk about. I take it to more competitions in hope of gaining some new luck from it, though its weight swinging from my belt makes me feel a fool. A white Indian indeed. But I win. I win. The winning is stupid and easy but I do it as if I had been born for it. Some of the prizes are poor enough things, kettles or badly tanned skins, but some are bottles of whiskey, and some are money. And people begin to know me, they talk of me as if I were not there. As if I were a tale. I ready my powder measure, and I hear a woman say I shot three men straight through, the holes lined up like shirt buttons. Another says I cleaved someone else's brains dead in half one Sunday afternoon. Families sit and eat on the ground watching, children chew their bread with their mouths open and call out: Shoot.

Another shooter, a sharp-faced man with ratty teeth, jabs me with a long musket and says:

—Now get one arm behind your back.

I take his musket and I do so, though the gun is near as long as I am tall and my arm holding it shakes. People go on talking of what I will do. Some place bets. I feel eyes pinned on me.

I can shoot this way, one-armed. I go cold all through with knowing that it can be done. My arm quiets, my chest empties out, I am able to hold myself still and shoot clean. *Israel, look.* The words come into my mind but are soon covered by the gun's crack. The ratty-faced man claps slow. The crack is what I love, and the burned smell and the bits of straw spinning from the target and slowing in the air.

Again I begin to feel alive. I get two new guns, my own long gun and another short-rifle, and in autumn I go on hunts with Squire and Neddy. Squire is very silent, a good tracker for his age. He keeps his thoughts to himself. Ned teases him for the way he checks the hour by the sun, as though time were of great importance out here. Ned likes to hum, or to stop us and say: Let's sit a while. Then he likes to go home. But though we know the whole of the Yadkin Valley well by now, there is no pleasure in it. The game is poorer and poorer.

We get back to the cabin one evening to find Hill sitting outside it singing. I say:

—What are you doing here?

He smiles. He is holding a new long gun, rubbing the barrel. He says:

—Inspecting Carolina's possibilities.

—Here?

—Even the whores of Philadelphia talk of coming out here. Even they have heard of your shooting. Some of them remember it personally, I should say.

This he says with his heavy reminding clap on the back as he stands. He presses the gun into my hands and says it is a gift. He has presents for the young ones and Ma also. As we go inside, he talks with Neddy about old times, he says he has always felt himself quite at home in our family. Ma gives him coffee and he sits at our table and talks on. He takes out papers with land advertisements in which the words *green* and *sweat* appear without fail. He has written them, he says, for the newspapers in Pennsylvania. I believe he means *sweet* but my spelling is uncertain and I do not wish to penetrate the mind of Hill. He is buying up land cheap, any land he thinks he can sell at a profit. When Daddy comes in, Hill stands and calls him sir. Daddy's face goes hard as a rod, but Hill offers him fifty good acres upriver for nothing, which slowly placates him for the memory of being cast out of Exeter Meeting. Wealth does this, as I can see, it smoothes things like a hand over a fur.

Soon it seems Hill's fault that people are everywhere and that houses and cabins pop up like weeds. Most of these have no interest for me, though one day I see a girl washing her linen in a creek, and she is a pretty girl, which is interesting, especially as she is wearing only her undershift and I can see her round arms. Neddy and Squire and I stare, but when she notices us she crawls into the rough low sty on the bank and does not heed our calls.

We have to go still farther to find deer and bear, and our traplines are often empty.

Tales crawl in with the new people like a dark blanket being tugged over the country. Everybody seems to know them at once, they infect the air. There is no peace. Cherokees and Shawnees and

Iroquois slaughtering everyone at any little settlement, old women and all. And Virginians killing Indians, even old peaceful Catawbas long settled there, for anything, for stealing an egg, and turning in the scalps to collect the Governor's bounty. Hill loves to talk of all of it. He will sit by our fireside and throw his hands behind his head and go over and over these tales, as women will talk of a mortal sickness, the vomit and the soiled bedclothes and the final words and the precise minute that Death arrives. I do not want to hear it.

—Some of the children whose parents the red-boys murdered got away into the woods, all bloody wounds. Poor little creatures. Who can say where they have got to?

He affects sensitivity and love of children. He sets his hands on the shoulders of my youngest sister Hannah. Hill feels all of this truly when he talks of it, his body quakes with his feeling, I cannot bear his swimming eyes. But he is richer than ever. He has turned his Quaker father's money into land speculations and bets, and he is winning everything.

I think of money, I think of fresh land. All I would like to have. I go to market with my skins on a grey day. There is no escape from the bad talk. At the stall I am told of a farmer tomahawked through the back of the neck who had to drag himself four days to safety with his head lolling, unable to eat or drink but knowing that he must somehow get away, for any prisoners the Indians take are burned alive at the stake. The woman who tells me this runs her eyes eagerly all over my face. Like rats they run. She says:

—The Shawnee are the best burners. Chief Black Fish is the one. He paints the captives black so they know just how they will look afterwards. Black as your hair.

She has a newspaper with a drawing of such a burning in it, which she thrusts at me. She then shades her eyes with her hand and calls for her husband to look at my skins. Ma, I think of your tales of women burned for witches in England and the north, little ashy heaps of them left everywhere. I drive the wagon home and have no wish to speak to anyone for some time.

64

I am in want of money, I am in want of everything, I am in want of a scratching. I itch in Carolina head to foot. I have no quarrel with the Indians, I never have, and not much with the French. But I am young.

Come on boys. Come on. We will get the FROGS out of this land for good and some of their Redskin friends too.

The appeal is poor enough. But I tell Ma the King's shilling is as good as any. She says war is no life for me, but to myself I say: You do not know what life is for me. It is not here.

I kiss her sad face both sides, and I go to drive a wagon in the army baggage train. I am young and I believe that I know what I ought to do, I believe that I can get free and make my own way. Though it is only Death opening its clothes to me and saying: *Look close.*

6

Traps

ONCE WE GET out of Carolina there are no true roads west, only narrow trails, which the scouts lose entirely from time to time. I hope to see something marvellous but there is little so far. The French have no interest in showing themselves. We will boot them back to Quebec when we find them, all this land and its furs for England and King George! So the officers keep announcing. General Braddock places his proper British regiments at the front in their proper scarlet coats. Some of us colonial militiamen at the back have jackets the wives or mothers tried to dye red, but we are a sorrier looking lot. The army creaks and groans and whistles along. We force our slow way through bogs and underbrush and woods. We hack everything down. Every blade of grass. We stop for every bump. For every anthill.

—Ought to have kept one to show my Ma. Or to turn in for the money.

I hear one of the scouts saying this to another as they pass our fire on their way to their tent. The other runs his finger over his lip as he says:

—No money in those, they have hung out there for months. Not even the flies are interested. Use it as a wig for your prick, your Ma would like that.

Scalps they are talking of, nailed to the trees where we last camped. In the Allegheny Mountains now, it is rough going. We are tired out and sore and want only to drink in private without catching Hell from the officers. No wagoner is fond of the scouts and their airs, and perhaps it is a mercy there are so few of them, though there ought to be more. Indian ones would likely do better, but who can tell which side they are on? I do know I could do better myself. Signs are everywhere if you look. And I do look.

As the scouts walk on I hear them arguing about the name of a town they both believe they know. No no yes yes, on and on.

—If they do not like the scenery they should paint themselves another scene. Such is the privilege of you boys of America.

This comes from Findley, the wagoner fondest of talking. He is the worse for drink now, that is to say worse than the rest of us. He is an odd fellow, all bones and small bright blue eyes. In his usual life he is a trader and so he is able to supply us with the drink we are not meant to have. But in exchange we are forced to listen to him. Rum makes him affable at least, and we all watch out for the officers together. He lies with a cloth over his face for his toothache and spins yarn about his travels. He has been south to Florida to trade among the Seminoles. He says he tried to shoot a dragon there, properly called an alligator, but he was baffled by its weird eyes with their black pupils like narrow doors. The heat also baffled him, it was so damp and gasping. And deep in the green swamps he came upon an Englishman living with twelve women and his old mother. The Englishman called it an Ideal Society, where work was done according to inclination.

I am the only one who really listens. I would like to know about all he has seen, not least these women. I say:

—And what was these ladies' inclination? What do they wear in the swamps of Florida?

From beneath his face cloth Findley laughs in muffled faraway fashion and says:

—Perhaps I will tell you. Perhaps.

I sit up and say:

—How long did it take you to get there, Findley? What was the hunting like?

But he seems to have fallen asleep. Dodd, another driver, says:

—Christ.

He throws a spoon at Findley, who stirs and reaches for it. His voice rises again gamely:

—For that, I will tell you something. There is another place I have been to with no one in it, no women, no French and no need of roads at all, so perfect is it. Some Indians perhaps, not many, and perfect nonetheless. No need of roads, no need of names. Beautiful. And clean. I dream of it, you boys, I dream of its cleanness. You too would dream of it if you only knew what cleanness was, if God in his mercy chose to reveal it to you as well—

I am listening. I know that Findley feels me listening. His voice seems directed straight at me. I am about to say: Where is this place then. But another among us groans like an ox and says:

—Oh Christ, no goddamned Irish sermonizing here, Findley. O *Jaysus.*

—Go back to your face-ache. Spare us the pain.

Dodd says so while digging about with a twig in his ear. As he goes too far with it, he yelps: Shit. Then he says:

—Lying there like a slug. Shame the Indians did not send you to your eternal rest on your travels. Their heavenly hunting grounds will take anyone, clean or not.

Findley gives a cooing laugh and flaps an arm:

—Indeed. The Indians are great friends of mine. We trade, and they have shown me all manner of things.

—And they like your things.

—All my things, certainly. They are fond of silver and gold.

—Well, and are your things silver and gold? The deuce, and mine only flesh. But meaty! Take a look if you dare to come out from under that arse-rag.

Dodd is laughing and reaching for his belt to drop his breeches as he will do at any opportunity, but Findley does not lift the cloth from his peaky face. He goes on with his arm held out:

—What I tell you will appear in your dreams, and they will be the most heavenly dreams you have ever known.

Dodd spits on Findley's face cloth.

I take a drink and I say:

—Your path to Heaven could be sped for you, Findley.

Now he lifts the cloth dainty as a bride with a bedsheet and looks me up and down with a grin before replacing it. He knows he has me on his hook.

The air tastes of thick dust. It gets all through our mouths and clothes.

We are in Pennsylvania now. Pennsylvania again. The fifes far at the front of the column take on a wheezy flat tone after some days in the dust. The late summer wasps and flies keep with us, I grease up my face and neck to keep them off, but they pay no heed. At the front the infantry are building a log road to get us through a newly cleared boggy patch. I pull up my horses, who are restless. The oxen pulling the open wagon ahead of mine are unperturbed at having to stop so often. I stare at their ridged blank backs. I wonder about the sentiments of oxen. What do they think of? Being gelded, there is not much to think of, as I imagine.

An insect creeps into my ear, and as I turn my head to shake it loose I see my little sick wife, Molly Black, the wife of my childhood.

For an instant I see her blindfolded ghost, a small camp-follower at the back of the wagons.

I am sentimental at twenty years of age. So I tell myself.

But now my team butts against the wagon in front and steps back, tangling the traces. One horse rears and sputters. I get down to unsnarl them. I invent fresh curses about vegetables and the crevices of horses. Findley on the wagon behind me laughs and says:

—I could listen to you all the day and night. Do not stop now, go on, go on. You are quite amusing to watch, Boone, did you know it?

For his benefit I turn the vegetable curses to the crevices of the Irish and he laughs the more and slaps his long thin thighs.

When I have untangled the beasts, we lurch on. We bump over the logs and onto the ground again. I could crawl faster than this backwards. The heat oppresses me. I occupy my mind with keeping the horses exactly half a foot from the wagon in front. I think also of the round-armed girl in her under-shift, and the pretty faces and parts of other women I have seen, and my thoughts become less sentimental for a time.

The axes at the front clash with the trees, the fifes pick up their dreary tinny tune, "Roslin Castle" again. Goddamned castle, are there no other tunes? Findley yawns heavily. I call back:

—Headache again? Like to die yet?

He only groans, and I must say that my own head is aching violently when I think of it. We drag on a quarter-mile or so, the sun heightens. The river nearby gives no coolness and no relief from the clanging and whistling and creaking and groaning. Far ahead of us, the line begins to ford the water.

We bump to a dead halt, pinned by a high bank on one side and stands of birches atop a ridge above the river on the other. The river seems an impossible cool dream. There is no way to get the wagons through this to the shallower ford up the path, so the axemen will have to set to work again. We are not permitted to leave the line.

I sit back. My hat falls down my back at this moment and my aching head burns in the sun.

I do not hear the shout, only the echo bouncing back. Then the doubled echo of four shots. Then more, running into one another so they cannot be counted. No human sound at first. I stand and I can see a mounted officer just ahead of the wagons and behind the marchers, stopped with his hand over his mouth and nose, as though a stink had hit him in the face. He turns back and I see his perplexed forehead. I climb up on the box: a half-mile ahead at the front of the train are hundreds of people like the Lilliputians in the story, miniature people appearing out of the trees and descending the bank. Where have they come from?

My eye lights on a tiny man in a tiny French blue jacket separating himself from the pack. Quickly he knocks down one of our soldiers with his gun-butt and then kneels on him and knifes his head and peels off his scalp. I see the whole of this scene, the small arm waving the detached hair in the air and the tiny body on the ground. I seem to be peering into a strange world underground, perhaps in an anthill. I want to shut my eyes but I cannot. I am still standing upon the box. A dog cries with a desperate sound. More bodies on the ground ahead are scattered like fallen red birds. The officer now cries out: Unfair! I believe this is what he says. He orders the rear guard and the wagons onward, slashing his sword across the air. Urging their animals ahead, the first wagoners crash into the infantrymen and some of the mounted soldiers who have turned back to flee. I turn to try to see Findley, but when I look back I see only the moving line of blue jackets and painted skin making its way along our confused column. They chop as if scything through brush, as if we were thousands of thin trees in their way.

Five wagons ahead they are already tearing into the white covering, slitting it like a belly and looking inside. I hear some words in French and then some of the Indians beginning to confer and to pull things out. They know where everything is. They have been following us for days, perhaps for weeks.

Dodd, the driver of that wagon, goes down with a sigh as the breath is torn out of him. I see him roll down the bank towards the water. By now the river is stuffed to the jaws with us, some face down, some splashing in feeble strokes, some standing up to their hips and holding their guns out, waiting for direction.

It strikes me that people do not always run in the face of such danger, they do not believe in it when it opens its maw at them. They wait to see what will happen. I am not the only one. I think of it later in my life when I am standing in the snowy woods, not running.

The French and the Indians sweep along the line, pushing between the trees. They want the horses, the oxen, the supplies. The scalps too. The French king buys them. I picture the French king in a suit woven of people's hair, stroking his long sleeves.

This is no fight, it is only killing, and killing is nothing after all, it is nothing, it is only dull and horrible. I want no more to do with it. Officers in their red sashes fall from their horses screaming. I turn again and see Findley is sitting on his box with his cloth over his forehead. My body is coiled tight. My gun is beside me. I do not know how loud I am or whether I speak aloud at all:

—We had best be gone, I am going.

I slash at the traces with my knife and one of the horses tries to bolt, one falls. I crawl onto the back of the one rearing, I cut him free and we run crashing down the bank into the Monongahela River up to his withers, where I throw myself into the water. I keep my head down and my eyes cracked open just enough to see. With my gun in both hands I push my way through the water to the other side, I hear muffled wet shouts and calls as I keep on, I feel terrible things that I do not think of.

Others are with me on the far side. Not many. One man's trousers are in shreds, he stumbles ahead, his backside ribboned with blood.

I can still feel the bodies in the water like logs, with the same sodden weight, the way I have to push them from me and stand on them. Israel, I keep thinking of your body, though I did not see it. I will not look at any of these dead in case I see you. I tell myself I have seen many murders at once here, but I have killed nobody and I have saved myself and so—*V is for victory.* But chewing it over is like another piece of army salt beef, likely to give you a sore mouth. I want only to not think of it.

I face west. I stand still with the sun burning my eyes out. I think of running past all of this, past everything, and finding the place Findley talked of. Paradise. It is not so far, surely.

My breath struggles in my tight chest. But Ma, I see you with your worried face white as an onion, your hair gone all white too. I see your terrible face after Israel died in the wagon. Ma and Daddy.

I leave the possibility of Heaven behind and make my way back towards Carolina. But after all I do not escape Death, I do not escape killing. There is no escape.

I walk on with my heart swollen and sore. I sing to the trees, I count them to occupy my mind. I list the names of horses we have had. Fatsy, Charming, Helen, Houynhym, Swifty, Sausages. Then I turn to hogs, Jub and Plum, good hogs and clever ones, who dug their way out of their pen at slaughter time. I think of Ma in the dusk of the summer pastures calling in the cows: *Here with you, you Ham.* Oh Ma, I think of you now.

I walk on. But I seem to feel breath at my elbow.

In the deepest backwoods it is horse's breath I feel, though the horse is not here. Jezebel. She has been dead for what seems a thousand years. This is the first time I feel it, the gentle hay-smelling breath. I have not wished to think of it. But Israel has done it. I feel him again as well, his presence behind me. He has called her up from the dead with some wordless sounds. I quicken to a run though the brush is thick and catches at my face and arms. The sun is setting at my back, everything is rusting red.

I know it now. My dead are following me. I say no but they say yes, yes. Little Molly Black's teeth chatter lightly. I feel Israel narrow his eyes and grin. I close my own. I say low:

—What is it? What do you want?

My voice is rough and hard. No reply. The horse's breath is cold but it comes and goes and does not stop. Now it seems to say to me, *You cannot forget.*

I will not think of it. All night I charge on through the brush, branches tearing at my face. I do not stop. The way back is very long. I believe I hear wolves, but my own heart is so loud I cannot tell what I hear.

When day comes, I am still walking, I drag my feet as if I am asleep, I am scratched with thin bleeding lines everywhere, the tip of my ear is torn open, but I go on until I feel nothing and think nothing. Until I stop at the edge of a river. Someone is there.

He is an Indian man sitting fishing on a log bridge over the water far below. All he is doing is fishing. His leg swings light, back and forth, one moccasin dangles from his toes and I see his bare round heel.

The way is very narrow here, my only path straight past him. I see the knobs of his spine curled over his fishing line, his rifle balanced easy beside him.

If I move he will see me. I am trapped, my ribs squeeze my heart, my heart is so loud that I want to rip it out and step upon it.

He goes on sitting and fishing and not going away.

Enough of war, it is not for me. Enough of killing. I say this reasonably to myself. I say to myself, I will frighten him off and go on home. Go on.

Israel, I know you are with me. I close my eyes a moment. Then I ready my shot, and as my finger squeezes the trigger, the man's head turns, his eyes catch on mine. I am startled that he can move and that his eyes can move, that they are real eyes.

The gun shifts and drops as I fire. His eyes change. He falls without a sound, there is no sound for what seems a long time until his clean splash into the slothful water. He does not come up. The ripples smooth themselves away into green.

As I stand looking it strikes me like water on hot metal. I am a murderer. This is what Israel wished to tell me. I think it is, I think this is what he was saying: *You cannot forget what you are.* Poor Jezebel has been sent to say it again. I have been a murderer all along. I think of shooting the deer after the fire-hunt with you, Israel. I killed it unfairly, too easy, and I killed the horse, and now a man, and perhaps I helped to kill you by taking away your luck.

I walk on. More than ever, I think of getting away to another place. But I drag back to Carolina. I drown any thoughts of the death I have caused, I sink them as the Indian man sank beneath the slow current. I never tell of it. I try never to think on it again. The way the mind can rub out such things is a wonder. But only for a time. They do come back. You cannot forget, no. More than once as I walk I feel the horse's breath on my cheek, all innocent.

More than once too I wonder whether I would have killed Neddy that night had he been the one to break his neck and look up at me with sad eyes.

7

When We Eat Cherries

THE REST OF the long walk home from war, I catch at it and I hold it in my mind to keep the ghosts from me, before I know who she is. Her profile, white against old Bryan's dark barn, only her face showing in the frame of black hair like a painting of a face, still as still. Rebecca.

She is a Bryan herself of course, with that whole band behind her. She does not forget it.

—Do I know who you are?

This is one of the things she says, always, in my mind. It comes with a slight lift of her brows as I watch her sweeping. Her eyes are black like birds' eyes, all pupil. She turns away and says:

—I am tired of looking at you. There are better views to the south.

Her voice is deadly and I kiss her cool grimy hand and she gives me the twisted smile. Every time I see it my heart near stops. My wife.

Months after I return to the Yadkin, I see her real face again when Hill decides to take Ned and Squire and me to watch girls cherry-picking in someone's orchard. It will be cheering, he says. There is no cheering me, I know. But I go along. Much of the way, Hill offers his opinions of the accomplishments of the whores of

Philadelphia and elsewhere. Ned asks questions and Squire walks along listening. I will admit that my memories of Maria the volcano whore have worn clear through, though they remain fond enough.

I drop back behind Squire and pick up a root, I look up for birds to club it with. Hill is untiring on other subjects also. Some soldiers carried mutilated bodies from the Monongahela River battle all the way to Philadelphia and dumped them in a square to show that peace is impossible. He has heard of this. He now shouts back at me:

—Did you see many men barbecued in the war?

His face is cheerful. Somewhere he has heard that I killed several Indians as well as a few French on the battlefield. I do not know where he has heard this, it makes my flesh crawl. Other people have been giving me fond thankful looks and one old woman in Salisbury asked to touch the bold *hand* of a young one who blasted the filth from our *land*.

Well I felt sick and ugly but I told her she was a poetess, and she rolled her eyes to Heaven before clutching at my hand and saying yes, she has written a poem. Indeed, more than one poem. She began to hurt my bones with her clutching. Her neck was all lollops of fat.

Now Hill asks again:

—See many scalped?

—No.

I am sick of his questions, I have no wish to think of the army or of anything I have done. The defeat is already infamous. Hill is writing a song about it, the General's battlefield death, bleeding all over his red sash, and all the rest:

The sad death of Braddock in fifty-five,
Soon there was nobody left alive.

Such is Hill's songwriting. He says he will have to make all of it up if I tell him no more. He is starved for interest in life, he moans. I say:

—I told you, no.

And so he begins to sing again: Poor Britons, poor Britons, poor Britons remember. His singing is insistent. I am not fond of this song and I am not fond of Hill singing it. And I am sick of this life and this walk. It is a long walk, a whole morning.

Hill has hopes of seeing cherry-picking girls caught out and having to relieve themselves somewhere in the trees.

—I will feed them all cherries with this very hand until they can no longer resist nature.

When we arrive out of the forest, he plants his feet and stands shielding his eyes from the high sun. Neddy laughs, and Squire says in his dry fashion:

—There are boys already up in the trees getting cherries, your admiralship, and a few girls getting their own. Best hurry before they take them all.

Hill marches forth, followed by Neddy. Squire looks to me, but I wave him on and stay where I am. The cherry trees are thin and young for the most part, all full of upward effort. Only one row is old enough to make any shade. Here two girls sit, the shadows making a net over them. They are sharing black cherries from their basket and looking straight at me. One is the face, the girl from Bryan's frolic. Rebecca.

They are very still as they sit eating. Rebecca moves her hand slowly to the basket, and I see what an effort there is in her stillness. She is full of trapped life. Her heart beats and beats beneath her clothing. She will keep me alive. She is another chance. My own flat heart swells and struggles in its pit.

I watch for a time, hardly breathing, then I force my legs to move. I walk over and sit directly beside her. Her mouth is full of dark fruit, she does not trouble herself to try to speak. I watch her jaw move and the stain spreading out onto her untroubled lip. She slips two more cherries in.

The other girl stares at me with her big deer-eyes. She is the sister who came out of the barn and took the dead owl from Ned. I say:

—How do.

The sister blinks and says:

—How do you do.

She has a stopped-up way of talking, with her hand hovering about her chin. She also has black hair and eyes but a paler, thinner face. I say:

—You are sisters.

She twitches herself about. I smirk at my stupid pronouncement. Rebecca plucks more cherries from the basket. The sister ventures a remark about the heat and peeps at me a while longer. Then she gets up and wanders over to where Neddy and Squire have sat in the sun with several of the girls who are minding children. Hill is hovering. I see him lick his palm and shine his latest gun with it and walk up to show it to them: *See this.*

I remain where I am. I take out my knife.

Rebecca has another cherry. A bee from the hives across the orchard drops onto her wrist. I flip the knife over my knuckles and in and out between my fingers. She pays no heed. Her eyes stay on the bee as it crawls towards the fruit. She turns her wrist and does not flick the insect away. It gets to the cherry, its fat lower body quivers as it sucks. She stretches her fingers lightly. She appears to be contemplating one of the world's marvels, that is to say her own hand.

Now she closes her fist around the bee, I see her do it. Its buzz goes on, though dampened. I say:

—Are you a witch? What evil do you have in mind for that innocent creature? Has it ever done you any harm?

She goes on holding it. It does not sting her, or it does not appear to. Her face shows no pain, at any rate. It shows nothing.

I throw the knife. It is a gentle throw. It catches the edge of her white apron and pierces the lace.

For half a moment she stops chewing. Aha. I say:

—Nice afternoon.

She says nothing. I go on:

—Nice apron.

I take up the knife and flip it again, and then throw it once more with a touch more force so it goes straight through the fabric of her apron and pins it to the ground.

If she tries to get up, the apron will rip to shreds. It is a flimsy fine thing, not homespun. It is expensive.

She keeps up her stillness and silence. The bee drones on in her fist. If it is stinging her she shows no sign of it. I toss the knife again and again, I make reckless holes all along the cloth, closer and closer to her thigh. All the time she does not move. It seems to me she wants to laugh. She eats more cherries, and I watch her chewing and daintily removing the pits into her other marvellous hand. I say:

—A shame to get cherry juice on it.

Now she opens her lips as if to speak, but she only pops in another black cherry from the basket. She spits the pit far off towards the forest. Dark juice sits in a bead on her lower lip and drips purple onto the white cloth of her apron. The knife is still embedded at an angle. I nod in the direction the pit flew and I say:

—Well now there will be another tree. Perhaps a little far from the orchard, though. You can call that your own when it grows up. Pick all the fruit for yourself.

A pit bounces against my skull. Juice travels down my temple. She looks up at the sky as if it were nothing but rain beginning. She opens her fist at last and the bee sits in her palm swaying its head before it flies off crookedly. She goes back to her cherries. I say:

—You shot me. You shot me.

I feign injury, I feign death on the grass. And I hear her voice for the first time. It is low and a little rough. She is still looking away when she says:

—Do excuse me. I could hardly help where the stone wished to travel to.

I say:

—Begging your pardon also. I could hardly help where my knife wished to go.

I see her do it, she pulls up her skirt so her stockings show. They are faintly streaked with grass. Her ankles are narrow. She wants me to see. Now she covers them again and smoothes the apron as though there is nothing at all wrong with it. As though she cut it full of holes herself and dotted it with juice and stuck a knife through it for an ornament. She flicks her black eyes at me and they eat me whole.

I always say I was so bold because I was trying her temper. She might shoot me yet, if I am to see her again in this world.

—Here you are.

I am loud and bloody. I want to make her speak, I want to hear the scratches in her voice. Her glossy eyes, all black with no keyholes and no key.

In her granddaddy's yard I have butchered the deer I dragged here, I have piled the cuts up tidy on the skin. I stand and I wipe my brow and wait. She and her sister live here, her pack of half-brothers live with their father. As I reason, the Bryans are rich but still need food. It seems to me a perfect gift, a mess of uncooked meat, a gift she cannot ignore and will have to deal with.

Standing in the doorway she looks me over. Suddenly I feel my coat of blood and sweat, I see the dark spreading stain I have left on the ground. A house slave appears behind her, followed by the nervous big-eyed sister, Martha. She puts her hand to her mouth while the black woman laughs a disbelieving laugh and folds her arms. To her Martha says:

—Jean, hush.

I swab at my forehead and I laugh back:

—Here you are, just as I said. A butcher's life is a hard one. You see how hard?

Rebecca vanishes. I go on standing like a great bloody infant who has just got itself upright and does not know what to do next. Martha goes on looking, her hands pressed together at her waist. Jean laughs again, shaking her head, and I say:

—You will not get fresher meat. Alive-o. Or near enough. Might get up and run off yet.

But Rebecca reappears with a bowl. She sets it precisely on the step. She returns to the doorway. There she stands as though the house were a ship and she a figurehead.

I go close and I see the milk. The white surface is as innocent as the moon.

—A cat, am I?

I grin and pick up the bowl, I am glad to bloody it with my hands though it is already none too clean and the milk is sour as I can smell. I put my tongue out, I hold the bowl in the air and speak to it soft:

—So you and I have found one another at last. We both need a good scrubbing. Is there no help for us here? No one to get us clean all over? But perhaps the girls of this house know nothing of clean. Perhaps they are all unclean. Perhaps it is my lucky day.

I lick the rim. Martha stares on. Now Jean stops laughing, and Rebecca begins.

Soon enough we are in old Bryan's big house, the lamps are all lit though it is not dark, not quite dusk. Daddy sweats next to the bank of lanterns, but he is smiling. He begins loud:

—Friends.

A flicker crawls over his face, the word is still bad to him. He is still no Friend, though he has been appointed a magistrate here in the Yadkin now, which he feels down to his bones, and so he keeps these straighter than usual. Rebecca's half-brothers stand in a great row. Old Bryan, Rebecca's granddaddy, sits in a rocker, looking cobbled up of the wrong parts. His brows are lowered at his new kin. Perhaps he is thinking that there is still time to have us out of here. But no. Daddy is stuttering out the marriage vows for Neddy and Rebecca's sister, Martha. Our young Neddy has made his choice, or perhaps it has been made for him. Perhaps the owl was only his first gift that evening. Martha looks rounder than usual, and not just her eyes. But no one speaks of it here, we need no further talk of fornication in the family. Ned looks content as ever and Martha keeps hold of his arm as she says yes, she will be his wife.

And now for my turn. I am occupied with keeping myself as still as Rebecca is. Out of the side of my eye I see her breast rise slightly. She is alive, she is seventeen years of age, I am twenty-one. She is near as tall as I am. I pull myself up.

At this time I cannot believe that she has agreed, I cannot believe that it will happen. Some disaster will now roll in, fire or stampede or instant plague. Daddy turns, his face is clouding. Do not go bandy, Daddy: this I think at him as in old times. He slows his talk, making every word a smooth separate pebble in his mouth. No stammers over my name. Daniel.

I know I am his favourite among us now that Israel is gone, though I do not know why. Daddy, I try to ignore the shine of your teary eyes and the way your face has gone so old, but for a moment I do get foggy myself. I have to cough before I can say:

—Well all right, if you say so, I will take this woman to wife.

This woman. My wife. A miracle and no disasters. I give my head a shake, I want to laugh and laugh. I grip her hand.

Well. It is done. Old Bryan has the air of one dragged out of a tomb and forced to put up with this life again. Rebecca's stepmother brings herself to kiss Ma. Two of the little boys press their mouths to the rum jug, hoping for it to sweat. Hill looks up and down my wife, all ideas about her possibilities. He hoots with his hands circling his mouth:

—Good night. Good *ni-i-ight*. Thumping big children to you. Give her a thumping, Boone! Who has the bottle?

When I am upstairs with Rebecca, I can still pick out his shrill shouts among those of the crowd below. For a moment I fear he will set to telling stories of my first marriage to little Molly Black. I almost fear little Molly will chatter her teeth in my ear. But Hill is laughing like a crow now, trying to convince himself of the merry time he is having, though I know he wants what I have.

I have a wife, a real wife, beside me. I am struck by a thought of my Uncle James's red face after my sister Sallie's wedding, telling me to find myself a woman, marry her first. When I was small he would pet and spoil me, rubbing my nose with his bristling whiskers, wielding his jollity like a club for bashing at disappointment. Not enough land, spiteful neighbours, a poor school to run, a dead wife, no new life here. Though I did not like his school, I remember him talking about ancient times, Jericho and Greece and Troy and Rome, which he knew I liked, and sometimes he would press sweets into my pocket until it tore. He said: Danny, you will have to do better than I have.

Hill yowls and a dog sings after him outside. The dancing reels along like a brawl. The boots seem to have increased their weight, the thump of a body falling rises up to us on a current of hard laughter. The air in the house seems a mouthful of liquorish breath let out. My own breath is liquorish, I admit, and Rebecca's is lightly so, though she keeps her mouth closed to a pinpoint and seems hardly to be breathing at all. The bed trembles. It is not our doing. A loud stumble and roar downstairs and Neddy's slow easy laugh from across the landing where he is with his own new wife. Ah-ha-ha. Ah.

Well Uncle James, here is my bride, my new life. To your health. I take another swallow from the jug for good measure.

Rebecca beside me is in her nightgown where Bryan's house slave Jean propped and primped her before leaving the room with a wink when I appeared. Her hair is cobwebby, black and soft against the pillow. The candle gutters as the dancers shake the walls, it reflects in shudders in her eyes. She is as still and quiet as ever and seems to want for nothing. I feel little guns going off all along my limbs and up my back. I am near to being purely happy, though there is plenty I want at this moment. I say:

—Here you are. Here we are.

She is unmoved. Someone below is singing "Black Betty" in the saddest wail.

Well. My hands seem dumb hammers as I fold them over my chest. I send out a prayer to Maria and the others in Philadelphia, I hope I will do better here. If I had my knife I could make a few holes in her nightdress. Look for dimples.

I roll onto my side and grin at her and say:

—Do you remember the cherry orchard?

At this she inclines her head towards me and says:

—Marriage has turned you sentimental.

In her voice is a flint lightly struck. The possibility of a spark, if not a spark itself. I say:

—It is known to do so.

—Rum is also known to do so.

—Well. Milk is too. Have you brought a bowl along for me tonight?

She says nothing. She winds a strand of hair around each finger on one hand. I say:

—At any rate, you are married yourself. You should know what it is like.

—True. I am married.

She says so as if it is nothing to do with me. I touch her hair.

—Mrs. Boone. Poor woman.

—Do I know who you are?

This is first time she says it. She gives me a sudden vicious little smile and I am seized with tomcat joy.

She catches her breath, I feel it.

Nine months later, we have Jamesie. Rebecca, you know that I have counted it out. I know he was mine.

8

In the Ground

You can have a new life for a time. But it does turn old, everything does.

Rebecca loses no shine for me. The truth is that I am full of aching for her, I am near always so, even now, after all that has happened. When we are new married, her face appears in the corn. Or the axe-edge of her shoulder blade does, or her ribs riding up under her skin as she lifts her arms, or the tiny cushion behind her sharp knee. She is built of weapons, I tell her, and she agrees: Yes I am. I know all of her, every inch, I cannot leave her body alone, even in my mind in the fields. At night I call her a Welsh witch, or Beautiful Helen, Queen Not-of-Troy but of the Backwoods, and I lie her down and kiss her low on her back and feel her silent laughter in her backbone. There is the proof of it.

Little girl, I wish I could see you now, any part of you.

Her grandfather's fields are dull. The soil is good, things grow readily. But everything here has the taste of Bryan property, a rusty weepy taste. Besides I have never been one for cropping. I am a poor enough ploughman, I make wobbling furrows, I strike any rock in any field. The work presses on me like an anvil. The corn is like lead. In truth I hate corn, God damn the corn, I would like to hear it all pop itself to nothing. But I stupefy myself. I sink my thoughts into Rebecca and our bed and anything that takes my mind from the plough.

Do not think of the army or the French or the Indians. That life is not for you. This is life.

This I hear in Ma's voice. I stop and bend to clear away a speckled chunk of rock. The horse throws back its head.

Do not think.

But it is easy enough to think of the French and the Indians. They are closer to Carolina again and more unhappy than ever with those settled here and those pushing farther to the south and the west. And now the British, that is to say the true British in the old country, want to tear us up by the roots. We are still Britons, our settler militia flies the King's flag, but we are not subjects enough, it seems. We go too far, we get in everyone's road, we interfere with their fur trading and their treaties, planting ourselves here wherever we like, moving into places they do not want us. It is all a game, all cats and mice. At any rate I find myself neither cat nor mouse.

I stand and look in a circle about me, checking for sound or smoke from anywhere. A pair of Bryan's slaves is at work far up in one of his fields, talking now and then. Their voices carry, slow and easy. The house at the end of the flats is quiet, closed in on itself like a basket with Rebecca and the children in it, Jamesie and my own little Israel now, as well as Jesse and Jonathan. The other Bryan houses are not so far off. The fences are up. The cows look stout enough, and cows can kill, as you know, poor Jezebel. Surely happiness is some protection. It is natural to feel so. But I feel also that if I could stand on a clifftop and look down, the farm would be a tiny rough island in the darker ocean of wilderness. All the toil of hacking down trees, dragging out stumps, clearing away brush, for this.

I want to look into the dark.

I sigh, which I do not like to do. I want to run off. I throw down the plough. The horse snorts and sets to work tearing up a clump of thin grass. I close my eyes and think of last winter, when I crossed the Blue Ridge for the first time after a slave herding cows in the mountain pastures showed me an old trace. His name was Burrell, and he had a broad face and a thin neck. I gave him a few swallows of my whiskey for his help. He said there was more he could show me, but I had no more whiskey. So I followed the trace west myself for two days. I found many creeks and springs and a lot of ginseng, which I took to sell, and the game was very good. In my mind I can see every tree, every nick in the bark, every plant, every animal shit, every sign.

But I had to come back. And now it is spring, there is no end to this work and this place. The wind in the trees has a sound like waves. When we wanted a real story, Ma always used to tell us of her own mother's crossing of the ocean. Her poor little Ma from Wales, going off to a fearsome new world. She was certain the ship would fall through a hole in the water straight into Hell but was glad enough to think of any end to being so seasick.

The wind drops, the sound lessens. I am still here. Well. I sit and lie back and strike my head on another small stone. My head throbs. Now I foresee myself turned under in the Bryan burying ground or in this very field, pressed flat with a cartload of the red soil, my face mashed by a spadeful of it.

A soft rushing sound comes, like the breath of someone running along lightly. Something is coming for me. My heart sets to beating hard. I have not felt them for a time, the dead ones who trail along behind me. I am alive, I have Rebecca, I have children. But here also are the dead. I feel their coolness and their interest once more.

They will dig me up: so I think. I laugh and the laugh goes flat in the dirt.

I get up. Nobody is here. The horse sees me and lays its ears flat against its head. I still have the speckled rock in my hand, and I am sighing again.

Fate hands me another exit. Though at the time I do not wish to take it.

Rebecca is boiling over with fear of attack, and her fear is pointed straight at me. It is late spring now, and everything is bone dry. It has hardly rained in a month. The Cherokees and Iroquois have raided settlements up and down the Yadkin Valley too many times in the last weeks. Not enough food, as the new-planted crops are drying up. And more settlers are coming in all the time, claiming more of the land. Some are thieves looking to take anything they can get. They stole a young girl from Halseys' over the creek. We gathered the militia and got her back before they could hurt her, but Halsey said she did not speak for a week. Now the Halseys have gone. So have others.

Rebecca pulls me out the door when the children are asleep. The insects are fiddling at a high pitch. The fat-lamp sizzles and spits inside. She is listening hard to every sound and she has a twist of my shirt in her fingers.

—Do you really wish to stay here? Do you?

Her black eye is sharp and her voice is soft. She knows how to pierce me through. I know she is foreseeing my death and possibly her own. Or capture and imprisonment. Her eyes flood with a rush of pictures of the children captive or dead, but she pushes them down. She cannot think of them so—who can think of their children dead?

—Daniel.

The withering fields, the corn and wheat failing. The endless work. I look out towards them through the dark. The dull home militia training, marching back and forth with a straggling group of farmers. Now Rebecca grips the back of my neck as if I were a pup and she trying to shake me out of this. Her hand says: *Am I wrong to want a peaceful life? No.*

—Daniel, even some of the Indians are leaving now. I saw a group of Catawbas going north with all their things. They want no part of the fighting. Why would you want to stay?

The week before, I went on my militia duties with Squire to patrol a pair of the far backcountry farms. We found Jennings and his son and slave lying face up in their wheat, all shining and buzzing, black and green, cloaked in suits of flies. Their scalps gone and their eyes also by that time. The boy was some thirteen years of age. I could hardly bear to look at him, I was so sorry.

The body of a Cherokee was face down outside the door of their cabin in its own buzzing suit. Someone had got one shot in. We buried all of them, though some leave the Indians out in the air to rot. I did not tell Rebecca, but she knows. There was no one inside the house, but I saw a woman's gown on a hook and a child's cap on the bed.

She turns her back to me now and says:

—You smelled the smoke.

—You smelled it first.

A stupid joke. I did smell it, we all did. It travelled in the dark from the north last night, probably one of the Carters' places, too much smoke to be burning brush. Too tarry and black, with too much stench, the kind that sticks to skin. Rebecca looks at me, her eyes fill with tears in an instant and she blinks them away. We do not bring up the smoke again. She moves back and forth like a switch in the air, and then goes inside.

She only wants to be gone. Her body has lost all its trained stillness. Daddy is the same, unsettled all through, worn down by Ma and age, his Carolina dream collapsed. So has the dream of Rebecca's grandfather. In spite of all his land here in the Yadkin Valley, he has brushed the dirt from his hands and stood up to go. The retreat is sounding.

—Daniel. Danny.

Rebecca's voice drifts from the doorway. I say:

—You know I never turn down a fight. Not even one against corn.

Again my words are stupid ones. I exhale through my teeth, a sigh by another name. I say:

—My Daddy will sell me six hundred of his acres, and we can have a better house. I know you would like that. Clapboard and an oak floor.

I do not think much of this idea, but perhaps she will. One of the children, likely Jamesie, breaks out of sleep with a cry, and Rebecca goes to him. He is never a happy sleeper.

I look out at the slight movement in the dark fields, the breeze shifting the low dry crops.

A great stone rolls from my back. It is not the thought of running from the Indians or the French or the attacks. The relief is in having a reason to turn from this silent, wily soil and all its demands. To leave it to itself and let it go wild and find somewhere else. Anywhere other, Daddy, as you once said.

All right. I move towards the door and lightly I call:

—We will go then, Mrs. Boone. If you like.

The woman with thin yellow hair and a sorrowful face picks at her skin. She seems to get no satisfaction from this activity, but she keeps at it. No one knows her, though we all sneak looks and wonder what has happened to her. Her chin begins to bleed, but she picks on with her trembly fingers.

Fort Dobbs, which the Carolina governor has built between two creeks some miles east of our place, is packed. Not enough air or light. The ceiling has the feel of a tight hat. We are jammed into one of the cabins along the north stockade with a dozen others. Between long silences, the women converse about better times and are fierce in their judgements. The walls are raw logs, we snag on the rough wood like pelts.

—Your fancy apron would enjoy itself here.

Rebecca gives a small laugh, trying to keep bitterness out of the sound. The room stinks of stale fear. Baby Israel wails continuously and serves as the voice for us all. Jamesie at least is heavily asleep for once, his face upturned as if in great hope. I have told him that we are in the dungeon of a castle waiting to see the king. Mosquitoes sing above the watery trench outside the wall. One is in here singing. We have all had a good swat at it but to no avail. The baby's crying heightens. The sound is a contagious one, and the other babies begin to cry, like wolves taking up each other's howling.

The yellow-haired woman bursts out suddenly:

—Plenty of bad mothers about. Plenty. All too easy to become a mother.

She returns to her picking. The wailing goes on.

My brother Israel's boy Jesse is curled next to my feet, his arm stiffened with a splint and tucked into a sling Rebecca fashioned from a shirt. He has been my boy since not long after his father's death, but he is never quite at ease. He and Jonathan have orphans' carefulness and bad luck. I say:

—Does your arm hurt you?

He says:

—No sir.

—Uncle Sir will do in this place.

Jesse looks up at me with a smile, quickly hidden. He shifts his weight and tries to give the air of one pleased with where he finds himself. He never wishes to make trouble. His face is very white in the dim, like a moon shining up from the bottom of a well, and I know his broken arm is sore. He fell from the loft in the barn and did not cry, he only came walking to find me with his forearm hanging loose from the elbow. Often he injures himself in some fashion, as though life lays traps for him everywhere. With a sudden nod, the picking woman says:

—I could take that one, give him a home.

Jesse turns to her, his eyes widening. To the woman I say:

—No, thank you all the same.

She gives me a hard-done-by look and folds her arms for the time. To Jesse I say:

—Hungry?

I have a strip of jerk in my bag, I rummage for it, but Jesse shakes his head. I rub his hair and am sorry that there is nothing more I can do. I stand, but there is no room to walk about. Rebecca is nursing the baby beneath her shawl, so there is some quiet interspersed with small smackings. With her eyes shut she reaches up for my arm and says:

—Fine lodgings you have selected this evening.

She wishes me to joke with her and make her easy. She is sorry to have brought me here. But my limbs are prickling, and I do not reply.

I sit again and cover Jesse's ears without thinking. Beneath the idle remarks, I hear them. Wolves, or Indian and French mockeries, as if the babies' crying has brought them prowling. I put my ear to the splintery gunslit in the back wall. Jesse shifts about, Rebecca says too loud:

—What do you hear?

The shadows beneath her eyes are like petals. For a moment I want to touch them. Others sit up and listen. She asks me again what I hear, and I tell her nothing now.

—You would tell us if you did hear something? Daniel?

She is staring at me. So is Jesse, so is everyone else in the room. Jamesie rolls over and opens a sleepy eye. The yellow-haired woman stills her picking. Now I also speak too loud:

—Nothing there. The watch will be coming past soon. You will hear them. Go on, sleep now.

They quiet. My eyes adjust to the night as it deepens. The moon rises and drags the dark about. The noises of breathing and sleep begin to press upon me. I step over bodies to listen at the different walls. I hear a brief yip, it is not distant.

For a wild moment I am pierced as if by something sharp as a jewel. It stabs up to my skull, I see cold blue everywhere. Something is about to happen, surely. The thing that has been coming for me all my life. Here am I. Ready for murdering, or for being murdered. For anything but this trap.

Nothing comes. The stoppage and silence cannot be borne. If there were a proper window I would leap out of it before my Fate can catch me as it is always catching Jesse. I would surprise Fate by dodging off in a different direction, I would make some change from what is. At this time I believe it would be possible to do so.

I take out my knife. I step over Jesse to put my ear to the gunslit again, and I listen hard into the deeper night. The quiet is like a heavy cloth. A horse tied in the centre of the fort snorts and stamps, the sound explodes. My heart surges, and I turn for the door.

Jesse's face is pale and creased as linen laid out to dry. His eyes are like his mother's, dark and still. They catch on mine. They stop me. His need is like lead weights. Well Gulliver, I spare a thought for you, all tied down by the Lilliputians.

To myself I say: Keep yourself still. Straighten your mouth. To Jesse I say low:

—Is your arm hurting you, Goodboy? Keeping you awake?

Sometimes I call him Goodboy as his mother did. He blinks fast, but after a moment he answers:

—Yes. Not much.

He tucks his head down again, and I crouch and place my own arm over his broken one, as if this will fix it.

—That hurt you?

—Yes.

—Oh.

I snort and Jesse laughs with a full ha-ha-ha, forgetting everything about his life for one moment. A young man in the corner groans a curse and the yellow-haired woman sits up, knocking her head, and baby Israel wakes and howls. I feel Rebecca looking at me and at Jesse with exhausted loathing. The boy retreats into himself, holding his stiff arm away from his body as if it were not his. Well I know how that arm must feel.

Forting up is rotten. After some days of the company here Rebecca can endure no more. She wishes to go towards Virginia where her family has gone, and so we do. She will not let the boys out of the wagon for an instant. She is cool all the way there until she sees her old granddaddy and her face splits open.

There is not much hunting round the place the Bryans have bought, but I am not expected to farm. There are plenty of slaves and hands. If I like, I can drive Bryan tobacco to market. Life here is like a set table. I will say that there is plenty of food also. The boys are cautiously happy. Rebecca is full of relief, she walks with the baby in a shrinking circle, regaining her old stillness. But I find myself curiously tired of eating. The smell of tobacco leaves seems to have sunk through my tongue to the floor of my mouth. I am tired of the heavy forks they have. I am tired of the talk of whether or not to have another slice of pie.

We stay through the summer, and all winter. My dreams are not frequent, but at old Bryan's big house I do dream once of the ideal society of which Findley told me. The Englishman in the Florida wilderness with all his women, living according to inclination. Is that not what my dead brother told me, to do as I like? I think of him, especially when his boys are near, but he is not here, though I keep watch.

Rebecca's dreams are riotous and full of portents. If she tells me about one and I come up with no great understanding she is cross

all day. I do not tell her when I have a surprising dream of Adam and Eve going about their innocent business in their own garden. In the dream this is a clean wilderness, fenced, with animals roaming prettily about. A dull dream within its noisy bright edges. There is much praising and clapping. *O Adam I am a happy woman! O Eve I am glad to hear it!*

I remember these words as if they were shouted down my ear. Later I thought that Adam did not say that he was happy. I do not know why I recall this dream even now.

Well a fall was coming for that pair, as everyone knows. Snake, apple, surprise, punishment for ever. Goodbye! But their exile never seemed to me a true punishment, since they could go wherever else they pleased. Going on living with the Bryans in Virginia seems a penalty indeed. Always having to praise Rebecca's granddaddy for having us here. He sits in his chair as if he has had himself stuffed for posterity. He has a drunkard's veiny nose and cheeks, though I have never seen him take a drink, and so I cannot help but think him untrustworthy. He has a leafy dry-rot smell, the smell of old money, as I suppose.

I owe him twenty pounds for supplies he has bought me. I owe his son more. Daddy has taken Ma up to Maryland for the time as she wished to be near Israel's grave. Neddy and Martha are here, and my sister Hannah with her family. I wonder about my brother Squire on occasion, though I do not let myself wonder whether he is alive back in Carolina, or dead from the fighting, or from being tied to his gunsmithing apprenticeship. I hate wagoning down to the pit of my gut. Squire, perhaps you hate your work also.

Trapped in the parlour, I make an attempt at conversation. To old Bryan I say loud:

—Spring is on the way.

A stupid remark, but something to say to the stuffed old man. What does he dream of? Hornworm in his tobacco. Or in his money, munching with a hundred thousand teeth.

I shift about in my chair. Rebecca and the women are talking as they thump and crack dough or nuts or bones in the kitchen. One says:

—I must almost have drowned when I was a small girl, that is why I am so afraid of water now. When I see a pond I just freeze all through, even in summertime.

The others cluck with enthusiasm.

—Perhaps it was another life when you did drown and you carry the seed of the bad memory in you. Like a cancer.

—Well I hope I do not have that. Is that what you mean? Do I look as if I have a cancer?

I pick out Rebecca's voice, calm and sure now. She says:

—Do you believe in other lives? I do not.

Her sister Martha replies:

—I do. I would like another one. I think I must have died of fright once, I get such pains just here at night, and I am so fearful then. What a thought, to die in my bed with my mouth and eyes open. Imagine being found looking like that in the morning. Might that be a cancer? It is just here.

Through the doorway I can see Martha pointing to her chest, dead centre. She seems to believe this is the location of her heart. Indigestion, I think, though I say nothing. Rebecca says:

—I would be glad enough to have a cancer instead of being tomahawked, as we all might have been in Carolina.

One of the women goes on about the children wandering the Yadkin woods, their parents killed. Another says:

—I would not go back again for anything.

I want to shout to them: Do not believe all you hear. But Martha starts in:

—Neddy heard in town that the soldiers at Loudon's fort have Indian wives who are sneaking beans and hog meat in to them while the Cherokees try to starve them out.

Rebecca thumps something hard and says:

—Would you do the same for Neddy? Or for an Indian husband?

They are all laughing. Martha says:

—Imagine being those women. I wonder what they wear under their skirts?

I think of a panther skin I once got as a prize at a shooting match and traded on again. It was deep black and had a weedy smell. But Rebecca, you might have liked it. You could have worn it, or wrapped the new baby, our girl Susannah, in it and made a savage princess of her. And your family would have fallen in astonishment like a set of pokers to the ground and perhaps snapped a pokery bone or two in doing so.

Such are my thoughts when Ned comes in from outdoors, his cheeks red with the wind. He nods to old Bryan and sits down beside him. The old man says in a sudden suspicious manner:

—Two black heads.

Neddy laughs. Ma used to call us her twins born in different years and say he was just like me. But though our black hair is the same, Neddy is still the one with the sweet voice and the darling countenance. Ma said he must never grow a beard, never hide his sweetness. He is always clean-shaven. Our sisters Sal and Bets used to call him Dolly Dear and make him twirl. He would usually do so without a fuss, and when he had had enough he would plop down on his backside, still smiling his sleepy smile. Ned, I do remember this, you know, and not just the rest.

To him I say:

—Been to town?

—Yes.

—Warmer out?

—Yes, a bit. Very pleasant.

—Anything happening?

—Nothing extraordinary.

Ned pities me, as I can see. He is himself content as usual and is perplexed by my restless questions. Standing and putting his back to the fire, he stretches and says:

—This is a good house. Comfortable. I know you could live in any place, though, Dan.

—Almost any place. Not you, our Ned? Keep-home Neddy, darling Neddy.

I speak in Ma's voice, and for one moment I am homesick myself, though I do not know for where. Neddy begins to hum a tune. A child wails and Rebecca sings out from the kitchen:

—Here is Neddy now. Come and rock the baby for me.

Martha calls:

—And your own.

Another wife joins in:

—And mine, Neddy. She will keep quiet for no one else, you have spoiled her.

He goes obediently, smiling as ever. I hear the children's chatter rise, the women teasing. If I had your complexion, they say. Roses and cream.

I remain in my chair having nothing else to do and feeling stuck to it, stuffed as old Bryan. He is now hard asleep, perhaps in an excellent dream of food and tobacco. I go out into the cool air and to the stables, I will bridle the team and drive to town for lack of anything else to do. I occupy my mind with the harnesses and buckles. This goes there, that goes here. In, under, out. And my Fate now appears in another form.

—Christ. You made me jump. You might have been a ghost.

He stands silently at the left edge of the stable door without a smile. A shower of bright dust surrounds him in the cold light. His shape is the same, his old slight stoop, though bigger. I know it is my brother Squire, fully a man now, thin and tall with a tight sandy plait. I stare and laugh:

—But I would have recognized your ghost, Squire, you know. Though you have gone and grown taller than I am, I think, even if you are trying to hide it. You look like a peddler crushed by a pack. Now hold yourself straight.

I say this last in Ma's voice. He gives a thin smile, his hands in his pockets. What I say is true, and it delights me, him here and unchanged. We know brothers all through, down to the smell and the marrow. So I think at this time.

I embrace him. He says only:

—Well.

—Why are you here?

—I have left.

He hunches a shoulder higher. He means his apprenticeship, the life Daddy arranged for him. He means he has run off but he looks unabashed. I say:

—You have left all your guns? Did your master go after you?

—I know enough about gunsmithing. Few enough left in the Yadkin to make guns for now.

—Everyone is coming this way, even Keep-home Neddy is here. What will you do in Virginia?

He shrugs again and looks direct at me and says:

—My wife thought it time we left Carolina.

—A wife? Well I congratulate you. Though I never would have taken you for the type to bolt from apprenticing, least so for married life. Did it seem a fair trade?

He gives a quick, private smile. I pull his hat down over his eyes and I say:

—Another Boone bride, poor girl. I hope you do speak to her now and again. Will we meet her soon? Or have you warned her off your kin already?

The brim shadows half his face. It suits him this way. But he settles the hat on the back of his head and his precise eyes run over everything from rafters to ground. Nothing in the stable seems to strike him, and so his eyes go on another round. I clap him on both shoulders:

—You can do as you like.

Israel, our dead brother, I think of you now, and I think too that Squire must do as he likes before his time ends, for who can know when that might be? He is young, he has no children yet. I tell him to come inside, as if the house is mine. I am so glad he is here that I do not mind old Bryan sleeping in the corner still.

The women have gone out back with the little ones and Ned. Squire is restless, stalking about the room. He pokes at the fire, he goes over to stare at the clock, preoccupied as a dog with a lost bone. I say:

—Will you sit down, stranger? I will find Ned.

Squire remains on his feet, looking hard at the clock as if at an old enemy. He crosses the room again. At once he says:

—What would you do for some fresh game?

His voice is severe, unusually so. I stop and say:

—Have you any on you?

He laughs briefly with shut teeth. Walking back to the clock, he says lower:

—The Cherokees are backing out of Carolina. They will stay west. No settling any farther than the Alleghenies, treaty says. The Yadkin Valley is all right now. Ellis from upriver has gone back, no trouble. The only places burned were done long ago.

—Ah.

—Not everybody knows this.

We keep standing. We do not dare to look at each other. Then he says:

—We might see for ourselves. Check the properties. And—

I say it for him:

—The pelts will still be fair about now. Hides getting better, winter hair coming off.

—See how many beaver are left on the Yadkin.

—And west. A little way west. A longer hunt. Why not?

—Why not?

—Why not?

We begin to smile, fierce as dogs. Our talk is careful and unexcited, drumming out in short beats. We speak very quietly so that women do not hear us. But our grins are huge and angry, we are fools made to wait for a picnic. I get up and together we go to the window. The leaves are just showing their green on the maple beyond the yard. The clouds drift west in thin threads.

At once old Bryan says very loud:

—You fought for the king.

To him I say:

—Yes.

To Squire I say:

—It will be better there now.

—It could not be any worse.

—No. Well it could be worse. But it will not be. And we can always go farther.

—Then why not go?

—Why not?

9

The Fair Country

OUR YADKIN HOUSE is still standing. It smells of mice but no other life, as if no one ever lived here. This is pleasant to me. I climb to the sleeping loft where Jamesie and Israel were born, where the bed frame sits empty. I go out and grub up the worst of the weeds and, feeling dutiful, I begin to sow a crop. I must say that the earth shows no delight in seeing me again. I walk up and down the empty field with the pebbly seed corn falling from my hand, I see the rough line of the woods not far off, waiting for us, as it seems to me.

The quiet is not empty. A few families are back, cautious but resolved to get their land again. No word of Indians or French either, but for a few traders. Squire and I buy a small quantity of shot from one when he agrees to give us credit, surveying us with ticking eyes. Everything we buy is on credit. Everyone surveys us with ticking eyes.

We make our plans for the hunt. John Stewart, the young husband of our sister Hannah, has come with us, in want of money also. He is a big-boned man, deaf in one ear and often shy of speaking in case he has not heard right, though his voice is loud. He is a good hunter, a good man. He always sees what needs to be done.

We begin to prepare the packs. And out of the dark one evening, Hill turns up at the cabin, hallooing on a high-stepping grey gelding with an elegant manner and saddle. He leaps down, jangling the reins, and sees Squire and Stewart and I are cleaning the old traps. He says:

—Your wife said you had come out this way. I bear her good wishes for you. Are you setting off again? Where? I will go with you.

Squire and Stewart look at Hill. I say:

—Well well. In search of further land investments along the way, no doubt.

—And further amusing pursuits among the Boone boys, ha!

Hill sits down beside me, full of happiness, and presses a bundle of notes upon the back of my hand with a small smile. I do not wish to touch them, so he balances the stack on my leg and takes out his flask. He swallows and says:

—To friendship. And investment. We will all be rich in the end. And I will write about you boys, I will make your name. I am writing now also, did you know?

He holds his flask against the side of his nose. Squire says quiet:

—Who will read it?

Hill laughs and says:

—Anyone who reads the Virginia newspapers, my old friends. Everyone wants a story.

Squire shakes his head lightly and goes back to his trap. I sit a while with Hill. I do not know quite what I have done to deserve him. But his sincerity affects me queerly, as does his talk of wealth. He seems to have a need to believe in our friendship. And I believe in his money and his luck with it, I can feel the bundle sitting on my thigh.

For two more days we ready our supplies. The last night before we leave for the mountains, we sit outside. Nobody wishes to give up this spring air with the breath of summer in it. There is no moon but the fire sends up pickets of light. Hill sings, but mercifully low, content with his bottle. A couple of late birds scythe through the air overhead and Stewart says in his sudden fashion:

—Those are big for bats.

As he raises his big hand, a creaking, jingling sound stirs up the dark.

I can see nothing beyond the fire. The noise goes on. It is quite unfathomable and absurd, ringing and jingling. I say:

—Dancing bears, must be.

Stewart's great abrupt laugh escapes him. An answering laugh comes, high and wavering, above the jingling. We fall silent again and look into the sea of dark. Two eyes shine white-green and high. They bob and vanish and brighten, like cats' eyes, but so high. I stand, Squire and Stewart beside me. We have our guns up now. My neck is cold. Hill rouses himself to say with dark excitement:

—I knew the spirit world would show itself to me, I have always—

The ringing ceases abruptly and a voice comes out of the black silence:

—I heard it was you. I heard you had come back, cowards.

There is a soft fall and a nosy breath from a horse. The man, if it is a man, is dismounting. The body's outlines become clear, I see the face fully. Findley. I know him straight away. I laugh and I say:

—So it is a bear. An untrained one though, no manners.

—None at all, none at all, though my dancing is not so bad as that.

We shake hands. His grip is gentle. He opens a saddlebag and dumps a load to the ground. It flashes in the firelight like a lost treasure come out of the deep. Trinkets, Indian jewellery, silver earbobs and rings, packets of needles, a tangle of ribbons like hair. I announce:

—Findley and son, peddlers.

Findley chuckles high and says in the singing Irish tone I remember:

—You are right there, Boone. But no son to my knowledge, none whatsoever. There may be daughters aplenty in various locations, all beautiful.

He sits and stretches his arms and says:

—Last I saw of you, my man, you were running from the Monongahela River like one let out of unlocked Hell.

It is a surprise to hear someone talk of the terrible battle, it had seemed a painted rag rolled up into a corner of my brains. For a moment I see with Findley's light eyes through the cloth he had over his face. I see myself a hazy shape running into the river. I see myself carrying on running home and doing a murder on the way, though I did not wish to do it. I see my ghosts.

Findley appears to be one of them, staring hard at me with his pale face glowing and amused, as if he had followed me home through the backwoods, as if he saw everything that happened. I say:

—I see you survived.

—Only just, only just, only just.

He taps his thin nose, his hair straggles down over his forehead. I say:

—But you have brought us some pretty things. Too kind.

—I trade among the Indians mainly, but I make exceptions for you backwoods folk. You are near enough to Indians at that.

—No more taste for army life?

—No, no. Too much marching about.

Hill interrupts:

—Then you will not wish to join our party?

He has a magnanimous look about him as he sits with his knees wide and his hands open, pleased to fancy himself part of a long-hunt. Findley surveys him for some time. He turns and says to me:

—Marching back to war?

—No.

—No taste for it either, Boone?

Again I say:

—No.

But Findley is amused now, he minces up and begins to tie one of his ribbons around my plait. I have to smile as he plucks and tweaks at me with his bony fingers. He stands back and says:

—Lavender suits you. Let it be a gift for your lady, or keep it all for yourself.

Hill says:

—Only put it around his neck next time, and tighter.

Hill roars with laughter and Findley rocks back and forth. He sits again in his mess of shiny tangled things like a magpie and takes off his hat to scratch his head. Without it his face looks lonely and tired for a moment in the firelight. He says:

—You are all off travelling, then?

—Tomorrow. Long-hunt, we hope. The first in a few years. We will have a good look about first and hunt properly when summer is finishing.

I feel myself grinning. Squire's own smile alters his serious face for a moment, and he says:

—Good trapping too, if luck is with us.

—We are lucky. Dan is.

Stewart says so very loud. He thumps me on the back, and I am pierced by this belief in whatever it is in me that people cannot leave alone. Indeed my back throbs with Stewart's belief. Findley laughs and tells him:

—My man, your lucky charm is no Irishman.

I say:

—Have we need of an Irishman?

—Everyone does, everyone does.

—You had best come along then.

Findley looks amused once more and reaches up to coil my purple hair ribbon round his hand as though it were a cat's tail. He says:

—What are you paying?

Hill bends into the light and says:

—The pleasure, the great pleasure, of our company. Have you anything to invest with us?

Findley shakes his head. He tugs at the ribbon gently. I feel myself

caught. He says:

—There are things only an Irishman knows.

I say:

—Irish women.

—Ha! Better.

—Ha! What could be?

Findley spreads his hands now, and they look adrift in the night. He says:

—Boys, boys, you will not need to wait for your hunting. I know where you will see thousands of buffalo and every other sort of creature. The Indians gave me excellent furs and skins when I first traded there, before the war. Plenty more of that. And have you heard of this most marvellous place?

I am listening. I say:

—Not one of your Irish fairylands.

Hill speaks with sudden drunken piety:

—We have all heard of Heaven, I hope.

The fire pops and spits a shower of sparks over us. I remember his army talk of all the secret places he knows. Findley is very pale, his hands floating on the air. He says:

—Better still. A true place. Heaven on earth. God's country. And no one knows the way but me. No one white.

10

Heaven

THE WAY TO Heaven as it turns out is easy. I have hunted west of the Yadkin many times and now I feel welcomed in again. I know the creeks and animal traces and salt springs here, I feel quite at home. Findley says these are nothing whatsoever. Farther on is a whole creation you cannot imagine, he says, rocking from side to side in his saddle.

Well I do imagine. All of May we ride and hike higher into the mountains, and all is shadowy and peaceful. I have crossed the Blue Ridge myself, but I have never been so far. We carry on to the west. It is difficult to see the way in places, but I trust Findley, who does seem to know what he is about. We are on the Clinch River, Findley says, and then in Powell's Valley, a narrow, forested place. At times I feel myself in a long half-dream like one of Rebecca's with its stabs of detail and its sudden changes. Rebecca, I remember you telling me of a dream of butter walking out of the churn and burying itself somewhere out of spite. Here, everywhere is bright raw green, and I can well picture all of it coming alive, but there is no spite, only peace and strangeness. When the weather turns one night, I wake first and see my companions all mounds of sleeping white. Snow covers everything completely.

Rain comes the next night and washes the world green again. We have reached the Allegheny ridges, I know, though we do not speak of it. It is difficult going but we do not mind it. Soon enough we reach a crest and make a steep descent into lower hills. We are on a road. The Great Warrior's Path, Findley says, the old trace the Indians have packed flat over the years. It narrows and takes us along high white cliffs to a great gaping gap in the mountains. The high sides part on either side of the path easy as skirts, letting us in. Findley is triumphant, standing at the centre of the pass and bowing as though he made it himself. Even Hill is admiring, though he says it is not quite Heaven as he pictured it.

We stop to carve our initials into the cliff and then carry on through the gap. We begin a slow descent. It is well treed and smells of easy, wet growth. Light snow falls now and again and covers our tracks. We keep watch for any travelling Indians, but the Indians have not yet begun to move from their winter towns this year, as the spring is cold. In truth we near forget that Indians exist, in spite of this road of theirs, or that anyone at all exists. Though there are more paths, wider than the streets in Philadelphia. Findley says:

—The buffalo have made them since God's own fingers deposited them here to run about.

He is pleased to lead us along these ways. They make the going very easy, taking us to the salt licks and drinking places. At this time I believe this place was made to be occupied, having such broad tracks. How could I not believe so?

We see a few bear and deer at the licks. They look at us without interest, we get the skins without trouble. But there is not much hunting yet. Standing on a small hilltop and surveying the trees, Hill says suddenly:

—Do you know, Findley, I am not sure I believe in your buffalo.

And we do not see any of the creatures until all at once one dawn we come upon a herd at a big lick, a great heaving dark mass. They paw and lick at the ground, their great heavy heads all butting and nodding as if they will eat a hole straight through the earth. How can there be so many? Thousands there are, uncountable. I see Squire's eyes trying to fathom their numbers, and Hill shaking his head and grinning. The calves bleat with a sound of shaky trumpets. A few of the bulls sniff at the air and turn, but remain unconcerned with our presence. They have never seen other humans, I am certain. Or perhaps no white humans, perhaps whites are nothing here.

We keep back in the trees. Findley is laughing behind my shoulder. He says:

—Good eating, if you can kill them.

Hill says:

—If this is hunting, it is easy.

Stewart at once scrambles for his gun and aims. This place has filled him with boldness. He gets one at the edge of the herd, a smaller cow, he has her between the eyes. The beast turns and flies at him, blundering along with her big bleeding head down, a curl standing up on her humped shoulders. Findley is laughing all the harder as Stewart runs for a tree crying:

—Shoot it, Dan, shoot it for God's sake!

Now I am laughing too as Findley calls:

—Wasting your lead, my man. Wasting your balls.

The buffalo charges for Stewart again after a snorting pause. I get her down at last after two shots through the neck as Findley laughs on and on in his weird fashion. The sun grows behind his head and he says:

—Breakfast.

We roast the hump and the tongue. Findley cooks the thigh bones and cracks them open for the hot marrow. This is my first buffalo meal, and it is very fine, much better than venison. Jamesie and Israel and little Susannah, and Jesse and Jonathan as well, I make my plans to jerk the next tongue and take it home for you. I do think of you all, you hop across my mind like little birds.

We eat. Findley gives Hill a piece of the raw liver, which he says will make a man of him. Hill laughs and enjoys it mightily and Findley says:

—Your stomach certainly must believe in buffalo now.

Stewart is doing his utmost to skin the carcass. The hide is difficult to pull away and too heavy to pack along with us, but he will not stop. We all watch him putting his shoulder to the body, trying to get the remaining attached side free until he gives it up. Sitting wiping his knife, covered in greasy smears, he looks perplexed and says very heavy:

—I told my Hannah I would get her some furs for herself. Not just to sell.

Findley says Stewart can embrace the carcass tonight and feel himself wrapped in victory. And besides, he says, buffalo hides are worthless on the market. Now he raises his flask:

—To buffalo. And their killer. And their would-be killer.

And in the end Stewart raises his as well.

The way remains easy enough, but the clouds spin themselves into a thick wool. A thin crust of snow remains in a hollow where we camp. Here Stewart catches fever overnight, and we have to stop to nurse him. He is sorry for his sickness, he keeps saying so, he clenches his rattling teeth to get the word out between them: Sorry. He is angry at the fever and at himself. When he improves, we go on slowly, though he is not quite well and looks pale and hollowed out. He keeps close to me, I feel his eyes on my back. He is not fit to hunt properly yet. We see no more buffalo, though I get a deer now and then. We begin to grow used to the country.

Hill does not like being used to anything, as I know. He does not like this landscape, as yet he sees no useful land he might sell. And there has been little enough adventure to his taste. He has fallen out of excitement into a pit of ugly boredom. At the fire his face is dull. He takes out his papers and ruffles them, but he announces:

—Nothing to write home of.

He has a trick of becoming like a straw pallet we have to drag along and try to amuse, though who can amuse a pallet?

He is quiet for a morning. Then he calls ahead to Findley:

—We ought to set up our station camp and set the Boones to hunting, if this is your great place.

Findley pays him no heed and carries on riding. He has taken us into some low hills and down along the side of a river, where we have to walk the horses. Hill persists:

—We expect to see a wonder at any moment.

Findley looks back with a smile and calls:

—This river, my dears, is the Red River.

We pick our way through the remaining patches of hard snow and the high stalks of cane along the water. We have to walk the horses, they do not like it here. The cane brake is higher than our heads in places, it is like being in a stiff cage. A stalk pokes Hill near his eye and he says:

—Who says it is the Red River? On whose authority is it the Red River?

I pay no heed to these two. A broken cane now scratches my face from ear to neck and I feel a drip of warm blood, which I touch with my finger. I taste it.

I am alive here, my blood is alive. I want there to have been no one here before us. I want the river not to have a name. I sprinkle blood from my finger into it where a creek joins. Lulbegrud Creek I name it, for Gulliver. One of his words. Behind me Findley says:

—I say so, yes. On my authority. I was one of the first to come here and the only one to go so far. The trading post was beyond here if I remember, and I do—

He turns and walks out of the cane. And there indeed is the post. Only burned. The foundations look like agonized jaws caught open. The stockade still stands in a few places, grey and beaten and sorry. A few mouldy pumpkins and cornstalks are sinking into the ground. The horses stop to crop at the thin, tender grass trying to come through the rags of snow and ashes. For a moment Findley looks disconcerted. Then he picks his way into the centre of the ruins.

—Ah.

He sifts through the snow, taking up a handful of ash and charred lumps, looking intently. He half-sings:

Any old needles, any old pins. I might perchance have left some here for the Indian maids of Eskippakithiki. Oh the Indian maids—

Hill stalks into the ruined post as well:

—Keep your goddamned bog-Irish puke in your hole. Sickening us all.

He walks footprints all over the snow and ash, looking sidelong at Findley, then pushes over a burned pole. It falls too gently for his liking. He jabs at it with his boot and says:

—Is this all?

Findley says:

—Is this what?

Hill blows out a rush of air:

—You are an arse of a know-nothing with nothing to show us, I have seen that from the first day out. What exactly is it that we are doing? Why do we find nothing at all of use? And why have you nothing to show for your trip here, you bastard liar?

Findley tosses the handful of ashes and charcoal into the breeze, and some of it scatters across Hill. I see the rage travel up Hill before he spits at Findley and reaches into his belt. Findley says very soft:

—A group of Shawnee and French took my skins and furs on my last trade trip. Did I not say? But there are plenty more for the taking. Plenty of land where no one has yet been. And the Indian maids, my friend. Think of the maids. I have seen the maids, I have unmade them myself. There may be one left for you, or one you might unmake again, if you use your celebrated imaginative powers.

Hill draws out his blade. He is no knifeman and will certainly blunder about it. I say:

—Have you not had your fill today, our Hill? Buffalo is better eating as we know, thanks to our bony friend.

Hill stands swaying on his planted feet, holding his knife thrust out at Findley and enjoying his own fury. He loves to be whipped by great feeling, he loves a scene. Squire is watching carefully, Stewart leans his head against his horse. Findley aims a grin at me and his eyes say: *I stayed at the Monongahela to see what would happen. I saw you run. What will you do now?*

He steps forward and sings lightly:

Oh, the Indian maids.

Hill's arm tenses, he is set to see his performance through. He curses and throws the knife wild. Findley dodges it easy. I take it up and give it a spin as I toss it so that it spirals into the tree nearest Hill's arm but catches the edge of his shirt. I say:

—Hill, Findley has not been lying. He knew how to get us here. He has been here, it is true. He knows this place.

Hill tugs out the knife. He looks at me for a time. Then he gives me his friendliest smile, as though we have never been anything but the best of friends. His eyes uncloud, he laughs with his teeth apart. Now he walks over and gives Findley a tap on the breastbone with his knife handle. He says:

—When you die, I will eat you. I will chew you.

He turns the knife about in his hand. A laugh flees Stewart like a nervous dog. Findley bows, unsmiling now, and says:

—I shall look forward to such a rare fate.

And he turns. Without looking at us he swings up onto his chestnut horse and jabs its ribs with his thin legs. He rides swiftly away from the river up a slope into the trees until we cannot see him. We are left staring stupidly. A weak ray of light makes its way through the cloud, and in it the ruined post looks more sad and lost than ever.

My hunting shirt grows cool against my back, a breeze flips past us and swings round in our faces. Hill curses at length, they are quite good curses and imaginative ones. I am loath to admit that I can see why he is angry. But I can.

We do not move. I do not know precisely where we are. Stewart looks at me with his exhausted face still feverish and asks:

—Are we lost?

I say:

—Perhaps. No. Let us say we are bewildered.

We stay where we are for the night. Nobody speaks.

When the sky lightens, I unhobble my horse and mount. Before I can go, Hill raises his head and curses:

—Goddamned bastard Irish peddlers!

But he follows quickly, satisfied again with having something fresh to do. Squire rises and helps Stewart mount, he pulls himself up and off we ride. I take Findley's trace. He has made it easy, knocking twigs from trees and catching his knife on others to make pale gashes.

After some hours we come to a rocky incline, very steep. It soon becomes a sheer cliff. Findley's chestnut horse is hobbled at the bottom with a surly look. On seeing us it stamps one forefoot again and again. We leave ours to keep it company. They begin to stamp as well, bang bang bang.

The only way is up the rock. I say:

—Well, boys. To Heaven.

The wet stone scrapes my fingers and palms, my feet slip again and again and fly into the empty air beneath me. The horses beat their hooves as if to drive me mad. There is a great rock hump I must hug myself to, angling out over the earth below, but I climb its spine and get over it to the top, where I lie on my belly at the edge with my head dangling. Below me are the upturned faces, all curious.

—Well, Dan. What now?

This of course from Hill. Squire gives Stewart a leg up. Stewart is slow, but he manages it, though he is very pale after I haul him up the last few feet. Squire shins up quick and then he and I pull Hill over the hump. We all sit panting. The horses stamp and nicker below. Findley's looks up, it flashes its teeth and gums.

The trees are in a thick dark knot round us. Stewart points a shaking arm:

—There.

And there is Findley, waiting against the crook of an elm some yards off as though he was born there. He has been watching.

We push through the trees into the daylight and stand before him, still breathing hard. Hill spits at the ground, *pah*, reminding us of his powers of spitting. Findley hums a tuneless little song and says:

—Here you are now. Please to go ahead. Your servant. See it without a bog-Irishman in your view.

He gives another little bow and a flourish. His eye is on Hill. He steps aside.

There is only our breathing and the far echo of the horses' stamping. Stewart and Squire stand where they are. Hill goes straight up the small incline towards Findley, brushing past him. I go to the left, to the other side of the tree whose branches make a thin awning over me. At the cliff edge I am the first of us to see it, the huge spreading plain below, a shimmering carpet of grasses with waves of treed hills rising behind. Peaceful but entirely living, a vast breathing thing with a rippling green heart and lungs. My own breath is puny.

A very light rain is beginning. I open my mouth and catch it on my tongue, it tastes marvellous, like a splinter of sky or like a secret, as I imagine.

—Kentucky.

As Findley says this word it seems to me that I have known it all my life. It seems to me that I have been dreaming of this place without knowing how to say it, without giving it a name. And it is the most beautiful name. Hill is breathing over my shoulder, the others are coming now, but I stare down over the spread of grasses, and I say:

—Empty. Is it?

Findley answers quiet:

—Buffalo enough, and bear and deer and beaver and all else you might want. Keep watching and you shall see.

—Indians, surely.

—Not to live. Some of them agreed with your good King to keep it as a hunting ground only. Of course your King did say you would keep out of it as well. I am proud to say that I supplied some of the silver chains and bangles he sent to seal the bargain, did you know it? But then my country does not recognize any English king's authority, no. And perhaps he will not be your King for long. This country does as it pleases also.

He waves his hand at it.

I watch the grasses lift and shiver as if they are a thing stretching its back. I want to believe what Findley says. I want to believe that we are the first to see this place from this cliff. I want to believe it is its own place.

I want to believe that this is Heaven now just here, as Findley promised. Is there any great wrong in wanting Heaven now?

11

What Is to Be Found

HEAVEN SENDS hornets to sting Hill's throat and swell him to bullfrog proportions. He is forced to keep to his bed at the station camp we make at a grassy place on a wide creek near a salt lick. Findley and Hill make a quarrelsome household there in the lean-to. Squire and I privately agree he ought to stay as their hunter and keeper to make sure they remain alive. Stewart and I rig up a platform high between trees for the hides we will get.

From the tree he has dragged himself up, Stewart calls:

—Let the bears and wolves try to get them up here.

I say:

—Hill will keep them off.

Hill smiles fatly, deep in his flask, and answers in a rasping whisper:

—If I am to die, my spirit will contact you from the next world, Dan. It will come in search of you wherever you may be and give you word that I am safe. I am sure I will be safe. But my spirit will tell you so, you need not worry.

Hill, at this time it seems to me your spirit must be a wobbling lump of flesh somewhere in your entrails, something that will crawl about of its own accord whether you are living or not. I do not forget your words.

This speech costs him some effort and he lies back with his tongue out. I look at Findley to make sure he will be all right staying here. He is no hunter but is a fair enough cook. He crouches over Hill, patting the fattened head, and says:

—Go, go, Dan, and take your big Stewart. I can live in peace with any man who carries such a supply of rum and who has so birdlike a voice.

So Stewart and I continue on the Warrior's Path, seeing no Indians. We cross the broad Kentucky River, which Findley said we would find, in a sandy shallows. I lose no pleasure in saying *Kentucky.* I say it to myself whenever it comes into my mind.

We keep to the woods at first. Stewart always says, After you, whenever we come to a narrowing of the path or a small ford on a creek. I tell him not to say so anymore and he says:

—All right then, Dan.

He is very happy now, though still not well, and I am happy for his silence. The sounds here catch at me. Birds calling and crying like water dripping, like thin strings and like bells. Insects buzz and crawl into our ears, and the wind has its own dry voice. We see a tree on fire with blossom, rustling and continually moving like the bright grass in the open meadows. I want to tie blankets about the horses' hooves to muffle them. I want to hear everything.

We camp on the edge of the open meadows. We go out shoeless at dawn when the beautiful grasses and clover are wet and bluish, leaving the horses. We are the more silent, though we cannot help but leave footprints everywhere. Stewart's shooting has calmed since the first buffalo, he follows my lead. We track the feeding deer early in the morning. The little camps we make as we progress are loaded with skins swinging in packs from the trees, all fine-haired spring skins ready for market. We pass deeper into the thick heart of the country.

The weather relaxes into summer, and we hunt in our breechcloths only, greasing ourselves with bear oil against the insects. Our own skins deepen their colour in the sun. Stewart has regained of his health. It seems that we are transformed, that we are alive in some new manner.

The grass grows higher and thicker and has great sudden ripples of movement running through it, but the game does not escape us. Every evening we sit scraping and stretching yet more skins at our fires after we eat. We have been out for months.

Out of the quiet one night Stewart says:

—I cannot see how we will be able to pack all of this back to the station camp. But we will be rich, just as your friend Hill said.

His eyes flash like his knife as it scrapes the hair from another buckskin. I say:

—Well, Stewart, I am glad you are so sure.

I cannot help but think so myself, though. It is easy to feel a part of all of this richness and easy to feel ourselves lucky. We know the country well now, the terrain and all the paths of the creeks and rivers. We have gone north as far as a great grey river, which I believe to be the Ohio. We feel entirely at home.

Stewart stretches his dirty toes and gives his barking laugh. He says:

—What will you do with all of your money?

I think for a time and I say:

—You remember the big bones we found at that big lick.

—Yes. But those are free for the taking. Going to build a house of them?

I chuckle and bite at the loose edge of a hide and taste the skin. I think of the huge piles of bones heaped all over the bare ground. We crawled into a great ribcage and rattled it as best we could. We thought at first that they were the bones of giants. Brobdingnag, I said, for Gulliver. Seeing the long curved teeth, Stewart decided on elephants, saying he once saw a picture of one at a tavern. I have never seen an elephant, but they must have lived here once and gone there for the salt as all the animals do. Everything here seems to demand witnesses to its splendour. Even the dead want us to see

their bones.

But I do not feel my dead here, I am free of them. I have not thought of them at all. I say:

—I might build myself an elephant. Take the little ones for rides.

Stewart's laugh barks across the fire again. He says:

—I will as well. My little girl would like it. And Hannah would like one to go preaching on.

I chuckle thinking of Hannah, who has grown up severe, as if all the Quaker in our line has puddled down in her, the last-born. I say:

—Paint it scarlet for her.

Stewart laughs once more. When he is silent, a great moth bats the air overhead and near falls into our fire. I watch it veer off and vanish. I wonder where it goes in the dark.

We do not often talk of our wives. On some nights I miss Rebecca with sharp surprising digs in my chest as if her rough heels are drumming on it. I am sorry for it when I realize that I do not think of home more frequently. Now I can almost see her curled little mouth and hear her little laugh. I am struck with a fierce wish to give her something marvellous and surprising. An elephant would do. Rebecca, you would love Kentucky. Eventually you would. You will. So I think at this time.

Aloud I say:

—I do not suppose the women will object to being rich in any case. Even if they have only buckskin to wear for the rest of their days.

But Rebecca and the children seem half the world from this place. The wildness around us is black and huge, a great gullet enclosing us. I think of a mother wolf carrying her pup along in her jaws or in her womb. Safe inside a danger. I wonder whether this is how a pup feels or indeed whether it feels anything, whether the minds of wolves are empty but for the yellow hunger that shows through their eyes.

I have never been fond of wolves. To turn my thoughts I begin to sing, and Stewart sings with me though he does not know the words.

In late autumn, Findley is singing alone in the camp. We hear him before we arrive, his voice cutting through the quiet. His singing is quite sweet. I call:

—Has an angel condescended to land in Kentucky?

Findley looks at us from where he lies, his feet outstretched and bare. Two pups are fighting beside him. My limbs tense when I see their shady fur. Well. Wolves. Findley smiles at us and says slowly:

—Angels have always walked here as they please. And fed upon buffalo tongue.

Stewart dumps a bale of skins at Findley's bony toes and says:

—Where is Squire?

—And good day to you as well.

Findley cocks an eyebrow. He looks slow and pained. He says:

—I am not enough for you, I can see, fallen angel or no. But! I shall gratify your curiosity in telling you that your good Squire has seen fit to leave for Carolina for more shot and traps.

He gets up stiffly and makes one of his aggressive little bows, putting me in mind of a terrier holding itself back, waiting for something to reveal itself as a rat to worry and shake. He says:

—And have you no interest in your other friend?

—Have you killed him?

I say it jokingly but I would not be surprised to see Findley point to a mound: Here Lies Hill. Findley shakes his head. His eyes look tired. They are a flower-blue like those of the little wolves. He says:

—My compliments to you this beautiful day, Danny boy. Winter coming, and still so warm.

One of the wolves runs up and bites Findley's ankle. I say:

—It is a beautiful day, Findley. What are you doing with such pets?

—Orphans. I thought I might train them up in the way they should go. I might trade them for something, who could resist a beast so trained? But they only bite me and fall in the fire when I am not looking. Still. They provide companionship.

The pup charges at me and clamps its milky teeth around the toe of my moccasin. I shake it off and grab it by the neck to return it to Findley. It bites him again and cocks its ears. He gives a tired chuckle as he swats it away.

I take him to see the horses packed with the skins we have brought in, and his jaw relaxes. He says:

—Good. That is money in the bank.

I say:

—Hill would like a look.

But Findley sets his mouth and goes back to the lean-to, where there is no Hill, and where Stewart has sat down. He plucks a turkey we shot on the way, which we roast on a rope over the fire for our meal. The wolf pups draw close to the turning meat. They whine and look to me and dart back to the shelter again, where they lay their heads upon their paws.

—No salt left.

Findley says so mournfully, but he brightens when Stewart offers the last of his little stock. I bring out mine also, which is less. In doing so I spill a little from the bag and I say:

—Clumsy. Bad luck.

Findley says:

—Ah then, our Boone is a mortal, only a mortal.

Stewart spits on the ground where the salt scattered. The sun makes it glitter. I say:

—That a remedy? Salt into gold?

Stewart grins and says:

—If you say so.

We sit under the lean-to. The wind ruffles the roof. The wolves tumble about and I move away. Among the bedding I catch a whiff of Hill. I have to ask:

—Well and where is Hill after all? I would not have thought him likely to miss a meal.

Findley is silent for a moment, his eyes closed. He says:

—A man restless all through. Our friend left a day after Squire. Had to get home, he said, though I offered him the best of my hospitality. And after I nursed him with my own two hands.

He holds up his pale hands in proof. I say:

—Did his throat heal?

—Of course.

—He looked human again then.

—Somewhat so, yes.

I laugh, but I have some worries over Hill alone in the wilderness. I say:

—Well boys, a drink to Hill making his way home.

Findley says:

—And remaining there, and remaining there.

His face lightens for a moment and then closes again.

—Do you wish to go back, Dan?

Stewart does not say *home*. I do not slow my horse.

—No.

I know that Squire will return with supplies. I wonder about Findley's state, but he seems healthy enough, and he has his wolf pups to amuse him. He can guard the skins. I dismiss Hill from my mind for the present. Stewart and I make for the Kentucky River once more, it is our best ground, where we will check the traplines. The beaver will be thick and perfect now that winter is coming back. We make a camp, and I sleep very sound but for a dream of my Daddy walking towards me. I reach out to shake his hand but he pushes mine away and looks fierce. When we wake I am glad to move on.

We come across a smooth flat lick. The horses bend their heads to the salty ground. I say:

—We can make salt here one day. Get the kettle from camp.

Stewart agrees and digs his heels into his horse. Now he says urgently:

—Bear. Bear. Bear.

He dismounts and lopes into the beech trees to the east. He has a craving for the sweetness of bear bacon, as we have eaten all the old jerked bear meat. He has said in his loud fashion that bear is the hunter's true food and that killing one gets a man closer to being one, as the Indians believe. He has been carting a heavy bearskin about as his bedroll for some time and smells of its dusty underground whiff. It is dull black with no shine. He calls to bears in his mind, he says, and he thinks they will see fit to answer.

The wilderness does grow such fancies in some people but I would not have expected it of Stewart. He is still very thin, he has never quite come back to his old self. And I have seen no bear sign, but off he goes. The horses carry on with their licking, having caught no scent of anything in the wind.

I walk up a hill not far from the riverbank. My gun on its strap rubs at my shoulders. A huge custard-apple tree stands on the hilltop, its branches stabbing out in all directions. Its fruit is scattered around it like fallen shot. A few hang still from the branches. Winter coming, and apples, and my shirt open. Kentucky.

Stewart fires, the echo rings back like a bell. I call down:

—You had best waste no more shot, Stewart.

I hear him roaring in triumph:

—Got you, got you!

I laugh and pick an apple and throw it in his direction. It bounces down the hill. Perhaps I ought to be thinking of Eve and Adam and my old dream of them in the garden, or of my dream of Daddy, but I am not. I walk round the tree for a bigger apple and I say:

—Your fondest wish granted. What powers of attraction you have, Stewart. The Indians will be calling you She-Bear.

And there just over the top of the hill I see them as I reach to pick the fruit. Dozens of them, all very still, their guns and eyes, only their hair and feathers stirring in the light wind, as if they have been waiting unweary here all along for Fate to take me to this place and to them.

12

Wide Mouth

FINDLEY, I think of your flowery blue eyes watching over the station camp. I think of you whistling or singing one of your high mournful songs, stirring some unsalted thing in the pot. I think of you standing alone in your ripe smell, crooking the wolf pups under your arm, waving us off, saluting a little goodbye.

I think of you still there.

—He will be long gone. I have never even seen Findley shoot.

Stewart says so to me through his teeth as the Indians walk us down the trace.

—We will see soon enough.

The Shawnee are lovers of peace and this is a peaceful time for once, their leader tells us in his soft voice when we stop at the small camp Stewart and I last made. He speaks some English, many trade words. Their language is something like Delaware and so we are able to hobble along in conversation. The others look about. He motions to me and Stewart to sit and we do so, though we have to keep our arms aloft as they are tied to Shawnee warriors who stand at our side. My guard's leggings are coloured red with bits of deer hair sewn to them. He reaches down and fingers my shirt.

The leader sits facing us. His expression is patient. He points to his chest and says:

—Captain Will.

I can see why this is his English name. He has a military look about him, straight back and closed face. He wears a blanket over one shoulder and beneath it a yellowish army coat, English or French, the true colour faded out of most of it. His hair is shaved but for a long lock at the crown, and the rims of his ears are stretched and split with silver bangles leaving huge open loops of skin. He looks over Stewart and me with resignation. Two more animals to deal with at the end of the autumn long-hunt.

His men are loosing our pack of skins from the tree. Stewart is trying to contain his bafflement at this turn of events and drops his head between his knees. He snuffs as if to summon the spirit of the bear he shot. The Indians picked it up and took the skin but left the meat, and Stewart cannot forget it. I say:

—Let them have the skins.

—God damn me, Dan.

Well I must say the blasphemy is a small shock. Saintly Hannah's husband, who has insisted on keeping the Sabbath through our hunt for her sake, though in truth we only pray when it occurs to us that it might be time for a Sunday. Now he appears to be coming apart, he sags as if his seams will soon gape. I say:

—Well it might have been God damn *you*, Dan, so I thank you, Stewart. Let them have it. It is only the one pack.

But there are the other small camps where we have cached our furs. I will not think of them. I will not let them show in my face.

Captain Will speaks briefly to a few of his men in words I do not catch. They cheerfully wave their clubs as if they were puppets in a Punch and Judy, and one of them chuckles aloud at us. They can see we have been out a good long time. I cannot pretend to be lost or witless. They know I am not so, and I know the game is up.

I want to laugh myself as I lead them to each of our caches with a knife pointed casual at my back. Stewart roils all the time like a sick stomach. They tie us back-to-back at night with tugs made from green buffalo hide, each wound about a Shawnee's wrist.

—John. Try to be calm. Try to sleep.

—I cannot sleep like this.

Stewart's voice is loud, the Shawnee move and mutter. His guard sits up, his hand over his eyes. I turn my head and whisper close to Stewart's good ear:

—It does not matter. None of this matters. We are alive yet.

—But—God damn them all, they have got everything we have taken this hunt!

—Not the station camp. Go to sleep.

But he does not sleep and I do not much either.

In the very early morning, Captain Will sits down before me, wrapped in his blanket against the frost. His eyes are calm as they roam my face, forehead to chin. He says:

—A long time you have been here, Wide Mouth.

He reaches out to finger the ends of my beard. He touches it as if it is a curious moss. His own face is very smooth, like my brother Neddy's. He goes on:

—You have more.

—No. You have all of it.

The fingers travel up to my cheek. They are cool and dry, and at once I think of Ma's hand on my forehead when I was a sick boy. He says:

—Poor white. I see you turn red when you lie. Even up under your hair you turn red.

I breathe out and laugh a little, I pull my head back from his hand. Stewart is looking at me hard and folding his lips, trying to understand what is being said. The Captain smiles:

—Your hunt is better than ours this year. You will take us to your big camp where you have put the rest of your skins.

His tone is cordial. When I say we have no more camps, he

gives a still more cordial smile and puts out his hand for me to shake. It strikes me that this is the longest conversation I have had with an Indian in some time. I feel myself like a printed page, he reads everything. I say:

—All right. We will take you.

What else is there to say? Stewart pulls at my arm, his face tight with hope:

—What did you say you would do?

—We will take them to the station camp. We have no other choice, Stewart, this is their ground. They know where everything is. They will find it for themselves at any rate. They might do harm to Squire and Findley there.

Stewart's face collapses:

—Let them find it for themselves! Let them mince Findley into bits! You can damn well mince me into bloody bits rather than let me watch you give it up. I will not do it. I told my wife, your *sister*, that I would get a good life for us here, that is what I have been doing, that is everything—

He raises his fists but quickly lets them drop. His body collapses, his big shoulders rolling inwards and his back sagging. The Shawnee look on quietly. Some smirk, some are sorry for him. They walk us along again, Stewart stumbling and dragging behind me. Our keepers talk with one another. They have our horses loaded with our furs and skins. The air is cooler, most of them wrap their blankets about their shoulders now, and some cover their shaved heads. But it is still pleasant out, the sun shines white. I find myself strangely untroubled, and I sing "Over the Hills and Far Away." It is one of Hill's favourites, I bellow it out as he would:

I would love you all the day,
Every night would kiss and play,
If with me you'd fondly stray,
Over the hills and far away.

My voice cracks but I carry on. Still singing, I turn to see Stewart, who looks as if he would like to lop off my head and parade it about on a pike.

—Sing with me, Stewart.

He looks at me, his lips tight. I say it again:

—Go on, sing with me. Who does not like a song?

—No.

—Stewart.

—No!

—John, I am only asking you to sing.

—I will not, Dan.

He is like a smothered fire, all damp misery. He no longer believes in me, but he is sorry for it, which makes him worse.

I sing on wild, my voice all over the scale. A few of the Shawnee are amused and turn the unaccustomed sounds around in their mouths like thick crusts. The *hells*, they say. Over the hells. This seems true enough and so I sing it that way as well as we march along through the trees and canebrakes and yes, over the hills.

Captain Will looks back from his place near the front of the queue, faintly amused. His stretched ears swing and shine with their silver loops.

I strain my brains and send my thoughts out to carry on any wind. Findley, hear us. Get out. Get everything out. Hide it.

I sing loud as I can. I sing to stop the noises of my dead rising behind me. It seems they might touch my shoulders and claim me any minute. I sing on, getting the words wrong myself, but the words do not matter.

I keep us alive.

But Findley is long gone, and he took only what he could carry easily. The station camp is cold and lifeless. No wolves, either grown or pups. No bones. The packs still sit on the platform like so many fat, stupid pigeons. The singing Shawnee get everything.

13

I Dance and Sing in the Wilderness

One working gun, a little shot and powder. Two pairs of moccasins each and one doeskin for patching soles. It is snowing in fat light flakes when Captain Will gives these items to us and presses our palms.

—Now brothers, go home. Stay there. Black Fish would not like to hear of you here. This is our hunting ground, and all the animals and their skins and furs are ours.

He explains this gently, as if we are very young. Stewart chews his underlip, his jaw muscles twitch. He looks feverish again. I find myself not wanting Captain Will to leave us, and not only because we have nothing. I say:

—Black Fish. Your chief? We have heard of him. Perhaps he would like to hear of us. Perhaps we might interest him.

I think of Hill pulling terrible faces with his tongue lolling, playing the victims the terrible Black Fish has had burned over superb slow fires, so slow they almost go out. The burnings last all day. Hill acts this with moanings and eye-rollings if there are any children about to watch. I am done for, he moans.

The Captain only smiles briefly and goes on:

—Do not come back. You may be sure the wasps and yellow-jackets will sting you.

I point to his drained-looking colourless coat and say:

—Was your jacket ever yellow? Perhaps we could get you a better one. We know a trader.

He shows no interest, but I go on:

—Hornets stung our friend Hill here. He left. I do not think he will come back. You would not want him, but we are not so bad.

—You English brought the hornets and bees to this place. None came here before.

—You are fond of honey, surely. Not all that we have brought is bad, is it?

He turns away, and his eyes show no sign of knowing us when I say once more:

—Captain.

They are going. There is only the creak of the heavy packs on the horses moving off towards the Warrior's Path, heading north. My guard with the red leggings gives me a nod. The soft chatter, the movement through the light snow, and the humming of a song drifting away.

—That is your song.

Stewart speaks wretchedly. He coughs and says:

—They have everything, even our songs.

We stay among the cold ruins of the station camp for two nights. Only now does my heart fail for a time. They have left us no horses. The real winter has begun to gnaw at last, and we are so far from anywhere. I try to shore up our spirits with talk of all we have seen, the beautiful lands and the abundant game, all of it like nothing else on the earth.

In talking of it, I feel myself like Findley, curiously free. Why not begin again? Why not? Another new life. I say so to Stewart, but he rolls over on his pine boughs and seems to sleep, though I can tell he does not.

Findley does not return.

—Likely gone over to the Indians. Could wait no longer for his Indian maids.

Stewart says so as he pisses steamily into the snow. Even his pissing has an angry sound. He cannot look at me for long. He lies down on his boughs again, his mouth set harder. He grieves the loss of his bearskin especially, among all the other skins and all his dreams of money. I know that I am to make up for every disappointment. I do not understand the luck Fate has given me, or that I took from my brother Israel. It perches hard and heavy on my shoulder, digging in its claws. It seems to think it is a help.

I go out, I shoot a scraggy turkey. Thank you, Fate. I carry it back and place it at Stewart's angry feet. As though we were in the middle of a talk, I say:

—Well all right. We had best go after them, then.

The horses' bells are easy to follow. The moon is thin but the snow reflects its cold light enough to see lines and shapes by. The horses are browsing in the white-powdered grass outside the camp the Shawnee have made. Their fire is a low red glow down by the creek. A few voices rise occasionally, then go quiet.

We wait in the trees.

We are happy again somehow. It is curious how happy we are.

We wait another quarter-hour in silence. I creep forward and crouch to unhobble two animals, working by feel. The silky cold grass and the bony forelegs and the cold stiff ties. My fingers work to loose the knots and I reach up to feel the horses' necks. They are bridled. Good.

—How can we tell which are ours?

Stewart's hiss explodes in the night. I speak as quietly as I can, through my teeth:

—Take any.

—I want my horse.

One of the animals whinnies, the others stir. Their bells tinkle, their warm smell rises with their movement. I go on working, I have the two loose, their reins in my fist. Stewart is feeling for me, grabbing at my arm:

—I want my horse.

His voice grows and his grip tightens, as if he is trying to keep himself from a fall. I shrug him off:

—Stewart, let me work, damn it—

A flare bursts up out of the thin dark behind a tree. Three Shawnee faces appear in the sudden snapping torchlight. One of them is my former guard. Stewart is squinting and crouching. I am still holding the reins.

They are smiling, they are delighted to see us again. For a moment I believe this to be true. Then my guard reaches out with his palm flat, he takes the bridles. He speaks in gentle crippled English:

—Steal horse, ha?

A thing is around my neck. A rope. A noose. My spine goes rigid up to my skull. Hold yourself still, hold your face still. The Shawnee man pulls at the rope and it chafes and burns my skin. A lump pushes against the side of my throat where the rope is tightest. It shakes and jingles. I reach for it, it is cold metal, a bell. Another of them sings something I cannot understand, and they are all looking at me, wanting something. Slowly I try to repeat the words:

—Pan pan fee?

They all laugh at my efforts. Stewart is still crouching, his eyes racing. One of the Shawnee pulls him up and begins to beat a rhythm on Stewart's back with his gun butt. The horses circle and look interested, the other two men are clapping their hands and encouraging.

They want me to dance.

Well, I dance. The bell jangles merry in the night as if it is Christmas. It *is* Christmas or thereabouts, as I realize now. Rebecca and the children in the warm dry Bryan house without me. I go on jingling and I say:

—Happy Christmas, boys. Happy Christmas, everyone.

They laugh again, watching me, and they do not kill us.

When Captain Will lays eyes on me once more, he looks at me as if I were a disobedient dog. In truth I have a queer wish to be one, to perform tricks and be forgiven and let back into the house. Into someone's house, or perhaps anyone's.

We walk and walk. I still have the bell on.

The sky looks colder every night, black with the stars like a windowpane shattered all over it. We are following the Kentucky River to the Ohio, towards the Indians' winter town, as I assume.

Stewart's eyes look stuck open. He watches me and he watches the Shawnee.

I say:

—Would you like to see their town?

He shrugs and asks:

—Have we any choice? Would you?

—I would not object. You, Stewart?

—I would not object either.

He takes a long breath and says:

—I was thinking of Hannah. I told her I would bring her money, but I have nothing for her now.

He stops. He says:

—I would like to see a house again, even if it is one of theirs.

He has begun to accept the way that life has turned. After walking along slowly for days, it is easy to accept the need for it, as

I find. The guards ride alongside us, holding our ties loose. I hear Stewart trying out a word or two in Shawnee on his keeper now and then. The Indians call him Bear in their tongue, *Makwa*, which pleases him, as I can see when I tell him what they say. He does smell of bear still, and it is a pleasanter name than Wide Mouth, which they call me in English at times.

When one of them shouts for us to sing, I oblige. I rack my brains for more music and find myself wishing Hill were present. They like "Over the Hills" and also "Come Butter Come," which Jamesie and Israel like to clap and stamp to when their mother is churning. I learn a couple of Shawnee tunes, or learn them near enough. I will teach them to the children and scandalize Rebecca. The guards laugh and try to correct my words and my tone, but their music is so meandering that I cannot always see the path through it.

I allow myself a thought of the children's bare feet dancing, hopping up and down before the cold fire, dipping their toes into the ash. I allow myself a thought of Jamesie's feet in particular, I kissed their soles when he was just born and had never touched ground. He is a great boy now, his feet will have grown still more. Israel's too, he will have grown, and Susannah no longer tiny. Time will have continued at home. In some fashion I have been picturing it as stopped there, as if everyone were keeping still. At once my bones ache violently.

I walk in silence for a half-mile. Under the jingling of my bell, I speak into Stewart's good ear:

—Stewart. John.

—What?

Stewart looks as if I am a bedbug or some other distraction. His eyes are very fatigued. I say:

—You know the butter song.

—No.

—You do, I know. "Come Butter Come." Be ready when you hear it.

—Why?

—Be ready. We have to go. Think again of your Hannah and your little one at home.

He stops walking. He says:

—I have thought. Look at me, look at how weak I am. Will she want me back?

He walks on and I carry on a pace behind. Two days more I take to ready myself. It is difficult to think of a way to leave, and to think of leaving at all. When the Shawnee are making camp in the evening, Captain Will says he can smell the Ohio. We will see its waters tomorrow, he says. Stewart and I are tied to one another but to no one else now. The Shawnee all loosen, they stretch out along the fire trench and talk as the dark comes down. They are easy at the thought of nearing their winter home and families.

I breathe in and smooth my face and sing a line:

Johnny wants a piece of cake.

I will admit that I am curiously slow and sad in singing it. Stewart looks at me, his face also sorrowful and perplexed. For a moment we stand blinking at one another.

I jerk my head. He ducks his and follows me to take up a gun from the careless heap left near the packs and the horses. The cane here is high and thick, we move into it carefully at first, then we run with the guns out to push the stalks down before us. There will be an easy trail for them to follow, but it is winter dark already, the fast-falling dark, so we keep up a slow run and turn south, and though we listen all the time through our breathing, no one follows. We are not worth following, it seems. I keep my fist around the bell at first but after a time I let it ring out. I will keep it always.

He disappears soon after we make it to the station camp again. One morning he goes out alone and does not come back. I search for him as I go out hunting. I find *JS* on a tree one afternoon, and I look at it for some time. The letters seem an insult, a wound on my own body. They remind me that Stewart was once here and has now gone, left on purpose, sick and disappointed at all he lost by following me. I wonder always what made him go. Could he not bear the thought of returning home penniless to his good Hannah? To have her gasp and step back from his filthy skin and beard?

Stewart, I brought you to Kentucky and to the Shawnee. Some will say I butchered and ate you, most likely. For my own purposes. What purposes? Keeping the furs and skins for myself? There are no furs and skins left. You were right, there is nothing. I am alone in the wilderness with a stiff-triggered, badly built gun and a paltry supply of shot and powder. I imagine Findley watching me from somewhere in the trees, laughing to himself and saying in Hill's voice: *What will you do now?*

14

The Heart of All

FOR DAYS I pad about in the snow looking for Stewart and occasionally for Findley. My entire skin listens. I call out quietly and then high like a bird, I use my own voice and all kinds of others. I take care with my tracks. But the Captain's Shawnee are long gone to their town, and nobody else seems to remain near the Warrior's Path now that winter is gripping.

Stewart is not anywhere. I look in puzzlement at the letters carved on the tree. *JS*. People have their reasons for disappearing, as I am left to suppose.

The creeks are icy. I get a few fish, a few turkey, a deer occasionally, some nuts. I survive the winter.

I use a precious shot on a great bird with beautiful bright underwings. I wish I had paper to try to draw it on. I keep the wings. I survive.

I go north, back towards the Ohio, where I see no one. Then I go west. I know where all the creeks and the buffalo roads lead and where they converge, I know all the licks, and which are the most crusted with salt. I climb to a ridge above one to see a living sea of buffalo pawing and butting and licking at the snowy salty ground as though all praying busily. Their noise and smell wrap me up like a robe, and I feel myself almost happy for that moment. I shoot one through the throat. It dies quickly. I eat some meat and jerk what I can. I am happier still, though less yet another shot.

I thin down to sinew, I feel strung like a bow, which makes me reckless in my body as I was when I was a boy. I dare Fate to injure me. I fashion myself a real bow and some arrows with saplings and gut and the beautiful bird's feathers. I shoot a wildcat with it just as it considers tensing to spring at me out of the snow. It falls, shot clean. Killing it so, without touching it or hurting it, is a beauty to me, there is no other like it. I love that bow sending its quick arrow to the heart just as if it is stopping time.

I could fire-hunt. I remember Israel showing me how. But I do not do so, I will do better. And I do not wish to summon Israel in this place.

I keep my bow and I do not die. Summer comes, and autumn again. I am alone, I feel myself at the core of silence. Again I think of being inside a huge sleeping wolf, but now as a bone in one of its joints. Or as a figment of its sleeping mind. I sing in the cold evenings as I lie in the canebrakes, which I keep to for shelter. I sing anything, and when I hear wolves singing back distantly I keep at it, though my heart speeds. I invent a song about Kentucky. I sing it at the top of my lungs: Yellow-jackets. Hornets. Pan pan fee. I think of the Shawnee but they do not come. The sky is a dark circle like a pupil open above me with the fringe of high cane all round.

Again the cold lightens, again the daylight holds longer. Pale green appears out of the ground like a thin fur. With the new spring, I begin to move east. I know I must. I am down to the last dust of the powder Captain Will left me. I have no feathers left for arrows.

I skirt the edges of buffalo traces. I go slowly. I will follow the Warrior's Path back towards the gap in the mountains that Findley showed us. All the time I want to turn around, turn and keep walking and let this place have its way with me. It is mine now.

First I stop at the station camp. I pull the pine branches back over the roof of the toppled shelter. Their cold scent puffs back to life as I move them. A blanket torn into shreds lines a hollow in one of the tree roots at the back of the lean-to. A faint smell of Findley and also of wolf. I go to find some fresh hemlock to line the shelter again.

I am beginning to kindle a fire when I hear a cracking in the quiet. I have near forgot how it feels to have no explanation for a sound, I have grown so used to the noises of snow falling from trees or of animal life at night.

I see nothing yet. The trees are not thick and there is no cane on this part of the creek. When I stand, I suddenly feel myself human again. Only now do I feel my weakness and my thinness and my lack of ammunition. Long teeth seem to poke into my mind. I have been living a half-inch from Death, I have been winning, I have been happy. I clear my throat and I rub my matted beard. My chest goes tight, the way it did when I saw Rebecca at her granddaddy's door after I dragged a dead deer to her. Here I am.

Only now, I do not want to be seen. I walk through the trees, following the line of the creek. I catch the scent of smoke before I see it clouding upwards and spreading thick. A large dry dead tree is fallen, and it is on fire, flames skip from branch to branch. The sound sharpens. I crouch to look. There is a blowing and stamping, a footfall. I stare through the smoke and burning branches and shadows. Four horses are behind the fire. One neighs and tosses its head. A figure wrapped in a cloak is standing with them.

Israel. But I will not say his name. No ghosts here. Instead I say:

—Stewart?

My voice is rough and patchy. I am ready to forgive Stewart his sudden disappearance, it is no matter now. But he may still be angry.

And I do not forget he may also be captive again, brought back here as bait to catch me too.

I do not move. The shape is dark behind the fire. A pulse jumps in my neck. The tree blazes and cracks and sends out thick black waves.

A voice calls through the smoke:

—Findley?

It too is wary and distant. It is too low to be Stewart. My heart falls, but I say:

—No. Gone.

This cannot be Findley, then. At once I think of Captain Will, but it is not his voice. Then I think of Hill. I am even ready to tolerate Hill if he has horses and powder.

I look hard through the bright flames, my eyes water and clench in the haze. Still I cannot see. The voice says:

—Is it Dan?

I hesitate before I reply:

—Yes.

I step towards the fire, straightening myself, pulling at my dirty hunting shirt and wiping my running eyes with the back of my hand. I come so close that the heat of the burning tree scorches my cheeks. The air pops and sparks, drops of fire land upon my clothing. The shape becomes clearer and taller and thinner. It cannot be Hill. The man opens his cloak and looks for a moment like a great bird preening its wings.

Squire. It is my brother behind the leaping flames, raising his arm to shield his eyes. He is alive. He has the horses packed with supplies. They are restless and wary. Traps dangle and clash on their sides.

Relief washes through me. I say:

—Well, Squire, all right, well done. Your fire led me direct to you. Quite a burning bush in the wilderness. You turned prophet since you left?

But he does not move. He only looks at me through the fire as if considering what he ought best do now. He drops his hand, but still I cannot see his face properly. At last he says:

—Looks like you need rescuing.

I consider this.

—Perhaps I do.

I pull another of the beavers from one of the new traps. I slice gentle into the under-jaw to draw the pelt down and off clean. The beavers have been obliging. We have got ten in the lines today and found a good new pond to try. Our packs are growing heavy again already. If anyone has to be here, I am glad it is Squire, though we are still somewhat strange together and I am unused to conversation. I ask whether he has seen any sign of Stewart on his way out, but he shakes his head. He only says:

—Your family told me to bring their hellos.

—They are all right?

—Seem to be. Though they have their concerns about you.

Squire pulls the trap from its chain and feels the edge. He says now:

—Bryan moved them all back to the Yadkin to set the farms going again. Ma and Daddy went too.

—All of them there again? Well. I will know where to find them. If they will have an old man back.

I pull at my beard as old Bryan sometimes does:

—I will be able to compete fairly, for one thing. Look at this beauty. Rebecca will not know her husband when he appears on her doorstep.

Squire's face goes still and obscure over the trap. I say:

—She is all right? I did ask you.

—She is all right.

Squire squints into the jaw of the trap and says no more. I have the beaver pelt off now, and it is a good long glossy one. I get out the hoop to stretch it. I say:

—I will be glad to see her. And home, if that is what I may still call it.

And I will be glad, although the way I imagine Rebecca now is perhaps less spiky round the edges than she is. This happens with one's idea of home also, as it seems to me.

—You were glad to get back there for a while, Squire?

He does not answer, he is busy filing at the trap. The rasping puts me in mind of Daddy in the forge. Squire goes on until he bangs the trap closed and turns to look very slow about the camp. He remarks:

—Should have enough beaver and otter to make up for some of what was taken.

I know Squire and I know what he means, which is that my question is not worth answering. We sit silent until he says:

—You ought to get back.

His face remains shut but his eyes rise to meet mine. I know that this is all he will say on the subject. His opinion has been presented like a small rock striking my head. Squire always had a good aim. I say:

—I know it.

Then I keep quiet, though something is evidently not right. I do not feel the need for more rocks to the head at this time.

We pack our way out through the mountain gap after more luck at trapping, and we travel past the white cliffs, where I stop to look for the letters of our names we carved. They are unchanged. We carry on down the eastern side of the Alleghenies. The Warrior's Path turns and follows a creek through the narrow valley I remember. Powell's Valley, I say, and I think of coming through here with Findley. I do not wish our trip to be finished, though I do not know where he is now.

Squire offers his hand to help me through the fast high stream. I say:

—I am not quite an invalid. I am alive yet.

He is still somewhat ill at ease but he laughs and says:

—I respect my elders.

We walk the horses through the water and stop on the far bank, our leggings wet and stiffening. The air is still cool, especially in the shaded places such as this. I sit to dry my feet a little. Squire says:

—We should keep on.

—Your favourite phrase, it seems to me. What is wrong with taking one more night here?

—Feeling your age, old man?

—I feel nothing, nothing at all.

I try to believe this, though I am still half-minded to go back to Kentucky. I find myself almost afraid it will have disappeared without me. I begin to gather kindling, and Squire sighs but sets to helping.

We do not see them until they are in the creek, running their horses straight across, straight for us. We have enough time to reach our guns but not to load. They dismount and stand, dripping and huge, their heads wrapped in coloured scarves. Giants, I think. Here are we in Gulliver's Brobdingnag.

We stare mutually.

I take my gun in one hand and step forward. I say:

—How do, brothers. Shawnee?

—Cherokee.

The one who replies is very tall with a long face, all bone. His cheekbones look as though they will burst straight through his skin. His headscarf is frayed along the edge, and he tucks it back up with care. His movements are all ease. His five companions go on staring until he lightly puts out his hands for Squire's rifle. With a glance at me, Squire gives it up. I speak little Cherokee and so I say in English:

—We can see yours?

The big man lifts his chin and hands over his own gun. It is poorly made trade-trash, the stock painted up all gay, and puts me in mind of Findley's pile of magpie rubbish. I point to my eyes and say:

—You know a white trader with blue eyes? Very white, very blue.

The man snorts and laughs. He says something to the others and they laugh as well, especially after he gives a little flourishing bow. Findley's gesture. He reaches towards my face, and I keep myself still as his hand goes around to the back of my neck, where Findley's lavender hair-ribbon is still in my plait. He tries to pull it out but it is well caught. He twists it over his fist instead and says:

—Everyone knows this man.

—Have you seen him?

The man smiles, still fingering the end of the hair ribbon. He says only:

—Maybe so.

—Have you seen another white man, tall and thin, smelling of bear? Or one who goes about singing in a loud voice?

—Maybe so.

His voice is even and tells me nothing.

—Did you kill either of them?

My tone is light also. Again he says:

—Maybe so.

He laughs and takes out a pipe. He offers it to me with a broad smile.

Squire makes the fire when I ask him to. Wariness shows in the line of his back. He says soft to me:

—We should get ready to be gone.

I am drinking from my flask with the tall man. I offer a toast:

—To Blue Eyes. Or—to you. What is your name?

—Jim.

The man says it so easy it is almost a mockery. All of their white-given names sound like small lies. I say:

—The same as my older boy. That the name your mother gave you?

He only laughs. The other men are examining the rifles again, and one looks up and asks something with a smile. Jim says:

—Trade?

He is smiling too, as if it is all one joke. I say:

—Oh, we could not do that.

I join the smiles. My face twitches and throbs and my muscles are warm from the rum. I look at Squire, he raises one shoulder, he is willing me not to get us axed, willing me to stop this. But I cannot stop, I feel reckless all through, and curious about these men. I want to keep them here. I want something to happen. I say:

—You can see we are not traders. Not like Blue Eyes.

Jim stretches out a broad, flat fingertip. He says:

—Your eyes are blue. Little Blue Eyes.

His finger is close to the surface of my eye, as if he is aiming at a target, as if he will gently touch it. I do not move. I say:

—Are mine blue? So I have been told. You will have to tell me what you see.

Jim laughs and takes his finger away. The other Cherokee make a show of considering the guns and pelts and horses with buyers' care. And so I make a seller's show, I point out the length of the rifles Squire brought, the quality of the otter pelts especially. Jim strokes one and idly puts his fingers through the eyehole. He touches the fur to his cheek. Bright as I can, I say:

—Squire. Your shaving mirror. Perhaps they would like to see themselves.

But Squire shrugs roughly. He says:

—My shaving mirror is not to hand.

The Cherokee Jim looks at him a moment, then nods to his companions. They load their horses with our furs and rifles, leaving us the poor trade guns. They wave and call as they ride our horses back over the river and up the path on the other side, the pack animals behind.

Well. Everything is gone again.

Squire sits by the fire and takes off his damp moccasins. He rests his nose against his fist for a moment. Then he looks up grimly. Smoke curls in tails about him. He says:

—You are quite a negotiator.

—They did not kill us.

My body still roars with energy, I do not know what to do with myself. I feel myself a player in an unsatisfactory performance. I want to do it again. I stand and walk about the fire in a circle and throw sticks into it. I say:

—Everything between us and the Indians feels false. Like theatrics. Or like a long joke. Do you not think so?

Squire is looking down again. He breathes out and grudgingly says:

—Then why play along?

—We all play along. It is a game. Or a tale, we all like a tale. A happy end.

—Happy for who?

—I do not know. For everyone.

I take off my moccasins as well and stretch my toes closer to the heat. Squire says:

—For us? This is happiness?

—Why not? At least we can start again. We can go back and hunt farther. It is another chance.

This thought cheers me, as it always has. Squire is holding his moccasins on a stick over the fire, and the air begins to smell of toasting skin. He says in his dry way:

—Not everyone gets another chance. Go home, Dan.

He swings his moccasins straight down into the fire, where they perish in smoke.

15

The Children

—You again.

She is standing in the cabin doorway holding a spoon. Something is dripping from it. Her mouth is curled tight at the corner, as I knew it would be.

I know you saw me at the dance that was going on at your grandfather's house when I arrived. I stood with my back to the wall and you looked through me as you spun by, some of your hair falling loose in a loop on your back. I saw your black eyes moving on and not stopping. I watched you do it. I felt myself disappear.

I left Squire at his house, and I slept outside that night. Now I have walked home across the fields to stand outside our own cabin, and she does know who I am after all. Rebecca looks worn, with a dull sheen to her skin. She is beautiful, it invades me, I breathe in hard. This is my wife. She is my wife. I say:

—Fancy seeing you in this place.

I push back my hat to see her in full. My voice is frogged and odd. My smile hurts my jaws. I need to hear her speak again. She does:

—The same to you, I was going to say, Mr. Boone.

—I suppose we would have to meet one another sometime in a crowded vicinity like this one. Only logical.

—I suppose so.

She stands with the spoon going drip drip drip. Her face is containing itself in its old way, the way it did when I first saw it against the barn. She is the same, she has been here all along. My eyes burn and I have to lower my face:

—I wish I had brought you more, little girl. So much was taken. Stewart is gone.

—Gone where?

—I do not know. Gone.

At once the loss of all our gains crushes me. It no longer feels part of a game or a play. My shoulders fall. I go on standing outside the house with its lit window and its weathering walls. It looks small and tight and fortified. *You outsider. You ape.*

Her eyes travel over me slow and reluctant. I see myself as she must see me: tired hunting shirt, dirty flapping moccasins patched together from scraps, hungry body. White Indian. Ha. I pull at my long beard and hold out the end to show her.

She smiles gentle, one side of her mouth. No laugh. She says:

—You got something for your pains, I see.

—I did.

She looks out past the kitchen garden to the rye and wheat and flax and corn. Her eyes seem to run over every plant in turn, as if she knows each one. She likely planted many herself, making holes in the dirt with her long fingers. Jesse and Jonathan are bent over the plough outside the stable, trying to mend it, and they look up but do not come over. It strikes me that life has been difficult enough here. Looking at Rebecca, I want to kiss her hard on her face and throat, I want to taste her clean skin, but I do not move. This is her place.

She looks at me. She only looks.

At last she says:

—Will you not come in, wandering sir.

I say:

—I will, lady. If you say so.

—I say so.

She turns with decision in her bones. I follow her in through the low doorway, I ought to have made it higher when I built the

place. The children are near the fire, snatching a wood doll from each other and beating its head upon the walls. They are so big and so healthy and so much themselves that I begin to laugh. Rebecca says:

—Here is your Dada.

Jamesie turns. He is so tall now. He is pleased but unsure, his feet apart as if he is stopping himself from running. Israel, always ready to show off for strangers and their beards, turns the spit all crazy to show me what he can do. And Susannah is a little girl already, her fine dark hair a tangle at the back of her head. She lets out a squeal and scrambles for the doll in the corner. She takes it over to the cradle and hops it up and down in the air before depositing it there.

An answering wail comes from within at a thinner and higher pitch.

My hand is about to reach Rebecca's waist, but it stops in the air. I move to look.

A tiny baby with a fuzz of black hair, like hers. Like mine. It stares up with its eyes fixed on my face long enough to send out a challenge. It opens its wet mouth. It keeps its night-blue eyes open also.

Two Christmases and more. Near two years I have been gone.

I pick up the baby and return the stare. It bleats and fights its swaddling bands. I say:

—Wants out.

I sit and unwrap it and let the bands fall in a pile on the floor. I want to see all of it. The baby hurls out its limbs, making itself star-shaped. It is very young and it is a girl.

Rebecca watches, still holding the spoon. The children try to get it, pulling at her arm and skirts. The naked baby gasps and lets out a clear yell, a single note, and Rebecca cannot help but step towards it. But she halts herself and keeps still. Her eyes shift between the baby and me.

I say to the children:

—Leave your mother be.

The baby flails again and I hold it up in the air, where it tries to lift its head to scream at the ceiling. Its neck lolls, it pisses a wet stream down my chest.

My first thought is of the Catawbas laughing at me with my stupidly won tomahawk at the shooting contest. Like them, I stare unbelieving and I laugh. I say:

—Yours?

Rebecca nods once.

—Well. She is half on the right side of the sheets, then.

The laugh catches in my dry throat. Rebecca says, her face held tight:

—She looks like you.

—That is fine for her, or for you. Whose is she?

She says nothing. I say:

—Perhaps I ought to ask the midwife then, you surely screamed the father's name in your labour. Is that not what they say in such sad cases? Who delivered you? Martha?

Her eyes are on me for an instant. She says fiercely:

—She is nobody's. Nobody's.

She is quietly furious, guarded as a gate. She stalks the six steps across the room. There is not space enough for her fury. To the wall she says:

—You were gone so long. You were just gone. For a long while I thought you were dead. Daniel, I believed you were dead, what else was I to think?

I think of Squire's locked-up face, and I say:

—Was that your reasoning—that I was dead? That it was time for a replacement? Well here I am from beyond the grave to prove you wrong.

I get up and step forward, she whirls to face me:

—It was twice—twice.

—More than enough, then.

She spins again, shaking Susannah from her skirt. The boys are staring. I am still holding up the squirming stranger baby. I say:

—Name?

She lifts her chin and says:

—Jemima.

This is new, nobody's name, not her mother's, not mine. I say:

—Did he name it, this travelling Nobody?

She bends at the fire to viciously stir a pot with her spoon, I cannot see her face. Her voice is trying to steady itself:

—A priest came. One of the Moravians.

—Oho, a priest now. Have you developed a taste for religion? Or did it develop a taste for you, is that your tale? *Ja ja ja, gut gut*—

Her voice rises:

—A very old man, a good man. An old priest with a grey beard to his waist and a smell of damp. Is that what you want to hear? He wanted a meal on his way back to their colony. He sat and watched all of us as he ate, and he said to me, You are in a lonely position. He saw what it is like here. I told him that I am afraid all the time. All the time.

—You had the boys here to help you, Jesse and Jonathan—

—Boys, they are boys! I am tied hand and foot here, I was alone with all of this—

—You had the children here. Mine.

The baby works up to a serious cry, ongoing and rising.

Rebecca whips about to face me again, clutching the spoon as though she will shovel out my brains for me. She is about to strike my face with it, I feel the sting of her wish to, I feel my arm tighten as hers does. Susannah knocks over a pot of beans soaking on the hearth and begins to howl. The boys stand very still as the water creeps towards their feet. The baby wails. Rebecca stares at me and says:

—Hold her. Not like that.

She hurls the spoon to the floor where it cracks into pieces. She bends to the mess. And I do hold the baby, who grows more angry and burrows her face into my chest, looking for milk or comfort or something else that I am supposed to have but do not have.

I go again. I vanish. I plunge into the woods across the Yadkin, I shoot pheasants and sparrows and squirrels and anything else that I see moving. I think of things I might take an axe to. Houses, heads, pricks. I sit by my campfire into the night with my eyes wide, and I wake cramped up as a claw. How can you uncramp yourself from such a state?

I think of going up to Squire's place to see how he has fared with his wife, or of going to Hannah's to tell her Stewart is lost. But I do not. I sit. And after some days I return to the cabin. I sit outside the doorway for a time, where I can see Rebecca passing back and forth inside the house. I say nothing. I will stare her out. But she refuses to acknowledge my presence. I watch her moving about, I see her face ease as she lets her eyes settle on the cradle. This baby is another first child to her. This dumbstruck look that mothers get with their newborn babies, as if a new planet has been made before their eyes. She has spent many nights away helping at births and come home sleepless, coated with awe as if she had been dipped in gold.

I see this life here without myself. I look at the dark fields with their accusing crops that say: You were not here.

I go back to when Jamesie was born and Rebecca was bright golden all through. I was waiting outdoors then also, smoothing a piece of wood with a sharp-edged stone. It made the shape of a leaf, a thing still living when it falls from the tree. I was afraid that Rebecca would not live and I wanted to make her live. Or to see her out of this world with some gift. I took out my knife to nick the edges. A stupid gift. I did not wish to think.

—You have a son.

A woman stood in the shadow of the doorway with bright eyes, watching for my reaction as her due. Women do this, as I know.

—He is all right?

—Yes, very well. Rebecca too. The boy is eating already.

—I cannot say I blame him.

It was pleasing to say this new *he* and *him,* I was proud as a prince. I laughed at myself. At once I was hungry enough to eat a cow whole. Another woman stepped outdoors and said:

—Come on. I will feed you, as you are so poorly off without your wife. We can spare you a cake and some beer, lucky man.

—No, no, keep those for yourselves. I want to see my son.

When I went into the hot room, I was full of aching delight. I had never felt so unnecessary and so full of my stupid part in the thing. Rebecca looked at me, sparkling, her cloudy hair brushed out against the pillow. She was surrounded by women coming and going. The baby was wrapped up on her chest. She had her hand round the back of his head. She said:

—Here is your present.

She did not give him to me. I saw the tilt of his nose, the side of his little red face only. I was struck by a thought of my old fond red-faced uncle in Pennsylvania. Uncle James, you were good to me, you tried to help me learn.

With a touch of Daddy's bluster, thinking to make my boy part of myself, I said:

—His name is James.

But Rebecca did not argue in the least. She got to me by not arguing, all agreement and a pale brilliant smile. She had an Uncle James also, it turned out.

I remember all of it. But now I wait outside again with my flask near empty and my hunting dirt still all over me. The day is finishing. Jesse comes out for a while after supper, but he will not sit down, he is not easy. I ask him how he has been, but he only says he is tired and will go to bed. He says goodnight very low.

When I am alone again, I feel the sky watching to see what I will do. I can only think of Rebecca cut off from me inside. Did I do the cutting? Well.

I want her. I want to have her, and not just to mark my territory, it is not only that. I am sunk with my desire, my body crackles with the old burning link between us, all the brighter for its coldness now. Other men want her, and why should they not? She is magnificent, she is Helen, she is a witch. She was afraid. And I was gone.

At once I feel exhausted and hollowed out, like a child done with wailing and pleading.

I trip on the steep steps to the sleeping loft. I find that I have forgotten how many there are and I am sorry for it.

The baby stirs in the cradle beside the bed. I reach out to find the edge of the bed and it creaks under my hand. Her skin smells of bayberries. I find her neck, her shoulder, her swollen breasts and softened belly. I keep my hand there for a time, I do not move.

Her fingertips fall on my back, light as moths. They mark questions all over me. I am burning and cold. The baby rustles and settles again like a small bird. Rebecca stiffens.

I make myself speak into her ear:

—It would not be easy. To untie ourselves.

I feel drunk. I am somewhat drunk, my blood is drowsy and slow like a summer day. Her hair feels like breath on my cheek. I want to cover my face in it and sleep. She says:

—Do not give me up, then.

I feel her lips twist against my arm. I cannot help asking again:

—Who?

I close my eyes, I want to ask it again, who who who, make an owl of myself. But I say only:

—Rebecca.

She is silent. She does not answer, but she is not putting on her Queen-of-the-Backwoods air with me now. I feel her vulnerability, her held breath. But she is my Queen of the Backwoods, my Welsh witch, with all kinds of black power. I cannot bear to see her topple from that and become a thing squashed down by life. She is not afraid, she cannot be.

Rebecca, in my mind you are black hair and shining eyes, spitting cherry pits. Witches can be burned but come back to life. Queens can do as they like.

Do as you like. My dead brother said so. Israel, you are long dead now, and your boys are growing, they work the fields with their hunched shoulders, waiting for the next blow.

Well there will be no next blow. I will not leave again. This I decide now. I say:

—How can I give you up, little girl?

My voice creaks in my ears, but I go on:

—Can you give me up?

She does not speak for some time. The wind picks up for a moment and hushes itself again. She says:

—I did. For a while.

—But I am not dead.

—No.

—No. I am here. Feel me.

She laughs a little with her hand on me and says in her old lazy fashion:

—I have felt you before.

She turns her face to my ear. Her voice sharpens:

—If you go again, if you die, I will not go looking for you, or your corpse. Hannah has been out of her mind with worry and now John is gone, just gone, that is all you can say—

Her fingers pinch my shoulder until it stings, until her nails are in me. She has not said my name. I say:

—You are free, you know. You were not wrong. You are free.

—I do know.

—Well. You are.

—You are not.

I laugh, my mouth open against her throat, and I do not know what else to do.

16

Lilliput

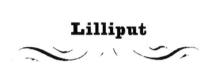

WE GO ON. The children watch us. We are formal. We do not tease one another. We do not quite look at one another.

The baby is part of the house. She screams suddenly out of deep sleeping silences and then screams on until the house throbs. The screams seem to be directed at me, and so I pick her up and stare at her face. She continues her yelling, her small mouth working and gaping and her eyes aiming to remain on mine. She has Rebecca's temper, only set on fire. She begins straight away to attach herself to me. Her small lolling head tries to turn itself towards my voice.

I see Jonathan and Jesse watching me with this other little outsider. Their faces are carefully arranged. I say:

—Well well. A baby is a gift to everyone, is that not what people say?

Still. I do not know where to go now. I work the fields with Jonathan and Jesse, and I hunt a little up the Yadkin but no more than a few days at a time. This gets rid of some restlessness but not all.

Daddy and Ma visit in the fall. Daddy jigs his legs about and still talks of buying more land, enough to give to all his children. He has had to sell much of his to raise money to live. His cheeks and eyes are full of red lines like little forking rivers. He has an elderly look but his voice is the same. He blusters in his best fashion:

—No one can take you off land once it is yours. No one.

Ma pets the little ones and rocks the baby. I feel her watching me as she does so. She knows this child is not mine but she says nothing. When they prepare to go home, she kisses us all and holds my face in her cool dry hands. Daddy says:

—Come on, my girl.

And they climb slow into their wagon and drive off. I see Daddy pointing at a flock of swallows.

It is January when Squire rides through the deep snow to say Daddy is dead. I turn my face from him when he says it. Daddy wished to be buried near Israel, and so we take his body in a wagon to the German town in Maryland, along the road from Pennsylvania. I ride ahead, I keep silent. We cut a black hole in the white ground and put up a stone for him: *Departed This Life 1765*. We put up a proper one for Israel now also. Squire walks off on his own. A dog looks at us from the edge of the field.

I stand with Ma as she touches the letters and numbers. I say:

—You do not mind them having headstones, Ma? I know it is not the Friends' way.

Ma says:

—They should have stones. To show they lived. I will be here too one day. You can put one up for me, my Danny.

She comes home with us. I lie awake for many nights, for weeks, as it seems to me. My heart is hot and empty and my eyes seem to boil. I wish for a dream of Daddy's spirit but none comes. It seems to me there is no one between me and Death now.

I hunt. Sometimes I take Jamesie along. I want to feel that he is mine. He is growing so fast, I can almost see his bones lengthening. He has fair hair with a gingery cast like Daddy's and dark eyes like

Rebecca's but more careful than hers. They watch me always as if looking for clues.

I tell him things: Here is how to load your gun. Here is how to shoot it. Here is how to kill the animal with a knife if you must.

My hand covers Jamesie's as the boy scrapes at a deer hide with the new clasp knife I have given him. Another debt. But I wish for him to have all good things, new things. The best life. I think of Daddy trying to read our futures and get land for all of us. Daddy, I understand this now.

I say:

—Here is how you dress the skin for market. Feel how the hair comes away. Stretch it between your fingers. Now get it on the board. Harder. Like this.

Having answers is a satisfaction for me and for him. Jamesie keeps at the one hide for hours, he hardly changes his position. He has grown into a cautious boy, always watching, always wanting to do things the right way. At last I coax him closer to the campfire and make him put down the skin for the night. It is cold again, and Jamesie can never get warm through out here, even if he sits so close to the fire he is struck by beads of sparking sap. He is thin, with the stretched look boys get as they grow. I watch him sitting with his hands to the flames. His mother would have pulled him back by now, but he is still shivering in bursts. I say:

—Come here.

He looks at me in surprise as if he had forgotten my presence, as if I had disappeared into the trees. My heart sinks for a moment, but I say:

—I am here, look. Come here.

Jamesie moves towards me and I tuck him into my shirt, his back to my bare chest. He is embarrassed, far too old for this, but pleased. He curls his legs down between my knees, and I feel his limbs relax. I smell his fair hair and give his plait a little tug. I am certain there is no mother's comfort like this, sitting by the campfire in the night.

—Better now?

—My front is hot and my back is still cold.

Jamesie says this in his precise fashion. He is like Squire in this way, but I have not seen Squire or Ned since burying Daddy. Squire has gone off on another hunt alone, I do not know where. When I think of him now I am not easy, but Jamesie shifts about and I say:

—Do you want to sit on your own?

—No.

After a time we settle on our bedrolls under our bearskins with our feet to the fire, and we are quiet. I think of Stewart and of Squire and Kentucky and I grow melancholy, but all of it seems a long-ago story. The fire spits in a spiteful fashion.

—Daddy.

James is used to the vast dark. It is the sudden leap and punch of the flames in the night that unsettle him, even at this age. He always arrives on my bedroll at some time during the night, and I do not mind. I say:

—You tired of the little people yet?

—The Lilliputians.

He is always a one for being correct. I say:

—That is right. Had enough of them, a big boy like you?

—No.

So I tell the old story, which is our favourite, and which we know we will never tire of. Jamesie listens hard with a short dry laugh from time to time. His eyes reflect the fire darkly. We are near asleep when he says:

—But they did not want him to get up.

—Who?

—The big man.

I can tell that Jamesie is on the edge of sleep or he would have said Gulliver. But to tease him I say:

—Who do you mean? I cannot think who.

—With the strings the little people tied all over him. He got up.

—Yes, he got up. The Lilliputians were only tiny, you remember. Their ropes could not keep a big man like that tied to the ground.

—Not a big man.

—No.

Jamesie goes silent but he is not yet asleep. He worries the question again, he turns and looks at my face, considering. He says slow:

—He got up but he was not supposed to. He was not supposed to be alive.

—He did get up, yes.

—He was supposed to stay with them and be their prisoner. And be dead if they wanted him to.

—What, like a dog? Lie down, play dead?

I tickle his thin neck below his ear and I make a little howling noise. He jumps, his body stiffens. I touch him and I feel his heart leap under my hand.

I wish with all my soul I had never made that noise, Jamesie, forgive me.

17

The Sun Rising Over the Fields

In summer, I come up from the goddamned corn one evening to find Ned and Martha visiting. They have brought Squire's wife Jane with them. They sit in a row on the bench outside the door with Rebecca, stiff as a row of plates. The children are all running about in a frenzy, knocking one another down, a pack of cousins doing their best to inspect the condition of each other's blood.

—Ned. Thinking about joining me on a hunt?

Neddy smiles in his sleepy manner and lifts his eyes. He leans against the wall and says:

—You were a long time about your last one.

—You might have come along, Keep-home Neddy.

He chuckles and says:

—I like it here. Did you find what you were looking for?

—No.

—Well oh well. You might come back to Virginia, Dan.

—Do you think of going there again?

Ned tilts his head and says:

—Bryan has me driving the tobacco there, doing his brokering. I go where life takes me. And where my wife takes me.

He turns his smile on Martha, who is sitting upright with her arms folded over her belly. She is with child again. Her big eyes run back and forth between us. One of her little girls draws great frowning and laughing mouths in the dirt at her feet. Ned says:

—Saw a friend of ours at market.

I look up:

—Stewart?

—Afraid not. No such good luck. Hill.

—So our Hill came through the wilderness on his own. He is full of surprises.

Neddy laughs his easy laugh and rubs his neck:

—Alive as ever. No sign of any woes. And with a new scheme for raising investments in Kentucky.

—What now?

—He wrote about it in the newspapers, he showed me one of his articles. He must carry them everywhere he goes. He told me to give you his especial compliments. And the family. He fondly remembers his visits, he says.

—He was here?

Ned nods and says:

—He came here when he first returned, seeking old tales about your man Findley. Old dirt to dig up. And about you. He is writing a book now, he says.

My heart is coated in ice. Hill dividing up my beautiful faraway country into rags and patches. And coming here sniffing after me.

Now my heart freezes to the core. I say:

—Rebecca. Did you see him?

The baby Jemima is shrieking inside the house but Rebecca does not move, she only says:

—All you men can talk of is Kentucky.

I see Jonathan looking up from where he is oiling a harness in the barn doorway. The baby's cry gets to him also. It does not stop.

I go inside and I pick up Jemima. She is wet and struggling. All my chest aches, cut up with the thought of Hill as her father. But I cannot believe it. How can I? No. I look into her face from an inch away, and she unleashes one of her best screams. I sing to her:

—No, no, no.

She gazes at me without blinking.

I have begun to be fond of the little stranger. To my surprise, it is not difficult. I banish Hill. I will not let this be her fate. I will erase her beginnings for her, whatever they are, and why not? Here you can reshape yourself. You can forget. Others can also. At this time, I suppose this to be true.

I kiss her. I carry her out and say:

—I believe this child needs her mother.

I kiss the baby's head again. Rebecca's eyes lock on me for a moment. Martha's do as well, they are round like eggs. She touches her throat and stands up heavily, dragging her daughter up from the dirt. She says:

—It is time we left.

Squire's wife Jane stands as well. She is clearly as uneasy as the other women. They know all about the baby, it appears. Jane is not one to say much, like her husband, but she does look at me. She is a little woman with a narrow face and narrow green eyes. I say:

—Jane, are you getting on all right at home without Squire? Is there anything you need?

Her eyes fill to the tops with tears before she blinks them away. She waves her hand before her face and says:

—Fine. Fine.

The baby howls, and Rebecca walks off bouncing her up and down. No one has any further remarks to make. They round up the children. One of the girls has pushed a nut up into her nose, she is shrieking and hiding her face and saying, leave it, leave it, as Martha shakes her and tries to fish it out.

It is two mornings later that Martha is in the cornfield where I am working very early. Her feet are half-sunk in the earth between the rows. She looks like a determined scarecrow waiting for me. The sun is rising behind her head. She has been running or walking fast. The words spill out of her as if from a boiled-over pot:

—I love to see the sun rise over the fields.

I want to laugh, but her eyes appear to bruise as she speaks, they go dark and shaded. She is thin and pressed-looking despite her condition. She is one of those who inhabits her skin nervously, although she forces herself into boldness now. She steps closer to me through the mud, holding her round belly. She is suffering, which has its appeal and which she knows.

—I have—

She breathes in and flattens a hand over her chest and goes on:

—You treat that child as if it is your own but it is not. You know that, I think?

She touches my sleeve, the sun makes a halo of her hair. The line of stalks I am weeding shades her body. Every word and gesture feels as though she has rehearsed it, even the sun coming up behind her at this moment. Her dress is muddied and its hem is fallen on one side as though she has planned that as well. I say nothing. I do not understand her. Then her hand is on my arm, travelling upward, and she is laughing lightly as she says:

—Rebecca and Squire. The names sound pleasant together.

She gives a little click of her tongue. The cornstalks feather and rustle with her movement. My head buzzes and I say carefully:

—Do you mean to say that Squire was with my wife? How am I to believe that?

Her eyes go bigger, they flood with instant tears. She says:

—I do not know but I believe it to be so. He was here when you were gone. He said he was looking out for her safety as she was so alone, it must be so hard for her without you. He said that. He brought food.

Her hand travels higher up my arm like a tentative but insistent mouse. I say:

—Martha.

—Squire and Rebecca.

—Martha.

I shake my head and try to laugh as she goes on touching me. I say:

—If you insist on pairing names, Martha and Daniel sound like a couple of Old Testament types. The types who get smote. Did Jane send you?

She is staring hard at me, her pupils wide, she is an inch away. She whispers like the stalks in the wind:

—I was there when your first was born.

And I remember of course that it was Martha who told me Jamesie was here, that he and Rebecca were all right, who took me to see him. Her eyes were hot and bright as they are now. She is a secret squirrel for knowledge, I see it now, she keeps everything squirrelled away. When I thanked her at the time for the good news, she said: You are welcome to it, and her smile showed a triumph. Her face was upturned and shining and seemed to say: *I have known Rebecca all my life, I have seen her do everything, I have seen her legs open to send out that baby, I have heard her piss in the night, I have smelled her smell when she is sick, I know her in every way and so I know you too. I know what you know.*

Now she says only:

—Daniel.

I am stirred, uncomfortably so. She moves her hand to the waist of my breeches and plucks at the shirt there, pulling it out slowly as if she were sewing. Her fingernails needle my skin.

How easy it would be.

She is so angry.

The crows veer overhead. When I blink I can still see the pattern of black and white, crows against clouds. I hear myself say:

—This will not help any. You have a husband, I have a wife. We all need to go along.

Her hand halts, her voice ices over:

—She killed our mother—my mother—you know, being born. Then in came the stepmother and all the other children, and she and I going off to live with our granddaddy. And she has you again, she has that baby, she is starting fresh as if nothing ever happened—

This seems to me the cry of the sister who never has anything to herself, never anything new or first. I can feel how she suffers, the air vibrates with her queer suffering. She wants me to put an end to it. She wants me to taste her blood, she wants to pull me into a hole and let me do it. I am all confusion. My stomach is hollow, her hand is still on it. I try to speak gentle:

—Go home now. You are tired out.

I am talking to a pack of wild dogs all trying to run in different directions. I foresee her baying but she bursts out laughing and says:

—Home?

—Yes.

—You make your home wherever you like. Do you believe there is really any such thing as home—that happy home we were all promised when we were girls? Be good and think of home, you will have your own when you are married, home will lift your heart when it is low—

—Go to your children.

She sets both her hands over her belly now and spreads her fingers:

—There is one in here already, there is no danger for you that way—

My heart skips and I close my eyes an instant for fear of striking her, or taking her, throwing up her skirts and pushing her beneath me in the dirt.

—Martha. Go to Ned and Jane.

—Ned. And Jane. Of course Jane.

—Jane needs your help, in any case.

—I am *trying* to help her.

She is shaking with rage now. She turns and dives through the thick ploughed earth, her feet bogging in it and her arms shoving vicious at the corn, sad and ridiculous as a blinded cat. She stumbles and falls and does not move. Her head is turned, her eyes are open, her belly forces her back up into a hump. I move to help her. She clutches at my knee to get up and then thrusts a muddy hand at my chest to propel herself off again, staggering and gasping, her clean elbow shows through a rip in her sleeve.

—Martha. Martha.

I think: Your wife is a whore. Which makes you a—

The corn seems to listen. I might go after her. I might find her and we might lie together in the furrow beneath the stalks, belly and all, her legs smeared with dirt. I might ruin her as she wishes, though I cannot understand why she wishes it. I see that I have shipwrecked her already in some fashion. My ribs and skull compress me, and queer thoughts swim in of the baby Jemima beating at me with her wails. Someone else who wants to dig something out of me, something that I cannot give.

Another thought crashes in like a wave.

What is she going to say that I have done to her?

Again I begin to think only of escape, but there is none here. I am forced to think of Squire and of Hill and of men without faces and with large hats, all with my wife's legs around them.

Martha does not return. Nor does Jane. I am forced to wonder too what they are saying.

I take my Jamesie into the hills. I tell Rebecca that we are going, and that I do not know how long we will be gone. She does not protest. We stay out for a month, inching farther west all the time. The leaves begin to turn their colours and burn round us when the daylight strikes them. It would not be difficult to keep going.

I help James get his first bear on this hunt. It has a white muzzle. I tell him that is lucky. We look at the dead animal, its fur showered with dew. I make the boy pull back its lip to see all of its teeth. I watch Jamesie's serious face. His tense arm holds the bear's head as if it might decide to come back to life, his fingers curl back the black lip. I feel peaceful for the first time in many months. I say:

—Soon enough you will be going off on your own hunts.

In his cautious manner he thinks for a time before he says:

—I like to hunt with you.

—We will go again soon, and for longer. I will show you a place. The finest place.

—I know. Kentucky.

He knows my stories of Kentucky and of the Indians and the game. I have made stories of some of it, though the real place is like a golden ball, sitting private in my mind. I have to laugh as I think how like Daddy I am becoming, trotting out the same old stock of tales.

To Jamesie I say:

—Yes. Kentucky. You will have some of it.

I sit and have a little dream of all my boys and girls with land enough, and beautiful land, when I am gone. They will be entirely free. This is all anyone could wish for the future. For now, though, there is nowhere to go but home, where I keep my head down and feel myself to be always looking at the ground as though I have lost something. I kill two hogs and put them up for winter and smell of hog for a week. The harvest is good enough. Rebecca and I remain cordial with one another, as if we are always part of some fancy ceremony. Cracking this shell might smash our lives all to pieces. I do not know what to do about it. I only know the children cannot survive without me. A shell is a shell in any case.

I drive the fall skins to Salisbury before the snows start. James goes with me. The leaves are beginning to come down, the clouds lift and roll apart in places. The wagon shakes along on the ruts, sinking to the left. I have Jamesie drive and he looks at the road in his intent fashion, holding hard to the reins.

—Let them go a little. The horses will not run.

—I know.

Jamesie makes a brief effort to loosen his grip as he looks at me, then tightens his fists again straight away. I smile and say:

—Well, my boy, I am glad that you are your own man.

We are close to town when a wagon comes at us from around a long bend. The road is narrow here, we are both forced to stop.

—There is Uncle Ned.

As he says it, Jamesie's face drops. He is always one for watching and he knows that something odd has been afoot. Martha is beside Neddy, her face shocked to see us, her belly bigger than ever. Jane is on the other side, looking held-in and grim. Neddy's face looks set as well. The children in the back clamber up to wave. One of the little girls stands on one leg stork-fashion and calls:

—Uncle Daniel, Uncle Daniel, look at me!

Her mother hushes her. We all seem to steady ourselves as if about to walk a rope. James is looking to me. So is Martha, her fingers at her throat. So is Neddy. And Jane as well, with her narrow eyes. All are waiting for me to speak.

My horses sigh and shift. Two of the children topple over in the back of the wagon and one begins to cry. Martha says nothing. Ned looks at me in a speculative manner, as if I were a skin brought for sale. What has Martha said to him?

The child increases her crying. We are trapped here. At last I do speak:

—Been to market?

Ned nods. I look up and say as if I have only just noticed the sky:

—A fine day for it.

At last Ned says:

—How many skins?

It is best to fall into this kind of talk, as if it is one long conversation that has never been interrupted. I feel some relief as I say:

—Only fifty. Deer are disappearing again. We have gone far enough to get these, as Jamesie can tell you.

I put my hand on the boy's shoulder, and I am glad of his presence.

Now Martha says:

—*Your* boy is growing up fine. Do you not think so, Jane? Look at him.

I hear the weight she gives that word, I see her great eyes brighten. *Your* boy. She is stirred, excited, almost trembling. She presses a hand to her bodice and I see it heave as the baby shifts within her. She knows I see. Now I know that she has said nothing. She has not said that I begged her for bodily comfort in my distress or that I tore at her clothes and ravaged her in the dirt, unable to help myself. She sits with a smile hovering about her lips. *Here am I, the prim wife who knows nothing at all.*

There is an appeal in that too, which she does know. I feel myself watching her. She wants to even our score. She has gone home as I told her to do, and she has kept quiet, and now she wants her reward.

I watch her and not Ned, though Ned and I talk of hunting for a few minutes more. Jane turns her face away. We drive off in our respective directions at last and I am very uneasy. The shifting clouds no longer appeal to my eyes. I hear Neddy's child shouting goodbye, goodbye like a knell from up the road. My careful Jamesie sits forward, gripping the reins harder.

18

North and West

We go out farther when we hunt, but everywhere letters are scored into trees. I grow tired of reading them and after a time I stop Jamesie from carving our initials, which he still enjoys doing. *DBJB*. His angled writing, as if the letters were only just halting themselves from falling over. Are any still there now, or have all the trees been cut? I do not know. I do not know what I would do if I found any.

We keep on. But the game is fleeing again as old settlers and new ones push back into the Yadkin. And I cannot keep my mind from all of my many-headed troubles for long. Gulliver, I do feel your position. I too am pinned down with no understanding.

I do not read life's signs to me at this time.

Bailiffs with names like Flesh come and sit on the steps for hours with their knees apart, worrying the children. It occurs to me, and not for the first time, that bailiffs are generally a wide-legged sort. I owe plenty, and to more than I can count. Shopkeepers, tavern-keepers, traders, the new taxmen who keep coming round. I am summoned to magistrate's court, and the judge has a look of granddaddy about him. Money runs away from me laughing, the one thing I cannot hunt down. I will not allow Rebecca to ask her family for any more of it. I do not talk to her of this trouble, though she is well aware of it.

I have no real land to call my own, and I cannot always ignore this old low smouldering in my gut. I cannot leave my children with nothing. And so I say we are going. Again I feel myself like Daddy, snorting and unsure but longing for a fight.

But Rebecca gives in without much fight at all. She is still uncertain of me and at the same time unwilling to let me go off on my own again. She has much to make up, as she knows. With her black eyes muted she says:

—Do not take me too far. I cannot live too far from here.

And I say we will not go far. And we will have family with us. Our own little family, and Hannah and her children, left without Stewart and hoping to find him again. And Ma, come back to us now that Daddy has gone to his rest, as she puts it. Some of the Bryans. Even Keep-home Neddy, whose wife has persuaded him of her desire to stay close to her sister.

Squire returns from his long-hunt with good furs and comes round to offer half to me, but I will not take them. I do not wish even to think of what he might mean by offering them. Seeing him, I am struck with a picture of him when young, slipping off from his gunsmithing apprenticeship for a woman.

—No. I do not want your furs. Keep them.

This is all I am able to say. He goes away with his usual stoop and his deliberate walk and looks no different. A few days later, Jane comes to tell Rebecca that she and Squire will go along with us as well. This would once have been a joy to me, but Martha has let a poison into my mind where it swirls about like black ink. Martha visits too and talks with Rebecca of our departure. I hear her voice outside when I am in the barn. Squire keeps away. He and I are strange with one another and it cannot be helped.

In spring, we move up along the Yadkin River where no one else has settled yet. We make camps and several times build a cabin, and though we cannot find the right place to stay, I am glad to keep finding new ones. We have another little girl, and the next spring a little boy, and we name them after ourselves. Any other names are dangerous. I do not have much to do with these children, though I know they are mine. I leave them to Rebecca. I clear scraps of land and hunt with my boys. All the time I am thinking of Kentucky, the game and the wild empty grasses. I think sometimes of the Shawnee and Cherokee, I think of how we will trade there and keep civil. I do not wish to ruin it by touching it too much, this dream, but I cannot help thinking of it. I do not forget any of it.

For a time we all live in a huge cave near the river with a sloping floor and a low ceiling. Though its mouth is narrow, it is a dry and homey enough place. I tell the children we are going under the earth to find the fairies. Come on, I say, crooking my finger and taking them with me into the narrower dark. Susannah and Jemima are in ecstasies, and even Jamesie and Israel show some interest in spite of their great age. The women have no interest in the fairies, though I insist we stay there a while. They try to sweep out some of the dust and dried mud, and they squint in pointed fashion whenever they look up. Covering the younger ones' heads with her apron, Ma raises her brows at me. I say:

—That ceiling will not come down on you, it has stood this long. Imagine old times here. Imagine being Indians and living here a hundred years ago. Then you would be happy enough. You would know of nothing else.

Martha looks at me then with a pitying expression and a soft mouth as if to say: *I understand you truly.* And she rocks her latest child with some great meaning, as it seems to me. It is better when Ned builds his own cabin some miles off. Ma goes with her darling Neddy. I miss her.

We stay. Rebecca says:

—I am not giving birth in a cave.

This latest baby is low and near its time. Fatigue has blurred Rebecca's temper, her spark has dimmed. She has let me drag us all into the wilds, and farther into the wilds. I say:

—Not even in this cave? Good enough for she-bears. Roomier than most of our houses.

—A nice place for a child to appear.

Rebecca looks at the long drips of rock overhead, trying to laugh. She blinks and two tears run down her cheeks. I say:

—A fine place. A palace of a cave.

—Surely. We might call it Cave-dweller. The baby.

—Sounds Indian. Sounds fine.

—None of your romancing now.

She is smiling a little with her eyes glittering like rain. She stretches her tired back. She says that I may kiss her hand. I do so. And I build her a house up near the forks of the Yadkin, on Beaver Creek. It is a solid one. This house has likely disappeared now, like all our houses, Rebecca, but I remember the place. Here is where I stay for the birth, I insist on watching all of it. Martha is also present to help and she watches me all the time, keeping her mouth in that soft squashed *O*. She grips my shoulder when the baby is coming as if she is faint, but she is not faint. I kneel below the birthing stool, and I see the dark circle of hair at the crown appearing out of Rebecca like a whirling pool out of flat water. If I close my eyes I can see it still now.

Rebecca lies in the bed, tired out but glad that her child has appeared in a civilized place. She lets me name the new boy. He is quiet. His hair is black like mine, I think. I pick Jesse.

—Not Cabin-dweller?

She smiles thinly now, her face slick and grey. She does not want me here, but at the same time she is glad of my staying, I know. I say:

—No. Not this time.

—This household has a Jesse already.

—He will be on his own soon. He needs a namesake here. Show his roots. Jesse Bryan Boone.

Rebecca likes this, my talking of roots. She likes the Bryan too, a huge gift. It costs me some to give it but I do. Martha glances at me sharp as if to ask, *Why do you let her win?* But Rebecca tells me to plait her hair for her and says:

—Martha, you go now. I am all right with Dan.

She briefly gives off her old bright light as the baby begins to suck and opens its fist against her breast. I plait her hair smooth. It seems as though we have walked over a thin skin of ice. We have not said much. But we are easy enough together for the first time in some years.

At this Beaver Creek homestead, we set to clearing, and we get the first crop in the ground. James and Israel are old enough now to do much of the work with Jonathan and Jesse, as well as to hunt with me. They are fine boys, I am proud of them all.

We are all digging out stumps for a new field when we hear the horses. We stand to look. Two men, one riding and the other walking. They are wearing headscarves and bright calico shirts. It seems to me at this moment that I have conjured them up. But the others see them too. Jonathan and Jesse and Israel stand, Jamesie stays crouched where he is. Jemima runs out of the cabin and shrieks:

—Mama! Some Indians are here!

I walk over slowly. When I am a few yards away I say:

—Brothers.

My skin pricks, alertness rises through me. The man on the horse points and says:

—Little Blue Eyes. How do?

He dismounts and offers his hand. He is tall, with that long rocky fall of a face. He splits it now with a broad closed smile and goes on looking at me.

I know him. Of course I do. I say:

—Well my old friend. Did you enjoy my gun, Jim?

I am pleased at remembering his English name. The Cherokee Jim gives a light coughing laugh and an easy salute. The other man is a stranger to me, but he laughs politely too. Jim holds out a pipe and says:

—Smoke?

We sit at the edge of the half-cleared field. The air smells of burning stumps and sweat. I call the boys over and they obey stiffly. They know to be polite and careful, though my bold Israel stares. Jemima is not to be outdone in boldness and runs up through the raw churned-up earth to stare also. The strange man grins and reaches to pull one of her black plaits. She scratches his cheek with her swift fingernails. I say:

—Stop that now.

—Daddy *he*—

The man gestures, it is all right. He touches his face, and seeing no blood, he rummages in his pouch and pulls out a lump of dark, hard candy. Jemima takes it, quick as a cat. The boys look over with interest.

—Not so old, ha.

Jim passes them all lumps of the maple candy. The other man nods, then takes out his tobacco. Flies cut through the air around us, scenting the sugar. Jesse sucks loud. My Israel pokes him and says:

—Slow down, they have more.

We sit chewing and smoking, talking here and there of the weather and the cropping. The Cherokee appear to be relaxed anywhere. They are easily still, like tools or guns set down. Our talk is broken and shallow, and yet I am queerly glad to see this Jim again with his easy manner. He reminds me of Kentucky.

Squinting against the pipe smoke, he asks how long we have been settled here. I say:

—A good while.

—You will stay?

The boys all look at me at once. Jemima too. I say evenly:

—For now.

Jim digs the toe of his moccasin into the yellowy earth. He says:

—A good place. Good water, good fields.

The other man is tweaking Jemima's ear. Out darts her hand for another piece of candy. Jim chuckles and goes on:

—We saw your man.

I sit up and say:

—Which man? Name of Stewart? A big man, like this?

I point at Jonathan, who is tall. I set my hands apart to show Stewart's greater width. Jim smiles in the direction of my boys. He shakes his head and says:

—Your ghost man. Your Blue Eyes.

—Findley. Ah. He still has his eyes then, he has not traded those away. You saw him in Kentucky?

The grey taste of smoke swirls in my mouth, and my heart leaps with the thought of Kentucky being a true place that still exists to speak of. I do not want others there, but I wish to speak of it. I say it again:

—In Kentucky.

Jim shakes his head and looks east, saying:

—Kentucky is Indian land. No whites.

—For now.

As I say these words again, we laugh, but it has a brittle sound. We know about the Iroquois giving up any claim to the land. But there has been no word of any Cherokee treaty, nor any Shawnee. The other man is snapping his fingers lightly, and Jim tugs a weed from the ground and rolls it about his thumb. I say:

—You have not given it up, then. But there is plenty of room there, plenty of game. Our man Findley might have some pretty things to give you in trade, would that change your mind? Though I do wonder if our Blue Eyes is dead. He was always white enough to be a ghost, and Kentucky is paradise.

I look at Jim. He smiles again but says no more. The flies are insistent. Jemima pipes up:

—Are you on a long journey? Where are you going? Where is your home?

Jim shrugs and widens his eyes to saucers at her but she does not laugh. I say:

—Then you have no home to get back to.

—Home is where we like.

—Kentucky, I suppose.

—If we like.

—You do just as you like. This seems to me a fine philosophy, it was my brother Israel's too. One we might all abide by.

Jim's smile has gone stiff. He suddenly pushes the pipe straight at Jamesie, nodding. My boy sets his brow. He has avoided it so far, but now he takes a pull and coughs, trying to swallow the smoke, and then coughs harder, his face stained deep red. The Cherokees chuckle and clap. Jamesie suffers. He never could laugh at himself but he tries now, coughing still. Jemima pounds on his ribs with both fists. Cherokee Jim looks around slowly, still smiling. He says very firm:

—A good place. To stay.

Well. There are better.

I get restless all through again, my brains itch as though stitched up too tight in their casing. It is now a Sunday, and we all put on good clothes and sit about silent to take our ordained rest after my sister Hannah gives us a good talking-to about God and prays for her husband's return. I listen, for Stewart's sake, but I cannot keep my mind from wandering. As we sit outside the house, I remove one of my good black shoes, which is creased over the top and loose about the heel. My bared toes look white and sorry and blind. I am at once ashamed of my shallow roots here. So much for Rebecca's happiness. I am sorry, Rebecca, but there is no help for it. We keep scratching at the ground and trying to dig ourselves in, but nothing is holding us here but stubbornness. And so there is no reason not to go on a space. I know of a space that I cannot forget in spite of what the Cherokee said.

I find myself wishing that the Cherokee would come back, and they do.

Rebecca huffs about my Indian tea parties and sends Susannah and Jemima out with seed cakes and rude stares. These occasions do feel thin, but we go along with them. We are attempting good will, as the Indians are. They always offer candy to the children and a smoke to the boys. Jamesie gets better acquainted with the pipe. Jim pulls the girls' plaits lightly every time he visits, and after Susy cajoles him, he once lets his hair down out of his headscarf. He has only a scalplock, which falls down over the back of his skull and down his shoulders. Susy grabs it and laughs. Jemima will not touch it but she stares a good long time.

We talk of all manner of subjects. But I cannot think of anything but walking through Kentucky. All winter I think of it.

Again Fate reads my thoughts. Two broad shapes poke up out of the earth next spring as if from bulbs, all confidence. They are on horseback, and two slaves ride with supplies some distance behind. They are not Indians. One is William Hill.

—Here you are, Dan, we have heard much of your travels! And your woodsman's prowess, your nobility of character. The first white man in Kentucky. I have spread the word, my old friend, are you glad to know it? The newspapers probably never reach you here. And I am still writing my book.

Dismounting, Hill bows low so that his forehead almost touches the ground. He has grown a small stiff beard and has the look of a broom when he springs up again.

I say:

—Hill, you are not telling the truth. I was not the first there, you know that.

—What does that matter? It is my book.

He snatches up my hand and pumps away, asking how I have been keeping, happy to see the family and all the dear Boone children.

The dear Boone children look for the most part perplexed. I will not let him near Jemima. She cannot be his child. Surely she cannot be. I look sharply at her face. Her eyes are not his. Even the thought makes my brains feel dirtied and sick all through. No. She is mine, or near enough now. I go stiff-necked, but before I can speak, Hill's companion says:

—Everyone has heard of you now. Why do you make yourself so hard to find?

He is sleek, with the look of one who has lost all his edges. Even his head and shoulders look coated in a layer of plump new fat. He is well-dressed, like Hill, and has shiny eyes that are kind enough but float about in a desire to see more of everything. He makes the cabin feel shrunken. Hill says:

—My friend William Russell, from Virginia.

Russell holds out his hand to me with the glove off and the palm up as if to show off its toughness and redness from riding such a distance. He has been much with Hill, it seems to me. He calls for one of the slaves to bring the horses round to the barn.

Hill has turned to Rebecca with a light in his eye. Russell is looking at her with a bailiff's appraising flash. They turn their look on Susy, who is a pretty and lively girl, never still.

These two both here alive, and Stewart lost. I want to strike them dead. I stand, but Rebecca pulls herself up next to me and says

in her best queenly manner:

—It is natural that everyone should have heard of my husband.

Hill laughs, all good cheer. He says:

—Naturally! Naturally everyone has heard that we have been into the fair country of Kentucky. They will read my book when I have finished it. When we have completed our tale, that is to say. Your husband, Mrs. Boone, is the man to lead a party back. We are the men to make it pay.

When I am able to speak, I say:

—You plan to return to Kentucky in person? In spite of its insect life?

I puff out my cheeks and Hill laughs from the bottom of his lungs, full of his old joy at a new prospect, the hornets who near killed him now a joke. Touching his beard, he says:

—Now I have this to protect me, and we have the land company registered.

My heart falls within me. Hill carries on:

—You might do the surveying once you get us there. We will pay you. You cannot say you will not go back. I know the cockles of your heart!

—Do you indeed?

—I do! And you may choose the first lot. Any land your cockles fancy.

Slowly I say:

—There is no stopping you, Hill, is there.

—Never.

—You are going to sell it—Kentucky—to all takers?

Hill's grey eyes brighten, his face softens. He says:

—Not to all. No border trash. Only to good people, the best people! We will make a proper place of it. Big plots, plenty of land, and no need to see anyone if you do not wish to, Dan.

I feel him waiting for my answer. I say:

—Perhaps I do not give you enough credit.

—Your credit, Boone, is not your strength, but I will not remind you of old debts now. Only old times.

Hill touches my arm and juts out his jaw in a grin. Hill, arranging my life for me again. It seems to me at this time that the rich always carry a happiness that they do not know they have. Not to need money is a happiness that must go down to the marrow. I see it in Hill's and Russell's posture and their ease. For a moment I wish deeply to be like them. Unhappiness wells up in me. I smooth my face and I say:

—Land is the way to my heart, is it?

—I know all the hidden paths of anatomy. Every twist and secret turn, I have made quite a study—

He glances sidelong at Rebecca and the girls, then curbs himself and bows slightly.

I also look at Rebecca. My unhappiness boils. Staring at her, I say:

—Well, all right. We will go. We can settle there. I can look for Stewart, for Hannah's sake. Why not?

Rebecca is keeping herself very still, her black eyes do not twitch. Little Jesse snuffs over her shoulder and chews her ear, but she does not move.

I pass my hand over my mouth. I say:

—Did you hear this? Some excellent land of our own, my girls and boys. Easy cropping, and no stump-clearing in those meadows. And a job at that. Here is a chance.

Surely speaking these words will make it true. Surely Russell and Hill and their money have the power to make it true. So bright and golden is their luck, I count on it to rub off on mine. Susy gives a little leap and a laugh.

Russell puts out a smooth plump hand and says:

—Women and children will make a home of the place. Land

and game enough for everyone, just as you say. Houses on the creeks, corn and wheat in the fields, orchards in the clover. Silver in the ground, too, some say, once we open it. For myself, I have plans for peach trees first.

Hill barks:

—Barmaids, a round of peach brandy for all!

He pulls himself up and bursts out in song:

Chickens, sweet chickens,

See them take the morning air,

See them drop eggs without care.

In my mind I see my brilliant sea of grass reaching out to the far hills. Teeming with chickens, spattered with eggs.

Russell says lightly to me:

—Other parties have already set out surveying since the Iroquois treaty.

He looks again to his slaves. One nods as if set to go this minute. I have to stop my throat from tightening and closing entirely. I have to stop my eyes from moving back to Rebecca or the children.

My Kentucky is all I can see. And chickens might as well be game as any other bird. In my mind I shoot them all from the picture.

19

Towards Kentucky

ANYONE WOULD hear us coming, our clanking parade through the bush, cracking branches and flattening saplings. The cows and hogs moaning as the boys whip them along, complaining worse than the littlest children packed into the creaking baskets tied on each side of the horses. The children bawl: Out out out, no no no, Mama. And some only bawl on and on without words. I do not like to hear them.

Rebecca rides our mare with the bald patch, holding the youngest to her, willing herself to look at the future and like it. I have told her she and the girls can be the first white women to dip their toes in the beautiful Kentucky River. She is very quiet. Well, I suppose I have won entirely.

I look back a few times from where I am leading once we have ridden beyond sight of Ma at the last Yadkin house. Jonathan and Jesse stood alongside her. They said they would stay and be with her. My Ma weeping, too old for this journey, clutching at the back of her cap. Even now I can see her outlines but not her features. All my days I will wish for a likeness of her face, even one of her as a little Quaker girl in grey, anything to turn over in my hands like a coin. But in my memory I see only her arms holding herself in as she watches us all setting out for Kentucky, whose beauties and terrors are beyond her capacity to imagine. I know that she did not wish to imagine them. We fired a salute and I called out goodbye only once, my voice falsely bright, anyone would hear the tinniness. Oh, Ma, I hope your face will be the first I see when I leave this life. Ma, yours will be a happy face then, I pray, and not the weeping ruin it is at this time.

In my mind I say goodbye to Israel too, and to all my ghosts. But Daddy appears that night when I am dreaming to frown and look puzzled and say:

—Well Dan, there must be a newer world.

When I wake I beg him to return and say more, but there is no more. My sleep for some time thereafter is as blank as an *O*. It is odd that we wish to know what the dead think of our doings. All my life I will wonder what my Daddy thinks. Daddy, I wonder still.

We move very slow along the narrow path. Horses are always going lame or sore-backed, children are always falling out of their baskets, boxes are always tipping off the pack animals. Hill and Russell have rounded up eight families aside from our own, Callaways and Mendinalls and others from Virginia, some slaves also, and a few lone men. Some of the Bryans have decided to go along. All have paid Hill and Russell for the privilege and also for the land they will have in Kentucky. They are game to settle. They have enough baggage for ten cities.

The way feels steeper and sharper than it did my first time through. At this slow pace my limbs do not work. My feet feel not my own, I stumble more than once. I have to laugh. With Findley leading it felt easy enough. Irish magic, he would no doubt say.

Rebecca's rocking chair rears up from the back of an ox like a weird double spine. Granddaddy's old black cabinet from England is balanced between two more beasts. We have some comforts. I know I am whoring myself to Hill for land, but Hill is fond of whores, as I know well enough. Besides, he is happy at this time, enjoying the noise and slowness and the feeling that he has helped me. He acts the chief of a royal progress, riding along with his reins slack, surveying in all directions, sending the slaves off here and there, though they are not his. Russell dismounts and walks ahead a little now and then, turning his agreeable face and his bright eyes everywhere. He catches me up and says:

—This is the original Indian warpath, Boone? I do not know how you know it. No one like you for finding a trace, for seeing signs no one else alive could see.

You do not know me: so I think. But I nod and carry on. My boys are happy enough, walking with their guns and looking out for any game. Susannah and Jemima dart back and forth along the queue, dragging the cat and two of the younger girls. Their arms are scratched and dotted with blood from it and the heavy bush. They run to me:

—Daddy, can Tibby have a drink of your water?

—Daddy, can I walk with you?

—Daddy, can I—

—Yes, all right. Anything.

The cat Tibby stares into the woods, its eyes burning green. The trees are thick here and the undergrowth thicker. In many places we have to chop it away to get through. The infants in the baskets squall like gulls as the branches press them. But the forest has a powerful silence and a beauty in spite of all our noise.

Russell approaches with two of his boys as I am taking out my axe for more felling. He sits on a stump and says:

—This is really a ridiculous procession.

—It is so.

Hill appears also, sniffing, and says grandly:

—Like herding wild buffalo along.

I say:

—When was the last occasion you did so, Hill?

He laughs, touching his beard fondly, and says:

—I remember when we shot buffalo together, Dan. Do you not remember that time?

—No such time, Hill.

Russell interrupts to say:

—The weather has been good to us. No frost yet. There is no such thing as frost in Kentucky, now, is there?

Hill throws out an arm and cries:

—No frost! Always summer.

Russell puts his arms around his sons' shoulders and says:

—Eternal summer. Of course. Do you hear that, boys?

The boys grin, Russell and Hill laugh again. I think of my private Heaven. Nobody will set foot on it before I can claim the best part of it, one part to keep safe. And I will find Stewart and make things right with him. All I have ever wanted. I clench my back teeth and try not to crack them.

I begin to hack at the saplings in our way. At the edge of my eye comes a movement, a blur of grey like a quick jet of steam from a kettle in the thick trees. The skin between my shoulder blades pricks as if a finger is just above it. A wolf, perhaps. Looking into the trees, I want to whistle, I want to go after it. I think of my brother Israel shooting wolves for magistrates' money. But no bounty is offered here. And no ghosts are here. I tell myself again.

So slow are we that we run short of flour and cornmeal, not to mention rum, before we reach the great mountain gap. Then we run out.

We are in Powell's Valley, with its steep sides and narrow path. There is no way to turn the whole rattling bawling group around now, and no way forward with all of these women and children and trappings. My skin bristles. All of this is wrong but I do not know why.

We stay in our camp for some days as we try to decide what it is that we should do. People seem to plant themselves, as people will do. My gut sinks. Some of the men sit up jawing half the night, and Hannah sets up preaching from a box, as though we have all the time in the world. As though this place is good enough. Rebecca and Martha and Jane make a nest of babies amidst boxes. It has the look of a miniature fort. I am for riding ahead, but how can I?

Russell takes me aside and says quiet:

—You and I might ride back with a couple of the blacks to Virginia and ready supplies to send on. If we have to winter here, it is not a bad place.

I look over the winding line of tents and cooking fires along the valley. All of it puts me in mind of the army train marching to the Monongahela and disaster. The smell of supper rises peacefully and says: *Stop thinking of such things. Do not think.*

Turning to Russell, I say:

—Can we leave these people?

Russell says:

—There is Hill to keep order.

Even he looks dubious. Hill is washing his head noisily in the creek, taking great gulps of air so that everyone will take notice and share in his joys. *See my great head, see my shoulders, see my health.* Ned and a few of the other men are playing cards with their backs to him. Old Dick Callaway grunts. He insists on being called Colonel, his Virginia militia title, and likes to walk about with a stick as if inspecting troops. His gangly red-headed nephew Jimmy shows in the set of his neck how purposely he is ignoring Hill. But Hill keeps trying with greater *Ahs.*

My heart grows with the desire to be moving. I am tempted. I take up my gun and say:

—We would be back in a few days. Five at most. A week at the utmost.

Rebecca, I feel your eyes as though they are hooks. They run along the gun and then look away towards the younger children, who are running about holding sticks to their foreheads like horned beasts. I see Squire cleaning his gun and glancing at me.

—No. No. I had best stay, Russell.

But the thought of remaining caught here for a winter makes me feel quite drowned. I look to the sky, it is grey and unhelpful.

The sound of a small axe breaking the air with precise cuts enters my head, clang clang clang. Jamesie is chopping kindling in a small clearing near us. He works with perfect rhythm, like a little bell calling for order. The Mendinall boys are sulkily chopping with no rhythm at all, but Jamesie continues in his fashion.

—Jamesie.

The boy's ears redden. Not really a boy—seventeen years of age at this time. His face keeps up its old cautiousness permanently, and it seems to me that fathers can always see through the grown bones down to the young child they knew first. I correct myself:

—James. Would you ride back with a party for more supplies and meet us back here again as quick as you can?

His face lights and is quickly serious again. He says carefully:

—I could.

I walk over to him and take his axe. I say:

—All right. You and these two friends of yours can go. They have complained long enough of being here. Make men of you all.

James half-smiles at the great Mendinall brothers, who keep their surly faces but stand straighter. Russell shouts for his oldest son:

—You will go along, Henry. Take two of the Negroes, Adam and Charles.

He motions to two of the black men who lead the pack horses. I say:

—We had best keep Hill to ourselves. He might work at his book, it will keep him occupied. But send Crabtree with the boys. He knows what he is about in the wilderness.

Crabtree is one of the lone men game to settle. He is grey-haired and past fifty, but a good shot and a storyteller, which the boys will like. He looks up from his horse's shoe and says:

—I will accept that compliment, Boone, from you.

He tosses his hat to the ground and I toss mine at him. James gives one of his short measured laughs, which always sound as though he has thought them out first. Then he throws his own hat a small way and laughs again.

In the valley bottom, the women are happy enough to rest and unpack a few more of their things, in spite of the lack of bread. Rebecca takes to the rocking chair in the evenings, she has found a grassy spot for it. Her eyes are heavy-lidded and her mouth is small. She is very still, smiling down at the baby. Martha has another new one, born not long ago. I saw her eyes through the gap in the tent as I passed by during her labouring. She gave a cry and willed me to look look look.

We build stone fire rings, they have the look of a bracelet in the dark. Squire works nearby but we say nothing to one another.

Ten days pass, and all the noise of the group settles to a hum. Even the cattle and hogs are quieter, browsing and rooting in the remaining grass and the reeds along the creek. Hill enters one of his damper periods as there is so little excitement here. He does not care to hunt. He writes in cramped hand on his papers. He reads them to one of the slaves, London, who listens with fortitude. Occasionally Hill trots about on his horse, singing. But from a distance away in the hills, one can hardly hear a thing.

I take my boy Israel on an afternoon hunt up the valley. He has dark hair with red in it, which he wears plaited up. He lopes ahead with his bird rifle. He turns back to shout:

—Daddy, you must have more shot for me.

I recall his bright face, his hand turning out his bag, his grin. For a moment he has a look of my dead brother, his namesake. My boy, it makes me uneasy for you. If one could know what was coming, would one want to see it, or would one avert one's eyes and carry on?

Israel gets a turkey. We find several more, and for sport we take a few songbirds with our clubs as well.

The girls run up and down collecting bright leaves. They have some plan for these. They do not let on what it might be.

The younger boys are restless. They follow the girls, they watch Susy's legs as she runs. They walk along the trail west of camp to see what is there. They talk of Kentucky often and loop back to where I am from time to time.

One of the lone men is even more restless and turns thief. He takes horses and skins and creeps off before dawn. Later in the morning he is back. Out of the forest he comes, his face greased with sweat, his eyes skipping like small flies.

—They are dead. All murdered.

His voice is loud in the extreme. He shuts his palm over his mouth in what strikes me as a tender motion.

Say nothing more. This is what has been coming for me all along. Here: a black bloom of nightmare opening its face every night, every minute. Let yourself think of any other thing and there it is, showing its red throat.

PART TWO

WHEN I AM NOT

I

Heaven

HOW YOU SCALP someone is like this. Cut a small round down to the bone beneath the hair on top of the head near the front. Put your foot on the back of the person to be scalped, pull the hair at the edge of the round. The whole comes free easy enough, easier than skinning a deer.

Jamesie, you once asked me how, and I refused to tell you, but I do not see why I should keep it from you any longer. If you are listening. But perhaps you cannot hear me, perhaps you do not wish to.

In my mind I write it: *James Boone, son of Daniel and Rebecca Boone, was killed October 1773*. But I do not know the day you died, I cannot write it properly in Granddaddy's Bible record, and my heart breaks and breaks for it. Every minute my heart is dying but it does not stop though I tell it to. I do not know how it can go on.

I have wondered too about the sound of the skin surrendering itself up and how the head left behind must feel. I have seen the hair dangling from the dried scalps stretched on hoops in Indian villages. And black Indian hair turned in by English scalpers for Governor's money. I could do it if I had to. I would do it hour after hour and day after day if I had the opportunity. When we find Russell's slave Adam hiding in the woods, he gibbers all the terrible things he heard as he hid behind a log at the boys' camp, despite having stuffed his fingers down his ears. I do the same at night for months.

James asking for help. For Daddy. For death.

I can hear it, his poor voice thickened and without words at the

last. The echo of it spreading out across the night country, shivering like wind over water or over the grasses of Kentucky. For ever. The father, which is to say me, only two miles away, did not hear.

Squire goes to bury them. They were so close to getting back to our camp with the supplies we sent them for. He tells me the bodies were left in ruins. Hurt everywhere. But not scalped. They do not take white scalps in peacetime. This is all Squire will say. He shakes his head when I ask him to say more.

I force my breath into a rough laugh. I chop at a tree. Pale chips fly back at me. Let them blind and choke me. I am not alive. I try to see the murderer's face. I ask him in my mind what point there is in killing boys for sport, without a fair fight. What point there is in killing a boy you know to speak to, but a boy you know nothing of otherwise. Aside from the fact that he did not like to smoke. And that he was my boy.

I let bears get too near before I shoot. I let deer get too far away.

If I were really to see his face, what might I do? I think of every burning and ripping and carving up there can be. There is nothing else. I can think of nothing. I can think of him no more. And Jamesie is hidden under the earth, I cannot see him. I did not see him dead. I did not go back for him with the burying party.

I will not think of the murderer's name. I will carve it out from my brains. And I will not think of you, Jamesie, I cannot allow myself to speak to you now. You are gone and the fault is mine and I am not alive, but not with you. I do not know where you are.

I chop in my boy's straight rhythm, clang clang clang. I cover his crying voice, I try to make my hands into his. It comes to me in my sister Hannah's soft words that he is like Christ, exalted by the suffering, sent straight to Heaven like a shot from a gun. So far away that I cannot hear him now, and he has no need to hear me.

But this is little comfort. There is none. I believe in the human agony on the cross. I have seen what people will do to one another. And I believe in the story of God being unable to help his son and therefore not being much of a God at all.

I will say that after the attack, I want to go on. Russell turns back straight away, his face fallen in and his neck shrunk into his shoulders. His boy Henry was murdered too. The Mendinalls go with him, having lost their two boys also. So do half of the others. I scream at the rest of the group that we are carrying on, as though Kentucky will blot out everything and rewrite it all beautifully. Terrified and half-starved people will go anywhere, looking for someone to follow. We walk for some time. Then I dare to look Rebecca in the face. It is a terrible face, a painted wall holding itself up. She has not looked at me once since she handed me a linen sheet for Squire and the others to bury Jamesie in. Nobody speaks.

When the burying party rejoins us, I agree to turn back for Carolina. We leave the bedsteads and furnishings on the trail. I stand Granddaddy's black cabinet up in the trees with its doors gaping open. Martha and Jane huddle the children together, telling them to keep silent, and cover the babies' mouths with rags. Squire leads. Ned and my boy Israel walk the cattle and hogs with their guns ready. Snow begins.

And when we are back, I am dead. I work the fields again, dead. I dye all my clothes with black walnut. I try to dye my hair blacker with it. I lie on the ground. When a new land company agent comes asking me to lead a road-building party into the wilderness, into Kentucky, I say I will do it, but first I wait for the birth of our next child. The child is stillborn into a hot June full of flies. A boy. I do not wish to see him before he is buried.

I leave for a treaty-making where the land company buys a piece of Kentucky from the Cherokee for silver and guns and shirts, but I do not see the murderer there. I look among the young Indian men sitting along the riverbank. Some of them do not like the bargain. They sit skipping pebbles across the shallows and muttering that the country is still theirs. The heavy son of a chief, watching his father making his mark on the treaty paper, shouts:

—All writing is lies!

Hearing this, I leave and make trail for the company axemen.

The next year, on my dead legs, I drag the family out again with all the rest of my dead followers. I tell Rebecca we are going, we will not be stopped, we will not give in. I tell her Jamesie would wish it. The words have a sour taste.

She says:

—How can you use him for what you want? How—

She does not speak to me again through the journey. But I have no wish to speak.

Others come, some of the first party who sold up and have nothing left here, or who think the adventure of it worth the while. Richard Henderson, a long-nosed hawkish man with grey hair, whose land company it is, says he will give me two thousand acres and pay some of my debts. He keeps just behind me as I lead. I use my old prize tomahawk to hack at the fresh brush and saplings that have begun to grow up again. We all hack, a great broad wagon road we build, the Wilderness Road. We let the rest of the world in. My country is already a ruin, and so why not? My paradise. Of my making.

When we reach Kentucky, we find the bones tucked in the empty gut of a dead tree. An arm-bone is broken and the gun is gone. The powder horn is there still, pushed behind the hips. I know the initials carved in it, the back-bent shapes of the letters *J* and *S*.

It is his. Stewart's. So is the skull. I stare it down, I put flesh back on the cheeks and jaw and eyes back in the raw sockets.

What happened to you, John? Did the Shawnee find you and kill you?

Or did you want them to find you? Were you waiting for your chance when you broke your arm and hid in the tree for shelter? Did you try to find your way back to them?

I had thought there were no ghosts here, but Kentucky is all salt. The salt is old blood seeped out into the ground, the beautiful grass all growing out of blood and bones. John, I wish I had never seen yours.

We hack on. I find the place for a fort near the Kentucky River. A great spreading elm in the centre of a meadow. This will be it, I say. This, here.

No one questions me. Henderson falls to his knees weeping for joy and cuts out a piece of sod he says he will keep always. He christens the place Boonesborough. We set about building. Hill appears again on a new horse. He has taken it upon himself to write to the newspapers in Virginia about our murdered boys. It is known everywhere, he says, and he is breathless with tales of some there who have taken it upon themselves to avenge us. A Mingo woman, sister of a chief, axed through the belly, her unborn child dragged out and left planted upon a stake. The rest of the group killed too and strewn about in pieces. Some Cherokees murdered also, any Cherokees the Virginians could find. Hill sets his grey eyes on me like guard dogs. He had hoped to find a certain one to kill himself, he says gently. He touches my arm and gives me a newspaper to keep. It is thin and soft in my hands, worn like a skin. I cannot read. I cannot think. I do not wish to.

We bang together fort walls with cabins attached in lines, taller blockhouses at the corners. We begin the stockade of pointed logs, but no one has much interest in seeing it through. The men are mainly interested in hunting and claiming land for themselves or to sell. Rebecca dreams one of her dreams, a house made of salt, where she can lick the walls and window frames and floors. The first time she tells me one of her dreams since she fell into deep silence. For so long we have lain in the same bed not touching, and moved about the small cabin not touching. Now at the table, she smiles for a moment, before her face is veiled with shame to have shown a smile, a part of her old self no longer in existence. She bends her head to her work, mending a linen sheet like the one she sent back to wrap Jamesie's poor body in. Wedding linens from her granddaddy, packed all the way to this place.

Rebecca. This terrible way my Fate has evened things between us. Taking away your other first child. Our first child.

Your hand moves quick, your stitches twist. You were always an impatient seamstress. Mending irritates you, the rips and wear should never have happened in the first place in your eyes. I watch your hands and my first stupid thought is of our wedding night, when we were so young. The next stupid thought is that I might get that buried sheet back for you, Rebecca. There is nothing else I can get back.

We sit still as the stumps that serve as chairs in that poor cabin. I have bought glass for the windows from Henderson's store, and I dragged Granddaddy's cabinet here out of the forest, but the floor is still dirt. In the end I speak. I say her dream has the sound of one of her old Welsh tales. After a time, she says:

—It is. A princess tells her daddy the king that she loves him as meat loves salt. Then he exiles her.

—I will have to remember that this is the way to treat unruly children.

—He is sorry for it in the end. She was right.

—About salt.

—About love.

—Aha. You know all about that, oh queen.

I am joking, but she looks stung suddenly, and I think of the shock of the strange baby who became Jemima. We both bristle. I sit a moment, then I reach out to stop her hand as it stitches. I say:

—Rebecca. Our boy is better where he is.

She stares at me with her eyes black and surprised and the needle bright in her fingers. She says:

—No, he is not. He is not.

Staring, we show the ugly angry raw meat just beneath our skins. I want to tear mine out and dump it at her feet like the deer I once dragged to her house. I go out to bang at the stockade with its missing side and its gaps. All the world's cracks gaping.

The salt runs when autumn comes again, and the game begins to run out too, fleeing from those here so starry with the ease of Kentucky hunting that they shoot everything they see.

I hear some of the smaller children talking in bed. Our little Jesse says:

—The food is all bloody here. I can taste the blood *all* the time.

The others talk of the bad smells, making a list. We all smell of old meat from every pore. Old Dick Callaway bawls with rage when someone shoots a steer of his within the walls, and his red-headed nephew Jimmy cannot stop himself from shooting an old bull buffalo that wanders up towards one of the blockhouses. He has the ideal logical shot, just behind the eye and straight out the same place on other side. He says so. Well. The shot does bring it down fast enough, but how can we use all that meat?

No salt.

The carcass rots and stinks and hums with flies and birds just beyond the wall. It bloats and turns green. Colonel Dick and Jimmy ignore it. The women run past it on their way to the spring, their aprons up over their faces. They always run all the way to the spring

at any rate, but now they run the faster. The well inside the fort is still unfinished.

The dead buffalo's stink is no worse than ours, trapped with livestock and their dung, and ours, and drying skins and smoke and rotting clothes. Susy's shift slides down her shoulders, the sleeves shredded. Soon she is going about in not much more than her bodice and a petticoat. One evening she comes to me with Will Hays and says they want to be married. She cannot wait any longer, not another day. She tells me so with her mouth firm, holding up her pretty face and shoulders as if saying: *Look at what I have to live with.* A bird swoops behind her in the twilight as she argues:

—I know how to cook and do everything already. Everything.

Her hands are over her belly. She is not sixteen.

I am voted magistrate, to Colonel Dick's disgust, and so I perform the wedding. Susy, it is all I can do for you. I have tears in my eyes, as Daddy did when he married Rebecca and me. After the ceremony I tug at Jemima's ripped skirt and remark that soon we will be like Adam and Eve in their innocence, without clothes at all. Holding the cat Tibby to her cheek, she fixes her stare on me and says suddenly:

—I wonder where Adam and Eve were buried, Daddy, do you know?

Jemima, no longer a child, always listening. And Jemima, you near are buried. They take you too.

2

Going

SHE COMES into the cabin, bunching her hair up under her torn cap and hopping on one bare foot. She says she stabbed the other on a broken cane. She holds it in the air so I can see the blue bruise circling the small bloody mark. Rebecca offers to bind it up, but she says:

—No, Ma.

Then you hop out again into the afternoon, and nobody stops you, Jemima. You disappear.

In my mind I see: down at the river, she unties the fort's only canoe, thinking to dangle her sore foot in the cool water. She calls to Colonel Dick's two girls to go with her. The air is warm, insects skitter over the river surface. A fish jumps and leaves hardly a ripple. The girls all lie together in the canoe bottom, waiting for the clouds to make shapes of themselves. A tower, a bunch of grapes. The current tugs the boat gently, and their talk drifts away, and birds begin calling. Jemima sits up to look. They are almost at the far bank. The bushes are thick and dark and faces are in them.

The Indians have them ashore and bundled off before anyone at the fort sees. Young Fred Gas on the watch hears only the cry and call from the opposite bank. He looks out from the blockhouse and they are gone, the air already still and the canoe riding high in the water, empty.

Three days they are gone, and we behind them, always behind, snatching up the strips of skirt and the strands of hair they tore off to make a trail. I follow the trail, I see nothing else. The first night, when we stop to sleep a few hours, I see white shreds of cloth against the dark behind my eyelids. I want to murder Colonel Dick every minute, always bellowing: No, not that way. He takes some of the men and rides off in his own direction. I plunge my group through the woods, seeing no sign, hoping only that we might head off the Indians and catch them higher up the river. It is only thanks to a snake, its head crushed by a club, that I know we are on their track.

I will be first. I will beat Dick. So I tell myself. My jaws and fists ache with clenching. We run on, I keep us running. And when we are on them at last on the third evening, I see Jemima's eyes instantly catch me as I raise my head from the ridge, where I lie like a snake myself behind the trees. In the hollow below, the Indians are making their fire and cleaning their guns. The girls are against a tree, tied to each other miserably, their fingers twined in each other's hair. Then Jemima's face lifts at once, her eyes wide, her belief like a torch. Her triumphant, insisting yell: That is Daddy!

We find them. They are saved. We kill some of the captors before they run. I shoot one, he falls into the fire, I do not know whether he is dead. This is the truth, the end of it. Hill writes the story, of course, and sends it off to the newspapers: *We will draw a veil over the scene of happy reunion.* But so many holes in the happy end. He does not know that when we first set off after them, I waste an hour going back to the fort to change my damned Sunday shoes for moccasins I can run in. I lose the trail twice. I lose it entirely, I have no idea where to go next, my head is empty. It is a miracle that we catch them up. Or pure luck, a worse thought. And Hill does not know what Jemima tells me later, that one of the Indians asked her to pick lice from his head at night, and she did so. Jemima, I have to say my first thought was to seek his face, not yours. The long, hollow murderer's face. But he was not there.

I ask her was it him, Cherokee Jim, in case he had magicked himself there and hidden himself from me in the rout. In case he was following me, trailing me like my dead, and had come back for her too. She says his name was Scolacutta. I ask her how she knew it, I ask her did he make her say it, did they—

She stares and says they only asked her to take down her hair, and they coiled it back up tidy in her comb for her after they had looked at it. That was all. They did not hurt her. She says:

—Daddy, they had heard of you. They asked me if I was your girl.

I curse Hill for his stories, for making me a famous man, when I have done no good. Jemima rubs her head and says she wants to be married, like Susy. Beside her, all awkward and young, stands Colonel Dick's nephew Flanders, who helped track her. She laughs and sobs and says it is all she wants in the world, to leave the kidnap behind her and have a happy life, her own life. And to live in the cabin next to Daddy.

It is not like her to sob. She is so young, but how can I say no to her wish? She sits with Flanders and holds her wounded foot in my face, and tells me how she moaned about it every step of the way to slow them further. Her eyes are ferocious with her victory. *See what I did, Daddy?*

Again and again, she says she knew I would come for her. Her belief makes me afraid. I am afraid for her all the time. Susy has a little daughter by now, she had a bad time with the birth. My girls, it is not the life I wanted for you.

I beg young Flanders Callaway not to take Jemima to wife yet, not fully. Though the thought strikes me that if she dies in childbed, we could at least bury her within the walls, and we would know where she was and could be near her. There is no possibility of going out planting, let alone grave-digging. Nobody wishes to go too far from the fort, crude and shabby as it is, and we all hope the

stink will prove a defence. But nobody can get used to it either. Martha touches my neck or my arm whenever she passes. And I do not know what to do. All I do is hope the earth will swallow all of us and this place.

A few young men arrive with plans to find adventure. They have all heard of me and of Jemima's kidnapping. Hill greets them gladly and talks and talks. One of them, Sam Brooks, has bright eyes and a wild air. He brings me a commission from the British army, making me a captain. But he is not pleased with how he finds us. Looking at the poor fort, he says:

—Is this all there is here?

He and his brother Will sit about a fire making bullets and talking of how they will shoot Indians. The Brooks boys have come out from Fort Randolph in Virginia, where a Shawnee chief was murdered by the militiamen he had gone to make peace with. Cornstalk, the chief's name was. An old fellow. Chief Black Fish is now bent on destroying any settlements in revenge.

Young Will, who has a sweet boyish face and curly hair, said he would have shot Cornstalk himself if he had been close enough and would shoot Black Fish if he ever saw him. Then he burns his fingers on hot lead and jumps up with a screech. I go to the outer wall and listen for answering sounds, but there is nothing.

We hear nothing for some time. The women relax a little and go back to walking on their way to the spring. Monk, one of the slaves, plays his fiddle now and then and sings to his little son Jerry, the first boy born in the fort. I do not like to see him, he makes me think too much of my own boy when he was a baby. Jamesie, I will not think of you.

I venture outside one morning thinking to clear stumps. I hear a crack from the sycamore hollow to the west of us. Before I turn, the shot smashes my ankle, and I am on the bare ground. The earth beneath my head shakes with the footsteps of the Indians running at me. I close my eyes and I think: Jemima, they had you. Now they have me. A poor trade.

A bang, a roar. I lift my head an inch. One of the new young men tears out of the fort gate and swings me over his great shoulders as if I were a child. We bump along, bullets singing past us. Ned and Squire come at a run and fire back at the trees until the Indians withdraw, after setting fire to our few rows of corn and pumpkins. The Brooks boys whoop and holler:

—Come back and we will give you some more!

Hill laughs and whoops also. I know his voice. I know the scratch of his pen.

Simon Butler carries me to my bed. I had thought him one of the speculators who cared for nothing but getting land to sell on again. He is enormously tall with a big jaw. But his eyes shine tender at me as he gets his breath back, and Jemima bustles about finding tongs to get the bullet. She tugs it out, mashed flat as a silver skin against my ankle bone. Butler says:

—You are all right now, Captain.

I say:

—Well, Butler, you are a fine fellow. Your name suits you. We could do with you in Kentucky.

He looks down at his knuckles and says:

—My real name is Kenton. I killed a man in a fight at a tavern in Virginia. I ran off and changed it to Butler.

I laugh. Saved by a murderer with no name. I should have let the

Indians carry me off. The smoke from the poor burning crop drifts in. Rebecca closes her eyes.

Laid up in the cabin for weeks, I look again and again at the official army paper, and cannot help laughing the more. Captain Boone.

Hill visits and laughs because I laugh. Colonel Dick does not like it at all. Border trash, he says as he walks past the window, and I salute.

I stay in the cabin for weeks, listening all the time. Martha visits in her brief nervous fashion, her fingers always plucking at me. I hear Neddy outside on watch, singing an old song in his clear simple fashion:

Waste lie those walls that were so good,

And corn now grows where Troy town stood.

Troy. An old war in an ancient city. Impossible to think of it, how ruined it is, how it is all gone. I think of Uncle James telling the story when I was a boy, the war of the Greeks and the Trojans over the stolen unfaithful wife. And a new war here, now. A great wheel seems to roll over me. When a Virginia newspaper makes it to us with another new settler, we find a revolution has begun back in the eastern colonies, that independence has been declared already. We are Americans, this is our country now, we will turn against the British and fight them all off it. We have a bonfire, and the girls dance in their torn dresses, though some of the Bryan boys do not like it and say they will love the King until they die.

Corn now grows where Troy town stood. But no corn in Boonesborough. By winter, the cribs are very low and almost no wheat is left for flour. I set a guard over the remaining supplies. Some people go mad and want to eat everything at once so it is gone and can torment them no more. Perhaps we all stay at the fort for the same mad reason, thinking that torment can be all eaten up and put away. Hunger comes in all varieties, as I have found.

Snow falls and deepens on the ground. We need food for the coming months, and a means of preserving meat. My ankle is not yet right, and the cold makes it ache the more, but I gather a party to go and make salt at a good spring some days north. We leave a few of the young men and some of the old behind to look after the women and children. We wrap ourselves in what skins and furs we have, and we say goodbye. Jemima comes out of the gate to wave her apron. Rebecca does not.

3

Salt

WE MAKE CAMP at the Blue Licks. The water in the bubbling salt spring is weak, but we do our best to boil up as much as possible. After a week, when we have a few bushels of pure salt, we send young Flanders back to Boonesborough with them. The rest of us stay to make more, but we do not get much.

I know the ground here is a favourite animal lick, but the game is poor now. It is very cold some days, snowing in sideways blasts. Some of the men are lying about under the trees at the edge of the flats, having given up on salt-boiling. Hill and Dick Callaway's nephew Jimmy are slowly filling one of the great kettles we brought, stopping to warm their hands at the fire below it. I say:

—I am going to find some meat.

Hill stands and says:

—I will go with you.

—No. You stay. Keep a watch over the rest.

He nods, all serious, with a salute:

—Yes, Captain.

I am gone with my horse and my gun before he can say anything more.

I know what is coming. I must have known it when I left the salt-boiling camp. I am hours from there, and days from the fort. There is almost no light left to see by and what there is looks dirty. The shade of drained flesh is what it puts me in mind of, but perhaps I am romantic by nature.

I walk the horse along, she is packed with the meat of the buffalo I killed. A tree is dead across the path, its roots seem the many dead legs of a monster, all helpless in the air.

The back of my neck pricks.

I stop. I can see nothing moving. Nothing. The buffalo blood on the snow is near black.

Cut the straps.

I feel for the knife though I know it to be wet with grease and blood. I left it that way. You goddamned fool, you ass, you ape, you charley, you son of a—. Jammed wet into the sheath the knife is frozen there now, dull as a dead fish. It would not cut the creaking green hide tugs wrapped round the meat. It would not cut a gillyflower. At this moment I seem to hear Uncle James, who would have said such a thing himself, being fond of poetry. And Daddy's face drags itself out of the twilight, his left eye slides off as though fatigued with looking straight on at life. Looking perhaps instead for gillyflowers. I had thought there were no ghosts in Kentucky, but there are. And they are no help. They do not speak when you wish them to.

Daddy lies back down in his grave and I am alone.

In my mind I call to my dead brother. Israel, face me here, help me or kill me. The tugs bite at my fingers, all greasy and useless. The rest of the buffalo carcass is back up the trail, fallen partly out of the cane, its ribs poking out sharp and whiter than the snow. An easy sign. I curse the dead buffalo and all its bones and its meat. My horse stiffens beside me, she can see my breath. They can see it. She cranks her neck upward, trying to see over the fallen tree. Her eye and her teeth show yellow in the falling dark. I pull the reins across her neck and put my face against her side. She is a beauty. She knows she smells of slaughter. She knows her smell sings out *Catch me.*

Catch me. Here am I.

The horse snorts. I whisper against her tight neck: All right, my love. I cover her nose with my cold hand, she tosses her head again and rolls her eye towards me, waiting for me to do something.

I am entirely still against the horse for two minutes. Three.

She cannot keep it up. Her legs twitch beneath her load and a ripple sets up in her flank, creeping forward as if flies were crawling all over her. The meat packed on the horse quivers too, as though it were planning to come back to life and dash off. The horse shoves her head forward and brays. I clutch at her mane. Hush. The snow is coming heavy now.

They know where I am. They are in the snow, they are silent and invisible. The snow is on their side and everything is on their side.

Now I say it to myself: Cut the straps, drop the load, shoot and mount and go, you ape. But the knife might as well be sodden paper. The rifle might as well be a stick. My heart dips and hovers like a bird deciding on its direction. I might as well be dead. Perhaps I am. I breathe out as the horse does. Our breaths mingle like smoke and then vanish.

No not dead, not all dead. My tired arm pulls back and gives her flank a hard slap. She rears and nearly overturns with the weight on her back, but she stumbles forward, trying to bolt over the fallen tree. Even with the huge load, she knows to run. She catches her foreleg on a root, her spine sways, but she keeps upright. Over the tree she staggers, through the canebrake towards the creek, where she cracks the ice and squeals, doubles back and bolts for the woods. The sounds of her gasping and crashing carry. She might be enough for them, with all the meat tied to her. What else is there?

I hardly hear her now, the blood continues to bang in my ears but more softly. I am still, still.

You might run also.

The words sing clear in my ear. My feet are near frozen. They say: *Move us, we are dead.*

Death is creeping up from my shoes. The thought of it makes me stagger. I drag myself over the fallen tree into the wider dark. Here on the other side I stand. A rustling like bodies made of leaves coming to life. No pretence that I am alone. We all have our parts now, we all of us know it.

One of them slips off in the horse's direction, three are running easily through the trees alongside the trail towards me. I know that they are faster than I, I feel their swiftness cutting the shadow. And now at last I move, my dead feet land again and again in the powdery snow, my joints begin to loosen and my lungs to open. My breathing is rough. *Run.*

A shot rips through the quiet. I picture my tired heart raining its last blood down my body.

But no. The one who has the gun drops back, but another is not far behind me, still running. I push on but I am pinched between a rock-fall and another fallen tree, its roots splayed upward and its branches tangled in the rough cane, and so into the stiff canebrake I crash. It is like loving a porcupine as I imagine, my face and hands are stabbed variously, but I push on. I step down onto creek ice—my foot goes through. I pull my leg up and limp along wishing for youth, though forty-four is not so old, is it?

I keep limping. The shots skip past, snow sprays up on each side, dashing me with white. Out of the cane, I find the trail again and I pound on in my frozen shoe. My gun slips in my greasy hands. They are all behind me. Do not think.

A black fall of powder showers the snow, my horn falls empty with a dead thud. The strap flaps loose, shot through, over my chest.

It is a work of beauty. The echo of the shot is quick and close. I am near laughing. They are doing this for sport. They are all murderers. My feet crunch and grind as if in salt, and the thought of salt slows me. The Blue Licks are not so far, I might reach the camp, it is not impossible. I might go on.

I do not go on. My legs sink behind a thick bent pine. The bark is hard through my shirt and against the back of my skull. I see the tree eating me whole, taking me into itself. I see my bones and blood becoming wood and sap and my eyes becoming knots. This I will be for ever. Jamesie my boy, murdered in the woods such a long time ago, will this be the way I find you again?

But no, again no. I am miserably alive yet. My pulse stings in my hands. I open my eyes, I still have my rifle, the long weight of it a surprise. I unclench my fists from round it. I hold it out, I wave and throw it. They will see it or its shadow on the pale ground.

Their steps slow before they get to me. They are leisurely as the winter creek and the snow falling, piling itself into drifts and turning the whole world soft and unreadable.

I have been looking for murderers. My boy's murderers. These murderers and I have converged at this place. It seems that we have all been aiming for this bent tree for some time. My Fate set me on this trail and at last here I am.

I am an unwilling murderer myself. Unwilling for the most part. Well, all of you, I am sorry.

When they see me, I feel it. I stand to stretch my limbs. I step out. I smile my widest and I say:

—How do. Remember me?

I remember them. Even in the twilight I know one of the faces straight away, the friendly squint of the eyes and the red leggings with their tufts of deer hair. My guard, from my first time in Kentucky. Now he points to himself and tells me his name:

—Aroas. How do.

He grins as he takes my arm and leads me into the night, just as though we are old friends indeed.

In the morning the snow is shin-deep and dry, my beard itches and my back sweats with the pace they keep me at. My shirt grows wet and then freezes and stiffens. When I have to stop for breath, they say *Pasheteetha*. Old man, in Shawnee. I laugh. I am curiously glad to feel my blood moving. I am curiously relieved to have been caught.

Before we reach their encampment, I can see the long fire trench through the trees. There are plenty of them, more than a hundred.

Aroas and my three other captors walk me in, they do not touch me now. The line of embers smoulders below the snow, the flames invisible against the day. All along it Indians sit and stand looking at me.

Aroas points to the far end of the trench and nods. We walk up the line and Indians stare with surprise or interest or distaste. I look at every face in turn, but I do not see the one I would like to rip away and find what is really beneath. No Cherokee Jim. And these are not Cherokee.

We reach the chiefs at the far end of the trench. They are wrapped in fine soft blankets. Their silver jewellery looks frosted over. They do not move at first. They survey me up and down for some time until one speaks to my captors. I do not understand all of the words, and I do not understand when they begin to confer with one another. Their talk is a short thread with knots of silence in it. They do not seem to have so very much to say.

One gets to his feet, holding his blanket at the neck. He is not much taller than I am, and not much older. His eyes take my notice.

They are like black rock, they are impossible. He holds his long hand out slightly. No knife, no gun. I square my bones and he takes my hand, which is cold and likely somewhat greasy still.

The other chiefs are lesser than this first, they come forward in turn and do the same. Their faces are all impassive but interested. For a moment it is as though I were being courted at a frolic or a fancy dance, though the suitors do not wish to play their hands yet.

I decide to speak first. I drag out my Shawnee, poor as it is:

—Well. Great brothers.

But no other words came to mind.

The last of them gets up from the ground then, his blanket loose over his shoulders, his split ears purple with the cold. His face is weary. Surprise runs through me, and I say in English:

—How do, Captain Will?

My voice is too loud and my grin is too wide, as if my face has been taken over. But he smiles as well:

—You say Captain Will to me?

—I always did so.

—Ha! Wide Mouth, ha ha!

He keeps hold of my hand and I must say that I am pleased to be remembered. I say:

—Many years since you took me last.

—Then it is time again.

—I suppose it is.

—You and your big friend Bear. We had you.

He cuffs my cheek and laughs again. My heart falls within me. I know that Stewart is dead. Whenever I see his face in my mind it is all angry and deaf and bewildered. I say:

—My friend Stewart. Did you get him?

The Captain laughs like a delighted child whose pet has come home after so many years gone. He says no more about Stewart, but he grips my arm harder. I find that I wish to tell him everything that has happened to me, I wish to offer it like a gift. But what a dreadful gift is this story. No gift at all.

I close my mouth. His hand is tight upon me, I am a captive and a stranger. I keep my eyes on the thin rims of his stretched ears and the huge silver rings stiffening them. They look so cold.

Some of the Shawnee warriors circle, curious about the talk and the handshaking. Two point and clap me on the back. One says:

—Old Booney, ha. Wide Mouth.

Then he pulls himself up straight and begins to sing "Over the Hills," that is to say "Over the Hells." I can hardly keep myself from weeping, so familiar a sound is it, so happy and so strange in its happiness. Captain Will says soft:

—I told you to keep away.

I try to clear my head. My eyes prick and sting. I pull myself up and I say:

—You spoke of hornets when you left Stewart and me. I have seen none today.

Someone is at my side, very close. A black man. He is full of a slow thick force like a pot on a low boil. A blue cloth is wrapped about his head, a deep blue that looks out of place here. And Findley, now I think of you, another lost friend. You and all your trade things scattered about here in the wilderness. Are you living?

This man lifts his chin. He stands before me silent at first, and I believe him a slave sent to kill me perhaps in some ceremonial fashion. Then he too begins to sing, only a little, in a high hushed voice, the same song. *Over the hills and far away.* His voice is beautiful. He intends me to take notice.

I keep myself steady. Smooth your expression, dry up. A weird warmth goes through my chest and I am reminded of Martha, the troublesome appeal she has for me. Her thin nervous body. God help me but I can see it bare beneath me in my mind, I can feel the sharp bones of her hips. Now I think of you, Rebecca. And all the children, their faces wavering as if they were fish in a quick stream. I understand nothing. I stretch my fingers and then I clench them and I fix my face still.

The chief with hard eyes speaks briefly to the black man, flicking a glance at me and opening his long hand once. Now the black man begins to interpret in an easy tone. He looks untroubled and indeed uninterested. He stands like a blind stone between us. With a jerk of his head, he says this chief is Black Fish. He is still stony but he is pleased to say this, as I can see.

I have the curious swaying sensation of being about to drop into my grave. Both men are watching me. The black man says:

—What are the men doing at the salt licks a day upriver?

Still hovering, I am slow. I stretch my shoulders to my ears like a dunce and I say:

—Are there men there?

The black man sighs and blinks long as if on Black Fish's behalf. The warriors began to shift, wondering what is afoot. Diversions are stupid, as I know. Out with it:

—If so, they are my men. From my fort. Making salt.

Black Fish looks in the direction of the river and speaks. The interpreter's tone is still flat:

—Tomorrow night no men will be left there. Nor their salt.

I look at the chief's face. It is entirely shut. Everyone has heard of his bloodiness. I study him.

—Did he say that? Did you?

I point, my finger stops an inch from the chief's chest. I harden my eyes like his. Such are my first angry theatrics. Black Fish watches me with no expression. Then I say:

—Would you not rather have me?

I grin until my gums ache with cold. The chief looks back. His black eyes defeat me. I want him to respond. I keep my arm out until the elbow joint begins to throb. I think of Daddy's stand at Meeting. Do not go bandy. I do not move.

The chief speaks again to the black man, who says:

—You are a head man. We know you are the big man here. You keep letting your people come into our territory. And so we are on our way to your fort.

He shrugs in a loose fashion.

My heart is too dead to quicken but it carries on, I cannot endure its carrying on. You already took my son, there is nothing left that you can take. Rip me to pieces and scatter them there and there, I will open my shirt to make it easy—

All of this I think. But I do not speak and I do not move. I can only close my eyes and feel the tissue of the lids too weak and poor to shut out anything. The bumping of my heart stills. And when I look again, they are all watching me in silence once more. The black man has his head cocked now, awaiting an answer. I look at the snow, the white covering of it. I think of what is beneath it all over this country. Bones and more bones. Even bones of elephants. I go whiter and colder, thinking of more death.

Now in pure coldness I say:

—Would you not like to have a whole set of good men first? I can show you some closer than the fort. Less trouble.

And so I sell us all.

4

Live or Die

THE DAY IS colder. The white early sun flashes on the snow, which has the look of great heaps of glittering salt. If this were the truth, my men at the Blue Licks would be glad indeed. So would Rebecca. I think of her at the fort saying her blood craved salt, just as though it were full of little tongues. When I said she would sell me for a bag of it, and not a large bag, she laughed, but her eyes ran past me.

I walk with my captors towards my men. I feel myself part of a mad play. The snow crunches, the sun strikes it blindingly. We crunch along all day, and the cold brightness does not lessen though the trees shade the light now and then.

At the Blue Licks camp, the men are lolling on their blankets in the last of the day's light. The river is too high, the spring water too diluted to give even a taste of salt now. Lying in the pool of light, the men look idle and content enough. Young Jimmy Callaway is usually watching carefully for any trouble so he might be proven right, like his uncle Dick. I am glad Colonel Dick is not here and that perhaps I will never have to see him again. But even young Callaway is lying back with his patched moccasins upon a stone, looking only into the dimming sky. Hill is humming, bobbing his head back and forth with his eyes shut. The big kettles sit cold with the few sacks heaped up beside them, ready to be packed back to the fort.

All of this is about to change, I am about to change all of it. I look back to the chiefs. Black Fish lifts his chin. And so I walk forward first from the trees.

Hill sits up and rubs at his forehead, which has gone pink. He is the first to speak:

—Dan! Here is our hunter. Surely not empty-handed.

I take a breath and I say:

—No. I have brought plenty with me.

I blow out through my teeth. There is nothing clever that I can do or say here. I have done it. Here is the only truth:

—Boys. The game is up. They have me, there are too many of them. Do not fight and you may live yet.

They look at me as though I were a ghost, as though I am mad indeed.

They do not kill anyone straight away. Black Fish stays his warriors, though some of them keep their weapons out at I might say jaunty angles.

My men are still looking to me, all narrow eyes and straight mouths. They are sitting in the snow, tied to Shawnees now. The whole camp is scratched over with purple shadows and our guns are a dark shapeless hill a way off. Callaway looks grim but satisfied, his uncle's usual expression. He and the Brooks brothers were the last to give up their weapons. I see him speak to Hill, and now Hill's eyes bounce about the camp. He appears to be considering some leap or statement.

I know I will have to speak before Hill does. I will have to play the game. Well. I know how.

Slowly I get to my feet, pulling my heavy keeper up with me. He stands beside me and makes sure to show he is gripping the tie and my arm in his hands. My mind rolls over like an old dog. In my slow Shawnee mixed with English I say:

—Brothers. Look at us. You see all of these warriors? Look. They will make excellent hunters. They know what to feed women. They know, believe me.

I try to smile, and Hill guffaws, though he understands nothing, before stopping himself. Black Fish's interpreter turns my words into better Shawnee, that is to say I hope he is doing so. A general stir and laugh come. I go on:

—They will be able to feed your families as well as ours who remain at the fort. I must tell you that the fort is strong. It is a very good fort, a great one. You were on your way there, I know, but it will give you much difficulty if you try to take it. There will be many deaths. We do not need more deaths. And there is no need to harm my men here. I know you will not do that.

I hope the real fort, poor and rotten as it is, does not paint itself on my face. But the Shawnee are listening. The talk rains out of my mouth, though I am not thinking right:

—It is better to wait. Much better to wait. In spring our women and children can travel easily. No deaths. Then I will take you there, and they will all surrender gladly when I tell them about you, and we will go to your towns and all live as one people. It will be better, we will all be better off.

For a wild moment I believe the mad talk that is tumbling from me, this wonderful story, all of my lies. I catch Hill's face, smiling and full of belief as well. My arms are out, my hands turned up. My ribcage feels thin as eggshell, but my brain is quick as lightning. I say:

—Be good to my men and they will do as you ask. Look at them. All good men. See?

The black man speaks for some time. I cannot catch all of the words.

When he is done, all at once the Indians begin to talk. Their argument boils up and sweeps round the camp, rising and falling like wind. When someone reaches for a tall straight stick among their things, a sudden order takes hold. They queue up to have their turn holding it and speaking. They all speak long and full of passion. Their faces shift and fade in the twilight but their talk goes on.

I understand enough to know that it is bad. Some of the Shawnee warriors throw back their heads as they listen. Aroas looks serious. Some of my men stare back, and few of the younger ones bare their teeth, attempting to show they are not weak, but unsure of what to do. Callaway lifts his lip and I see his dead side-tooth. He rubs his red hair up under his hat. Then his face returns to its measuring. I can see his thoughts working in a line like ants: *There is a way out, there are several.*

The chiefs go off to speak amongst themselves. My men look to me, but I do not understand anything now. The snow is still pale in the dark. The stars try to pierce through.

Black Fish steps away from the chiefs and walks back towards us and his warriors. He pronounces something and sets his hands apart with the space of a foot between them. His eyes give off cold.

It is very silent. He says one word, it is a short word. *Neppoa.* Now comes a show of Shawnee hands.

The black man counts slow, his finger bobs as if he were marking music. Black Fish says another word. I do not catch it. More hands go up. I cannot count now, it seems to me I no longer know what numbers are. My brains try to recall Ma singing a counting song when I was a small boy. One and two, two and three.

The black interpreter draws in a breath and speaks. At once shouts rip loose from the Shawnee. We sit amidst the roaring as if in a windstorm, trying to look stoical. Johnson, small and thin as a child, looks as if he were at a picnic lunch, turning his head about to see the various views. Hill turns his own head about as if it will spin off.

The interpreter appears triumphant. Now he walks the line of us, surveying our upturned faces. He bends and speaks into my ear:

—Fifty-nine.

A solemn slow voice but with an undertone of mischief.

I say:

—Fifty-nine what? Wives apiece for us?

—You can keep them.

This from young Ben Kelly a finger thrust into the air. A few of the men laugh. The black man does not smile. He cocks an eyebrow at me and says:

—Fifty-nine say die.

He walks back up the line, he looks at each of us in turn with his lips set. Then with his back to us and his hands clasped behind him, he ambles off towards the fire.

Hill shouts in disbelief:

—What? How many say live?

The man is walking away. He does not answer. Others begin to shout with Hill: How many? How many? Their voices have the sound of alarmed birds. From up the slope the black man says:

—Is that your concern? You whites. There is never enough for you. Never satisfied. That is your greatest trouble, you ought to know it.

He walks on a few steps and then tosses back:

—Sixty-one.

Hill cries:

—What did he say?

The man is gone. Hill says:

—What did he say, Boone? What is it?

I say:

—Live.

The men roar and gibber and then fall silent, all thinking *Fifty-nine, sixty-one.* To this day I hear those numbers in that slow amused voice. I look but I cannot see the interpreter, he seems to have disappeared into the dark, and I find myself fearful, not knowing where he has gone.

They are feeding us from our stores when the black man comes back. He stands before me with his arms behind him yet, as if he plans to continue on his idle wander. Black Fish is watching his men packing up our things and cracking pine boughs from the trees. I do not know why they are doing this. The sounds are worse than shots, so hard does the wood crack in the cold. To Black Fish I say:

—Food, but no peace, then.

—We agreed to be peaceful towards your men. Did we say anything of you?

I see the black man's slow smile, and a bright flicker of amusement across Black Fish's face before it falls. What he says is true enough. I see the Shawnee sweeping the snow with the broken boughs, raising powdery clouds. Now I know what is coming. I say:

—For me only? Then I will take my pleasure straight away.

—As white men do.

The black man keeps up his smile, the Shawnee laugh. I laugh also, a great braying laugh. As white men do.

The dark comes quick. The interpreter walks me to a long alley made by two lines of Indians running some hundred yards. They have swept the ground in the middle, the bare earth looks black. My men sit tied to one another in the snow at the end of the lane far away. The pitch torches burn like bright blowing tents against the dark. The eyes are all flashes when they move, the teeth show in laughing crescents.

I am near bare. My skin shines and flickers orange. They have let me keep my leggings and moccasins. The cold air stings my chest, gooseflesh crawls up my body. I breathe hard, my mouth and nostrils open. One of the warriors I recognize calls in English:

—Run pony, run.

He claps. I do not run yet. They are all watching to see what I will do. I know this feeling well enough. Clubs, gun-butts, sticks, a few furtive knives, to judge from the metal glints here and there. All waiting.

My muscles whisper and tighten, almost a happiness. But no. There is no happiness now. I do not know what it is, I feel old and young at once, as if I were being reborn out of bones and ashes in the snowy dark. Confusion cramps me. I do not wish to be alive.

They will kill me. I think this and it is a relief. It propels me gasping forward.

I run hard from the start. They all let out their own coiled force, lashing with their weapons and their feet and fists. This is no game, there is no easy go for me here. Black Fish's still face flashes by behind the line on the left, but I am past him quickly, I dodge skull-crackers and an axe all coming down in flying arcs. I see each movement and each planned movement, each flare of a weapon turning and falling in the light. My eyes are everywhere, dried out and raw with cold. My shoulder is snapped hard and pulled back as I go, but it seems to belong to someone else and so does my heart, it is leaping like a caged bird in another chest.

Jamesie. No. Do not use him as fuel, do not waste him here, you goddamned ape.

My mouth burns dry and sour. My skin is hot, the snow falling is like thousands of wings brushing me. I cut and feint, I dance along the alley of weapons, a fist, another ball club, a yell, an open palm, a closed one, a gun-butt raised to smash in my forehead, a short blade slashing low. A club bangs my rib with a crack but it disappears behind me with everything else. I am living still and running. I am inviting Death to a fight. I do not know what I am about. My skin is inches thick, made of pounded metal. An old knight crashing forward in a joust, O Sir Dan! And no real armour and no horse, only a poor ghost of something that was, but I am winning. If I run fast enough I will reach you, Jamesie.

The last man. Direct in my path, big-shouldered. His hands out low, his arms tense and ruddy in the torchlight, a strip of paint across his eyes. He is not Cherokee Jim but he is framed like him, or close enough. Yes.

I lower my iron head and drive it straight at the waiting chest, ploughing through the suddenly soft body, no breath left in it or me.

This is the end. I keep running, I cannot stop. I might run on into the forest and I do not think that they could stop me now. All the way home I might go. Or elsewhere. Some clean snowy place I have never been and that nothing has ruined.

The sound reaches me, my men applauding and Hill bawling out, Haha!, and one of his ridiculous whoring songs for joy:

So I'll roar and I'll groan,
Till I'm bone of your bone,
And asleep in your bed!

My heart bangs. I think of Daddy's hammer, bang bang bang on the dull orange iron. I turn back, I drag air into my lungs roughly. A rope of spittle hangs from my jaw. I raise a hand and Hill shoots his own upward, dragging Callaway too, who is tied to him and clapping on his thigh with grim relief. A thin victory, but a victory all the same.

The last Shawnee man is on the ground, vomiting upon the snow he has rolled flat. He is thinner than I thought, he is nothing like Cherokee Jim. The other Indians are shouting. They are applauding also.

My rib hurts, my neck and shoulder hurt, but I am breathing. My hands hurt from being balled up. My ears hurt from the roaring. I am still here. Well. Life wants me for the time.

The Shawnee come up to slap my back and hold out their weapons for me to see closely. They say the English words they know: Brother. Soldier. Good man.

Two of them inspect my ears. One has a clasp knife open, ready to cut them off. No. He shows me, delicately he fingers the edge of my left ear with his nail and points to his own. He will slit the rims like theirs. He begins to shave off the fine hairs growing along the top. The black man marches up and argues with surprising life until they back down. He walks off without looking at me.

Here I am, I have won. The snow keeps falling as my blood cools.

5

The Long Walk

THROUGHOUT THE long march to the Shawnee town, Death runs alongside. I think only of walking and snow, both endless. But I cannot ignore the presence. Who else can it be but Death, flapping its jaws and its rags?

For a moment very early one morning, I believe it is Martha. By this time we are so starved that we are seeing false things. My legs are used up, they bow out like Daddy's with every step in the snow, which has gone heavy and wet. I stand for a moment with the huge iron salt kettle on my back crushing me, risking a stop for breath. Hill, who is tied to me, groans for food again, and something seems to swish past, brushing my face. For a breath I think: Israel. But the thought fills me with cold anger. I will never think of my dead brother again, he is no help, and he is not the ghost I want. And I will not allow myself to think of my boy, now dead through my fault.

Martha. The feel on my face is like her cobwebby hair, similar to Rebecca's but with no shine, like black smoke. I try instead to think of home, which is meant to be a comfort to the desolate.

Home. Ah Martha, now I see what you meant when you spoke of home as nothing but a tale. Home now is a makeshift, half-built, lazy fort. It bears my name: Boonesborough, Kentucky. Thinking of it twists my gut. The raw splintery stockade unfinished, the place wide open. The well no deeper than a leg, step into it and break your own. Someone called it the ha-ha, and the poor joke has stuck, just as the well is stuck at that shallow depth. The fort is a heartless place, half-enclosing the huge beautiful elm, and for nothing. It makes me sick. Perhaps they have fixed things by now, but likely not. Who is there to fix it? Squire. Perhaps he is fixing everything for me, my wife and all. I think of Martha's big swallowing eyes. I think of being above her nervous pale body at the edge of a new small field outside the fort wall. Her skirts up, her face open, trying to bare itself down to bone, hoping for something out of me. Corn all round again, just starting. I gave in to her in the end, for she was trying to offer comfort and nothing mattered, as it seemed to me.

Perhaps it is the thought of food that conjures her up. Both food and Martha seem very distant, fairy stories that turn out slippery and do not end the way you think they will.

Hill looks up dully, as if he has felt something brush his skin also. Nothing to see but naked trees and banks of snow and the Shawnee some distance ahead. Death has passed me by, but for how long I do not know. Starvation is its easiest choice, though sickness is likely enough also. Some of the Indians and my men are already squatting in a great hurry wherever they can along the path. Hancock is the most troubled, he sinks down to open his bowels yet again ten minutes after the last time. Well, perhaps Johnson is the most troubled, being tied to him. He is a small, sly, boyish fellow. He lifts his eyes to the heavy clouds at every stop as if he were in a church, but he cannot help hearing the bodily noises from his captive partner. And nobody can avoid the puddles of stink.

Never have I been so cold, my eyelashes freeze and stick together, I can hardly see to walk. The kettle freezes to my shirt over my back. The cold pierces down to the core of everything and wraps itself hard there like a root. End-of-the-world cold. But the world does not end. We keep moving, though moving is no longer any help. The cold has camped inside our bones. The sky is like the palm of a great iced hand coming down at us. Hill mutters and complains now and then, but not so much as at first. A silence is opening like a cave in me. I will never speak again.

The evening fires are sad affairs, all the sadder for the lack of anything to cook. Not for the first time, Hill says:

—Where has the game got to? Why do they not shoot anything?

Callaway says in his impatient smart manner:

—There is certainly something edible here. Boone promised us the best hunting grounds imaginable. Ducks so fat they cannot fly, they just swoon over the Ohio falls for the catching. Remember that, Mr. Boone? Most likely these Indians are all poor shots.

Hill shouts a laugh and the Shawnee look over from their own fire, but they are too tired to threaten. They have withdrawn from us on the whole. Hill says:

—Maybe these ones do not eat. They live on air instead.

Callaway shakes his head and sets his mouth, and Hill roars louder:

—I know the truth! We have marched all the way to Hell.

Callaway pulls his knees to his chest. He thinks on this and at last arrives at an answer:

—If this is Hell, it is Indian Hell. Even their Hell is backward. You can see how cold it is.

He brushes his hands together after this pronouncement. No one speaks for a time. Then the talk rolls back to the endless complaint about the lack of game and the lack of food.

Too cold for game, you asses, everything is hiding and waiting it out. Nothing will move in this. I want to shout this and shut their mouths. But I do not, and at any rate they seem to enjoy their thoughts of Indian Hell and how we have ended up there. It gives them something to chew.

—Sounded like deer, I think. Sounded like deer. Did you hear it?

Will Brooks speaks insistently, with the soft hopeful face of one

whose ma loves him too much. It is stricken at the thought that he might have conjured up the sounds out of the bottom of his dizzy hunger. Shots and brief animal cries. We are all sitting up, we have all heard something in the night. It is the sixth night. Nobody can answer.

The men's faces are like children's, all straining to see.

The guards are standing about us, making a fence, but through their legs we watch the flints strike and strike. They are cold too, they take a long time about it. The fire at last flares up the creek bank. We do not move our heads, we are still as wooden men.

When the smell hits us, it seems a golden wreath over the bleak dawn camp. A couple of the men near me are blinking hard, and I will say that I am close to weeping myself, stupid with want and angry for it. Brooks is looking up the creek with tears pouring out of his eyes and freezing below them. The guards eventually go off towards the smell of the cooking meat with a backward look at us. They can see that we are weak, they can see just how weak. Hill says:

—Damn all of it, I am going too.

I pull him down and shake my head. Even he is too feeble to protest any. We all sit on, some still trying to contain their tears.

One of the guards comes back after a time. He is chewing meat. He is carrying more on a long strip of bark. He holds out pieces to us between his fingers and it is like a vision, a trick. Before anyone can take any, Callaway points a finger and says quietly:

—What is it?

The guard tilts his nose at the sky and gives a short howl. I have to pinch my eyes shut. Callaway says:

—Wolf.

The guard hangs out his tongue and pants. Hill interrupts:

—We are not your dogs—

He is ready to plunge into a fight if he can only be fed afterwards. He has always been fond of fighting and eating. But Callaway clips off Hill's speech:

—They have killed their own dogs. I am not eating dog meat. Lice, maggots—

He touches the sore place on the side of his mouth where his tooth is rotted. He goes on:

—Let me advise you boys, do not eat that filth. Do not take it.

Hill says:

—Well, and why are they feeding us at all? It could be poisoned.

Callaway is flatly patient:

—Where would they get poison out here? Do they travel with vats of it?

—Jimson weed. If they could find any under the snow. Or other things we do not even know about. They know things.

Hill nods, though he does not look certain, his right cheek quivering. His eyes remain on the meat. Callaway is abrupt now:

—They know enough. They know living prisoners are worth more than scalps to their British friends in Detroit.

—But they do not mind sickening us with dog meat?

Hill's face has dropped. He gives up his argument and lies back down like a sluggard. The guard shrugs and turns to take the food back to the Shawnee. I speak for the first time in some days:

—Best eat it.

My voice is hollow and unconvincing. But the guard returns, he holds out the curled strips and most of the men begin to eat, though they keep their eyes away from what they are putting in their mouths. Hill takes a bite with a little cry first. Young Ben Kelly barks, but nobody is amused. I swallow quick. It is not dreadful meat. Dogs are friendly animals. I tell this to my starved insides, but they protest at the work and I pause.

Callaway is not eating. He is watching me and trying to control his expression. His high clever forehead creases and his light eyes narrow as though he is trying to work out an irritating puzzle.

Two more days' marching. Then more.

The one brief meal makes the returning hunger all the more terrible.

The soles of my feet ache and burn, the skin is coming off and the new raw flesh shrinks from the cold. My lungs suck in the icy air, it stabs at my sore rib and my old broken ankle bone. Little Johnson behind me says he has dreamed of dogs and can see them everywhere, hiding in tree roots and treetops. He says loud:

—That was the best dog I ever ate. The very best, by quite some distance. I will have another, thank you, yes.

Nobody questions what other dogs he has eaten in his day. Nobody speaks much now.

The iron kettle on my back shoves me towards the earth. I have to turn my eyes up to avoid its invitation. Callaway has set down his own pot and is standing still. He says:

—I will tote this kettle no farther.

His face is clear. He holds out his arms, his hands palms-up, they say: What will you do? Aloud he says:

—Go on, scalp me. Take the whole head.

He tosses his head back and his hat falls off, showing his red hair. The Shawnee smirk at it but do not deign to take up his offer. One pushes him onward and two others carry the kettle between them for a time before they abandon it in the path with its great empty mouth showing.

At night we lie on the snow that has frozen again to hardness, and try to cover ourselves with branches. I keep curled within myself, I try to believe that I am warm, or gone. I think of elk liver, buffalo tongue. I have to stop these thoughts or I will weep. My stomach is again too empty to complain and I know the others are in the same way. A couple of the younger men are retching.

Captain Will appears out of the growing dark with pieces of bark and a pot of mashed paste. He says:

—Eat this. Then this. Or—

He pushes out his belly and rubs at it. He says:

—Bang.

Kelly says:

—Or they will get us with child? Oh Christ.

Johnson says:

—Bang bang. They are eating the gunpowder now. I thought it would be our horses next, but powder it is.

Captain Will looks to me and says:

—*Meethelookee.*

He means shit, and sickness. My voice is rusted up again:

—Elm bark loosens. Oak ooze stops you up. We have to eat them on long-hunts sometimes. You need both. They will help your bellies.

The Captain offers some of each to me first and I take them. I find myself wishing it were a real poison. I try to control my throat and I get it all down. Most of the others follow, though Callaway holds out with a mutter about waiting instead to be murdered honourably by the British in Detroit. He says:

—I am an American. This is our country. We are fighting you now. We are fighting everyone.

Captain Will nods and waves bleakly as if to say: As you wish. He puts a hand to his ear. When he turns his head to go, I see that part of the ear's rim has snapped straight off with the cold, it has left a gap in the loop.

The slippery green taste of the bark and the bitter oak ooze are bad but they are enough to keep us from swelling with hunger.

Enough to keep us moving through the deep sludge of wet snow when it softens as the days go on. When we reach the Ohio River, the Shawnee are too fatigued to rejoice much, but their skin looks less dried up over their bones. Black Fish has the warriors drag out a skin boat they have hidden off the river path. They cross with us in groups. The water crawls choppily in the gap between the icy grey edges. I dip my hand into the current and my skin no longer jumps at more cold.

There is a deer at the edge of the trees on the other side. I see the movement of its turning head, the flick of its ears. I breathe in to speak, but of course I have no gun, no anything. A shot comes. One of the Shawnee has got it with no trouble. He runs to pull up its head and drag its body towards the bank, leaving a blood trail in the snow. It is a doe, its sides heavy with fawn. Its belly shifts and stirs for a few moments and then goes still.

No whoop and no murmur from any of us. Silent, we watch the shooter begin the butchering. He gently removes the fawn and places it on the snow a little distance off, cloudy and curled up in its bag. Out come the entrails, and other men get the fire up and haul them over and put them into a pot to boil. Everyone's eyes are on the carcass, the skinned meat of its sides and haunches, which the Shawnee man is cutting out so slow and careful that I am put in mind of a woman embroidering. An apron. A baby's cap.

—For God's sake.

Hill bursts out with this suddenly but then drops his head. The silence is as heavy as the fatigue. Both are hard to fight.

We sit where we have been put and watch the chiefs queue up to take turns drinking from a dipper at the boiling pot. Little Johnson says:

—Are they not even going to eat? Are they not going to let us watch them eat?

—They are not like us. Torturers gain more pleasure from starving others than from eating.

Callaway says this in his calm faraway tone. He has decided that they mean to make him eat and that he will not. Once he has made up his mind, there is no changing it. He is young, he is so sure of himself. I can hardly bear him at times. He is here and my boy is not.

The warriors are next. And now the guards pull us up and take us up to the pot in our roped pairs. I see most of my men pause and drink, beyond caring what it is. Hill and I are last. By the time I am confronted with the remains of the sticky boiled liquid with its bland evil smell, I cannot help myself, I gag and heave. When I look up and clear my eyes, I can see my men and the Shawnee are all crouching or holding their bellies, opening their bowels everywhere. I see Black Fish crouched off in the trees in the same position, his back to us.

—Poison.

Hill mutters it almost with relief, his forehead all sweaty dots. Well if it is poison, they have poisoned themselves as well. Here is your chance, Death, we will all go together, all brothers, ha! I take the dipper and force down the warm thick liquid, it slops over my shirt. Tar and vinegar.

Hardly have I swallowed before my guts begin to quiver and my legs collapse just where I am. I have not the time to remove my leggings. Those who have come through the first cramp and pains are sitting up looking at me, and some are laughing silent. Callaway is sitting up, keeping his eye on me and shaking his head. He did not drink. A pine shakes a clot of wet snow over me. I shudder.

In the end, some of them are well enough to cook the strips of meat over the fire, and someone shoots another deer, so there is plenty. The smoky scent cuts through the sickness and I must say we all feel quite refreshed. We sit up like good children, paying no heed to the muck around us and looking only at the meat smoking on sticks. When Captain Will brings some over to us he says:

—Now we can eat. The medicine first, or food would make you too sick.

I chew my meat. Its taste is fine and familiar. I would eat the same thing at every meal for the rest of my life. I am living. My head bangs to tell me it is so. Through a mouthful Hill says:

—You are our mother now?

Captain Will manages a ghastly smile. He says:

—You need a mother, maybe. You also, Wide Mouth.

Ma, your poor face appears before me, I shut it out by chewing hard. I say:

—People often tell me what I need. What I need is a meal.

I feel the lump of chewed meat on its travels down my gullet. Captain Will says:

—People want to get hold of you.

—Ha. Like dogs with a rabbit.

—Maybe so. Or dogs with another dog. They think you have something they do not.

Hill interrupts with his mouth stuffed again:

—You are one to talk of dogs. What would your dogs say to you now, if they still had powers of speech?

Captain Will retains his smile and says:

—You like hornets better, maybe. Wide Mouth told me your story.

Hill goes on chewing and eventually laughs and says with his old good cheer:

—The hornets have not had the better of me. I would eat hornets if I had to, I know that now, ha! And if I were a hornet I could not resist a taste of me. We are all living yet, at any rate. You are a character, I will put you in my book.

Captain Will goes off. I do not blame him. I look up and see the black man stretched out in one of the remaining unsoiled places higher up the bank. He is smirking at us. He glances over towards Black Fish, whose mouth is set and who will not look in our direction.

There is no further food. When we are marched up the last ridge to the Indians' winter town of Old Chillicothe, we are all indeed alive, though we drag our feet pitifully. We have to drag all of Callaway, he has eaten nothing these two weeks and is near dead. But not quite dead. He manages a frozen hiss from between his teeth before his head drops back insensible.

6

Chillicothe

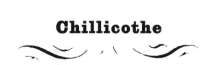

We arrive in the night. The Shawnee strip little Johnson bare and have him run screaming into the village to announce our presence. He has the look of a child's ghost fleeing against the dark. I shut my eyes. He screams his loudest, my ears near shatter.

When I look again, women and boys and small children are emerging from their houses to watch. I hear an old woman saying: *Mechtacoosia*. Whites. Then the warriors light torches. They sweep a path in the snow in one of the lanes. They line up my men and prepare them to run another gauntlet. I protest to Black Fish, but the black man refuses to interpret and says only:

—We said we would not hurt your men there. We did not speak for our women.

Black Fish retreats into his inscrutable regal stance and my appeals in Shawnee fly straight off him. And so I watch each of my men take his poor weak turn. The women and children have a good go at the runners. The little trade-silver bells on their shawls ring as the women strike. Young Sam Brooks does not run but tries to fight, and his arm is broken by a club. A girl thumps Hill in the shins with a thorny stick, looking as if this is a disagreeable but necessary task. He almost falls, but he staggers on to the finish. Callaway staggers worse, he is like a corpse dug up and seeking its old home where there is now none. He manages to bash out at a woman who holds a club and gets a rain of blows to his head and shoulders, but he keeps slowly on and does not fall.

They do not let me run this time and I am sorry for it. Black Fish keeps me near to watch the spectacle with him.

Afterwards they take us into the big log house. Inside it is dim and smells of old meals. They tie us again and leave us alone. Sam Brooks groans all night with his pain. Sounds of celebration creep in through the openings below the roof but my body is so fatigued that I fall into a black sleep.

Two keepers wake us with cold cornbread in the dull morning light. We are still here. We all blink and eat fiercely. Many of the men show lumps and bruises and dried bloody patches. The keepers stand at the door. Their posture is sluggish, but they look at us with interest. I suppose it is pleasant to have the kind thoughts of those who might kill us any minute. Hill gives us all a spraying of crumbs when he suddenly shouts at them:

—How long do you intend to keep us bound up in here?

Then they untie him, but only to take him away. I must say that I am somewhat relieved to lose his noise and his presence, but I am not easy. Johnson begins to murmur about there being peace at last but Callaway is sitting up as lively as Lazarus after deigning to eat some of the bread. He says into the upper air:

—We are not safe here. There is no safety here. Remember that.

—Mr. Boone said we would be safe enough now.

Young Will Brooks, sitting next to his injured brother, says this. He has a black eye in his round and hopeful face. His look puts me in mind of Stewart, also of Jesse. I will not think of my lost boy. In Brooks I see how easy it is to begin to feel at home somewhere. This is what he is hoping for. I am hollowed out inside but I manage to say:

—They have promised we will be all right. And that is all I know.

—Aha. Well, if they promised.

—It could have been worse. No one killed, and not a drop of blood spilled at the surrender, Callaway.

—Here is one.

Callaway splits open a crusted cut on his face, blood slips down from it. He is still speaking to the rafters, and a few of the others squint up as though hoping to see a message there in hammered golden letters. The rest are looking at me.

They come for us soon enough. They walk us along a street sloping slightly downward. The sun is struggling in the cold white sky. We are still slow and shuffling, but the keepers have purpose and we have grown accustomed to following. For the first time I see the town properly. There are some two hundred wigwams, like sleeping creatures curled up at the centre of the cleared snowy fields, and some log cabins without windows round the edges. The big house is at the centre, built of notched logs. It puts me in mind of Exeter in Pennsylvania and our old Meeting House. Is it still there? It seems to me it must all have crumbled away to dust by now, so far behind me is it.

There is no one about as we walk through the town. The quiet is strange. This is a strange place.

We go down the ridge to the water, and at the riverbank is a fire trench. And here are all the people in a row as if they have been waiting for some time. The women are quite dressed up in beaded calico shirts and hide skirts, with silver brooches in their clothing and scarves wrapped round their heads against the cold. The warriors have on good hunting shirts and quillwork moccasins, their blankets tossed over one shoulder. They look prepared to be entertained. Some nod as we pass by, many squint and stare. The faces are not quite friendly but not unkind. The people appear not to want to touch us or have their own clothing brush against ours. One small boy muffled up with a cloth about his face throws a snowball, which strikes Johnson's knee. Johnson pretends to fall down, smashed to pieces. The boy's eyes flash.

Will Brooks says:

—Are they going to burn us?

But there is a shout. Hill is already here at the water's edge. They have cracked the ice and shoved it aside to make a great hole. He is naked, and a woman stands to each side of him with her skirts tucked up in her leggings, holding his arms. Hill has his legs apart, grinning and showing other signs of pleasure despite the cold. Perhaps we are all caught in one of Hill's dreams.

He is strong but, like me, not such a tall man. As he waves, the women take him by surprise and drag him into the cold water. He goes in face first and comes up with a great raw gasp. The river level is up to the women's knees, they bend to hold him under again. One takes hold of his hair and pulls up his head to let him breathe. The crowd of watchers enjoys it, some are calling and pointing, the children are running back and forth.

Hill roars and flips over like a fish and rolls the woman with him, pinning her below the surface. She thrashes beneath him, white drops shower the air and the bank. I am put in mind of ducks coupling, the same surprise and violence. He holds her down and his lips pull back from his teeth in a frozen grin as he looks to us through the splashing. Four women come running to pull him off. They do not drown him, though well they might. They drag him away up the riverbank, I do not see where they take him, though I hear him yipping as if he is being pinched by one of his whores.

The soaked woman stands shivering, her clothing clings to her. She crosses her arms over her breast with a terribly sad countenance. An old grandmother covers her with a blanket and speaks into her ear, but her face does not change.

Is this to be the way we all go? Young Brooks behind me says in confusion:

—I did not know them for Baptists.

Callaway says:

—I hope you have had the dunking call from the Lord. But no matter if not, they will take you regardless.

It seems a time-eating way to kill some twenty-seven men. Each man is taken down into the river in turn. The women strip them of their clothes and then scrub and knock and bang them as they struggle for their breath in the water, but nobody fights hard now, even poor Sam Brooks with his broken arm. Afterwards they are sent in blankets to the fire trench, where they sit looking stunned and brainless, even colder than before. Waiting for what is next.

I am the last. The old woman approaches me with a younger one, their wet leggings frozen and cracking. I raise my arms so that they might pull my shirt from me. I let them take down my leggings and remove my moccasins. The cold and their eyes whip my skin.

If I speak to them, perhaps they will not kill us today. It is a tiresome thought and I am very fatigued. But I take a breath and I say:

—You are experts, ladies.

The water numbs me quickly and now my heart does rip along as if I have been given a dose of something. Perhaps it will stop now, perhaps the cold water will be my last bed.

But they start on a hard washing such as Rebecca would give to a sheet from a sickbed. I am spared laundering poles. Instead their fists and feet strike me all over, their knuckles scrape up and down my ribs. The one still unhealed sends up a screech. A hand knocks my side and my head, my muscles ball up. The rocks on the riverbed gnaw into my backside, but I am pushed down so hard that I do not try to move. The old woman grimly takes up my feet in turn and drags a rock back and forth over the soles of them, bending my toes back. The younger one has hold of my knotted up plait and works my hair loose. She takes my head in her two hands and lowers it into the icy water. My lungs suck in and my old hurt ankle aches to the marrow. My heart beats beats beats. I keep my eyes open and I can see her face, which looks half melted like the rest of the world.

When she lets me up I am alive. I gasp:

—I am only a man. Have pity.

But my attempts at Shawnee only make them duck me again. My loose hair wraps around my neck and face like weeds. Here I will drown surely. I am going. I open my mouth. A rock thumps my breastbone, a rough cloth scours my belly and my lower parts. The old woman at her work shows no interest in these that I can see. Her mouth is still and her arms scrub away.

My cold brain wanders back to Pennsylvania when some girls caught me swimming bare and threw a bucket at me. I stood and showed them my arse and I said: Remember this, tell your grandchildren one day.

The younger woman pulls me up from the water again, I cough and spit and shake. I see her face with its round brown eyes and small nose. Now she is still, waiting for me to speak this time, it appears. Some of the other women are chattering, running into the water up to their knees and then back to the fire. A couple of my men still have the spirit to catcall from the bank.

I stand straight so they can see all of me and I say:

—White men need the most washing, I see.

I force my voice into a brief hoot. The women give a short silvery breath of laughter at once as I stand turning to ice, all bare and all pitiful. But I do not die. Through my rattling teeth I say:

—Clean enough for you now?

They drag me out and bundle me firm into a woollen blanket like the others. I remain standing on the bank. My teeth rattle on, my skin stings and itches and my wet hair sticks to me as if afraid. Indeed it might be afraid if it could know its fate.

The sky is heaped up with heavy clouds. I watch them slowly roll past.

The women busy themselves at the end of the fire trench, pulling off their leggings and wrapping blankets about their waists. Then they come for me again, their arms out and beckoning.

The younger of my laundresses pushes me down and rubs at my head with another blanket. She smells of wood smoke, as I notice, being so unusually clean of smell myself. When she has finished, she wraps one of my hairs tightly around her finger and tugs sharp.

I see the hair come away and stick to her arm, making a crooked *S* there.

She pulls out another and another, then a few at once. Then a fistful.

The pain rings through my scalp and worms down into my neck and arms and fingers. The roots of my hair seem to run all through me. Rip rip rip. I try not to shudder as her hands take hold of the next hank. I keep my face flat, I stare at her bare legs through the opening in her blanket. At once I know how wolves must feel at night, with howls bursting to get out of them. No. I will not think of wolves. Around me my black scrawls of hair in the snow look like a cipher.

My watching men have gone silent. I see their bruised faces and eyes from their run down the alley of beatings. They can see what further misery is coming for them.

I say loud:

—You have made a fine turkey of me, ladies. I am good and plucked.

—Your feathers are poor.

The woman speaks Shawnee to me slowly. I try to catch her eye but she folds in her lips and seeks out the next hairs. Her smoky smell puffs round her lightly as she moves her arms. I sniff and I say:

—I can only make do with what I was given.

—You should have asked for better. More.

She says *more* in English. She pats my forehead where the hair has already backed off of its own accord, as I will admit. It is a cool and efficient pat. Then she plucks out a handful from the back of my skull. My eyes water.

—Well, and are you the local barber? Or medicine man? Or woman, should I say?

She does not answer but hands me the ribbon from my plait, now faded to grey. Findley, I have kept it. I clutch at this damp sorry thing you gave me. You got me here and you are gone, somewhere you are laughing at me.

She goes on to the next plucking, smiling at Will Brooks's curls. I am certain that my head wears a great bright halo of agony and is twice its usual size. Well perhaps this is how angels are made. I raise one aching arm to touch the sore bared flesh, I feel the long lock left at the crown.

—Ah. For ease of scalping.

I mime the action on myself. I am shot with the old blue recklessness I have felt before. A couple of my men snort and the women smile pityingly. My barber woman says:

—You can keep that.

—Can I? Thank you.

—Warriors do.

—What?

—Warriors.

She faintly mimes a raised axe. I say:

—Does this make me a warrior now?

She shrugs with her whole body and says:

—It is supposed to be so.

—Well well. Does it work?

She only looks at me, and so I flip my remaining hair in her direction. The old woman who washed my parts grins suddenly with bright teeth and makes a gesture that I understand. My barber woman smiles thinly too and says:

—She says your hair is—

—I know. *Limp* is the word you are searching for.

I stand and I open my blanket. Her face does not change. I will admit that I am less than impressive in this condition. I feel my men behind me, I hear some of them chuckling. In English I shout:

—You have evidently done this before, beautifying men's heads for them. Making them less limp. We could give you a job back at Boonesborough. What do you say boys? Plenty of shaggy types there. Limp types too.

I turn to the whites huddled under their blankets scratching at themselves. A few are holding the ends of their wet hair. No one laughs further.

Well. I should not have mentioned the fort. The Shawnee could take it easy enough. Hair by hair, scalp by scalp. Burn everyone. Burn the place to stumps, let the grass grow over the burned black rectangle until there is nothing at all to show it had ever been. I see it, the bright wild grass and clover all along the river, the meadow whole and empty again. Beautiful and horrible. Which?

At once everything here is pointed and venomous.

Other women set to plucking the men's heads now. My barberess has moved down the line. I shout:

—What else are you going to do?

—What do you want?

She is calm as ever, but her voice shows a small note of surprise and I know that I have trapped her attention. In English I say:

—I said what else will you do, Delilah? Curl it up for us? Perfume it? Mine is clean. It is limp. It will not hurt you.

I twiddle the lock around my fingers. Everything I say feels hollow, though the words come easy enough. A wave runs through the men, and a few bark out expectant laughs again, their eyes on me.

The woman only turns away and begins the walk back up to the town. I stop moving my head about. My skin is damp still and very cold. Callaway pulls his blanket tighter. He gets to his feet and begins to walk up the beach as if he is making to leave. Some of the Shawnee women point and call in alarm: *Napeia. Napeia.* The rooster. His final lock of red hair has the look of a cock's crest falling over. He turns back and says:

—No, the question is what are *you* going to do now, Boone?

7

We Are Clean

THE TRANSFORMATION they perform on us is real enough. Now we are something else entire. Clean. New. No longer white. The stinking stained heap of our clothes stays at the riverbank for burning. We are given new clothes. We are given new families. All of us are new people.

I am to be Black Fish's son and live in his house.

So surprised are we that we go along. They speak to us differently, they are softer, their faces are softer. We are replacements for their dead men. We are their dead men come back.

This strikes me now as a generous and clever idea, though at the time I could not believe in it. We whites are stingy with our dead, we hoard them and put them away, as I know. We roll their stories about like pebbles in our heads until they are polished and rattling and all we have left. And our dead are gone. That is what we say. Gone. I tell myself mine are gone. I will not think of them.

The house is covered with sheets of elm bark and flecks of moonlight get in, all speckled. It is like living under a hen. I would prefer to keep outside, but they tie me in at night. The woman sighs and turns. The little girls roll about frequently. The man is a silent sleeper. He has the look of a grave, a mound covered to the forehead with a blanket. But many things make me think of graves.

For lack of anything else to do in this long night, I call to Squire in my mind now. I imagine a small, flickering trail like a cannon fuse licking its way along through the woods, all the way back to the fort. I will it to keep going and not go out.

—Squire. Hey-o.

We have never spoken of the difficulty between us. The silence now is a great disappointment to me. I want a word from him very much. Any word would do. Any word at all: pincer, pie, prick. O Squire, I am such a fool that I laugh aloud.

—My son.

The voice is cool. The fire is down to the last embers. My spine aches and shivers up through its core. I squint into the dim. Nothing has changed. The cooking pot is squat above the embers. The shapes of corncobs still hang like icicles from the thin beams. A chicken murmurs once on the roof. It is only this same life. I wonder how long it may have left to run.

I say low:

—Only dreaming. Only speaking to myself.

The voice is almost tender from beneath the blanket:

—No more. Sleep now.

And I do sleep.

Light comes. The two little girls stare at me through a hole low in the wigwam's bark covering. I am pretending sleep but I feel the eyes roaming. They have crept outside early, they are very quiet in their spying. They cannot have enough of staring at me. They laugh whenever I speak to them. They laugh more when I speak in English, as if it were a great entertainment. I do not trust them but I like them well enough. They are pretty little girls and full of life.

One of them whispers *wochkonnikee*, the word for the colour white, and then *Shawnee*. I am startled enough to open my eyes. White Indian. There are a few other whites here aside from my men. They are dressed Indian-fashion and look as if they have lived here a long time. If they see me, their eyes find the distance at once, they do not speak.

Now the girls are breathing puffs of air at me. I see the vapour coming through the bark as though their words are trying to give themselves a shape and stick to my skin. My head itches. I pull at my remaining lock of hair and I say:

—You women are always trying to change a man.

The girls shriek with laughter and run off.

The early light comes in stripes like cold fingers on me. The girls have roused me fully, though I have not slept deeply and my head still pains me inside and out. I sit up on my mat, and I see my Indian mother and father taking their breakfast from the steaming pot. They are crouched and silent. When she notices me, my new mother stands. She holds out a large bowl and says *Skillawethetha*. Boy. Her face is young but worn, and tight with effort.

Well, here is another new life for me, I suppose, another beginning. I feel myself to be very young. I say in a hearty manner:

—Well Mother, may I go outside just now?

She stops, her mouth shifts. She wishes me to eat, I can see. But she puts down the bowl and says that I might grind some corn for her. She imitates a grinding motion, watching me to ensure I understand. She reaches for a handful of the dried corncobs that hang from the ceiling like a nest of bats.

I say:

—Ha. Woman's work.

She knits her thin brows, holding out a cob to me in hope. She turns to Black Fish, all tears, as she always seems to have ready. I dash the corn to the floor and I shout:

—If I am your son, why do you work me this way? I am a warrior. Look.

I bend low so that the crown of my head is visible and tug at my remaining hair. My Indian mother puts her face in her hands and sobs. I am not much of a replacement for her dead one. Black Fish says:

—Let him go.

His face reveals nothing. He is biding his time, I know one day he will react to my talk and my ways. I bow again to my Indian mother and I leave, feeling sorry. I do not like to make a woman cry. But I am a captive, son or not. We are captives. I remind myself of it. Well if my father is a king, I am a king-to-be. King of the prisoners.

The young man assigned to guard me catches up easy. I am not entirely free yet. He shuffles along in silence dragging his moccasins, sending out ripples of misery and dislike and occupying himself with touching his pimples in tender fashion. In this way we pass up the street of wigwams. In the open beyond them and before the fields, my little sisters are playing with a few other children, squatting at some game with pebbles and dried cobs. It is a serious game. Trades are made. They are hoarding their piles and building banks of snow around them when the older of my sisters suddenly shrieks, swatting her stack of cobs so they go spinning off in all directions. She flings a fistful of pebbles at the others, and one starts to howl. She stalks off, pitiless. I call her Miss Hiss for the noises she makes. She is a fury, like Jemima. But I do not think of Jemima. I do not know what I can do for her or anyone now.

The littler sister spots me watching and comes over, chattering in breathless Shawnee, to hand me a pebble. I crouch to take it and I say in English:

—You are a fine society lady.

She smiles with her chin tucked in and then leans on me and begins to suck her thumb. She pulls at my ear, all dreamy. It seems to do as well as her own.

—You would have my ear if you could, miss.

She looks at me, and I point and say:

—My ear. Ear.

—Eah.

—That is good.

I point again to my ear to show the other watching children and the guard, who is smirking now. The children repeat it after me. I say:

—I can quite fancy myself a teacher, though that is near all I would be able to teach you poor scraps. But for a card game. All-fours perhaps, if we had some cards.

They all go on staring at me, and so I put out my tongue and try to say what it is. It comes out as *Ung*. The children scatter in apparent disgust, even my little sister, who near takes my ear with her. The guard looks disapproving and shifts his eyes away. I suppose I have done some other wrong now.

—O girls of mine, leaving me again!

I groan and clutch at my heart, and I fall to the snow and play dead. Jemima loves this game. Susannah and Israel too. Jamesie—

No.

I lie still, my head is icy. I feel Death sucking at my breath again. So many times it has come so close.

My furious hissing sister rushes over from wherever she has gone and leans into my face, batting her black lashes and blowing close to my mouth. I do not move. I cannot.

She screams very loud. My ears bang with it. I will never be allowed to be dead, as I have learned.

I sit up and see another little girl watching me closely from where she sits nearby, her arms round her knees. She has quietly gathered up all the corncobs and pebbles and has them heaped up before her now. I say:

—Hello Miss. Have you won the game?

—Tongue.

She says it perfectly and matter-of-factly, and then spins away looking ferocious and careless, hard as a little bullet.

I think of her sharp little face as I walk in an arc behind the wigwams until I reach the fields. She has an air of complete liberty about her, the way some young children do. As if she cares for no one. I walk and listen to my dull footsteps. I look out over the fields and try to feel some liberty and lack of care myself. The sky is wide and ash-coloured.

Black Fish at my side with an axe.

His face is remote. I know I have displeased him this morning. He walks ahead, saying nothing. After several yards he looks back at me, and I follow. He does not swing the axe, he holds it across his body in both hands, as if it is a thin child.

We walk through a furrow that winds about the strange hillocks humping up out of the fields. He moves quietly but sends back a ripple of disturbance through the air. My guard is disturbed also and shambles along to the side of me with his head down.

When we reach the edge of the woods, the chief stops and turns to me, the axe flat on his palms. I take it. The handle is rough-grained and heavy. I think of what I might do with it, and what it might do to me. My neck is quite thick, I think.

—You are to build a trough for your father's ponies. Choose any log you like.

I look up. The voice comes from a short way behind, it speaks in English. It is the black man, our interpreter. I have heard this voice in the nights, singing from the big house, amidst other sounds and talk. This is a noisy place on the whole. A busy winter town, full of its own life. I can hear Miss Hiss bawling from up the track between the wigwams.

The black man says now:

—I have left my whip at home, but I will be pleased to be your overseer.

Saying no makes him smile. A lump of sugar shows between his teeth. His eyes are on the axe. I have no wish to deal with a go-between. I turn to Black Fish and say:

—I am not building a trough. I told you, you have made me a warrior. My hands are not made for stupid work, look at them.

I throw down the axe and thrust out my palms as I used to do for Daddy's inspections. I boil up old anger and force my gaze to hold steady. If I do not argue, I will have worse to face. Or I will sink into this life and never get out. I know that my men are always listening and expecting escape, I can feel them hovering like a flock of great birds all of the time, even out here. And so I stare hard at Black Fish's cold face and I raise my voice again:

—Look. Go on. Take a good look. Smell them. Read my future.

Black Fish covers his lips with his fingers and speaks in quick Shawnee. I catch a few words before the black man cuts in:

—He says you need not work, you are his son. There are plenty of workers to build things for your people, plenty of women to grow food for you and your family when they arrive. What do you wish to do?

The black man puts his hands together as if praying. An air of friendliness hovers like a dragonfly over water but I do not catch at it. I say:

—I wish to do as I like.

Black Fish listens to the translation and nods. He speaks again and briefly makes the same praying gesture as the black man, who says:

—All right. We only wish for you to do as you like.

We all nod and go our separate ways. This all seems very simple and sensible and perhaps it is so. I am still too slow and heavy inside to think it through. The black man is whistling something that sounds familiar, but I am too fatigued to recall the tune. My young guard walks beside me again, his hand clamped on my arm. He looks with longing back at the axe.

The days fall past like water dripping. There are shooting contests here. There are fights. The Shawnee take my arm and offer me fights as if they are healthful remedies. I do it but I dislike it. I do not trust my excitement or my pulse. I do not like the feel of my body trying to act as if it is alive. I fight a thickset man with thick arms, we near kill each other, but we catch one another's eyes in the midst of grappling and both see that it is a stupid false thing to be doing, though we do not stop until I let him push me down into the snow and that is that. I feel myself to be drunken all the time, though there is no drink.

In my permitted idleness I wander about the village with my guard. I hope to see my men to speak to but instead I find the black man lying on a rock by the river in the cold afternoon sunlight. He is the only black in the Indian town. He is treated like a visiting prince of some minor sort, indulged and ignored in turn. Is he free? He must be so. He does no work but the interpreting so far as I can see. He dresses as an Indian, with his headscarf and large rings splitting his ears.

For lack of anything else to do I sit down near him. My guard hovers about us looking uninterested and disapproving at once. He pokes with a stick at the ruff of ice fringing the river, crack crack. But the air is quieter here and queer to my ears. No insects yet, and still cold. The water is low at the edges. The sun looks thin and white, a cut-paper sun.

—*Neppa*.

—What?

—*Neppa*.

—The same to you.

The black man gives the word a stony drawl and keeps his eyes closed. I do not understand it. A branch cracks in the knot of trees where my guard has gone. I decide to play along. I say:

—Tree. Is that it?

He opens his eyes and rolls them upward, smiling to himself. I say:

—Cloud, then. Ice. Water.

He shakes his head very slightly and then lifts his hands and fans his fingers as though something were spilling out of them. I say:

—Salt.

He gives a short high laugh like a horse. He says:

—Idiot. Salt got you here.

I laugh back and say:

—I would not disagree at this moment.

—Your little white friend is an idiot.

He sits up somewhat and nods towards a spot upstream where Johnson is cowering on his hands and knee. He is swaying his head low like a sick dog and muttering. A small group of Shawnee men is behind him watching. I say:

—If you say so.

—Idiots, all of you. Devils.

—Idiots and devils come in all varieties. All colours. Just like flowers. Are you fond of flowers?

I look straight at him, all innocent. He stares back, making his eyes pots of innocence also. We have a brief contest of innocence until Johnson begins to bark. He is dripping foamy spittle at the mouth. One of the Shawnee shouts at him to point to where our fort is, and he gets up and points in every direction, including up to the sky, with a sloppy grin. We look to him, and I say:

—They call him Little Duck now, I think. *Pekula.* But I defer to your knowledge of the local tongue.

—Ought to be Little Bastard. Or Crazy Mongrel.

—They have a way with names. As do you.

He glances at me and in his slow stony way he remarks:

—Sheltowee.

—Is that what they call me now?

—Do you not listen to your mother? Big Turtle. It was their dead one's name, but it suits you well enough. You looked like a turtle coming out of the river after they washed you. Sheltowee.

—Well. I am flattered. Turtles are no fools.

—Fools are generally popular. They do not work that one at all. Like you.

The man nods towards the foaming Johnson. I say:

—And like you, may I say. What do they call you? Thunder and Lightning?

—Pompey.

I have to laugh:

—Pompey, is it? Hardly sounds Indian. Pompey. That what you call yourself?

Now he closes his face to me, and I feel his coolness return. We sit for a time in silence. I hear my guard poking roughly at the ice.

The woman who tugged out my hair is coming along the bank, holding a child's hand and carrying a bucket. The child is the sharp little girl. Her hair has a rusty tone in the sunlight. She trails a stick behind her and keeps looking back at it as if hoping a small dog will attach itself. When they near us, I say:

—How do, Delilah. How do, young lady.

Both of them ignore me. They leave shuffling marks in the snow. I watch them go. To Pompey I say:

—That woman speaks some English?

Pompey rolls lazily towards me, he shows the most interest I have seen from him yet, but he is refusing to give up his game. He eyes me and says only:

—*Neppa.*

And he passes his hand through the air before his face. It changes to a flat sleeping face.

—Ha! Sleeping. Sleep.

He smiles with his teeth now and says:

—Close to *neppoa.* Which means *dead.* A sensible language, Shawnee is.

—Well. Thank you for the lesson. Now tell me how to say female barber.

He says:

—You can repay me first.

—Well well, and what can I do for you?

—I will think on it.

He holds his grin a moment and then appears to go unconscious again, eyes closed and lips open and nostrils going in and out. I think of the last time I really slept so. It was the night my Jesse Bryan was born in the little house I built on Beaver Creek, when I plaited Rebecca's hair for her and went to open the door and look at the sky. A stripe of pink was above the trees, morning a certainty. I say:

—*Neppa.* There you are. Or *neppoa.* Well. I wish I were one or the other.

Pompey props himself up on his elbows and surveys me once more. He says:

—You look as if you are smoking something sour. Shall I have someone fetch more of the drink for the sick? Give you a purge? I saw how you enjoyed it.

I want to laugh but I remind myself to get up and stalk off, though I am tired of conjuring these bursts of anger. I am tired of my aching ankle and rib and shoulder, reminders of wounds that did not kill me.

Johnson is bucking like a young mule trying out its first kicks. His knees are knocked together, all awkward, and strings of drool swing from his chin. His audience is contemplating him. Some of them make low remarks to each other on his performance. Delilah and the girl are standing slightly apart, looking on calmly as he yells: Ee-aw!

I can see what he is playing at. It would be easy enough to do the same, to become another Little Duck, or Little Ass, to save oneself. All of the capering and foolery. But surely Johnson cannot keep this up. Do ducks live for ever? No. We had a mule once that lived to a great age but not even asses live for ever.

There are ways to preserve oneself. Bury oneself in salt, for instance. I think of it. At this time I still imagine that I might preserve everyone I have not yet lost.

8

The Whores of My Life

—All right.

This is all I seem able to say. My men look at me for signs and I have none to give. They look at me as if I were a gypsy ball that shows the future. I am the freest of us, but the guards do not allow me to be too close to Johnson or the others. They put up with a few words in English if we pass in the town, but this is the only time we can speak. All I can do at such times is try to harden my face or say: All right. Perhaps it is a question.

I see men working outside their new families' wigwams or in their plots in the fields where the snow is beginning to clear. They grind corn or chop kindling or pull up dead stalks and roots with their mothers and guards nearby. But two I do not see, Hill and Callaway. I do not know where they are until the night I hear their voices shinning up out of the dark and over the distance. Hill is singing as if drunk, and Callaway is speaking the song's words as if he were arguing. *Poor Britons, poor Britons, poor Britons remember.* He is the sort who believes there is no point to singing at any time. Then there is a shout and a banging and the song goes no further. Well, perhaps Callaway is satisfied with this outcome.

When I go about in the village in the morning, I notice a small log outbuilding behind the big house. It has no windows, and two rough, raw-boned young Shawnee lounge about before its door. Now I know Hill and Callaway are in this little prison house with little space between them, to judge from the size of the place. No one has adopted them. Perhaps they are such dirty types at bottom that they are not yet clean. Perhaps they need another good ducking in the river, but who will adopt Hill now?

I give a halloo. Shufflings and questionings come from inside as if I have awakened them, but my young guard hustles me on with his face forward and his eyes sliding towards the two rough fellows. There is no reply.

We turn and pass through the town again. I hope to see the children but they appear to have been kept at home today. I make for the riverbank. The day is warming and Pompey might be lolling at the water again. Perhaps he will teach me more words, perhaps he will give me some sign of what to do. He seems to want something from me, though he is not straight about it.

My guard follows me along the water's edge. I go farther along the bank than before. The river is higher today, the earth softening somewhat where it meets the water. Round the bend is a great canebrake, high dead stalks blocking the way. I push back a few to make a path. And here is Johnson, sitting in a flattened patch and staring saucer-eyed at the current. He is throwing sticks into the water and still drooling. His guard is also throwing sticks, but keeping his spittle contained. I say:

—Surely you can find better bait.

I kick my moccasin high into the air and take my time finding it. My keeper looks at me with his pimply face but lets me be. Johnson turns his saucer eyes on me to gibber:

—The falling of the stars, the smash-up of the moon.

His voice is trembly and aged though he still looks small and young. He quacks loud and I say:

—No need to keep that up with me, Johnson.

I shake my head sadly at the guards and say:

—Poor madman. Poor little fellow.

I roll my head and eyes about to show them what I mean. To Johnson I say:

—I know what you are doing, and you are doing it just fine.

Johnson whispers again, his head stuck into the cane. He throws a twig feebly and dangles his fingers as if he has dabbled them in something sticky and dripping. He clutches at my leg and I near jump away.

—What?

I bend to hear him and he grins at me through his beard, which the Shawnee barberesses have not touched. This beard is like old rotting rope picked apart and slathered in wet. The grin is humourless. His hands keep still on my leg. He says through his teeth:

—Get us out. That is your job.

My guard and Johnson's are smirking and watching him in hope that he will perform some new antic. The Shawnee seem distantly fond of Johnson, as they are of Pompey. They appear to like characters, which is sensible enough, as everything here is unchanging and endless, it seems.

I smirk also as if we are sharing a joke, and I say low to Johnson:

—We will get out. Not yet. So do not give us away now with anything stupid. Or too stupid.

My young guard is suddenly reminded of his authority and tugs my head back by the remaining lock. Behind his pimples and his disinterest, his face is full of longing. He wishes to be a warrior. He still has all of his hair, for which he is ungrateful. When he lets me go, I shake my head again and I say:

—Poor Pekula. Little Duck, is that right? He has always been the same.

In my mind I can see Johnson at the fort, chopping logs and hunting quite sanely, and showing no interest in ducks or play-acting.

Something has loosed itself, but it is not true madness, and not only an attempt to keep himself safe. He is enjoying himself in some fashion.

I replace my moccasin. My toes are damp and cold but not frozen. The days are slowly lengthening. How long have we been here? A month. More.

Johnson's guard shakes his head also. Johnson begins to chant and thump himself upon the chest. His voice is melancholy and deep as he calls out of the cane:

—O your mother is a whore, your wife is a whore, and your daughter i-is a *bastard* whore.

I hear it in the night travelling on the air from the prison-house.

Some of the other men are singing it in the morning. They are in the fields hoeing at the mounds of black earth emerging from the snow. They have the look of grave-robbers at their work. I watch. The women watch too and walk back and forth, their hands in their pouches full of rattling seeds. They are waiting to plant the hillocks with their crops. If there are any dead beneath, they will make for better plants perhaps. Young Will Brooks spies me and lifts his hand in greeting, but soon it falls as if ashamed of itself.

The singing cuts through the chopping and digging. The men sound merry enough but with a hard edge. The kind of merriment that comes when there is someone to kick. This is new. Though not new in my life.

Your daughter is a whore whore whore, your daughter is a whore.

Someone has given it a melody, sweet and almost melancholy. *Whore whore whore* runs slowly up the scale. As we walk back to the village, I even catch my guard humming it.

Well. It seems to be providing amusement. The white men's music carries on the breeze, and my little sisters dance to it, hopping over pebbles set in rows in the street outside of our wigwam. In the midst of their hopping, the girls grin at me. I tip them a small bow.

Inside the house I cannot hear so well, and I must admit that I am somewhat relieved. The dark and the smell have also become a relief to me. The young guard coughs outside to remind us that he is still doing his job. The chickens rustle on the roof and one pokes its head down into the smoke hole. My Shawnee mother smiles without looking at me and then turns her back as she tends the fire. I can see she would rather I were not here.

The men's voices rise. Black Fish is resting on his mat and says nothing at first. But as soon as he opens his black eyes they are on me. He stands and takes up a gun from beneath a blanket in a corner. It is an old flintlock with a poor splintered stock. He holds it out and I take it. I put it to my shoulder and take a sight and say:

—Is this to shoot my men with, now?

He smiles very briefly. I could say: Or shoot you with. But I do not say so. For one thing, who can tell whether the gun actually works?

I watch his face for another break in the flatness, another joke. He says:

—Go off and hunt.

—Hunt what, Father? I am at your disposal.

—What you like.

I expect a smile, but there is none. My mother bangs down her pot.

—A bastard daughter. Excellent wife you must have.

Pompey says this in his stony fashion. The crows are examining the papery old cornstalks and brown leaves the melt has revealed at the edge of the woods. He sits smoking a pipe of willow tobacco and watching, as if they will try to get away from here if he takes his eyes from them.

I have come by a long route towards the woods, away from the field where my men are at work. I take the gun from my back. I have made a new stock for it and it is a good one now. I give it to my sullen guard to hold and I say:

—Shoot yourself a bird.

And the young man aims straight at the sky as ordered, his face near happy for an instant. He keeps the gun plumb.

—How many daughters, Sheltowee? Big Turtle Who Holds Up the World Entire?

Pompey sucks in his cheeks at this title. The dead one's name has not settled on me yet. Even Black Fish does not use it for me, though I have heard him calling his little daughters by name, Pimmepessy and Pommepessy. From my sleeping mat with half-closed eyes I have seen him kissing the girls good morning and letting them snatch pieces of maple sugar from between his teeth. I think of Hill's stories of him burning people tied to stakes, toasting them so slowly they go on dying and dying. There is an art to doing this. How does one learn such an art?

At last I say:

—Plenty of daughters. You?

—None for me.

—No sons either?

—No.

—That makes sense. Who would have Pompey?

The crows laugh and flap off. He curls his lip up over his gapped teeth in a great false smile. For once he looks caught out for something to say. I ask:

—Where did they get you? You have been here a good while. Bedded right in, I would say.

Pompey only shrugs and keeps up his frozen smirk. I say:

—You were captured?

He looks at me. He says:

—Not like you, son of a—chief.

—How is that?

He spits out a few pellets of laughter and says:

—I am no one's son. And I did not come running to them like a blind man at the end of a sack.

—Ha.

He begins to chew on his pipe. It gets caught between two of his teeth. His mouth twisted sideways, he says round it:

—As I see it, you wished to get yourself caught. And your white fellows with you.

I strike the pipe hard from his teeth, it falls into a puddle of slush where it sticks stem-up. He looks at me, keeping still.

—Well, Turtle. Touched your turtle heart?

—Do you think I wanted us all taken? Do you think I choose to be here?

—I do not think you mind. It has not hurt you any. Some are born lucky, the rest of us have to put up with seeing that.

He hums a little of the whore song, then he says:

—They hate you well enough now, your own people.

Be safe here. Preserve everyone. I remind myself. I do not feel at all safe around Pompey. Carefully I say:

—It will all be for the best. My men know that. Our joining the Shawnee will stop all the warring between us. Make us all better off. We can ally against the British.

His eyes lift to the sky and he gives an idle half-smile. He says:

—We shall all be brothers in the spring. You did tell us so when we took you.

He begins to unwind the blue cloth from about his head. His hair jumps free in its tight coils. It smells of clove oil or something like it and I wonder whether he has a headache. But I do not ask, and he would not tell me if he had. The pipe is still sticking up out of the slush like a jaunty leg. I say:

—You seem to be a brother here yourself, I might say. But you must have been taken prisoner first. You were somebody else's slave to begin with.

His eyes go hard and dull. He says:

—You know everything about the lives of slaves, I am sure. Slaves of your own at your fort. They do say you are clever.

—There are slaves there. And I am that. Clever enough.

He rubs hard at a place on his head as if it itches him. The scent spreads. I say:

—We are staying. We are not going to run. Are you?

His face twitches, and he laughs, a forced sound like a bellows:

—Run? Back to Virginia? To whippings and eating beside hogs? To eating hogs' arses? I do not even remember who I was then. I do not even remember my name.

—Maybe you were a hog's arse. Or merely a hog.

—Maybe I was.

He is about to knock me down, I feel it coming. I stand still, I dig my feet in.

He stills himself also. It is an effort. His fists are tight, his boil rises.

A long silence knits itself between us. The river chuckles. The guard takes the opportunity to pull the gun's trigger and fall over with the kick. The bang rings round us and fades away slow.

I crouch and pick up Pompey's pipe. I try to make my voice solemn when I say:

—Well. Life is good here. Better.

—No mistake. True.

Something hangs in the air, a deceitful whiff. Our agreement surprises us, we do not trust it. I see a great unhappiness stiffening him. Then his bones give way and he stretches his arms in a lazy manner as if he has no cares at all. In his usual fashion, he says:

—They may still kill you, you know. Your new brothers.

—I do know. They did not kill you, though. They have not yet.

Pompey's hands are above his head, the fingers spread like branches against the sky. He swings them down and says:

—That is where they bury their dead. See the sticks?

He points to a small open place a distance through the trees. Painted sticks stand in the ground there, some weathered and some bright. I say nothing. He does not frighten me. He smiles and says:

—The sticks are hollow. So they can breathe, the dead. On their journey to the next world. It takes three days and nights. Did you know?

I cannot speak. I cannot. He looks at me all curious and says:

—Well, Sheltowee. Which of your many daughters is the famous whore that everyone knows?

The black man's voice hunts me, it slides after me when I am in the woods with the gun and the guard. It catches me up.

You wished to get yourself caught. And your white fellows with you.

I cannot lose either the voice or my young keeper, who is closer than ever now that I have let him shoot the gun. I step over the slushy ground and crusts of snow. I am heavy-footed and noisy. Let the game run off from us, I do not care. But the memory of hunger on the march is ferocious, like a beast writhing in the gut. My eyes quicken and sharpen with it in their old way, seeking out animal movement in the trees.

But why hunt? Why feed them at all? I load the old gun and I hand it back to my guard.

—Enjoy yourself.

He whips it away, most happy to have it again. But his face drops when he looks at me. He thinks of Black Fish, and he will not abandon his duty. He motions that we should walk on, that I should follow him, and I do. Indeed I keep to his very footsteps and I near step on his heels more than once. Running now would be no help. There is the tiny chance that he might shoot me, for one, though I have seen his aim now. I do not wish to be a month dying of a gunshot wound. And if I were to get through the woods, who would help? The other small forts that popped up round us have already been drained of their terrified settlers. Boonesborough is the last.

My mind keeps settling on my Indian mother's teary face. It sinks me into a miserable low feeling. Do not think of weeping Ma in Carolina. Do not think.

I keep my eyes on my guard's back. He walks quietly enough, this way and that, his head up, seeing nothing. We go deep into the woods with no sense to our movement, no catching of any traces. After a time I cannot help myself, and I give his shirt a tug. I say:

—What is your name?

After a moment, he says:

—Kaskee.

—All right, Kaskee. Look. No, look down. Here. A deer has been lying here. This is the sign, the way the needles have moved against the direction of all the others. Do you see? Easy. Signs are everywhere. Your people know this.

The guard looks at me all earnest, likely understanding nothing. My Shawnee is still weak enough. I pantomime running on the spot, making antlers with my fingers against my forehead. Then I lie down in the whispery slick needles under the boughs. Kaskee nods in a serious manner and lies down too. Well. What else is there to do?

We lie here a long time, our legs growing stiff and cold. A tidy heap of deer droppings sits near our heads. But I do not wish to move. I begin to whistle an old song of my Ma's from the times we went to the high pastures in summer, one of the tunes she would hum to the cows as she herded them in for the night, patting their heavy sides. Come you and you, come in come in. It is a pleasant little tune, it shakes the song about whores from my ears. Ma singing it and I roasting the birds I caught for us. Martins and blackbirds and songbirds. My heart lifts for a moment and I close my eyes and whistle on. Kaskee is listening. But before I finish he gives me a little shake and tells me to get up, we must hunt. He stands brushing dirt and needles from himself, but I remain where I am.

—You go on. I will be just here.

Now comes a crash out of the brush. It is directly before us, unmoving. I can see its soft fringed brown eye and the velvet on its short points, the bald fly-bitten patches on its flank, the winter hair beginning to fall. A buck. I take up the gun from the ground and half-sitting, I get it through the chest. It falls at our feet with a final thump. The shot is clean. The holes are small and hidden in the hair, the buck's face is peaceful. Its brown eye is even closed, as if all it has ever wanted was to be shot by me today.

—Well.

This is all I can think to say. Signs are everywhere, yes, but who can say what they mean? I know nothing. Kaskee blinks and touches his mottled chin.

The breath cuts through the air from close by, hard and ragged. Kaskee turns to look, but I know the rhythm of his mad panting. Johnson. Gambolling, though not in a very duck-like fashion, and lolling his tongue as he does so. He capers about in the small clearing. The corners of his mouth have dried white patches upon them, his matted beard is like a frantic creature clinging to his face. His eyes are red but they clear when they light on me. He sweeps a great bow and then performs his weird boneless dance in a circle around the deer, stepping high. Kaskee relaxes and smirks. Only the Little Duck. His own keeper catches up now, looking fed up to the teeth.

I say:

—Johnson. This deer yours?

—Is this the sound of the Lord I hear? Or only my private lord? A lord just for me?

His head is cocked and his tongue is still hanging out and so he speaks stupidly. He means to sound stupid. He squeals. His guard is speaking to mine, waving an arm as if to say: *Look what I am forced to put up with.*

—Ease up, man. They are tiring of you. You will get yourself killed, acting this way.

—Would you not be pleased at that sight? A dead duck at your feet just like this deer. Not my deer, no. Nothing to do with me.

No hidden friendliness in Johnson's voice.

—Johnson.

—Pekula is my name.

—You must stop drawing so much attention to yourself. They are leaving you in peace now, they think you are a joke, but they do not—

—You call this life a peaceful life, *Dan*? Lord Dan! And here poor Pekula thought we were clearing this country of lords. God save the bloody king, is it, eh? Your wife's family are still king-lovers. You as well?

—It is peaceful enough here. It can continue to be so. Ease up.

Johnson moves closer to where I sit. His mouth is open under his beard, it has the smell of a pit. His eyes shift left to right and go clear again when they settle on mine. He speaks low now and not at all stupidly:

—They like you.

—They like you as well.

—You like *them*, Boone. You always did. Like it here, do you? Happy?

He jabs a quick finger at my collarbone. I say:

—You seem to feel at home yourself. Do you like your new father and mother? Have they found you a wife yet? Settling you down?

He shrinks his eyes down to pinheads and says:

—I always liked your wife. Your girls too. Everyone likes them, everyone does. I used to pay your Susy a penny to run my hand up her arm. What was the cost for a touch of ankle, or higher up the leg, beneath the skirt? Oh Susy, oh Susy—

My hands are clenched, they ache from clenching. He smiles and goes on:

—But any one of them would do for me. I will take them all off your hands, Dan. I never turn down a gift horse, even a second-hand one. We would all like to try their gait. Trot dam, trot filly!

He trots up and down a moment. I stalk after him and he says:

—Have you not heard the song? I hope you have, I know you have! I devised it myself. All for you.

Turning, he kisses me firm on my mouth. His breath works its way up into my nostrils and will not depart. I pull back, I strike his chin with a hard crack. He coughs and whispers:

—Have you not wondered what your women are doing without you?

He widens his eyes and heaves himself up to gambol about again. He lopes and sweeps and looks vaguely threatening, like a crippled man scything. The guards are watching.

All my blood is hot and dark. The dead deer with its closed eye lies as if asleep. I still have the gun and some shot. Johnson is still in sight, lolloping back towards the town with his guard in disgusted pursuit.

My young keeper has no idea what to do. Through my teeth I say in Shawnee:

—Come on.

He holds out his hand for the gun but I strap it on my back again. Enough shooting. Enough. He grudgingly takes a hind leg, I take the other, and we begin to drag the buck through the slippery needles and patches of boggy snow. A dark furrow follows behind us. To be rid of Johnson and the taste of his mouth, I make myself speak:

—There is an easy sign for you. Look, anyone might track us.

I point to show him, but looking back, Kaskee stumbles and falls hard, landing on his side and knocking out his breath. I try to help him up but he shakes me off roughly. He turns his back but I have seen he is weeping. A young man's weeping, angry at itself, ripped out of the chest. He sniffs up a noseful of wet and Jamesie flies up suddenly from the depths of my brains to the surface. Jamesie's face stricken with that same awkward furious sorrow, like someone trying without success to lob a huge stone away from him.

Quickly the thought vanishes, leaving nothing, nothing, and I dream of battering the guard in the face, because it is the wrong face. Pummel it to blood and mash. I clasp the young man's shoulder very hard for a moment, jabbing in my thumb. Then we drag the deer on towards the town, for where else is there for either of us to go?

9

Tales

Your mother is a whore? Your wife is a whore? Your daughter is a whore, whore?

The woman is singing lightly on her way to the river some days later. I am keeping away from Pompey and Johnson and everyone but my sulking guard. I am keeping myself to myself, working on another oak gunstock for my father. But I hear what she sings as she passes. Her English has a slip in the tone, it gives the words the sound of questions. This is a small mercy and so I answer her:

—They go on saying the same thing, so it must be true. How do, Delilah?

—Your men say so. All the time now.

She looks at me. Her usual expression seems to be an unsmiling one, but her eyes have a wry cast. The sharp little girl with her is tapping her heels together with great concentration. To her I say how do, and she repeats it back: How *do*. She seems to be saying: Get it right, you oaf.

On the girl I try some of my oafish Shawnee. I hope for the laugh my little sisters always give me for it. I must have the voice of an Indian bumpkin. But the child turns away and bangs her little heels together again without a flinch. To Delilah I say:

—And this is your daughter? Speaking of daughters. She does

not look much like her mother, if you will pardon my saying so. Not that looks signify.

She runs a hand over the girl's hair. I say:

—Planning some more barbering? The girl's hair is prettier than mine. You might let her keep all of it.

She turns her look on me and says:

—Your hair is growing. But—thin.

—Limp, you might say.

—Yes.

She does not smile. I feel dim as a sheep. I say:

—You and your ladies will be at work on me again soon, then.

—Maybe so.

She pulls at the girl and picks up her pot. Her arm is thin and ropy and I am suddenly struck with the thought that she must rarely have enough to eat. I have seen her outside a small wigwam up the street from Black Fish's house. She seems to have no man and no adopted white son or husband. She helps my Indian mother at her work some days and receives some meat in return. I say:

—Would you like fresh meat? I can hunt for you. I have a gun now.

—You should give meat to your mother.

—I do. But I can get more. Only ask my guard what I can do! Deer fall out of trees and into my arms.

Kaskee points his surly chin away from me. He has not forgiven me for seeing him weeping, or for shooting a deer so easy, or for having a gun when I am white. Delilah says nothing and so I carry on:

—I can dress the skin for you, butcher the meat.

—I can do these things.

—I am sure you can.

Kaskee sniffs violently and gives my arm a jerk. But I say:

—Your little girl could help you.

—She does help me.

I want to ask the girl's name, but I am held back by the sharp little face staring at me. She looks as if her heart has been smashed and reset very firm. Delilah begins to walk on and I stand where I am. I see my young self at old Bryan's door, covered in butchering blood, willing Rebecca to come outside and see. So long ago, it seems. I want to say: A man needs a bowl of milk now and then. But Delilah is down the path, the girl bolting after her. She walks on a few steps, then turns and says:

—Why do they keep saying this about your daughter?

—Well. It is easy to turn on the leader when people are unhappy. Or the leader's daughters. I do not know, I do not even know which daughter. I think it is Jemima they mean. Though my Susy has the same thing said about her plenty.

Johnson is not the only one to make remarks about Susannah. She was always bubbling over with life, she cannot help herself, I know. Susy my girl, I am sorry for you. It is hard for us, it is in the blood, this thumping wish to do as we like.

But it is no matter now. I shrug as Delilah did. She says:

—Your daughter was taken from your fort but you took her back. Is it she?

I am confused to hear her say it. My old life, far away, covered in ash. When I can speak I say:

—How do you know about Jemima being taken?

Again she lifts her shoulders. She says:

—Your girls were taken outside your fort soon after you built it. Our men knew they were yours. They were going to bring them here. But you and your men found them first. They are clever girls.

She smiles. I am startled by it, her pink gums and her round eyes creasing. I say:

—They are. Only Jemima is mine, though. The other two taken were Callaways.

She is mine: it does not occur to me to deny it. She is mine. I let a thought of her face creep across my mind. Delilah says:

—They tore their skirts to make a trail so you would find them. They cried and fell off the pony to be slow. Again and again.

I have to smile too. I remember what they told me afterwards. I say:

—You know the whole story, I see.

—It is a good story. For you. For us, not so good.

—Was it your Shawnee—here—who took her? Your own people, here in this town?

She tilts her head. My Fate has been whipping me head-down and blinkered to this place all along, I know it. I want to ask her whether she knows about Jamesie. But I will not speak of him. I stare at the rising river, swelling now with the thaw. I pick up a rock and throw it. I am reminded that I saved Jemima. I got her back. The Callaway girls and her. Not my boy, but her. I shake my head. Well, can I be bad all through? A little wing flutters in my chest, but not for long.

Delilah has her girl by the hand now. I cough and blurt after them:

—It was a mess. We near shot her. Betsy Callaway too. Took them for Shawnee—for two of you. They both have black hair, it was down loose, they ran at us, and their skirts torn off at the knees—

She says simply:

—Yes, a mess. We know the story. Everyone knows.

—You like stories about us, we like stories about you.

The little girl has skipped ahead, only her shadow is visible as she rounds the bend. Delilah goes after her. I want to shout and tell them I was sure the girls were all dead. In my heart they were dead. The men hate me because they expect me to save them from here in the same way I saved her. Because I cannot. They call her a whore because she is my daughter now, Jemima my poor girl.

It does have the feel of a story. It unrolls itself like a bolt of Daddy's crooked weaving through my head as I lie on my mat tonight. Sleep does not often descend here, and when it does it is a woolly unrestful sleep that does little good. Why sleep? Why throw yourself off a cliff into a pit every night and have to pull yourself out of it again every morning? When I do sleep I hear Death whispering all garbled to me in Pompey's voice, in some other tongue. And this night I wake startled out of my pit to hear Hill singing with a tomcat's wretched desperation across the night. I do not know what he is singing and I do not care to hear. How long can he keep it up? I do not hear Callaway. They seem far from here, they seem to have gone under a hill.

I know near every part of the town now. I have visited different houses. I have seen means for escape: a boat to take, a horse to take. My guard is near always and does not trust me fully in spite of my letting him use the gun. He would love to be the town hero for catching me escaping. For the time I remain much at home. For the first time in my life I like to be at home. It is a refuge from the faces of my men and the things I cannot do.

I decide I will try to be a better son to my mother. I grind corn if I am asked, though it is woman's work. I scrub pots with sand. I make a stool covered with carvings of the tiny folk and giants from *Gulliver's Travels*, and I tell the little girls about them. I say Boo Hoo and Brobdingnag to make them laugh. But I will not work in the fields near my men. I have had enough of songs about whores, and I have no wish to see Johnson again for the time.

Black Fish sits silent in the wigwam in the evening. The sun is low, but light still makes its patchy way in through the walls and the smoke-opening in the roof. The little girls huddle near him, they pull the feathers from his hair idly. My mother is stitching a shirt and I am making a new bone awl for her. She never looks at my eyes, she keeps her look instead on my chin or cheek, but she has grown more used to my presence in her house. She still calls me Boy, *Skillawethetha*, as if the word is new to her. She has not brought herself to say my son, *Niequeetha*, the way my father does.

The flax thread hisses lightly as her arm cuts through the air with her sewing. I watch its shadow against the wall. The whole village is quieter tonight. There is no sound from the big house or from the prison house. The fire flickers in small bursts, it is keeping itself quiet also.

I dream, and I know I am dreaming. Jamesie is in my head. He is a baby, hiding with Rebecca at the edge of a field, waiting for a chance to run. She says: *It is too light,* and she whips the skirt of her gown up over the little one, face and all. Martha appears without her clothes and says: *I love to see the sun rising over the fields.* She lies in the dirt and parts her legs. All of my men stand in a line waiting their turn, holding their pricks stiff and looking amiable. I am the first. Jemima stares at us in great surprise and disbelief, holding the cat. Now I stab myself with the awl and find I have been heavily asleep, blankly so, my arms loose and my neck falling over. This is the first time since we were captured that I have been in such a state, that I have had any dreams. Such dreams.

A booming crack snaps through the air, like ice breaking on the river. But it is already broken, I think. I feel my brains struggling to surface, my limbs jerking as I pull myself to sitting. My Indian family is looking at me with some curiosity. Black Fish is at the door now. I stand and am pulled by the tug tying me to the wall. It is loose. It is flimsy. It is a test, as I know. It says: *Will you stay?*

—Come.

I did not dream the cracking sound. My father motions with his head, I untie myself. We go outside to listen in the direction of the woods. Other men are coming out of their wigwams. We all stand listening, our heads turned. No one speaks.

There is a yip, a crowing howl, full of cold laughter. My spine ices up to my neck. The moon is only half full, one bleary eye blotched by a scrap of cloud. Wolves will howl at it regardless, if they are so minded. This is the way they are. But wolves' minds cannot be penetrated. Even if you were to crack open a wolf's skull while the animal lived, you would find nothing there you could read, only a howling grey blizzard.

From up the road comes an echoing call, clearly false. A poor imitation of a wolf. Hill, and Callaway soon afterwards in a lower tone. Alive, then, though still locked up. Black Fish loosens for a moment and then pulls himself straight. I see his hands flex and close. My little sisters venture into the doorway with big eyes and are swiftly pulled back. The air is cool, the trees and houses are silver round the edges, the purple is gone from the sky. Black Fish strikes out quickly up the middle of the street. I follow, I see a few white faces and I raise my hands to say I do not know what is happening. I go rapidly to keep up and as I pass the last wigwam, I see Pompey standing in a patch of deeper shadow there, I see the outline of his headscarf and neck against the dark. He turns and steps forward so that his face is lit by the moon, so that his lazy enjoyment shows, and he says for my benefit:

—Ducks can fly when they remember how. Little duck bastard has up and gone.

10

We Go

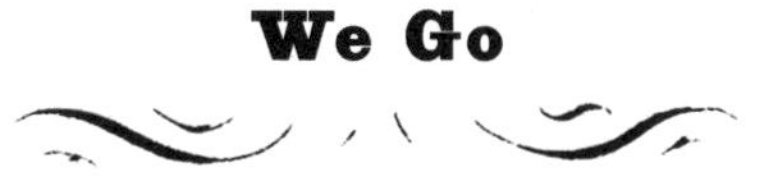

VOICES DRIFT out of the big house on a long slow tide. Banging from the prison house accompanies it, kicks against a wall all night.

Three days after Johnson runs, several chiefs and their warriors ride in from other towns, all wrapped against the cold spring wind. On and on they come.

One blanket is a bright violet. The chief in it is quite aware of himself, like a bird making a display, looking at no one but certain of the eyes on him. The women draw in their breath. They have never seen this colour, I know. They have no word for it. To each other they say: Red? Blue? They all hold themselves in and touch their own clothes, they picture the blanket around their own bodies. Even the little girls touch their waists and necks. I have never seen them so moved. I have never seen quite this colour. Where did he get a thing like this?

I watch, tied to the house door with my guard sitting near and my mother and my sisters standing just inside. I want to ask the chief: Did you get it in exchange for Kentucky? Are you Cherokee? Were you there at the treaty, or at the murder of my boy? My throat aches. I watch the riders, all the silver flashing on their horses' reins and bodies. I think to ask this new chief about Cherokee Jim. But I do not want to say his name, I do not want him to exist at all.

I will not speak. I feel my guard's eyes, and those of other warriors. I am under tight watch again. As are we all. Johnson, God damn your duck heart.

—Father.

It is late when Black Fish comes back to the house. A scent of grassy tobacco wafts in from outside the door before I hear him. My mother and the girls are huddled asleep, I am tied to the wall, but I chance a move towards the doorway. He does not look at me but only pulls at the meeting pipe as though the smoke were some pap and he a toothless starved old man. It is peculiar to see him so uneasy. I go on:

—What do the chiefs want here?

He exhales and inclines his head. The smoke drifts about his face. When it emerges again it looks sharpened, as if a chisel has been at it. He says:

—They bring some news.

But he does not tell me what it is. He at once turns and strides back up the street towards the big house, where smoke is still spiriting out from the roof hole. The fire and talk are still on. I can just see him disappearing inside. I hear Pompey singing one of his high monotonous Shawnee songs from there. A scattering of sparks leaps out of the smoke hole against the night. It strikes me that Black Fish is well named, although this is likely not his first name or his only one. The Indians do not seem to be so very attached to names. But he does have the look of a fish hiding near the bottom of a river in winter, belly to the mud, almost unmoving and almost invisible. Then snapping to life in an instant with jaws wide for a fly.

The moon is fading and the little girls are surfacing into a lighter sleep, turning on their mat. The talk goes on, it does not seem to have slowed at all. I stay in the doorway untying and re-tying the knot around me, trying to pick up words. I think of Johnson's beaky face close to mine, cold under its mad, rough mask. *Like it here?*

I lower myself into his mind, it is like sinking into a green pond. I know that if he can find his way back to the fort without starving first, he will go there. Back to the stench and the idle half-life of Boonesborough. At least he will be able to tell the women what has become of the rest of us, that I have sold all their men. Or perhaps he will keep up his mad act for amusement. I find myself wondering what eats ducks.

The silence spills from the big house all at once as if all the visitors and warriors have instantly fallen asleep. I listen for Hill or Callaway but there is nothing from them either. Only the creak and rustle of the trees and night birds, the river pulling itself along. Someone yawns a few houses away. Someone grunts as if tired of an old pain.

Black Fish's pipe is still lit. I see the small glow approaching. I say:

—Your business finished?

He brushes past me and goes inside, where his shape darkens. Then in one of his abrupt movements he is beside me in the doorway again. He says:

—My son, I have decided you will go also.

I try to look surprised and grateful. I am surprised and grateful, at that. Usually he calls me *Niequeetha*, son, with a flicker in the word. He is not old enough to be my father. I am not his own flesh. But now he looks at me as if he has known me since the minute I was born. I say:

—Father, I am not like Pekula. I am staying here with you.

White teeth split the dark for an instant. His voice is gentler:

—We go in the morning. You too.

—A hunt?

The blue energy I have met before in my life rips all through my body. My arms and legs feel young and unthinking, my eyes can cut through the night. I see my mother's bare forearm flung out from her blanket, my sisters coiled into one another like hair, the carved faces on the stool I made. One of the girls begins to sit up. Black Fish kneels to stroke her and says very low as if hushing the child:

—A journey.

—Here. Ride this.

The pony is a black and white paint with its hair in its face and its ribs showing. No saddle, only a rope around its neck for my guard to hold as he walks alongside. Pompey hands the rope to him and rides off on his own animal, which is fatter. The chiefs are on their horses in front. My men walk, tied at the wrists in pairs and with a single rope about each neck stringing them into a short column, with warriors alongside and behind. Near the back are Ben Kelly and the Brooks boys. They have made nothing but trouble for their new families. They look smug and victorious, as young men who have exasperated their elders will. Behind them are Hill and Callaway, pale and starved and sore-eyed and changed.

I hold the pony back, which does not please it. Kaskee pulls at the reins. But I turn to call:

—Boys, it is not too far.

A stupid remark, I do not know where we are going, and I fear it will be the fort. There are warriors enough and these other chiefs with their men. We are heading north, but perhaps we will make a loop back again, perhaps they are trying to perplex me. I watch the trail. It is narrow here. In my mind I see the fort, I see them all there, waiting for us to come. Rebecca, will you have thought me dead—again? What will you say when I appear amidst all of this? You will cover your twisting lip, trying not to laugh or cry, or you will bash out my brains.

I look to my roped men with an encouraging face. But fresh hate rises from Hill and Callaway like their caged-up smell. They were inside that dark little house near all the weeks we have been here. Their night singing and talking dwindled to a few occasional dirty bellows from Hill. *Till I'm bone of your bone, and asleep in your bed.* His singing always seems to pierce straight to my liver, do what I might to ignore it.

I see my father in profile as he passes under an arch of boughs, his long nose and his shining earring. I cannot read him. I nudge the hairy little pony on and the guard is relieved, but Callaway's cool low voice is behind:

—Off your high horse, Boone. They will sell you too.

He has dragged the whole column closer to me, as if seeing me has given him some peculiar force. The cord about his neck is rubbing the skin raw. It has the look of a hangman's burn. He looks at me out of his bright red eyes. Hill beside him keeps closing his own.

I call:

—Do they have to be tied so, Father?

Black Fish looks back, I point at my neck. Callaway says:

—Spare us your pity. Only let me see you roasted alive or boiled in oil or whatever the British are having their savages do for them now.

—That your last request, Callaway?

—My dying wish.

—I am sorry to displease you. There will be no dying. But wish away.

He snaps his jaws shut and yanks Hill forward with him. They both stumble, then regain their slow shuffle. Hill has said nothing, for once. He does not look right. His back is queerly bent and his eyes are still shut. I call to him but he does not look up.

I get off the pony and walk along beside my pimply keeper, closer to my men, though they want nothing to do with me. Black Fish has retreated deep into himself. The other chiefs ride quietly ahead. The purple blanket flashes like a signal in the trees, I watch it come and go.

Pompey sits his pony with idle ease. He says:

—Walk on, Sweet Apples.

His voice and his lazy manner infuriate the younger ones, and Ben Kelly shouts:

—At home I will have you picking my apples for me. Baking my pie. I will have you for my own sweet prize black boy. Or girl, if you prefer.

Young William Brooks, whose face has thinned and hardened, makes kissing sounds. His brother Sam chuckles. Pompey gives his high laugh, a gang of pigeons flings itself into the wind.

Be empty, I tell my mind. I watch the trees: hemlock, ash, pine. No fresh blazes chopped out of them. This path is old and well-worn. We have not made any great turn yet, though we are tilting east. Some leaf buds are beginning to appear, still hard-packed. The men speak occasionally, their voices carry to me on the wind. The word *spring* strikes me like a hand in the face, as does *home*. How long before the Shawnee insist it is time to go and take the fort as promised?

Snow still lies in brittle heaps and hollows.

There are still trees with no buds at all. No green. The bare branches do not hide the sky.

The sun is pale, near lost.

Do not think of the fort. No bread by now. No corn. No salt. Only meat, if they are lucky enough to get out for any without being killed. Johnson will tell them to hold on. He will tell them that the men are alive and that we are here. That it is not all lost. That we will all be brothers and sisters with the Shawnee, ha. Johnson will tell them about us. If he gets there.

It is curiously easy not to think of Boonesborough. As if it is in a private strongbox in a past time. Lock it up. Bury it. Do not think of it. Well. It does fling its lid open into my face sometimes when it will. It does now. It blacks my eyes and dents my nose. It is an agony.

Rebecca, you are strong. You have been without me before, and plenty. You have Squire and Neddy and the old men and the boys. The girls too. Put them in boys' clothes, if there are any left to wear. Make it look as if there are more men about. Walk them about on the walls, do what you must.

Only when I think of the place, I cannot see myself there. Not on the blockhouses or at the gate or in the cabin or digging in the cursed ha-ha. I am not anywhere.

I close the lid. I nudge the pony.

A moment later a wet shot strikes the back of my shoulder. The Brooks boys have their heads lifted, the rope tugging at their necks. The guards are smirking.

—Oh, did my spittle land upon you, sir? My apologies.

—No no. He got in the way of your spitting.

Do not think. The pony keeps its head low and plods. How can it see? It has no need to see. It snaps at a flea or tick in its shoulder, its feet carry on. On his mount, Pompey lollops ahead. I slap my pony's back and loudly I say:

—Giddup, Beauty.

I aim for Pompey's tone. To myself I say: Straighten your mouth and keep it straight.

We make a camp near a small lick. Two of the warriors get a couple of deer in the trees. The smell of venison and cornbread softens the evening chill. Pompey comes over to where Kaskee and I sit eating.

—Going to call on Hair-Buyer.

Pompey says it as he finishes chewing. His tone is cordial, as if he wishes to chatter. He swallows slow, I can hear every muscle of his throat working separately, every mite of the food moving down him. He adds:

—You have not much hair left for anyone to buy, Sheltowee.

—So we are going to Detroit, then. Good of you to tell me.

He goes on chewing and swallowing. His noise interferes with my relief that we are not marching on the fort. But I do not trust Pompey. I do not trust the hard film over his eyes and whatever is behind it.

A knot of warriors laughs suddenly from down near the fire. Two of them throw and catch something. A knife. The moon is like a fingernail hooked above. Callaway and Hill and the others appear to be asleep sitting up, bound tight to one another for the night. Their heads dip and loll. The horses' bells swing and tinkle in the breeze and my scalp pricks.

—Why is Black Fish taking some of us there now?

—Perhaps he thinks you will run away from him, and then where will he be? Alone, alone again. No son.

He smiles at me and I know he wants something. As I think this, he says:

—Would you like another language lesson, Sheltowee? You have not forgotten that you owe me for the first. *Neppa, neppoa.* Do you remember the difference?

Sleeping. Dead. I do remember. This night I lie wrapped in my blanket with Kaskee next to me. Pompey sleeps not far off. I do not think that I will sleep but I must, for I dream of Hair-Buyer, that is to say the British Governor at Detroit, sitting in mounds of scalps, clouds of hair, all colours of it, fair, brown, black, grey. Crisp and dry and rustling. Hair floats and spins like straw and gold in the light. High above everyone he sits on the mountain of it as if riding a great shaggy beast. The dry skin of the scalps shifts and rustles under his great legs, white rebel scalps and enemy tribe scalps alike, some French. Any scalps. Everyone is digging up trouble for him in this land. Idly he brushes loose hairs from his face. His fingers run over the strands, they decide on quality and then flip shillings to sellers who scuttle off like beetles with the money in their mouths.

In this dream I see Governor Hamilton from every side as though I am a vapour curling through the air, as though I have no body. The Governor crooks his great fingers around a china cup, it is a blue and white one, and then he says in his puzzled British voice: *No more today?*

Black Fish steps forward with fistfuls of scalps and lays them down like flowers upon a grave. The violet-blanketed chief arrives with more. I know each one. Each hair. My men's, and the women's too. The children's.

Aha, Hamilton says with satisfaction.

My hair is not there, it is *not there*—

I wake with one hand over the top of my skull. No relief in finding my scalp still attached. My guard is asleep on his back. Pompey is half-awake and staring at me with an interested gleam in his eye. He pats his own head in its scarf and turns over when I say nothing.

Someone else is awake, one of the tied-up men. I hear my name cutting through the quiet:

—Boone.

When it comes again I rise quietly and step closer though not so close as to rouse the guards. I crouch and whisper:

—What is it?

—Can you hear me? You can.

It is Callaway. I can near feel the current of his breath, rude and stinking and sickening like his buffalo carcass left outside the fort. I think of his dogtooth with its blackening tide line. It must hurt him. I say:

—Callaway, do not start in. There is no way to get anywhere tonight. Unless you see something I do not, which I doubt. Leave it to Detroit and I will—

He gives short laugh. Then he says in his cool fashion:

—I know your promises. I know all that you are capable of. I have travelled with you quite enough to know, as my uncle did when you went chasing after my cousins and your daughter.

He coughs and rubs his arms against the rope about him with a painful chafing sound. He carries on:

—I assume that you know all that your girl did to please the Indians. My cousins told me that she seemed quite at home. Just like a wife. Or a whore. But you do know all about that. Did you have her yourself when you got her back? Is that how you consoled yourself, by making her your own flesh truly? Perhaps this is what we will have to do for you to get us out. You can see we are quite powerless before you. Will our mouths do, or must you have our persons, Boone? I have wondered.

He drops the words like a string of pearls he has had stashed in his cheek. He has been thinking over this little speech, likely for weeks. His breath is a stinking wave. I aim towards it and I break his mouth. His teeth snap rottenly. He gasps and groans, and a warrior shifts nearby. I hold myself in, but only just. Hill is awake, calling me in urgent and thick fashion:

—Dan. *Dan.* Do not hurt him. He means nothing. I know you will have us out soon enough.

His voice is small and slurring. I say:

—Hill, are you all right? Are you ill? I will have them get you something.

Callaway gives a clipped groan and says some gummy words. I will crack his mouth again and split the corners far into his cheeks, I will rip out his tongue and make jerk of it. Callaway, I would have made a Wide Mouth of you, I would have made your face just like mine, and how would you have liked that? But Hill is speaking again:

—We do not mean Jemima is a whore. Only a song, a laugh to pass the time.

I am scored through with anger, it has got right through me, or eaten its way straight out of me. My breath sears my throat:

—I will kill you if you call her by name again. She is not yours. You never had anything to do with her or Rebecca, she is mine. She is mine! Do not speak of her, you make me sick, God damn your shitty stink.

Again I strike at the dark. My fist catches something or someone. The others tied to them are moving and murmuring. Hill is trying to speak rapidly but his voice is giving out:

—Dan—I never did, did you think I did?

—Shut your mouth, Hill, before I have them kill you.

His words tumble out of him:

—Your brother had her, Dan, I heard of it when I went back, I thought you knew. I am sure he meant no harm. You were gone—

—I have heard that bastard story, thank you. Squire and I can settle our own family troubles.

The guards are up, they are coming. I hear Callaway working his mushy mouth:

—Does not know which brother, ha. Ha ha.

He sucks in a wet stringy breath and says:

—Brother Ned. Squire would not know how.

11

Like the Walls of the City of Troy

As DAWN BEGINS to break up the dark, I hear what I think I hear. My keeper hears too. At first I believe it to be Hill or perhaps Ben Kelly, who is so young. But it is Callaway rubbing at himself, trying to grind some pleasure out of this life perhaps. Well, he will have to grind hard.

He does. Kaskee turns his head in embarrassment. It is very odd. The sounds are tight, as if forced out of Callaway's great new bloody mouth. As well as lonesome and cold. He is alone but it seems to me that he has got his wish to be so. Stewing in your own irresistible juices, Callaway. He is forcing himself upon us, we can only listen. The sounds speed and then cease.

He has won. The terrible thing he has told me stands upon me like a great lead horse. Ned. Was it so?

I am visited by thoughts of Martha, pictures of doing every terrible thing with her I can think of, and things I cannot think of, I only see darkly. Getting children on her through every hole, stuffing her full of children, using her like a rag. Martha, trying to protect Ned while having her private victory over her sister. Using Squire that way, stolid Squire who bears everything like a block. Everyone wishes to keep Neddy happy. Now I see what you were about, Martha, I did not know then. I feel I have crawled up out of a hole into a weird scribbled sketch of a place I thought I knew but do not know.

It must be true. Darling Neddy, Keep-home Neddy. Wanting only happiness for himself, and to spread his to others. To offer comfort to the lonely, abandoned woman. Wanting to drown the world in sticky happiness like flies in jam. Ned, did it have to be in that fashion?

He looks so much like you: Ma's old words. Might well have been Rebecca's also. Rebecca. You protected him also, but you did tell me in your way. You said the baby was like me too.

Callaway is silent now. I burn my eyes out at him through the dark. They will crumble into ash. I know he is not a liar. He is a collector of information, like Martha. He is a liquid for mixing it in and turning it clear.

My mind roams back like a dumb ox let out of harness. It noses along the ground, chewing anything it finds, it will not stop. It sees Hill returning alone from Kentucky, blundering about looking for stories to write about me, getting a sniff of trouble before I returned. It sees the girls kidnapped, Callaway's young cousins thinking they were going to die, telling Jemima all the truth they knew about her out of concern for her soul, as I suppose. It sees her insisting she was mine. Calling me Daddy. Jemima, is this how it went, did they tell you? Or did Jonathan or Jesse, the other orphans of our house, do so? My mind sees their big eyes and open ears. They were there while I was gone. Did something slip? A visit too many from Uncle Neddy? A visit too late in the evening for travelling home again, a soft sound from the barn in the night?

Everyone knows my story. Everyone but me, as I think.

I feel myself a vacant house. I have nothing.

I hardly see anything the rest of the walk. Callaway and Hill drag along at the rear. The warriors call to them to keep up. *Napeia*, they shout to Callaway, which means rooster, for his greasy red lock of hair. Hill they call *Watchiwie*, which means hill. There are no other words for him. And no words at all for either of them in my mind.

My empty eyes gape when we reach the great wood stockade of Fort Detroit on the bare flats between two rivers. It is enormous. It is like Boonesborough ought to be, ugly and impenetrable. We stand waiting next to a little burying ground outside the wall. The red coats of the British soldiers who push open the gates are a surprise. I have forgot they were so red. I have forgot that there is a war carrying on, a war with uniforms. A war wider than the skirmishes between Boonesborough and Old Chillicothe. A war of rebellion, a war for independence from Britain. I have forgot other people are in it. The English, the French, all the various Indian tribes, the white rebels, the black slaves. White Indians, white blackhearts, who can say who is who?

The younger men are marched in, dragging their heels. Will and Sam Brooks lean back laughing. I feel only a cold wish that they were in Jamesie's place. Callaway is bowed, he covers his mouth with his hand but still I see his pale eyes land upon me. I know what that hand was doing in the night: I think this at you, Callaway. But this is no secret like the one he had for me.

The soldiers take my men off between them. Before he is swallowed up into the maze of streets behind the high pointed stockade, Hill staggers, but turns to see me again. He lifts the corners of his mouth and raises his arm. He must have talked of me during the long unbroken night in the prison house. The book of me he has been so long writing. People need tales at night. Hill, I see your raised hand still, your odd short thumb, your goodbye to me, though you do not know it.

Henry Hamilton, the British Lieutenant-Governor of the fort, is wearing a wig. Of course. Rich and shining and white. The curls bump down to his shoulders like a log road, a line of dark bristle shows above his forehead. The wig deadens his narrow face and makes it look bland as an egg, as any old egg. He stands at the window of his room with his arms crossed and his hands cupping his elbows. One pane in the grid has been stopped up with wood, but I can make out people going to and fro outside beyond the thick, blistered glass squares. I make out a woman in white going along. She has the look of a tiny puff of smoke.

Hamilton turns to me. Whose hair made that wig? Or, What did you pay for that? I want to ask. Pompey told me he pays a hundred dollars for American rebels. Nice to know how much one is worth. I could sell myself and build a better fort for me alone.

The walls of my skull bang and echo when anyone moves upon the plank floor.

—Chief Black Fish. Captain Boone. I understand it is Captain.

He is referring to the army title sent to Boonesborough for me, my ancient life. How does he know this? Perhaps he too knows everything about me already. He has a tinny and courteous sound, like an Irishman trying to sound English. The skin puffs beneath his eyes, but his voice is brisk. He does not look as though he is losing any battles.

Black Fish speaks and Pompey, after a wilted flourish, interprets in his best weary fashion:

—We have brought several white traitors from Kentucky.

—They have been taken to the guard house by now, yes? The payment will be given to you before you depart. But we will dine this evening first. I hope you will stay.

Hamilton never looks at Pompey, as if he is not here at all. His eyes travel over Black Fish's feathers and ear hoops and my shorn head. No surprise. Only a brief contracting, it is like a wince but not quite a wince. I picture him hacking his dull way through bush and mud and rebels and French with no expression, his sword in his efficient grip. I see him doing his duty to some wife somewhere in similar efficient fashion, his face unmoved. Is the wife his?

A hard smile tightens my face. I cannot stop it. Pompey is looking at me and smiling as well. In Shawnee he says to me:

—Have you any words for the Governor?

—One or two.

My stiff smile stretches my mouth further. Pompey smirks and pretends to be struck with a fit of coughing. Black Fish glances at us, his eyes all rocky sparkle again. I turn to Hamilton and I try to rein myself in. Look at Hair-Buyer. My whole body is coiled, the soles of my feet prick in the fur-stuffed moccasins, my toes curl under. Here I stand like a horse for sale. Well—he has seen all my teeth now. I close my lips.

Through Pompey, Black Fish tells the Governor that the payment for the prisoners is acceptable. His hands folded, he says:

—You will not kill them.

—No.

—You may wish to when you see the way they comport themselves.

—Not today, at any rate.

Hamilton laughs politely, a little block of laughter set off from the talk. The wig stays still atop his head, he briefly touches his hairline as if to check. Pompey and I cannot look at each other.

—Chief Black Fish, may we send the Captain out for a short time? I wish to discuss our affairs with you.

Black Fish nods without a look at me. I am nothing to him, I am nothing. A trap is opening beneath me, I am swinging lightly above it. Death is back, I know its greetings now. I greet it in return. I am relieved.

Two redcoats and Kaskee march me. A narrow corridor,

a different set of stairs. A darkness welling at the bottom. Another passage, a dogleg bend. Doors and further doors. The English guards appear to be at a brief loss until one says:

—Here.

The room is low and wide and full of boxes and barrels. The dust makes everything look ancient, like a dusty town, all built of dust. Like the fallen city of Troy, like all ruins. I have no care for where they put me. Perhaps these walls will fall in on me and my relief will be complete. To one of the guards I say:

—This will suit me fine. I had a red coat like yours once, did you know? Not so nice, though.

They say nothing. Kaskee's face is pained, his nostrils open. The English hold his arms now and shut the door. Their words click along as they walk off with him:

—Why have you still got all your hair? Why have you, eh? What tribe? What do they call you? What is your name? Your *name*?

I listen for Hill and the others, but the lock-up is nowhere near. I listen for Pompey's voice interpreting above, but I cannot hear anything. There is a high, oblong window with a grate over it. The street outside hums and crows with faraway life.

For some time I stand waiting. Death does not come. No one comes. The smell gets to me and idly I look into a few of the barrels. Sawdust. Pebbles. Earth. Powder. Ah. Half-full. A barrel half-full of fortune, a hook to drag me up again. Not your barrel, Death, is it? I run the powder through my fingers, grey and black and sandy. I smell it. If I had a flint, I would light it. I might eat it, I suppose, and see whether I go bang. I put a fistful into my pouch.

Now a click and a scrape. The British soldiers draw the door back. I stand with my blackened hands above the barrel. Guilty. I begin to smile. One holds his bayonet at the angle of a fiddle-bow, with a drooping wrist. He is freckled and looks like a young boy though with very dull eyes. He says:

—You take him up.

The other prods my arm and says:

—You come along.

We walk. Another passage, a cold wall against my arm. More

redcoats passing, mild curious faces. We come to stairs and light. Up here, says the freckled one.

He has the same accent as my Daddy, slow heavy *r*'s. From the first Exeter, in England, where Granddaddy and Daddy began. I want to ask the guard: When did you cross, did you know my family there, perhaps you were in Meeting as a child? But there is no point. There is no point in thinking so of the past, I know. It will find you soon enough.

Now at last, I will be killed. The Shawnee have not done it, and so Hair-Buyer will have it done. I said there would be no dying, Callaway, but you have never believed my promises at any rate. Perhaps I do not believe them myself.

I walk on all grim and wishing my feet an inch above the earth. Wishing I could cut my heels away from it myself.

12

The Queen of France

—You are an enterprising sort of person.

Hamilton has seen the powder dust on my hands. He has classified me, I am put in a little box. I keep my face a shell like his. An eggshell. Rotten inside, but who would know it yet?

He rubs his elbows sharply again, looking cold and irritable but trying to deny it. His face is so hard to get a grip on that I go on staring at his elbows for some time until he interrupts my dumbness:

—Your people are less so.

—Less what?

—Less enterprising.

I say nothing more. I expect him to take up his sword with a sigh and take off my head himself in his resigned fashion. But on he sits. I see Death has not finished its usual play with me. My tongue is thick and slow:

—You do not have to kill them for that.

His elbows remain tight to his body. He says:

—The families at your fort and the other Kentucky settlements are without supplies and have no hope of getting any. This is well known.

My brains have set up clanging again. I say:

—Is it well known? People always enjoy sad tales.

—Nevertheless, it is known. You know it yourself. You can be sure they would wish you to help your settlers see sense.

—What sense is that?

He pauses a moment, but now he pulls himself up as if set for a speech:

—The sense of calling a halt to these illegal inroads into my Indian allies' territory, where your people are likely to be slaughtered, if they do not insist on starving first.

—That would be sensible.

—It would indeed.

Say what people want to hear and they are content, they leave you be. For a time at least. He lets himself out as if loosening a bodice a half-inch. He walks across the room behind his table and pivots back to me. Lines run in rays around his eyes and down his face, only from a distance is it bland and bald and pinkish. Again he touches his grey hairline and says very brisk:

—The sense as well of stopping this new revolt. The King is not the only one who wants it ended. The Indians do not want you here either. They have seen the way you overrun their land and spit on our treaties with them. No settling in that area was to be permitted.

I turn over the word in my mind. Revolt, revolt. This is what they call it. I say:

—The company I worked for bought some of Kentucky from the Cherokee. Henderson made his own treaty.

Hamilton tilts back his head so I can see up into his nose. He says:

—That was not a legal government treaty. It has no force. You may be sure not all of the Cherokee wanted it. And our good Shawnee friends had nothing to do with it.

I can feel the gunpowder grains in the skin of my fingertips and palms. They warm me as if they were all alight. It seems to me that none of us cares much for any of the politicking, we only want to be left alone. To do as we like. Anyone would want this. Ha. If Pompey were still here, I would likely want to laugh again.

—Captain Boone, I will ask you outright whether you mean what you have told the Indians about taking them to your fort to lead the surrender of your people. You are clearly the person to do this safely. It is your fort. Boonesborough you call it, yes?

In the street outside a goose screeches, a child squawks after it. A flapping, beating commotion. I cannot see through the wooden square in the window. I look at Hamilton.

—I mean what I say.

—Then to Boonesborough you will go. Take Black Fish there. Convince your starving people to abandon their futile attempts at settlement. We do not want women and children killed. Do you? You have children, I think.

Straighten your mouth, stop your blood. Look like him. So I say to myself. To him I say:

—I will go. We will.

He does not let up:

—And when, I must ask, will you do so?

I shrug and look at the ceiling: no scalps hanging. A cobweb drifts in the light. I say vaguely:

—My Indian father knows. Women and children will travel easier in the spring.

—Black Fish is not an unkind man. For one, it is good of him to lend you to me for the afternoon.

Hamilton's arms clamp again to his sides and his face opens, he is near smiling. My hands are cool beneath their coat of black powder. I say:

—Not sold?

—No. He will not sell you. Not for any price I named. He says you are a good son and a good hunter and gunsmith as well. You must be very proud.

—Is that so?

—It is.

—Well then. I am proud.

Hamilton turns and looks out at the sky with its fat grey underbelly. He puts his hands behind him and says in a soft, more Irish manner:

—Rough winds do shake the darling buds of May.

More rain, more mud, more cold coming. The cold will preserve you, Rebecca, Jemima, boys, Squire. Neddy. At this time I do struggle with the thought of you being preserved, Ned, I will admit it.

Now Hill's grey eyes appear in my mind, all curious. I say:

—What are you going to do with the whites my Indian father did sell you? Sell them on?

Hamilton looks at me from the side and says, still soft:

—It is a surprisingly cold country. A cold quite different from any I have ever known. I was born in Dublin, which is wet, but here it is not the damp, it is the ice in the air. It crystallizes on the skin remarkably. I dare say you find it as hard to sleep here in winter as I do.

His carefully dull face is almost beseeching. His hands go back to his elbows. Do not fall into this small trap, this small invitation to confidences. See his long waxy fingers with their yellowy nails. See him on top of his mountain of old hair. He says almost absently:

—A strange country. People simply go off and vanish here. It happens so often. Quite odd.

Oh, is that your game, Governor? He slips two fingertips under his wig for a scratch. See regiments of vanished people marching about, changing clothes and giving themselves new names, as easy as pie. Or being hidden in vanished graves. Easier still. He goes on:

—Your daughter was returned safely to you, however. I was pleased to know of it. Her story is quite a sensation in Europe, I hear, as is her father. Paintings, books, poems about her. They do take an interest in the more romantic aspects of our wild territory. Have you seen any?

Hill, I think of your stories spreading from you like clouds and drifting across the whole of the world, infecting all of it. But you are locked away here, hidden now. I say nothing, but Hamilton sees me looking at him and his face takes on the slyness of a cat who has seen a bird but is pretending not to see it. He says:

—Here is another question for you. Tell me, is it true that you were born the same day as the Queen of France?

He gives another boxy laugh. His question is real and eager. I answer slowly:

—The Queen of France. If they say so of me, it must be true.

—Then perhaps you will be living in a glass palace soon enough. Speaking *en français*. Do you know, I can quite see it. Destiny is a capricious mistress. And why not French? You seem to have a knack for the Shawnee tongue.

The lines of his face stretch out and I am put in mind of a net hanging underwater. A snap, a tightening, and it closes again.

13

Beautiful Horse

THE QUEEN of France would eat her liver for my horse. Glossy white it is, with a waving white mane and tail. It looks like a painting of a horse, it looks quite varnished.

—Is that where Hair-Buyer got his wig from? A fine gift for Sir Turtle.

Pompey strokes the horse's mane with a slow hand. The horse rolls her eyes and dips her lashes.

—Too beautiful for me, is that right?

—That is right enough. You have everything you wish as it is. Why did he give her to you? You were no help to him.

—He wants to keep me sweet. He thinks I might change my mind.

—Will you?

—I might. Make free and jump on, Pompey. That pony of yours looks as though it suffers beneath you.

I am walking beside the tall animal. It moves like water. It is morning and we have left Detroit behind. Callaway and Hill and the rest remain, they cannot see us now, but I do not ride the beautiful horse nonetheless. At this time I cut these prisoners from my mind. I cut them out like holes in wool. I do not wish to be their saviour even if I could. This is the truth.

People vanish here. A simple recipe.

I do not wish to see them. I do not wish to think.

Here is what I have. This white horse. Gunpowder on my hands and a few dregs in my pouch. A bag of silver trade trinkets and sweets from the Governor's secretary, handed over at day- break with the message that I was to make use of them with the Indians. I said:

—They treat me well enough.

The secretary looked as if he had something else stuffed beneath his white shirt and his snappish politeness. He said:

—They refuse to sell you yet. Will you not sell yourself?

He touched his pocket gently as though by chance. And this was my chance, as I know. I might go back to the British, or act as if I had. Live at Detroit and have feather pillows and be praised all day long. Ride to Boonesborough with a column of redcoats behind. Secure a safe passage to Fort Detroit for the families, turn all of them British again. The Bryans would like it. Feather pillows for all, why not. Another new life.

But it was an impossible picture, it smelled dry and bad. It was a turning back, which I have never liked. And a recklessness had me by the neck. Hamilton had reminded me of the war going on. War makes people want to dig in and win. This is the way I explained it to myself, stupid as it is, stupid as a mallet banging on a rock.

I think of Old Chillicothe. But we do not go straight home. We accompany the other chiefs back to their winter towns first. The route is longer and muddier also. Spring.

Do not think.

Well I do not think. I get on the horse.

The violet-blanketed chief has a small village, a poor enough place in a hollow, but all of his people come out to see us arrive. They stand at the doors of their huts. The older ones look shrunken or sick, their hands tight about their ribs. A couple of the boys point at Pompey, and one makes a sign at me, his small fingers turn to small horns on his forehead.

—Your reputation precedes you.

I make no reply to Pompey. I am an empty house where sounds echo and have nothing to catch upon.

The trees sharpen before the late sky. All the village youths dance indifferently, their heads spiked with turkey and crow feathers, nodding and shuffling in a row. The women serve hominy with chunks of last year's pumpkin in it. Their faces are proud but it is the sort of proud that goes with being too poor. I wonder again about their chief's marvellous blanket, which I have never seen him without. He might sell it and feed them. I wonder what he traded for it. Perhaps a piece of this country. But perhaps it is the best thing he has ever got and he cannot give it up, the purple scrap of a dream of betterment. He tucks it about himself now with care.

I eat my plateful but I am struck with a sudden desire for grapes, or apples, or plums. Something fresh from a plant or a tree. Too early yet. But it is something to think of, a plum with a white bloom all over it, and yellow flesh inside the blue skin. And a stone at the heart, of course. Plums are well-made things. Near perfect things.

I see an orchard of plums in Kentucky, that is to say the Kentucky of my dreams, but the shreds of my old dreams do not help me. The violet-blanketed chief is smoking and talking intently with the others, a mixture of tongues. Shawnee, Cherokee, something other. I pick up a little, but I do not try much.

I sit with Kaskee, who is tossing a small stone from hand to hand. Pompey wanders over from the chiefs and says:

—They talked of you first tonight, big man. Beloved of the Governor.

—Did they? This should not surprise me, I suppose.

—Does it surprise you?

I am weary. I say:

—Need you ask? You seem to know everything about me. What am I thinking of right now? You tell me. You are the interpreter, my friend.

—I am not your friend. Do you miss your white friends? The ones Black Fish sold?

I shake my head. I set my eyes on the children dancing, and I say:

—He might have sold you.

—He did not.

He looks ruffled, he blinks long. I say:

—You must be quite special to him. Pompey, beloved of the chief.

Pompey grunts and says:

—A special possession. A curiosity. So special he will not let me go.

—And where would you go?

—Where could I go?

—Anywhere you like. I am not stopping you.

He gets up and walks off. What he is thinking I cannot tell, and I do not care. The dancers start up again as the chiefs rise from their circle.

One of the boys, quite a tall boy, is at the centre of the line now. He raises his arms stiff as planks above his head. His top teeth grip his bottom lip. He stands still. He is meant to do something but cannot do it or cannot remember it. He keeps his arms up. Then at once he lunges to the left and his ankle bends over. He topples and balls himself up. The other dancers stop. I am sorry for him, I know how he must feel. I look to Pompey, sitting across the fire, but he for one is watching me instead, considering, and tapping his knuckles on the ground as if testing ice.

The warriors go on and on about the white horse, they offer me anything in exchange. Houses, shirts, beads, wampum belts miles long, favours, wives. When we stop at the towns we are entertained and the chiefs are good to me, but the warriors keep up their teasing with serious faces. They say:

—My wife I give to you for this horse.

I say:

—No.

This does not quiet them. They laugh at my Shawnee accent and kiss the animal's neck and sigh and whistle after her: I will love you better than he does. I will love you under your tail. Name her after your daughter, Turtle, I will ride her.

Kaskee grins. I would murder them all, him too, at this time if there were some instant way to have it done.

In the morning when we set off, a pair of the warriors set into the same talk. My horse, my daughter. They whistle and hoot as they are always doing. But Black Fish turns and halts his mount. He looks back at me for the first time since we left Hamilton. Now he looks at the rest in turn and they are quiet.

The horse stalks on as if blind to mud and other horses and anything walking on two legs. She has dark, damp eyes. She drops a mass of dung without breaking her high stepping. The warriors laugh themselves sick, and she carries on without a flicker. Perhaps she is deaf truly. There is always a flaw, as it seems to me. Stewart, for a moment I see you. Your flaw also, deafness. One I would not mind having instead of all my silver and sweets, all my gifts.

For five days Pompey keeps back from me as we go on to other towns. Then he rides up on his Sweet Apples into the wood where I and Kaskee and two others have been dispatched to shoot some dinner for the night's camp. We are at the edge of a narrow clearing, readying our shot. Black Fish has given me some powder. I have not told him of the handful I took from Detroit, some of which I have sprinkled out in a little trail as we have gone. A trail to nothing in particular.

Pompey seems to be taking lessons from my horse, he is sitting his pony silent as a stone. Before long I am tired of him sitting there. I say:

—Do you know, I miss your singing just at this moment. Go on, call up some game for us. Charm us a buffalo.

The two Shawnee warriors confer and point at a stand of trees to the east. They get their rifles up and check their powder-horns. One jerks his head at me. I say:

—All right, you start.

The men go forward silent and easy, they trust me to my keeper, who is eyeing the gun. I am about to let him load the shot when Pompey reaches for my upper arm. His grip is cool but insistent. His voice is very low:

—Take the gun. Take it back.

His eyes are still, deliberately so. A trick he has learned from the Shawnee, Black Fish especially. He blinks up at the sky where the light is reaching the perfect pitch of dullness, it is evening shading into dark. Shadows mix with things. His head tilts slowly towards the darkening bushes. He unwraps his blue headscarf, his hair fades against the twilight, like his face. He says:

—Let your guard go. Tell him to go after the others. Here is another opportunity. Life seems to serve them up to you.

I keep my voice low like his. I say:

—What has you so serious? You speak heavy this evening.

—I believe I do.

Our eyes light into each other like teeth.

Kaskee has the gun, ramming the barrel and paying us no heed. We both look to him and then turn our eyes back to one another's.

Pompey speaks again, soft and deliberate, as if he is teaching me more unknown words:

—Take the gun. I believe I saw a turkey in the direction of those bushes.

He does not turn his head from me, he does not twitch. Sweet Apples browses the emerging grass intently as if not listening out of courtesy. My horse hobbled behind us seems as deaf as ever to anything but herself. I say:

—In that direction?

I point to the west where the sun is gone, leaving a bright smudge on the sky. Pompey gives the slightest nod. I say:

—Why would I wish to go there?

He says:

—You know the way to Old Chillicothe and all their winter towns now. If I were a white man who knew so much, I would do something with my knowledge. I also know the way. There is much I know.

His mouth sets. This is his offering to me, I can see. It has cost him to give it. What does he want?

In the thicket of saplings, a gun blasts and sends out rings of echo. My keeper looks to the sound. No one emerges yet. My eyes find Pompey's again, his are clear and open. He looks to the horse and the pony and I now know him to mean: *Get on the horse and we will be gone together.*

At this time, my capture in the snow with the other horse comes back to me. Fate having me try it once more, seeing what I will do this time. It strikes me that I do know where all the Shawnee towns are. And this time my horse is not loaded down. And I have a companion who knows much. I turn all this over in my mind. But Pompey's movements are not clear. His hands twist, pulling the pony's head up by the mane. The pony's eyes roll behind the hair. I say:

—Why do you wish to do this now?

He stares at the pony until it shuffles. He hisses:

—I am nothing here. A servant. They might as well take my balls, I might as well be a eunuch.

—A favourite, surely. Quite a prince. Part of the Shawnee family. Black Fish—

—You are the prince. To Black Fish, I am still a slave, doing his bidding, interpreting and singing for him when he pleases. I am no Shawnee. No warrior. They call me a bearskin.

—You are safe, you are fed. What else do you want?

At once he goes stiff and proud. He says:

—I want—what you have.

He gives a sour laugh and his eyes on me are like Hill's when we were boys, curious and determined. He comes closer and takes my arm and says:

—I have money. I buried it with my brother in Virginia. He stole it and gave it to me before the master curry-combed him with salt and pepper and hay for losing a cow, and he died. No one will ever have found it, the grave is not marked but I know where it is. It is at the end of a field. I paced it out.

My joints ache. Run now, run this time. Pompey is behaving like something in a cage bursting to get out, but to do what? His eyes are still, as if he is looking into the bottom of that grave. He says:

—It is not much, but I know where it is.

—You would dig up your dead brother?

—The Shawnee do it. I have seen it done. It is nothing.

The smell of powder residue floats back. I push my own brother Israel's face away. The Shawnee hunters call to me: Sheltowee. Sheltowee.

So far their voices are without urgency, they are talking to each other about the deer they have brought down. My young guard is sitting splayed on the ground, troubled by the shot he is trying to fit into the barrel. Ten steps and we would be invisible to him, we would be in the dark of the trees. I am twisting as if on a rope. I twist and twist and I do not know what is beneath me.

Pompey speaks again:

—You could say you were my master for the time. Until I could get myself elsewhere. It is your turn to help me, as you promised. You are free.

He shuts his mouth. But I do not loosen my grip on that rope. I have not finished. Not yet. If I run they will come after me, they and Hamilton will come for the fort and all of us, and they will not be kind.

And worse. The Shawnee will call me traitor. I cannot bear that somehow, the thought knots in my gut.

Looking Pompey dead in the eye, I speak up in a hearty manner:

—Well. Sounds as though we do not need a turkey now.

To the other hunters I call:

—Here I am.

Pompey instantly averts his face and rides away in the direction of the camp. Pompey, I am sorry, you thought I could give you some luck and another life. You could not go yourself and hope to be free. Where could you go? Free blacks have no true life, someone would have made a slave of you again. But I did not see this at the time. You bewildered me. I did not see what you were about. I did not wish to go looking for the dead and their money, I saw only myself twisting. I did not see you.

14

Father

I RIDE ALONE as we continue on to the other towns. I watch for signs on trees or the ground, but there is nothing fresh or readable. The horses and ponies and walkers churn up the damp earth. Frost ridges the outlines of the prints as the sun climbs, they look silvered in the light. I watch the lines glitter and fade as a little warmth spreads out in the air. Soon enough they are mud.

The breeze rises as we ride on, the sun is warmer. The tiredness in my bones lifts. I see a woodpecker with its feet dug into the side of a tree, and I think of throwing my little bird club when I was a boy, again and again, until I could get anything I wanted with it. I would have been glad to get this bird with its scarlet crest and its black and white body. I would have taken it to show to my brother Israel. Israel, you would have been surprised. I think of you but I do not feel you near.

The bird raps sharp at the bark. My father riding ahead turns, and his eyes pierce me through. His silver earrings sway when he stops. I am startled somewhat. When he urges the horse on again, I see Pompey cutting away from him and dropping back among the warriors.

In his anger at me, Pompey has been telling Black Fish that I mean to be off. I am near certain of it. I can feel his anger from here.

But no one comes back to truss me up. I walk the white horse for a time and no one holds me. I am slow, my guard Kaskee walks some little way ahead with the other young men. The horse steps high, the mud sucks at her feet. The dew will be heavy tonight. I keep my weight light and even to stop my tracks being too visible, an old hunting trick Israel showed me. Going along slow, I watch the light coming through the bare branches and the hard buds, a web above us. The trail curves to the left.

Round the bend, Black Fish is alone. He is off his horse, standing at the centre of the path and waiting for me to catch him up. His eyes are hard. He has let his blanket drop to his waist and his hunting shirt is open. I see a thin crooked line on his chest. I think of knives. My heart begins to speed.

—My son.

He seems to be speaking without falseness or threat, he is all calm. He waves Kaskee off. The others go on at his nod and we remain where we are. A grapevine is coiled around a tree, hard and brown with a few new shoots snailing out. He seems to admire it. He touches one of the tendrils and pulls it to see it spring back. I watch his hand, the easy return of it to himself.

The party has moved a way ahead, I can hear the murmur of talk, the horses' footfalls. We go on staring at the vine until Black Fish abruptly speaks again:

—You miss your wife? Your daughters and sons?

I think for a time. Pompey has been speaking to him, I know, and saying what?

No answer comes. My tongue clicks and feels dry and loose in my mouth. The shut box flies open in my face once more, and I see the fort and all of them there. They are like a set of knives stuck in me and pulled out again, leaving holes. But here and now they are not quite real, the way the fort has never been a real place. They have become a story. I do not know how to finish it, I cannot bear to think of them suffering, I do not know how to save them from it and from you, Father. I do not want them to be here. I want to be here.

Such are my tangled thoughts, but I do not try to untangle them for his benefit. I say only:

—We will see them soon.

A good response, surely. Safe.

Now Black Fish is quiet. His eyes inspect every inch of the tree bark. My gut rumbles and he points his finger at my belly:

—Do we not feed you well here?

He looks quite sincere, I might say concerned. My throat is rough as I say:

—You feed me fine. And I hope my hunting satisfies you, Father.

—You know you are a fine hunter.

—I know I am.

I am struck with the sense that he does know me, and that we do not have to play the old false game. A bird rustles in the dead vine growth up the tree. Black Fish puts his hand on my neck. I feel the fingers before they reach me. He takes them away and says softly:

—They may have hanged your men by now at Detroit. This is what they do, no matter what they say. They have no use for such prisoners as those.

My eyes want to dart off from his. Keep them still. Keep your mouth still. But I cannot. Instead I blink and look for the bird. I say:

—I know.

I did not know, though, did I? I did not know that this was why we were going to Detroit. Behind my lids I see Callaway's neck, burned further and stretched, his angry face purple, his eyes cast with blood and bulging. Hill's neck, his voice all gone, his curious eyes dull as a pond. The others all hanging like terrible dolls. Will and Sam Brooks. Ben Kelly. The young men. All of you, I am sorry. I am sorry now.

—Sheltowee, did you wish it so?

I did wish them all dead at one time or another. My Fate seems to have twisted and pulled at her weaving to bring it about for me. Black Fish's eyes are so tender that I have the curious feeling that he is not speaking to me, but to his dead son. And as his dead son, in a dead skin, I reply:

—It had to be so. Father.

—We took them to Detroit. You brought them to us first. This is what you think. But the way they were is not your doing.

—I know it.

My voice comes in taps like a hammer on thin metal. Black Fish is still speaking softly. He says:

—The men talk always of your daughter, your wife.

I tighten my lips. This has the feel of a sly stab with a dull old knife. I stab back:

—They *talked* of them. Before they were dead. Which they now are. You could have burned them yourself. Saved us all a trip.

My father now takes the vine in his hand. He says:

—This is good for hanging. Very strong.

—You would know that, I suppose. Being who you are.

My blood is rushing, my stomach lets out a moan. Callaway makes a queer noise deep in my skull and Hill calls up: *Dan, Dan.* Now Black Fish is close, I can see each of his lashes around his black eyes and the dark shadow beneath the skin of his jaw where his hair is coming. He has almost no smell, it is so peculiar that I find myself sniffing without thinking. He says:

—Your daughter, the one they say is a whore. I know of her.

—Everyone knows that story.

I speak sharp, thinking of Delilah saying the same thing back in Old Chillicothe. The kidnap, the rescue. Why can this not be buried, as the bodies at Detroit must be by now, buried in unmarked graves, bundled up with other bones to be lost? Why must it be paraded about like a severed head? But Black Fish lifts his hand and goes on:

—You took her back from our people. We would have kept her as we keep you.

He is rolling his neck, the looseness of the movement is not like him. His face has gone slack.

—I took her back. Of course.

I have to calm the pitching and flaring inside my body. I exhale hard and I see Black Fish blink, a ripple passing over his face like a breeze over a lake. I saw the same ripple when I first went into his house as his son, the same wave rolling over and vanishing. I keep myself still until I am able to say:

—Father, she belonged with her family then. But we will all be one family, will we not? Is that not our intention? You will be able to see her when we go to the white fort.

My knuckle joints all ache, my ankle aches, all my old pains. Black Fish grabs at my cheeks and pushes his forehead hard against mine. His skull grinds on me, I feel his nose brushing and butting mine, I feel him suck in a breath. Now at once he turns, he is walking. His back is to me as he goes. The others are out of sight and hearing. I do not run, I go on standing. He stops and looks back at me to say:

—I have daughters.

—I know your little girls.

—They are what is left to me.

I want to stop him talking now, his voice has gone all glassy, with nothing to catch at. He has begun to speak in soft English and I am surprised by it. I say back:

—You have me. Is that not what you wanted also?

I grin without thinking, all teeth. But he has turned back, he is walking on. I shout:

—You had a son.

His blanket trails along in the soft mud, looking royal for all that. I shout harder:

—I had a son. Brothers of yours took him.

He turns, he is in the centre of the path beneath an arch of trees, he is so still, looking out over the woods, surveying his country. His blanket falls gently about him, his hands fold over each other beneath it. I walk towards him, I have no choice. He pulls me in and down like a deep well. Tears are all down my face. He says:

—You have sons still. You are what I have left.

I can see him breathing, his chest rising and falling, light and slow. He is controlling it. His eyes open like traps, the bottoms drop out of them, they are only black. He says:

—Your people killed my son when you rescued your girl. Perhaps it was you who killed him, ha? My son.

My head seems to crack like a shell, a rush of air and light blast in. I see the Shawnee I shot, fallen into the campfire, rolling in the flame and going still. His hair sparking and crackling, his face down. His thin torso, a splash of paint on skin, fingermarks visible in it. And then I forgot it. Jemima running towards me, her face open, *Daddy, Daddy*—

Now he has turned again, he is walking on. His voice has lightened. I catch it as it glides ahead:

—In war, you kill me, I kill you. We all make our trades. All right?

15

We Are Too White

THE BEAUTIFUL HORSE talks in her sleep. In my sleep. She pulls back her grey lips and says through her ivory teeth: *We might go, the both of us. We are too white.*

Her voice is a horsey whisper, her breath smells of old bark and roots and leaves.

When I wake the horse is still there with the others, hobbled and glowing in the dark. Her head is low like those of the warriors keeping watch, they are nodding by the fire now with their elbows propped on their knees. Outside the glow are dark humps under blankets and furs. The dew is rising already. The damp cushions footsteps and movement.

Pompey sleeps by himself, away from the fire. Black Fish is across the camp with the chiefs. Perhaps he is awake too, with his face beneath his blanket as always, imagining his own murdered boy, trying to sink into the grave with him. I saw his eyes before he snapped them back into blankness. Just before he told me, I knew what had happened to him, I saw that he was eaten inside as though ants had found a way in and left nothing behind. Well. There is always a settling somewhere, as I have found. And always I will be full of a burning shame, my Father, like a house on fire for ever. So much have we lost. What a ruin we have made, or I have made.

The night is very still. The camp feels like a field after battle, the quiet shot through with rough echoes. Though we are the same in our ruin, I feel myself sundered from Black Fish and I am sorry for it. I feel myself sundered from everyone.

Jamesie. Or do you have a different name now, do you not recognize the old? I wonder.

For the first time in months I allow myself to speak to him, though only in my mind. I ask him greedy things, I ask: Where are you? Tell me. What ought I to do with myself now? Will I end like you? Do I have a choice about it? Are you all right now? Where are you?

I await a sign. I await something clear, I feel smothered in fur. I groan, and the white horse whinnies suddenly and breaks wind. Well, this gives the feel of a sign, so desperate am I for one. I pull myself up to a crouch, though my thigh muscles protest. My old hurt bones begin to throb at once. My whole body is struggling to move and get itself to life, it seems to me here in the dark. Thinking of my boy, I have gone back to being half-dead as I was when I first arrived.

Keeping my blanket about me I stand and take two short steps, as if I am hobbled myself. My legs will not loosen. I tell myself that I have escaped before, I did so with Stewart and it was easy enough.

I stop and listen again, my feet bare and cold on the dirt. Stewart's corpse seems to club me over the head like a ninepin, or like an elephant bone: *Get out.* And I begin to see things. O you murdered dead are all about this night, you are all here to tell me the same thing, are you? Telling me to go. Or to join you. If I knew what it was, I might consider doing it.

The air has a populous and whispery feel to it. Hanging bodies sway among the branches, if I look. Do not look. The dead keep their flesh, I have learned, you can see them as they were, only they are cold and dense, like wet sponges. Israel's face in the dark, Jezebel breathing. I turn my face but here inside a tree that leans towards me is another: Stewart again. Stewart, you always looked at me that way. As though I were a signpost waiting for someone to come and read it. As though some great answer were there, if you only had the time to spell it out. Even your skull with its sockets all hollow looked at me out of that tree your bones were stuffed into.

I have no answer. I never have had it, though others have thought I had. Dogs with another dog, Captain Will said. Thinking they might get something from me. I have nothing for anyone, I bring only disaster.

I banish the dead, that is to say I try to do so. My head swims and rolls. The soles of my feet ache. I dig my toes in as if I were in a swamp and seeking the bottom. I will go. I will take the horse and I will go.

I step forward on my sore legs, making ready to reach for the reins. I find that I have to think over each part of the movement. Here is how you lift your hand. Here is how you open your fingers. Here is how you breathe, do not do it so hard.

Gently I cut between two trees, holding my stiff body as still as I can. My mind sends out a few half-hearted arguments: No gun, no food, no knife, no shoes, you ape. My hand slips into my pouch. Some powder remains at the bottom, I pinch for the grains. No shot, you greater ape. And no gun, have you forgot?

Needles make a slippery fallen skirt about my ankles. The clouds pass and split about the moon, the horse glows. Its head bobs gently. Its breath is warm, I know, I can near feel it. I move again and my feet swish over the needles before I step onto harder earth. I breathe high in my chest. I reach for the bridle, I have it. My nose is against the white shoulder. And now the face I see is clear. It is Pompey's. Black with bright living eyes. They flare up with hope for an instant and then cool like coals. His mouth opens tall as if to begin singing: *I see what you were going to do, you were going to run. And without me. I see clear through you.*

16

What I Am in Old Chillicothe

EACH MORNING I expect to wake in my dream Kentucky, my Heaven. I expect a smell of dry winter cane going softly rotten, and fresh shoots coming through. But there is none.

My Shawnee mother and sisters watched us march in when we returned, after Pompey caught me thinking to run. My eye lit on them first as they stood with the other women along the street. My mother's eyes were brimming as usual but the tears did not drop down her cheeks. I saw her looking at Black Fish and the superior types who rode in first on their best mounts, far from me. The other Shawnee, all painted up, paraded the gifts of Hamilton and the other chiefs. Silver, powder, plate, linen, wool, shirts, blankets skins, furs. Things. The faces were approving.

A thin rain fell, a spring rain, setting drops like shining seeds on the presents. It fell on me also but only made me damp. Here I was, the draggled tail of the proud return. When the treasures had passed along I felt all the other eyes turn to me. The white faces of my remaining men were startling. They stood with their families. They did not nod. I was tied to two tall fighters, I was white and unpainted, coated in dust and mud, bare and miserable as a bone.

—Hello ladies. Pleasure to see you again.

My voice was weak enough but I hoped that they would laugh

so I might laugh. Some of the women smiled into their palms. Some kept their faces still. But the door between us had shut again. My mother kept her wet eyes away from me after one look. My little sisters appeared older already, thinned out and thin-lipped.

—Girls.

The elder made a wary face. Pompey was behind me, the last of all, keeping an eye on me, as he put it. He was carrying a wolf pup in one arm. It was my wolf pup to start with, it came to me out of the night where I was tied at our last camp, it burrowed straight under my blanket and nosed up to my side as if it belonged there. But nothing is mine anymore.

Pompey leaned over and set the pup down. Sweet Apples tossed its thick tail about. The small wolf splayed its legs and raised its face. Pimmepessy, my littler sister, took it up as if snatching a scrap of food from a trap. She and the prim-faced Miss Hiss made off into the wigwam with the animal. It did not even let out one of its customary howls. It did not try to bite me, it did not turn its head in my direction. It pricked up its ears and was gone. Pompey kept up his bored expression but was glad I had lost it, as I knew well enough. He wished to see me brought to nothing.

The guards were taking me away from the rest now up the street to the prison set off from the big house. I saw Delilah then, looking away down the road as if there were someone yet to come. A cloud passed overhead and lightened her eyes. For the first time I noticed an old scar on her cheek, a small pitting, like pox come and gone. As I went by her I said:

—I am the last. No one else.

—No one else.

She spoke in English and pressed her lips together as all of the women and girls seemed to be doing. She turned away. Then the sharp-faced child appeared from behind her hip, looking straight up at me:

—Here I am.

They are not supposed to speak to me, as I can see. But the girl's clear little voice gave me a smile. She was still the same. I thought of you, Jemima, still the same. For so long I wanted not to think of you and the rest. Now you are all I can think of.

It is spring now, there is no denying the damned corn shooting up in the fields and the river opening. I saw it before they locked me in. They will keep me in here until it is warm enough to march. Then I will see you all there, I will see your faces light with surprise and then fall with disappointment at what I have done, just as the faces here did when we marched back into the town. I will not have saved anything. Still, you are a comfort to me in my prison, though I keep you a little distance off like a blanket on a warm night.

The prison hut has room enough for Callaway and Hill and the rest to congregate and haunt me further. My first night here, they beat me to death in my mind. The Indian man I killed as he sat fishing so long ago stares at me all curious, Jezebel's breath cools me.

I feel compelled to defend myself. I tell them I tried to do right. There was no other way. But I feel mean and sick as I think it. The next night I wait, my whole body waits, my teeth grit against each other. I chip a piece from one, and the part left behind is pointed and jabs at my tongue every chance it gets. But the dead do not turn up again to listen to further sorry remarks.

I sleep a short while, not a deep sleep.

—A dozen deer. Three buffalo. Jellies, your favourite drinks, any innards you fancy.

The singsong voice snags me in the dusk of this windowless house. It is outside the door. I make myself answer:

—Could be reckoned excessive.

The voice says:

—We wish to keep talking of our victorious journey to Detroit, so we let our food grow cold. There is always more. We have more meat cooked and start our dinner fresh. A simple idea, but clever also, do you not think?

—You might have brought me some. Cold or no.

—They will feed you eventually. Perhaps. Did they say they would?

—Pompey, nobody says much to me now. Thanks to you.

Pompey cannot seem to keep himself away. His face is close to the chink in the logs. I can hear him breathe in and place his lips to the crack.

—Your trouble, Sheltowee, is that you do not understand it here.

A burst of laughter pops from the big house like a bubble of sap in a fire. Pompey laughs too. Then he says:

—They are sincere. They tell the truth. You think they are lying or dissembling, you think everything has another meaning or is part of a game. But they mean what they say. They believed in your Pekula's madness because you said he was mad. And when they start over, they start over. It is a good weapon. They told you they would not hurt you, a head man like you. They told you that you might do as you like. They made you their son and they believe you to be their son, but you did not believe it. You said you would stay and then you made to leave. You are not to be trusted.

—Am I not?

I am curiously sad at this thought. I stretch my arms behind my head and open my chest to the dark room.

—No.

—You were the one who wanted me to leave.

—You think so.

I wait to be left alone again in all my badness but Pompey is still breathing there. A curl of tobacco rises. Old Bryan rises too like another spectre, shaking fistfuls of money, his money wasted on me, his debtor for ever. Bryan, are you dead now as well? I have been here for months, and you were so old.

—You do not trust me alone even in here, I see, Pompey.

—Would I ever have put my trust in you?

I hear him spit and strike a flint. He says:

—White Indian.

—Black Indian.

I feel the way a rat must feel when between the teeth of a dog, twisting its spine to squeal and make the dog listen though its rat language cannot be understood. I shift myself closer to the wall where Pompey is. I say:

—You are a black Indian. If not a very good one. I am not wrong. I can tell the truth also, if pressed. You had no wish to remain with them in the clearing on that evening, making eyes at me and my horse. Do you not remember it? I do.

A shuffle, a loud puff. He is standing. He says:

—White Indian is right enough. All you whites think you are born clever enough to see through anything. Can you see through this wall?

At once he begins to sing one of his Shawnee tunes. Over his voice I call:

—You belong to them. Or you would like to.

He cuts off the song:

—I could say the same to you.

—Why did you want to go, then? Why did you want to go with me? And afterwards, why did you go telling my father that I was trying to leave him?

—Were you going to leave, Sheltowee? All alone?

A heavy silence thumps down. I do not answer. His disappointment in me is like a thick fast fog, I feel it spread through the chinks in the walls. Even the feast sounds have receded. Perhaps everyone there is neck-deep in one of the roast deer or buffalo. Then Pompey says low:

—There are plans for you.

—So I can judge. Will you tell me their plans for my fort? If it is still there.

—Perhaps you will not be in prison for ever. I will not leave *you* all alone here. We think of your comfort. We are your brothers in this land.

Even his willow tobacco has an offended smell. I hear the way he is choosing his words. He is knitting himself to them with that *we*. He is trying to deepen the hole he is caught in here, make it more fast, make it his own. Well Pompey, you and I might have been brigands together, running through Kentucky, taking what we liked, selling our knowledge of the Shawnee to the highest bidder. Then cutting it up, twisting it about, and selling it again. Getting the Indians cleared out, opening up the land, selling it too, like Hill. Richer and richer. Did you see us that way?

—We will see to it that you wish to stay.

He speaks in Shawnee now, a tight formal version. Then he is gone, and sounds from the big house come again, and women's voices make a haze of words that I cannot understand, and it is night again.

I am not crazed yet. Not at this time.

The door opens with a scrape. The prison hut has been built in white style like a log cabin and the door is made of logs lashed together upright. The light angles in, I get to my feet.

Delilah, carrying water and a plate of food. She tilts her face up at me as she bends to place them on the ground.

—How do. You are not the usual turnkey.

She gestures towards the food. I say:

—From last night's feast? The remains of the twelve deer, the three buffalo?

She is turning, but before she is out the door again, I say:

—Did my father send you specially?

She points to the plate again and says:

—It was good food.

—It *was*? That does not bode well for me.

—It was. Last night.

—But no longer.

A smile spreads up her face and then drifts off.

—Try.

I take up a strip of meat and sniff it and chew a bite. It is cold and tough and sinewy. I mime choking on it but she is not persuaded. Feeling quite a fool, I swallow it down in a lump and I say:

—Thank you for the provisions.

—From your father.

—Is that so. Well, and will my father be visiting me himself?

She shakes her head and says:

—He is occupied.

—Ah. I have heard of his planning. Though not what it tends towards.

Her quick hand touches the side of my head where my hair is growing back. No longer a warrior, most likely. Her hand is curious and, I think, pitying. It draws away quick. At once I am struck by a wish to tell her about Jamesie, about the feel of his head under my palm when he was new. But I put my hand on my own skull and I say:

—Always soft-headed, some have said.

She is going, but from behind the door she says:

—You are still his son. He will not be cruel.

17

Meat

I SAVE SOME of the meat and some of the water, for who can tell when I will have more? I find that I am not so ready to die. Or not to starve to death at any rate.

No further food this day or the next.

I think of Delilah for a time, I even call to her once, but I hear only the usual coming and going in the town. The light through the walls deepens its colour and so I know that dark is coming on again. I sing a little tune:

For the want of a nail, the shoe was lost,

For the want of a gun—

Will anyone answer? No. But I have always liked to sing when alone. When I was a boy in Pennsylvania, it kept others from me sometimes. If I sang wildly enough in the woods the other boys would snort and lob a rock or two but leave me alone. But if I tried to sing sweet like Neddy and sounded as though I were trying, they would crash out of the bushes and call me an arse and we would fight. Toadmouth. Arseholemouth. Well, Hill, you were with them sometimes, I have not forgotten it.

I think about what Pompey said, that the Shawnee are straight in their meaning, that it is a good weapon. That the rest of us are the ones making a virtue of deceit, pawing through everything as if it were a great trunk with a false bottom, the real treasure hidden away. Perhaps that is true enough.

I eat another strip of the cold venison. Chewing it is work. I rummage in my pouch. They have left me a few of Hamilton's silver trinkets and sweets. A dented ring, a single earbob, a few thin coins. I feel for the King's profile. Sir! Would you have me back in your army?

I flip them over my knuckles until they fall and I have to feel about to find them again.

An odd wish strikes me, a peculiar taste for sugar, perhaps to cover the taste of the old meat. I am not generally one for sweets, but now my teeth ache for it down to the roots as if I were really a boy again. I find one boiled English candy from Hamilton's secretary among my few belongings. What became of the rest I do not know. There must be mice about. I must be sleeping hard at night, harder than I believe. This thought unnerves me. I open my eyes until the lids feel pinned back. It is near dark now. I crunch the sweet. Shadows cross the dirt floor and stay there.

When Hill and Callaway were in this house and went quiet, I thought it was as if they had gone beneath the ground. I was outside then. But now it seems to me that this whole place is a fairyland, the place under the hill where the unwary stay for thousands of years once they stray in. Where people disappear to. Rebecca's stories, and Ma's. Hamilton's too, for all that. A ring of toadstools by the light of a full moon, a little door under a tree root, a drugged drink, and you are gone. Gone. Perhaps the fairies have added meat-packed horses to their list of tricks to get people here.

To myself I say: They are keeping you alive. You are alive, you must be. You are still here.

I am heavy-headed. My limbs fall about and I sweat. I open my eyes wider until they dry out and pain me. I think again of being a child. Indeed I feel that I am a child, I can see through my old childish eyes. Some girls in the town ate mushrooms in the woods all unknowing that they were deadly. One little girl from Meeting, Lucy was her name, Lucy Black, the sister of Molly, my little first wife. She survived the summer fever but not this. Her coffin was among the others being carried to the burying ground on a hot summer morning. I had been watching pigeons strutting along a fence as if to show what they could do. But the wooden coffin wobbled on the men's shoulders. I saw it, I must have. I saw a boot dangling from it, I saw the black leather cracked over the toe, a button loose and dangling too. But how can I have seen that?

Things get into the head somehow.

Do not sleep. I close my mind to the idea. There is no sleep. Sing again, keep yourself awake, wake everyone else. Take a breath.

I sing a mumble with no words. It is not Shawnee. It is nothing.

A low answer arises from outside the door. The surface of my brains is covered in cracks, like dried mud. I try to speak. Slowly I manage to say:

—Pompey.

I am filled with relief. But the silence hisses around me. I try again:

—Taking the air?

Still no reply. Pompey wishes to frighten me. I say:

—I would be happy to receive you, had I the power to open the—

My tongue is too thick and dry to finish. The water is gone. When? I have Hamilton's silver ring gripped in my fist. I stumble and bang against the door. Now comes a whisper, a single word, but what? I cannot understand it.

—What? What did you say?

I am desperate for it now, even for Pompey's taunting, but there is nothing more. I think on it for hours or days, I do not know which. My mind reaches for it, it stretches itself beyond its powers. I think the word is *go*. Or *gone*. Or some other word I cannot reach.

I eat again. I do not know what it is that I eat, meat or metal or earth. It is still dark, my throat is rough as hot sand. Daddy's anvil pounds unevenly in my skull, clang clang clang. A little red Daddy banging away. I am very little and my bed is hard and hot. I think of my sister Bets and my little brothers Neddy and Squire. I think we are very sick together.

A slow thought wraps itself about me. A slow word takes time to spell itself out. My finger is tracing the letters, trying to catch them in the air. My finger is bewildered. I concentrate until my head aches further. I can never finish the word, it never finishes.

P-O-I-S

P-O-I-S

P-O-I-S-O

This is what it says. It does not finish. I am busy down a deep hole, I am clay. My moving finger is drying clay, it is going stiff. I am dry. I will crack right through. What is inside?

Straw stuffing.

There is nothing else here, I am so low in the hole. Nothing to see or hear. But I am listening. My eyes are open in the clay of my face. My tongue hurts all the way along. I keep very still but my bones vibrate and clack, the dark muffles the noise. But there was a word, a word in the dark. My mouth reaches back for it and tries for the sound. It comes up with Guh. Guh. What was it? Gone. Possibly so.

All moves backward now, there is no forward. A smell of wolf. Wolf's stomach. This is where I am again, then. I sigh and sink and the stinking wolf stomach cradles me in pieces. And I am so glad.

But the word will not let me be.

I flap my baby wings a little, this is the way my arms feel, weak as a new chicken's wings fresh out of the egg. They hurt to move, they hurt to unbend. I am trying to pull myself up out of the wolf's gut and its gullet, out of its throat and over its lolling tongue. The smell is sharper here, and the gate of the teeth is sharp.

I am crawling across the dirt floor looking for water. The sound of my legs dragging is a harsh sound.

I have kept it off, but I cannot here this night. Now it comes, it screams up: *Jamesie.* I cannot see him. He is down inside the wolf. He hides his face in the dark with his torn arm. I cannot see him. He will not speak to me, and my heart drains inside me.

In his place another shrills out of the black, it is Jemima. *Daddy, Daddy!*—Her face is white inside her curtains of black hair, her eyes burn as she shrieks. *I knew you were coming.* Her mouth is open, shrieking, black, empty. Seeing her face, I stand stock still and I am afraid. My famous daughter's face, my poor girl. It retreats suddenly, leaving only a pale print on the dark, as my brother Israel's did. My ghosts.

The thought strikes me as it must. I have been trying to run from it but here it is in my face: Jemima, dead like Jamesie and like Israel, having joined the dim ranks that I can only try to reach. Is she? Are you? Jemima. Is the fort gone? I have sometimes wished it to be. Everyone gone with it. All burned, all turned to ash and air, floated away in all directions. Everything gone.

Rebecca, are you living, and my girls and my boys? I cannot read you, I cannot read. Now I see Israel standing with his arm out and covered in sitting birds, which give me directions, but their language is sly nonsense, their eyes are beady lies. The face of Israel's lovely dead wife flashes at me and is gone. These signs mean nothing to me. When she was teaching me to read and write better, I felt like this, like being blind and cursing my state every minute of my life.

And at once I do see it, all the signs snapping and locking into sense, all thick black lettering: *Everything is gone.* They are all gone, all dead together. Their faces drifting off. My heart aches and aches, it is stripped clean and robbed. For a moment I believe that now I will catch my boy among these dead, I will see him, see a brilliant picture of his face, even for an instant.

I drag myself along, only myself.

At the door is a shadow deeper than the others. I know it is Death. It has a shape, a face, a mouth. A long face, a smiling mouth. It opens the mouth, it can talk. Death has his face, of course. His hollow eye sockets and cheeks and smile. I gasp the name: Cherokee Jim.

I want to weep. I have kept it away for so long, though it has always been with me. The long sad face. I stare at it and I say: Why? Why did you kill him that way? You could have adopted him as Black Fish did with me. He was a good son, he was better than I am. You did not have to use him as a sign to the rest of us, you did not have to make such a poor piece of writing paper of him. *Keep Off.*

I expect to be dead in a moment, if I am not already. The short hairs on the sides of my head are up on end, my whole skin is screaming. I am alive. The pain smashes me. I stagger to my screaming feet and with all my breath I say: Cherokee Jim. Big Jim. I know Jamesie said it also. It is the wrong name, it is a false name, but what else is there to say?

The face can talk but it chooses not to. It has the same old easy manner it always did, the ease of ownership and certainty, like Hill's and Russell's. Stupidly I hold out the silver ring to it, the dented trinket. I feel it wanting to laugh. I know that I will get no answer. Answers do not come when you wish for them. They come later in curious forms you do not recognize.

Now I only want him to be gone. I raise my arm, I will chop him down like a tree. I cannot look at him, I am sobbing, I have no breath. But he will not go. He puts a hand on my arm and presses me back to the ground. He crouches beside me where I lie, he touches my head. It is a gentle enough touch. He says: *I told you to stay where you were. You did not listen. You kill me, I kill you. We make our trades.*

Or perhaps he does not say any of it, perhaps this is what I imagine he would say. I do hear other words, they tunnel down into my bristling head:

—What is your dream?

18

Sheltowee

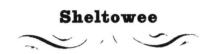

A BLADE is moving above my face.

I am awake and not dead. When I shift myself, I expect my body to ache as it would after a fight, but it does not. My head is clear and still attached. The ring is still in my hand. I rub my jaw and it is oddly smooth.

Delilah draws the knife over my cheekbone towards my eye. It catches and rasps and I feel a small cut opening. Then up and over my skull it goes. I can feel the short hairs lifting and being cut away. For some time I listen, I turn my head with her hand when she pushes it. The knife scrapes gently over and over.

—Did you poison me?

She is dipping the knife, it clanks dully against the wooden bowl of water.

—Did you come and ask what I was dreaming? It is not your affair.

The knife rolls. Still she says nothing.

—Ha. I will tell you in any case. I saw Death, if that was your intention.

My head lightens further. I am exhausted and cleaned out. I have seen Death's face at last. I saw what Jamesie saw. This is what I have wanted. I have seen the very worst thing. I have seen that the rest must be gone. Rebecca, Jemima, all of you boys, all of you. My bones have turned into birds' bones, all hollow and light. I have a curious feeling of having been rescued, though I am still in the prison house. It is very curious.

—Delilah. Did my father order it? If he is still my father, that is to say. Or Pompey?

Her arms are still for a moment. I have the sense that it was all her doing. She says:

—I told you the meat was from the day before. Maybe you needed to be poisoned, to see such a thing.

She gets to her feet. She opens the door. I see the little girl watching in the gap. She steps in and presses a finger over the nick on my cheekbone. Then she looks at the blood printed on her fingertip. Holding it high she leaves. For a moment the door is open. The air is fresh and warm and the sky is paler as though it is a different place, a different year.

My mother's eyes are full of tears again. She is still my mother. She will not touch me but she cannot keep from looking at me and calling me son, *Niequeetha,* and something else related to eggs. Fresh Egg perhaps, or Egg Head. She does not call me Sheltowee. But she is trying.

My young sisters skulk outside in the twilight, peering through the bark in their old way and hoping for something interesting. There is no sign of the wolf pup, perhaps they have done away with it.

The pot over the fire is smoking. My mother's tears travel in lines down the sides of her nose. I say:

—May I help you, Mother?

She smiles and blinks, more tears spill. She pulls herself up. She speaks to me soft as if I were her true son whom she has known all along:

—No woman's work. You say this always.

—Where is my father?

She looks at me intently. Her eyes cross my face and double back again. She says:

—My son. You are sad tonight.

—Well Mother, you have found me out.

—Why?

I bow from the waist, I rub the side of my bare head. I say:

—I do not know. Perhaps the moon. Perhaps I am getting old. An old turtle—

She cuts in:

—You think of your whites. Your white family. Children and wife.

I am surprised. The cooking pot is overflowing with smoke, but she makes no move to stir it even when an evil bubble erupts from it. She only looks upward. There is the moon hanging over the hole, I see it too, a pale fruit hazy in the smoke. She weeps for a few moments, she wipes her forearm across her eyes. She breathes tears. I wish I had some helpful thing to say, any words.

She clears her throat and coughs out a clog. She takes up her spoon and says heavy as if she is tired of saying it:

—My son. When you bring them to live with us, they will be your family also.

—They are gone now. Gone.

I know it as I say it.

The dinner is so burnt there is no hope for it.

The guard Kaskee, with a crop of fresh pimples, smiles straight in my face. I sit up and crack my forehead on his jaw. He yelps and flails backwards and makes to hit me but I catch his wrist and I try to laugh:

—Back again, my old friend. Life rolls along.

I am glad to see him. The wigwam is otherwise empty. No Black Fish. I have not seen him since they let me out.

The young guard looks at me, a mixture of murder and resignation. He pulls me towards the door. My forehead stings somewhat, which is no consolation to him, as I can see.

We walk up the street. A few boys are about, kicking a leather ball against a house and chasing an elderly dog back and forth with sticks. The dog throws itself down wheezing in the middle of the street. We step over it. The children scatter and group again and follow us like mayflies.

Before we reach the river, I see the two figures side-by-side. They look like preachers set to outdo one another. Or like judges. Their faces are bland as judges' faces. They say: *You will have to guess what I can do with you.* At once I am struck with a thought of my piles of debts behind me, my bankruptcies, magistrates I have stood looking up at.

It is Pompey with Black Fish. Seeing my father for the first time now, I am relieved. They are waiting for me. The guard walks me down towards them. The river is fuller now, moving quickly and rolling over in places, the sun flashing on it. A broken log is jammed against rocks, its inside shows yellow and torn. I think of that old dog lying in the street wheezing. The children have gone, perhaps they have returned to kick it and make it move off and kick it again.

Black Fish is keeping himself to himself. He nods once. It appears that I have been forgiven. He looks set to make the best of what he has left. I understand this. I say:

—My father.

He looks at me so that I want to weep again but I dry myself out, I turn to Pompey and I say:

—Pleasant to meet you here as well. Out for a stroll?

My words fall flat. Pompey hums, he looks up at the birds crossing the sky. No purpose is obvious here. But I will say that I am glad to see them both.

Up the stream a short way, a horse is tied to a thin elm. It is splashing its nose in and out of the river. It is a paint, with a blotch spreading round one eye. In it the eye looks astounded.

—A gift for you, Sheltowee.

Pompey is watching me. I say:

—Indeed?

—Yes.

—I am lucky in horse gifts.

I think of the beautiful white mare from Hamilton, no longer mine, shifted off elsewhere. So many people and animals and things shifting about, bought and sold and traded, this country is full of their tracks. And do not wonder where they get to. There will be no answers, you ape.

Pompey holds out his hand. Black Fish is still. I walk down towards the paint horse. Its spots make it look as if it is trying to hide in the trees. Guilty horse. So calm am I now that I do not imagine the burned fort when I say:

—We are off on another journey, then.

Pompey laughs high and Black Fish echoes him, adding something in quick Shawnee. So surprised am I that I laugh too. Pompey says:

—Not yet. You will have to stay here for some time. Bridegrooms generally like to keep at home.

Keep-home Neddy, darling Neddy. I cannot help but think it. It is like a stone in the body, growing more and more until its pain cannot be stopped. I ought to have kept home more. But now there is none. And I cannot imagine facing Neddy now.

Rebecca, a gentle thought comes of you in the bed on our wedding night, your hair all outspread, before any of this. And in our first cabin on your grandfather's land in Carolina when you felt safe. Queen of the Backwoods. You would hate it here, even more than you hated the fort. One morning there I heard you outside, you said to Martha that you wanted to fall on the path to the spring and never get back up. You said: But I have no choice. How old do I look? You laughed for a moment and touched your neck, I saw you. I knew you were crippled up inside with homesickness and suffering. You went along for me. You were trying to make up for Neddy, for Jemima, for everything.

Black Fish's eyes scan my face. They open wider when he says soft:

—Happiness will keep you here. You will be happy, you are my son.

Pompey translates in his slow measure but I have understood already. He is thinking: If I stay, you stay. I can see that Black Fish's sentimental vein has opened. And I find myself not unhappy.

On my wedding day, the ceremony is quick enough. Black Fish presides and joins our hands and wraps them together in a bright calico cloth. My mother weeps through it. My little sisters stand at the front and look crafty. Delilah's little girl is watchful. I cannot see Delilah's face. My poisoner, my barber, that is to say my barberess. I might have known that we were intended for one another. I hand her a deer's hoof when prompted, but I do not look. For a moment I think of you again, Rebecca, of dragging that dead deer to you when I was courting you. But quickly this thought slides away. Pompey passes the hoof to me and tells me very loud what to do.

He says her name is now Methoataske. Delilah's name. My wife's. It means Turtle in a Nest.

There is a feast, a circling dance that runs all night. I can still see the dancers at Bryan's when I married my first wife. But it is a curious silent vision. The laughing and calling and shuffling here in the big house overlap that old picture.

Methoataske is silent beside me on the sleeping mat. My mother has draped this wigwam with fresh pine boughs and bunches of thin green leaves and a few pale orange flowers with black eyes. She backs out the door, where my little sisters and Methoataske's girl whisper before she drags them away. I do not know what to say about them. I do not know what to say. But I speak nonetheless, her silence is so deep:

—This is why you shaved me again. Made me look a little more decent.

I feel her head move, she is nodding. I say:

—Well. You have seen all of me already.

I think of her beating me in the river, cleaning me and pulling out my hair. I think of myself opening my blanket to show her my wet body, limp also. I taught her that word. I want to laugh. I say:

—My father gave me a gun tonight. The horse as well. My mother piled me down with blankets. If I had known that this was the way to get all of this and a good barbering, I would have proposed to you some time ago.

My joking has little effect. I keep expecting Pompey to pop up from behind the cooking pot and say: *Aha. See where your sentimental heart has got you.*

Bang. I shut my mind to him and to everyone else. Here I am and here we are. I turn to face her, I touch her. Her skin is warm and very slightly rough.

She is accepting.

It is not difficult, of course it is not.

—Have you tried your gun yet? Does it work as you might have expected?

Pompey touches his breechcloth and the warriors laugh. A couple of the Boonesborough men are among them. One watches my face, his eyes moving in any direction mine do. I cannot look at him, he makes me think too much of the fort. His Shawnee father is very fond of him, he puts his arm about the young man's shoulders. I want to say: This is not a bad place. This is better than what we have left. This is what we have now.

But instead I say to everyone:

—Everything is in working order. Rest assured.

Black Fish leads, smiling. We go up the street and through the growing fields and out into the woods. They all elbow me and ha-ha some, but they let me loose with the gun. No guard. The early air is warming, I feel myself freed from any prison I could imagine. My father fills my pouch with powder and shot. We cross the fields and go into the woods and get a couple of deer straight out. The lead smells damp and precious.

When I return to my wife's house in the evening, I have plenty of venison. I bend to get through the door and I am knocked down hard. My back rocks on the ground, the meat is spilled, my breath is gone. I cannot see my attacker until I lift the body from my face. It is Methoataske's girl. I grip her shoulders, she stares me down, the hard steady stare of children. Then she gets up and runs into the house. I am still sprawled amidst the meat when Captain Will comes along with his wife.

—Here, my old friend.

He pulls me up from the ground by the arm. He says:

—New wife, new daughter. A family. I congratulate you.

His wife smiles as women do with the newly married, thinking of their own weddings. She and the Captain adopted two of the whites, Hancock and Jackson. Another ready family. They pass on up the way with their sons behind.

Inside the wigwam, my wife is brushing dust from the mats.

She looks up. The girl is curled into a corner, whispering to a wooden spoon that she is revolving between her palms. Her fingertip is still dark. My blood still?

—Ought not you to wash your hands, miss? Or stir the pot?

She continues to turn the spoon about. I say:

—Now, what is your spoon's name?

She is silent. Then at once she announces:

—Eliza.

—Well. Fine old English name. Not Sheltowee, after me?

—No.

Her eyes slide back to her occupation.

—And you, what is your name? I do not know it yet.

—Eliza.

She speaks just as though she is naming another utensil, as though it were no matter to her what her name is.

—Is that so?

Her mother looks at her with a small smile. The girl puts the spoon into her mouth and gets up to stand before me, her cheeks puffed out. Her stare is unblinking, like the wolf pup's. She seems to decide something. She holds out the spoon to me. I take it, with its damp half-circle from her mouth.

—Thank you, Miss Eliza.

Methoataske bends, her plait slides over her back, her hips lift. My wife. I go out and I pick up the remains of the meat.

At night Eliza is banished again to Black Fish's house to give the married couple their privacy. I can hear her howls. Methoataske stirs, troubled.

—Go and get her. Bring her back.

When Methoataske carries her in, Eliza's eyes are triumphant above her blanket. She keeps them open for hours, I can see in the low firelight.

She attaches herself to me like a nettle.

Methoataske has to keep her from following me everywhere, even the latrine pit. She seems never to blink. My little sisters hover outside and call her to come and play but she suddenly pretends not to understand Shawnee any longer. They go off in a whispering huff.

When I go to hunt she keeps beside me. I do not mind. I like her presence. She sits on a rock where I tell her to stay. When I come back with game after a few hours, she is still there, chewing on a fingernail. She says:

—I am here.

—Why, so am I.

I carry her home on my shoulder, the rifle knocking awkward over my chest. She kicks at it with her ankles. She takes the ramrod and waves it about like a wand.

In spite of herself, she drops into a heavy early sleep after our expedition. Her limbs sprawl out as if she has fallen hard upon the floor. My wife and I sit outside in the light evening. We can hear her deep breaths and occasional snores.

Methoataske is shelling seeds from last year. The husks strike the ground softly. I am stealing a handful from the basket when my wife says:

—She is not easy.

—Easy? Is any child?

I crunch seeds between my teeth. I think of other children, but the thought is vague only, I chase it off. She slides a glance at me:

—Is this not a word? *Easy*?

—It is a word. You are not wrong.

—She is not—at home. She feels this.

—She has a good home. You are a good mother, I can see for myself.

Methoataske brushes husks from her lap, her arm is like a wing. I catch at her fingers. She says:

—You are her father now. She believes so.

—Her father, was he a good man? I hope so.

She shrugs one of her shrugs. I take her hand, I want to know suddenly. The man must be dead. Am I the first replacement?

—I am sorry.

She picks up her basket. The husks sound like light rain falling. Her fingers are quick and unthinking.

—I do not know her father.

For a moment she seems flustered, it is very odd for her. I look away and listen to the night insects and birds starting up. After a time I say:

—Your history is not my concern.

She carries on with the seeds, she moves her foot up and down. Inside Eliza coughs and gulps. The dark slides down.

—I am not her first mother. She was given to me.

—She was a captive?

—Yes.

My chest tightens and tells me to shut my mouth but I do not. I ask:

—From where? Another town?

Methoataske's hands keep working busily. The seeds split softly: crack, crack. She says:

—In the south. No name. A moving town, not Shawnee. It is gone now. My town.

—Your town also?

—Yes.

—You are not Shawnee?

—I am now Shawnee. I was Cherokee once.

She speaks matter-of-factly, as if I should have known. All I am able to say is:

—Ah.

A flash tries to ignite in me. Ignore it, stamp it to death. I close my lips. I reach for my happiness, smooth and clear and thin as a ball of glass. Straighten your mouth. I say:

—Then you are a captive too, you were adopted here.

—Once.

I do not wish to know, I do not wish to know this. I wish to brush her past away like the seed husks, as she seems to have done, as they seem able to do. But I cannot stop myself. I say:

—Eliza. She came with you?

—No. Later.

—But from the same town?

She shrugs again, she is maddening. This talk is maddening. She says:

—The town moved after the attack. Maybe the same town, maybe not. We move our towns.

—The Shawnee attacked the people there again. Your people.

—One of the wars. A little war only, not your big war now against the British. Her parents died.

I push at her, still burning in the pit of my chest. A lump of coal is there, a stone, an eye. I say:

—Died. Killed. Murdered.

—Yes.

So simple is this word against everything.

I stand, opening and closing my hands. I want to see the girl, I move towards the doorway, but Methoataske stops me, her hand tight on my arm:

—They gave her to me. I had no people.

—She was an orphan. What did they do to her family?

The eye in me bulges and burns. Everything burned to the ground, flesh and bone gone to charcoal and dust. Orphans. Orphans are left, orphans survive. Jonathan and Jesse. My own children. My heart bangs dull and familiar. She presses my arm faintly and then lets go. She says quietly:

—She came from another town first. She is maybe some white.

The reddish hair. The English. Someone else's captive, traded in and passed on. I spin back to look at Methoataske, I grip her:

—Where did she come from? You do not know? What was her name? You have never asked her?

—No. Why? She will not say. She is young.

—If I ask her, she will say.

Another shrug, a slow one. I turn back, I stand in the doorway, I hear the girl turn over and sigh. I cannot wake her. I cannot drag this out of her. The eye inside me is wide, it is demanding, I cannot close it. It wants to know everything, it cannot leave the past alone. To Methoataske I say tightly:

—In Carolina there was a big Cherokee with a long face, an over-tall man. A sad face. You know of him? He called himself Jim. Big Jim.

I spit the words in two pieces. She might know him, she might well be his sister. His wife. She might have learned her English words from him, in his voice. I sit in expectation of an answer. I expect to have all of the answers. But now she is quiet, her eyes perplexed. She says:

—I do not know that name.

Her words are so simple, so straight. She is so separate from me, sitting calm on her stool with her seeds. I kick over her basket. She is confused by my rage. She does not touch me. She says:

—I had a different name then too.

—What name?

—Gogiv. Crow, in Cherokee.

Still she does not move, but she says:

—Everyone remembers things, but why say so? Maybe not to talk is better. The girl is my girl now. She is your girl now.

She knows that I will not turn away from this. I feel her quiet certainty like a cool wind. She picks up her basket and takes up a seed with her fingertips. Crack crack. The past is stuffed with the dead, I know. I cannot look at them. Look at what is here now: Here is my wife, here is my daughter, here am I. We are all in pieces. We all move about, everything moves, as it seems to me. These pieces have landed here for the time, but who can say when they will fly apart again?

19

All Comes Again

IF ALL IS nothing, you might well have a share of it.

You might well start again. Again.

You might well start here.

You might well continue on with your wife, touch her and sleep with her and eat her food.

You might well keep the girl as your own. You might well love her. She holds on to your ankle if she is close enough. She never blinks, she is worse than the eye in your chest. Her fingers are strong.

These are things that I tell myself. I do not know whether I believe them. But I tell myself.

When I cannot see her sharp little face, I ask her. She is riding on my shoulder again as we walk back from the woods. Her feet dangle against the gun. They are bare, the day is bright. We are looking at the towers of clouds when I say it:

—Do you remember the other place you lived in? The other town? You remember your Ma and Daddy, I imagine.

Her sudden stillness is terrible. A bird flaps up out of the bushes and spins quickly in the air, flying away from us and into the trees, flashing its bright underwings. I think of the children left to wander the forest after attacks, surviving on something. Indian, white, black children. Sometimes they run if they see us, they hide in the trees rather than say anything, they store up the scraps of what they have seen and turn them into God knows what. Once Squire saw a boy from one of the Indian camps that had been burned and routed. The back of the boy, shirtless and blistered and raw, the brown skin left around the edges. Running away at full tilt. Squire never caught him.

Out of nowhere Eliza says coldly:

—My *father* is a great big man. My *mother* is a great big woman with big feet. They have a chimney and big dogs to eat everyone.

—Is that so?

When I say nothing else, her legs slowly relax against the gun again and we carry on home, both of us easier with this story.

We do go along. This is our life. The crops grow well. Boonesborough recedes to a grey point. I can see all of it and none of it. I stop looking. In Eliza I can see Jemima of course, and Susannah, and Jamesie too. I see the wariness, the sudden bursts of confidence, the big eyes always watching.

I am asleep when the door is pushed open. Methoataske is instantly awake beneath my arm, Eliza rolls and sits up. Pompey's face is almost invisible, there is no moon and the fire is near out. But the slow amused voice in the dark is his.

—You are wanted, Sheltowee. At the council house.

—Now?

—Does that not suit you?

—All right, I am coming.

I find my leggings and moccasins. I feel Methoataske and Eliza trying to see me. I say nothing, I walk out after Pompey. The night is loud with insects, moths touch my cheeks. We pass by the hunched wigwams, feeling our way along the walls until there is a swath of light from the open door of the big house.

—Not going to send me to prison again, Pompey?

He laughs low and slaps the log wall of the hut as we go around it. He says:

—The bridegroom never likes to leave the nest, as I said.

He seems at ease with me again, his laugh is warm enough. I have not escaped to any freer life, I am still here, as he is. Pompey, I remember this.

He leads me in. The raw light makes me blink, the fire is heaped up and blazing with sparks.

Black Fish is standing before it. His lock of hair is slightly dishevelled from sleep. He gives me a small smile, an indulgence for the bridegroom. The warriors are talking. A few of the whites see me with bright awake eyes. Jackson looks doubtful and tired, Hancock smiles very broad.

Black Fish raises his hand for quiet and says:

—This evening, hunters have seen the duck. Not far.

I think only of fat ducks flying by in some insulting fashion, perhaps relieving themselves upon the chief. Pompey sees my lack of understanding and bends to tell me:

—The little bastard duck, if you are wondering which one in particular. Pekula.

I see Johnson's lean face again, all long jaws. I had forgotten it but here it is. I say:

—He is alive? Here?

—There were other men with him in the woods beyond the fields. We could not catch up with them.

Black Fish looks to an elder warrior, who speaks quickly. I say:

—Is Johnson—Pekula—here?

—No.

Pompey says:

—Away with the spirits, the little madman.

The Shawnee laugh, the fire leaps. Black Fish steps forward again. He says:

—The white fort is strong, we know. They have more men. We will not wait to take it.

His eyes hook into mine. Hold your face still. In truth it is easy enough to show nothing, I am so perplexed and so surprised that I am empty again. So often I told them that the fort is too strong, and full of sick women and bawling children. And now to myself I have said: It is gone.

I cannot think.

Pompey is looking at me with his lips tight. Black Fish is looking at me, my men are looking at me. A tremor is holding itself back, waiting to open a great cracked seam in the floor.

Slowly I say:

—Of course. We will not wait.

Black Fish nods once, his eyes go behind their doors. The talk pools into planning and drinking and loose celebration. My mind runs everywhere. The fort. Johnson made it back there alive. There must be people there. It must still exist. All of you still alive, is this what you were saying to me in my sickness? Did I have it so wrong?

There will be more deaths. The fort will be ready for a fight now, there will be no surprising it. Death, is this what you were here to tell me? That you would wait a while?

Black Fish's face is sure and set. His profile stands out sharp in the firelight.

My heart leaps like a caught trout. The fire spews sparks and ash, a curl of smoke drifts out the hole into the night. Pompey grins at me, leaning forward and mopping his forehead with his blue scarf. He shakes it out like a flag and begins to sing.

It is happening. It is already happening, Daddy. The past circling back, pushing down the door.

20

The Burying Ground

THE MESSENGERS ride out very early, before most of the men are up to hunt. They are going to the other towns to enlist their allies and prepare the attack. When I close my eyes, I can see an army massing and rolling forward like waves. I hear the hoofs pound off. Their rhythm is stern but has a catch of joy, it travels through the earth. The sound carries.

I go to hunt. I think on the feel of the gun, which is not so very good a gun, but I will make a new stock. I think on the stock I will make, the wood I will choose for it. The dew is wet and not frosted. The grass does not crunch, it slides like hair underfoot. I hook my finger around the trigger, I watch for movement in the sky, my finger pulls back and bang, a duck falls out of the air. It lands with its beak open, looking disgusted but reconciled to its end. Eliza sits on the rock where I told her to sit, she is watching hard.

The women are preparing over-much food, gutting and plucking and skinning. Joints and limbs hang in the trees.

Methoataske brushes out her hair like a blanket over her body, like a Quaker cloak. I touch it. I call her *Squethetha*, Little Girl. I give her a woodpecker I got. It has bright black and white wings and a silky crest. I have no Governor's silver left to give her, only this. She smiles and takes the bird. I give a wing to Eliza, a crow's, black with an oily bluish cast and a leathery handle. She turns it into a fan, she will not let anyone touch it. She fans her face, in and out of shadow.

The dance is serious and ancient but a current of happiness ripples through it. Everyone is dressed up, painted up, very fine. Even the children are in the big house. Everyone eats and talks and goes back to pick again at the meat and bread and bones, and then more food comes in on platters. A warrior vomits quietly at the side of the room and I think briefly of poison, but it is only too much eating. He is a famous eater, as Pompey tells me.

The drummers started long ago, their bodies are coated in sweat. The rhythm drags and then bounces back up. Bodies mill and shuffle round them. Pompey stands about, refusing to be pulled in, looking as though he has to be persuaded, which he likes. At last he lets himself be pressed to the centre of the room beside the drums. He raises his arms to shoulder-height and looks distant before he begins a high song, another familiar tune that was once English, perhaps. Many of his words are unfamiliar. I understand some: people, time, war, sing. It is something about the past, old times, I think. *Sechcommika.* It sounds as though he is making it up. It goes on and on.

Black Fish is smiling a little, tilting his head, then he catches himself and sits up straight. Pim sits upon his knee and pulls his earring. The men make a circle to one side of the room, women make one on the other. All turn and turn, no one looking at anyone else. The concentration is great. The bodies seem walled off from one another. Only the feet move on and on together with the drumming.

The women melt away, their silver brightens into gold in the firelight and then vanishes. The children go too, some crying with fatigue. My wife turns to me with Eliza in her arms before they disappear.

Alone the men carry on faster, twisting their upper bodies within the circle. I am jostled in, Pompey pauses in his singing to grin at me, his face glistening. I shuffle my feet about, I was never a dancer. But this is not difficult. I turn, I feel the mass of the turning, a great shivering wheel. I feel the drums in my ribs and my back and the top of my head.

When the circle breaks into pieces, the drums roll back down into a low steady pulse. We all stop and breathe and stand about, a little foolish. Some stretch their arms and necks. The smell of us pervades the great room and I am glad for the smoke hole, though not much cool air comes down. Several old women, their eyes down, drag in a huge salt kettle. One of those they took from us at the salt spring, most likely. Perhaps the one I toted here. So long ago, back down a thin tunnel in a rock.

The women struggle to set it down, they puff and back away when they have done it.

Black Fish has vermillion on his raised palm, which he pulls across his eyes. Red streaks his forehead and eyelids, his finger-lines show in it. He dips a cup into the pot, he holds it in both hands. The air is heavy and liquid and over-breathed. My head wheels, I pull my eyes back to my father. He is drinking. His throat swallows, down and down.

We all form a tail. We all drink. Black Drink, they call it. War drink. When my turn comes, I take the cup from my father. Bitter, brackish, strong. It moves into my blood. His eyes glitter at me in their red, they are full of love. He dips his chin.

And Eliza's face. It catches me. She has crept back in, she is crouched in a corner, she fans herself with the crow's wing.

—You ought to take your mother's old name. You are like a young crow.

Eliza feels heavier on my shoulders this morning. The paint horse walks beside us, its head nodding. I am tired, I have not slept. The Black Drink did its work on me but now I am emptied out, though
I must hunt with the others. I must go with the men to the graves beyond the trees. She, however, is wide awake, banging her heels.

—Why?

—Because—you make such a noise. And your eyes do not shut.

I talk stupidly, I talk to stop my mind from darting about. I tease Eliza and I tickle her legs. Others are out already on their way, laden with food and pots and clothing and other offerings. We are late rising. Methoataske is coming along as far as the fields. Women are at work there with their white sons, they are crossing their arms and leaning on their hoes and sticks, turning their faces to the sun. Methoataske stops to speak with them, she bends to pull up a string of weed. Her hair is plaited up again. I have an urge to touch it and to make her look at me.

We are to dig up the dead warriors and rebury them with better things in hope that their old strength and luck are still about and will settle on us. We do not like them to be alone. They will be with us when we march on Boonesborough. We will go there and I will see the people there again. There will be more deaths, more burying, and whose? This I do not know. I watch my feet.

I go on with the girl. I walk slowly, I try to sharpen my brains. I hold onto her sharp knees. We are close to the trees at the edge of the woods. Here I set Eliza down on a greying trunk.

—Your place for this morning. All right?

She flaps her fan at me. I remember the waft of air on my face. Eliza.

Four or five others are drifting into the woods, spreading themselves out. No one is moving quick today. They are walking towards the painted grave-markers, the sticks weathering in the trees. I cannot see them yet. Black Fish is first. His head is bowed slightly. He is thinking of his real son. They brought his body back here to bury it. He will see him.

I walk the horse forward, the shade cools my sore tired eyes.

Across the sun it comes, a burst of black and bright red, a flight. We have not seen turkey for months. So many of them fly out that they are crashing into one another, knocking heads and wings, crying garbled sounds no one can understand. They are like the bright flying souls of the dead, they are absurdly close to us, within our reach. They are alive and flapping and fighting and callling. The men laugh, hardly able to get out their guns and load and aim. This abundance is a shock. It is like seeing Kentucky for the first time, full of turkey and full of everything.

My chest goes hollow. Surely this is some sign. All my life I have been looking for signs. And the turkeys seem to be looking on me with their peaceable ringed painted eyes like spirits. So beautiful is it here, and so strange. But nothing can stay so beautiful and so strange.

You might run.

Go.

Be gone you ape.

The old voices in my head. Human voices, but so far away.

I rein the horse in, I turn her head, her hooves twist, her ankle near rolls. The day is bright and sharp-edged above the forest. The figures dip and sway in the fields. Clutching at the horse's mane I drop the rifle, the stock cracks and splits as it strikes the ground. No gun, no knife. Here again am I. I have not moved an inch since they first caught me in the snow.

An army surges at my back and it is an army of ghosts, all of my dead. My neck pricks and cringes, so bare is it. They do not touch me. They are watching, they are all eyes, what will I do this time?

I argue with them: We need to go along. We have been going along here.

A turkey gobbles and gibbers like a dead aunt offering advice from the next world. It is no advice. It is no help. The dead blow cold nothing on my neck. Israel is smiling. More of them are waiting, quiet in their graves in the woods. I wheel, I try to see but again there is nothing. Still your face is not there.

I want to see you. I want to see you again. Then perhaps I would understand.

The want strikes me like a blow, my heart is a great hole full of want. I had not thought want could go so far into a body. I hear Eliza calling after me, insistent as the turkey: *Daddy, Daddy*—

Out of her words shapes grow. Jemima, Rebecca, my boy Israel, and Susy and the rest. Perhaps alive at the fort. Not safe, but there at least. But Jamesie, your missing face rips a hole through me. I think of you calling me in the same way as Eliza does. I turn again to try to catch you but you are not there.

Here is the bargain I offer Death: Take others if you must. Let me see my son.

We make our trades.

I see what I want, what I must do. I dig my heels into the guilty horse, I push her so she runs and we are ahead, we are in the trees. I narrow my eyes against the branches, and the day dims. And as I race on I see myself running on through black woods and mountains, for days and days, all the long way to Powell's Valley. I see myself in a light spinning snow at the grave Squire went back to make, where it is higher and colder, where the wolves have been first, trying to scratch a way in.

I see that I will dig down to the two bodies wrapped together in Rebecca's linen sheet. One has dark hair and one is fair. The fair plait is yours. It is stiff and unpliable, like frozen straw.

The face is yours but covered in a film of salt. The eyes are still there beneath the half-closed lids but they have withdrawn entirely. You have become strange. The waxy flesh is dull, still torn. I had thought it might have healed itself up in some way, I suppose. I take up the forearms, the poor hands, the nails all gone, pulled out one by one. The stabbed palms. The black bites from knives look like small gills, as if you had been trying to suck at air with your whole body, trying to get free of the terrible net.

I hold your hand. A dart-arrow is broken off in your side, I touch it gently beneath your torn shirt. Your shirt makes me want to weep. You are still seventeen years of age, but strange.

The dark boy is Russell's son Henry. His body is in much the same state and is worse to look at, it makes my shoulders heave, I cannot touch it. I can only touch you. I cannot let you go. I am the only living thing here, a black mark in a field of snow. I put my face to your chest. It is cold and hard, no sound comes from it. If I do not move, wolves will eat my body. They have not eaten yours but they have been close. They will eat us together and we will be mingled inside them then, we find out where wolves go.

The thief who returned to camp said they were dead, all the boys, and Crabtree and the Negroes gone. Their camp was only two miles back from ours, they would have reached us the next day. This thief found Russell's slave Adam in the woods babbling and shaking and clutching his hair as if it would all fall out if he let go of it. When the attack came in the night, Adam had hidden himself under a pile of driftwood near the creek. Twenty Indians or more, Cherokee, Delaware, Shawnee. He watched everything. He heard everything, the wolf calls and the false wolf calls.

He said Boone's boy called one of the attackers by name, asking for his life and then begging. Big Jim, Jamesie said. It is me, he said. Already on the ground shot through both hips. Jamesie never could speak a name without a hesitation and a flush, as though he were making too free. But he said it, he looked up and asked through his hovering hands: Did you kill my Mama and my sisters and brothers?

Jamesie. Your poor voice and hands. What were you thinking of? Mama and your family waiting you in the next life, but your Daddy missing?

He did not speak of me then. He did not think I could ever be dead, he thought I would come. In the end he did call me. *Daddy, Daddy, Dada.*

I see what I will do now. I will count your fingers and toes as I did the night you were born. I will count them again. I will dig and I will rebuild the grave deeper, I will put you in it, I will heap rocks and logs on top.

I will hear wolves yip somewhere in the light snow. A gun firing, not far. The wind stirring and sighing. I will get to my feet.

ACKNOWLEDGEMENTS

My thanks to my excellent agent, Denise Bukowski, and my excellent editor, Anne Collins. Thank you also to Amanda Lewis and Michelle Roper at Knopf Canada, and to Alexis Alchorn, Tilman Lewis, and Robin Studniberg for their careful copy-editing and proofreading. I'm grateful to the Canada Council for the Arts, the Banff Centre for the Arts, *The Walrus* magazine, and the Faculty of Arts at Okanagan College, especially Jeremy Beaulne, Jim Hamilton, Rob Huxtable, and Craig McLuckie. For reading and discussing, many thanks to Damien Barton, Corinna Chong, Francie Greenslade, Sean Johnston, Terry Jordan, John Lent, Clare McManus, Melanie Murray, Andrea Sazwan, Matthew Skelton, and Rebecca Upton. A particular thank you to Mary Ellen Holland for her untiring thoughtfulness and support. My family has lost me to the frontier for some time: Mike, Theo, and Kate Hawley; Jocelyn, Peter, Jon, Marcela, Laura, and Sarah Bunyan; Carolyn and Dan Hilton; José Burtch. Thank you all for letting me go, and for taking me back.

Alix Hawley studied English literature and creative writing at Oxford University, the University of East Anglia, and the University of British Columbia. She published a story collection, *The Old Familiar*, with Thistledown Press in 2008. She won the 2014 Canada Writes Bloodlines competition, judged by Lawrence Hill, and was runner-up for the CBC Literary Award for short stories in 2012 and 2014. She teaches at Okanagan College in Kelowna, BC, where she lives with her family.